AUSTRALIANS

Visit dramatically beautiful, hot, luscious Queensland and see the glamorous sophistication of Sydney's social elite in these two stunning novels by bestselling author

Helen Bianchin

Convenient Possession

A collection of two super, passionate, dramatic and powerful novels

RED-HOT
AUSTRALIANS

June 2010

July 2010

August 2010

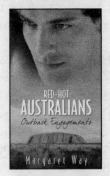

September 2010

RED-HOT
AUSTRALIANS
Convenient Possession

Helen Bianchin

M&B™ and M&B™ with the Rose Device
are trademarks of the publisher.
Harlequin Mills & Boon Limited, Eton House,
18-24 Paradise Road, Richmond, Surrey TW9 1SR

CONVENIENT POSSESSION
© Harlequin Enterprises II B.V./S.à.r.l. 2010

The Marriage Possession and *The Greek Tycoon's Virgin Wife*
have been previously published in the UK as separate, single volumes
as follows:

The Marriage Possession © Helen Bianchin 2007
The Greek Tycoon's Virgin Wife © Helen Bianchin 2007

ISBN: 978 0 263 87470 9

024-0610

Harlequin Mills & Boon policy is to use papers that are
natural, renewable and recyclable products and made from
wood grown in sustainable forests. The logging and
manufacturing processes conform to the legal environmental
regulations of the country of origin.

Printed and bound in Spain
by Litografia Rosés S.A., Barcelona

The Marriage Possession

Helen Bianchin

Helen Bianchin was born in New Zealand and travelled to Australia before marrying her Italian-born husband. After three years they moved, returned to New Zealand with their daughter, had two sons, then resettled in Australia. Encouraged by friends to recount anecdotes of her years as a tobacco sharefarmer's wife living in an Italian community, Helen began setting words on paper and her first novel was published in 1975. An animal lover, she says her terrier and Persian cat regard her study as much theirs as hers.

Helen Bianchin's most recent novel,
The Andreou Marriage Arrangement, **was
published by Mills & Boon in March and a new
novel will be published in October 2010
in Mills & Boon® Modern™.**

CHAPTER ONE

THE legal soirée was invitation-only, hosted in a luxurious hotel and presented for the city's legal eagles and their partners.

Judges, barristers and eminent lawyers of note. Where friendships flourished and opponents left the rigours of the court-room behind.

'More champagne?'

The familiar male drawl had the power to quicken Lisane's heartbeat…and more, so much more.

Lisane tilted her head a little, met Zac's dark, gleaming eyes, and almost drowned in their depths. 'Do I appear to need it?'

A loaded query, if ever there was one!

Mingling with her peers would be a breeze in comparison with the formal dinner, where seating arrangements would place her at Zac's side in the company of his parents, and Allegra Fabrisi, their preferred choice of a partner for their son.

Tonight she would field empty compliments, the brilliant female smiles that didn't reach the eyes…each of which were a mere salutation in deference to attract the attention of the man at her side.

Zacharias Winstone, wealthy in his own right, a prominent barrister and son of an eminent judge, he was the embodiment of everything that was charismatic male.

In his late thirties, tall, with dark hair and dark eyes, broad-shouldered, wide-boned, sculptured features, a sensual mouth and piercing dark eyes, didn't come close to describing the inherent sensuality he projected with effortless ease.

Zac, the babe magnet.

One had only to *look* at him to *know* he could drive a woman wild. It was there in his eyes, the faint, teasing smile … the promise, simmering beneath the sophisticated façade.

Women undressed him with one lingering, seductive look, and blatantly moved in for the kill. For some it was a challenge, others had more serious plans in mind… So far none had been successful.

For the moment he was *hers*. Friend, lover…

Commitment wasn't a word Zac mentioned and *marriage* didn't enter the equation.

Relationship? Lisane pondered the word, sought its true meaning, and failed to pin it down.

Together…for now, seemed appropriate.

A pensive smile tilted the edge of her mouth.

It was enough…wasn't it?

They shared much, yet in many ways were poles apart.

His wealth earned him a position on an accredited list of Australia's wealthiest names, while she came from an ordinary family of humble means and her education had been gained via scholarships and part-time work to help pay expenses.

Within the legal profession, Zac was recognised as one of the best in his field of criminal law…while Lisane occupied a position in the Crown Prosecutor's office.

He had chambers in Brisbane, resided in a city apartment and owned a magnificent waterfront mansion on Sovereign Islands, an élite suburb on Queensland's Gold Coast, seventy kilometres distant.

Vastly different from the small, weathered cottage in fashionable suburban Milton that Lisane had bought, mortgaged and was in the process of renovating.

A Sydney-based girl of French-born parents, she'd relocated to Brisbane a year ago…a move due in part to the need for change. And the desire to remove herself from what had become an awkward situation.

Two couples…two blonde, blue-eyed sisters dating two brothers. Except whereas Solene and Jean-Claude had fallen in love and planned to marry, Lisane didn't share the same feelings for Alain. Friendship, yes, and affection. But not love.

Something it had taken a while to divine, given the almost life-long connection. Solene's engagement to Jean-Claude had prompted Alain's marriage proposal, and Lisane accepted his ring, temporarily caught up in Alain's persuasion and her sister's euphoria…only to have doubt soon cloud her perspective.

It hadn't been easy to break off the engagement, nor to leave the city of her birth. Except it wouldn't have been fair to Alain to stay.

He deserved more. So did she.

The law had fascinated Lisane from an early age, fostered and shaped by gritty television police and court-room dramas…none of which bore much resemblance to reality, she reflected with a tinge of wry amusement.

At twenty-seven, she hadn't found it difficult to settle into a new job in a different city. In many ways she'd relished the changes, new faces, forming tentative friendships…and running into Zac.

Literally. Three days after assuming her position in the Crown Prosecutor's office.

The momentous occasion had occurred in the city courthouse when she exited from the lift on the wrong floor.

It had taken only seconds to realise her mistake, and she'd swiftly turned…only to collide with a hard male frame.

An immediate apology had left her lips, and in the same instant she became aware of the man's physical impact… his impressive height, breadth of shoulder, his sculptured facial features. Not to mention the fine quality of his clothing, the faint aroma of his cologne. The slight smile curving his sensuously moulded mouth. And foremost, his indisputable aura of power.

Definitely off the Richter scale in terms of the *wow* factor, she had acknowledged a few minutes later as she rode the lift to the correct floor.

Who was he?

Discovery hadn't taken long. The family *Winstone* was well-known in legal and social circles. Zac Winstone was a legend in both.

The fact he sought her out had seemed little short of amazing. So, too, had his invitation to join him for coffee. A week or two later it had been followed by dinner, then a show…

'Pleasant thoughts, I hope?'

Lisane spared him a stunning smile. 'Why shouldn't they be?'

He was something else. Tuned in to her in a way that made her wonder if he'd become adept at reading her mind. Although pure people skills, the ability to weigh up character traits and successfully divine them, contributed much to his success in the court-room. Very little, if anything, seemed to escape him.

Zac curled his fingers through her own, and leant in close. 'Just remember I get to take you home.'

A teasing light entered her eyes. 'That's supposed to see me through the next few hours?'

'It won't?'

His place or hers. It hardly mattered which, as long as they shared what remained of the night together.

'The jury's still out.'

His soft laughter almost undid her. 'Let's commence the tour of duty, shall we?'

Zac's parents, Max and Felicity Winstone, had just entered the large lounge area, followed, Lisane saw, by Leo Fabrisi, his wife, Charmaine, and their daughter, Allegra.

Two brilliant judges married to two equally qualified solicitors, who had each borne a child destined to follow in their footsteps into law.

There was little doubt the coupling of Zac Winstone with Allegra Fabrisi would make a perfect match. Or that both sets of parents were intent on actively encouraging it. Allegra made no secret that snaring Zac was her prime focus.

Tonight the glamorous barrister had chosen a designer gown in sinful black which hugged her tautly honed curves like a second skin. Long, gleaming hair the colour of rich sable cascaded in loose waves halfway down her back, and even from this distance her make-up resembled perfection.

Wonderful.

Lisane couldn't compete. Her budget didn't allow for the purchase of designer originals, or the Manolo Blahnik or Jimmy Choo stilettos that inevitably graced Allegra's slender feet. And her jewellery was limited to a diamond pendant and matching ear-studs she'd inherited from her mother.

Fortunately, her talents included the skillful use of a sewing machine, and she doubted even the most observant society maven would spot that the exquisite gown in floral silk she wore had been fashioned by her own hand.

Muted music provided a pleasant background to the social chatter abounding among numerous patrons in the large lobby, and Zac's progress was frequently stalled as they paused to speak with a friend or associate.

Lisane briefly entertained the uncharitable thought that they might escape detection for a while longer, and thus delay a confrontation with the Winstone and Fabrisi parents.

Fat chance.

She watched with detached fascination as Zac's elegantly attired mother caught sight of her son, and began leading the group of five towards him.

'Darling.' Allegra stepped in close and pressed glossy lips to Zac's cheek. 'We're a little late.' Her mouth performed a pretty teasing pout. 'Traffic.' Dark, eloquently warm eyes assumed a cool tinge as she acknowledged the young woman at his side. 'Lisane.'

She bore Allegra's studied appraisal with a practised

smile before greeting each set of parents with a politeness gained from instilled good manners.

Wealth and social position lent that certain indefinable air some people exuded with an inborn ease acquired almost from birth. Maximilian Winstone, or Max, as he preferred to be known, could trace his ancestors back several centuries to an era of obscene wealth, enormous holdings and a social position almost second to none.

'Go fetch some champers, darling.' Allegra issued Zac the directive with a seductive look that was definite overkill. 'I need something to kick-start the evening.'

There were waiters and waitresses in abundance. Zac merely lifted a hand to catch attention, and within seconds a waiter bearing a tray of filled champagne flutes moved to their group.

Allegra wrinkled her perfectly shaped nose. 'Not, I think, the house variety.' She placed a beautifully lacquered nail on Zac's arm. 'Shall we adjourn to the bar?'

'We're about to be seated.' His voice was even, yet there was a warning hint beneath the surface.

One Allegra chose to ignore.

'There'll be at least thirty minutes of boring speeches before they serve the first course. We've plenty of time.'

Lisane felt her body tense. For what? An intimate tête-à-tête? To cause a temporary division between her and Zac?

She should be used to Allegra's ploys, for they occurred at frequent intervals and without doubt were deliberately orchestrated to diminish Lisane's existence in Zac's life.

It was a relief to see the ballroom doors swing open, and they joined the mingling guests entering the large room.

Polite, superficially pleasant conversation tempered the evening, and the addition of a further three guests at their

table provided some light relief from Allegra's not so
subtle attempts to command Zac's attention.

The food was superb, although Allegra barely sampled
a morsel from each course while sipping Cristal champagne.

Discretion and client privilege ensured that only gen-
eralities within the legal system were discussed, and
Lisane did her best to appear interested in Charmaine and
Allegra's recount of a recent shopping expedition in
Sydney, where it seemed Allegra had been intent on adding
to her collection of expensive shoes and bags.

'Prada, darling,' Allegra extolled. 'And the most
gorgeous Louis Vuitton.' She subjected Lisane to a
sweeping appraisal. 'Your gown. Is it a Collette Dinnigan?'

I wish! 'D'Aubigne.' It was her late mother's maiden
name, and one she felt entitled to use.

An eyebrow slanted in overt puzzlement. 'I'm not
familiar with the label.'

'It's French,' Lisane enlightened solemnly.

'Of course. One can tell from the superb craftsmanship.'

Lisane restrained the desire to smile. Allegra was completely unaware she'd inadvertently gifted a compliment.

It was almost a relief when the evening drew to a close.
Allegra's attempts to monopolise Zac's attention had
moved Lisane from mild amusement to irritation. Had the
beautiful barrister no scruples?

Don't answer that!

The 'goodnight' process took a while, and Lisane felt
her tension ease as she slid into the passenger seat of Zac's
sleek Jaguar shortly before midnight.

Thank heavens for the weekend. It would allow time to
put the finishing touches to the kitchen trim, then mid-

week, when the laquer paint had hardened, she could hang the lace curtains.

The cottage was gradually coming together. She adored the homely country-style furniture and refurbishing she'd chosen. It suited the one-hundred-year-old wooden structure, and she'd painstakingly polished the wooden floors, added rugs and wall-hangings in cross-stitch and tapestry.

She could walk indoors and feel at peace with her surroundings. Her plans for the garden were underway, a vegetable patch already yielding some fine produce; and while she still had some work to complete in the flower borders, there was time to bring it to its full potential.

Tomorrow, after a lingering breakfast at one of the city's pavement cafés, Zac would deliver her home.

Tonight…what remained of the night was theirs.

Just the thought of how it would end caused her heartbeat to accelerate and heat to course through her veins.

Gentle fingers brushed her cheek, almost as if he sensed what she was thinking, and she covered his hand with her own for a few timeless seconds before releasing it to offer him a lingering smile.

The Jaguar swept down into the underground car park beneath the tall city apartment building and came to a smooth halt in Zac's designated space.

He took hold of her hand as they entered the lift and buried his lips in her palm. His eyes were almost black, and she was willing to swear her bones began to melt at the degree of emotion reflected in those dark depths.

She needed to have his mouth on hers…his hands on her body, moulding each sensitised breast, exploring pleasure pulses, bringing her sensual heart alive and aching…for him, only him.

The lift slid to a halt, and minutes later they entered Zac's luxurious apartment. Floor-to-ceiling glass provided a panoramic view of the city, myriad lights and bright neon winking against an indigo sky.

It was a sight which never failed to enchant her, and she crossed to the tempered glass and gazed beyond the cityscape to the darkened outline of distant hills.

There was piped background music cued in low, courtesy of Zac's sound system, and she turned as magnificent curtains swished closed from the touch of an electronic button.

Dimmed lighting provided soft illumination, turning the large lounge area into their own private world.

'Come here.' Zac's voice was deep, husky, and Lisane took hold of his outstretched hand.

He drew her in and held her close to his hard body, then lowered his head to nuzzle the sensitive skin beneath her earlobe.

'I've waited all night to be able to do this.'

Slow-dancing.

Lisane closed her eyes and let emotion take over her body. It felt so good to be like this with him. To breathe in his male scent beneath the fine tailoring; to have the freedom to slide her hands beneath his jacket and savour the heady warmth. *Feel* the hard musculature and sense the quickened beat of his heart.

This was where she wanted to be. With him. The physical whereabouts hardly mattered, nor did the soft, lilting music drifting from expensive speakers.

There was only the man, the heady, dreamy sensation, and the need to feel his hands, his lips on her body, arousing, with the promise of how the night would end…and the journey.

He was a generous lover, intent on gifting the ultimate in pleasure, and she swayed slightly, almost missing her step…and felt the slide of his hand to the base of her spine as he held her firm against him.

His arousal was a potent force, and she lifted her arms to encircle his neck, then sank in against him as he lowered his head down to hers.

Magic.

She felt his fingers loosen the slide-comb holding the length of her hair, sensed the silky fall of it around her shoulders, and the slow threading of his fingers through its length.

He adored the feel of it, the faint fresh smell of her favoured floral-scented shampoo. The way she tossed her head in the throes of passion, and the tumbled mass of waves that fell like a curtain across each cheek…or cascaded down her naked back as she arched up against him and flung back her head.

He could bury his face in its silky length and savour the sweetness…*her*.

Beautiful, so very beautiful inside and out. Intelligent, clever, yet without artifice or contrived coquetry.

He wanted her…in his life. In his bed. He hadn't given much thought for how long. There didn't seem to be the need. The status quo suited him…suited them both. He couldn't see any reason for anything to change.

Zac took the kiss deeper, and Lisane experienced the familiar deep pull of desire.

Had they stopped moving? She wasn't sure, didn't care.

All that mattered was his mouth on hers, possessing with such tactile skill she became lost. *His,* solely his in a way that rendered her wanton…and *wanting*.

His clothes, hers, were an inconvenient barrier they

each sought to remove. Urgent hands, accompanied by barely audible sounds as the need to feel skin-on-skin contact became unbearable, closely followed by the shimmering satisfaction as the last shred of silk slithered down onto the carpeted floor.

In one fluid movement she leapt up against him and curled her legs around his waist, and sensed rather than heard the soft, laughing groan deep in his throat.

Seconds later he eased his mouth free from her own and feathered light fingers down the length of her spine, teased the curves of her buttocks, then unerringly found the warm, moist heat of her.

Wickedly clever fingers sent her high, the spiralling sensation causing her to gasp with the intensity of it, and she clung on to him, unaware of the soft, guttural sounds emerging from her throat as he brought her to climax.

He reclaimed her mouth, sweeping the soft inner tissue with his tongue, before tangling with her own in an erotic exploration that mirrored the intimacy of sexual possession.

She wanted more…so much more, and she lowered her body a little so the intimate heart of her rested against his powerful arousal. Then she moved, slowly, in an evocative teasing slide that had his heartbeat thudding in his chest and rendered him almost without breath.

'Minx.'

A soft knowing laugh emerged from her throat. It had been Zac who'd taught her to totally relax and enjoy sex. To receive and gift pleasure without inhibition.

'Bite me.'

'Now, there's a thought.'

'Promises, huh?'

Lisane moved up against him, then gave a surprised

gasp as he adjusted her position, eased his length into the moist heart of her...and surged in to the hilt.

She was aware of stretched tissue, intimate muscles enclosing him...and their readiness to convulse at his slightest move.

'What are you waiting for?' Her query was a breathless murmur, and she felt the press of his mouth against the vulnerable curve of her neck.

'You. To catch up.'

'Wretch.' If he wanted a challenge, she'd give him one!

The move was hers, and she relished being in control... until he took over. Then nothing mattered except their escalating pleasure and a libidinous climax that shattered them both.

Afterwards he carried her into the shower, where they gently bathed each other beneath the pulsing water, then, once dry, they walked naked into the bedroom and slid beneath the cool percale sheets to indulge in a slow, sensuous after-play...drifting fingers sliding over smooth skin, the gentle brush of lips, and soft, indistinct murmurs of appreciation.

On the edge of sleep Lisane sighed a silent word of thanks. For the man who cradled her close, and the place she'd reached in her life.

It was good. Very good.

No other man had made her feel so aware of her emotional heart...or so *alive* and incredibly sensual.

There was a certain danger in analysing her feelings in depth, for she was wary of repeating her mistake with Alain.

Although what she shared with Zac was different...so very different.

Love?

She didn't want to go there. Dared not. For it would mean contemplating an admission of sorts…one she wasn't ready to make.

It was enough their togetherness lasted a while.

CHAPTER TWO

LISANE came awake to the feather-like drift of fingers teasing a path over one hip, and the breath caught in her throat as they slid a little and sought the warm, moist, intimate heart at the apex of her thighs.

Soft lips nuzzled the sensitive curve at the edge of her neck, and she felt her pulse thud to a quickened beat as those skilful fingers found the highly sensitised nub, stroking it gently until she arched against his hand, wanting, needing more.

'Good morning.'

Zac's musing drawl sounded close to her ear, and her mouth curved into a generous smile as she opened her eyes to look at him.

Tousled dark hair, beard-shadow darkening his sculptured facial features…those eyes, so warm and liquid brown, and a mouth to die for.

'It's Saturday.'

Silent laughter lightened his gaze and his lips curved a little. 'And this is important…because?'

'I get to do this.'

He'd taught her so much. Where to touch and how. She knew what caused his breath to hitch. The way his body tensed when she enclosed his arousal and began to tantalise, driving him to the edge, the faint hiss as she brought him close to climax in what became a test of his endurance. The times he reached it and assumed control…the occasions when he allowed her to take charge.

Their loving was at times hungry, primitive, when passion ruled and surpassed all else. Mostly, it was slow and incredibly erotic, a true feast of the senses.

Lisane moved in close and brushed her lips to his cheek. 'Do you have anything important planned for the next hour?'

Zac moved a little so her mouth met his. 'Nothing without you.'

Morning sex, Lisane mused as they rose from the bed, was a great way to begin the day.

Together they shared a leisurely shower, then, towelled dry, she followed him into the bedroom and collected fresh underwear from her overnight bag and pulled on jeans and a pink singlet, added a cropped top in black and slid her feet into kitten heels.

With quick, smooth fingers she caught her hair into a loose knot, applied minimum make-up, added a touch of lip-gloss, then packed her overnight bag.

Zac took it from her hand, and trailed light fingers down her cheek. 'Hungry?'

'Uh-huh.' Her eyes sparkled with mischievous humour. 'For food.'

He pressed a thumb-pad to her lower lip. 'Of course.'

She was something else. Intelligent, savvy and possessed of an innate honesty. What was more, there wasn't an ounce of coquetry…which made for a refreshing change from most young women of his acquaintance.

Together they decided on a Park Road café not far from Lisane's cottage, selected a pavement table and ordered a full breakfast, preluded by strong, hot coffee.

The sun shone brightly, promising a warm late-spring day, and there was a freshness in the air that would dissipate as the temperatures rose, along with the humidity.

It seemed almost a shame to consider spending most of the weekend indoors. For a moment Lisane thought wistfully of Zac's waterfront home at Sovereign Islands, his cruiser moored at the jetty, and the occasional weekend they'd spent together there when the constraints of work had allowed them free time.

'More coffee?'

Lisane was seriously tempted to delay their departure, and it helped a little to know she could. Except she knew time was an important factor, given Zac was engaged in a particularly difficult case, one that required long, tedious hours as he meticulously built undisputed evidence and framed his questioning technique in preparation for a trial due soon to go to court.

'I'm fine.' She slid her sunglasses into place from atop her head, and rose to her feet. 'It's time to hit the road.'

Zac paid the bill, then caught hold of her hand as they walked to where he'd parked the car.

'Thanks for breakfast.'

He slanted her a warm smile. 'My pleasure.' As the night had been. And the early hours of the morning.

She made it easy for him to relax and unwind, didn't make any demands, and rarely rose to anger. None of which were an act. He never felt the need to play a part, and her wit and wisdom provided a lightness that had been seriously missing before she entered his life.

They reached the Jaguar, and he saw her into the passenger seat before crossing to the driver's side.

A few minutes, maybe five, was all it took to reach the street where her cottage was situated, and Lisane leant towards him as soon as he brought the car to a halt outside her gate.

'Take care, and don't work too hard.' She brushed her lips to his cheek, and bit back a faint gasp as he framed her face with his hands and took possession of her mouth.

Oh, my.

She could hardly find her breath when he released her, and she met his warm, steady gaze, glimpsed the faint wickedness evident…and wrinkled her nose at him in teasing remonstrance.

'I guess that'll hold me for a while.'

A wide smile curved his generous mouth. 'Sassy. Definitely sassy.'

Lisane reached for the door-clasp, caught up her overnight bag and slid out from the car. 'Go suss out the legal arguments that'll tie the bad guy up in legal knots.'

His soft laughter remained with her as the car disappeared from view, and she smiled a little as she extracted her house-key and unlocked the front door.

The morning was spent on household chores, and clearing the detritus of a hectic week. Wielding a very careful paintbrush, she completed the finishing touches to the remaining windowsills and two architraves.

Strong paint fumes provided a reason to escape the house for an hour or two, and she took the car to the nearest supermarket and stocked up on essential groceries. On her return she swiftly changed into old jeans and top, and spent time tending her garden. It wasn't a chore, for she loved the smell of freshly-turned soil, the caring work that produced a fine vegetable patch, the neatly trimmed ornamental shrubbery, and her pride...several herbs in terracotta pots.

Lisane liked to cook, and her kitchen bore all the necessary utensils needed for almost every dish in her late mother's repertoire of fine cuisine.

Who would have thought such a serious law student would thrive on domesticity? Or choose an aged, rundown cottage instead of high-rise apartment-living?

It probably had everything to do with her inherited French gene pool, she mused as she showered and washed her hair before pulling on shorts and a fresh top, then fixing an omelette stuffed with mushrooms, chives and a hint of garlic for her evening meal.

Afterwards she slotted in a DVD, watched it to the end, then climbed into bed and fell asleep within minutes of her head touching the pillow.

Sunday morning was divided between the gym, fixing decorative borders on the walls in the guest bedroom, then adding the white embroidered bedcover with its numerous ruffles and matching pillow covers.

It looked great, the numerous sewing hours necessary in its making well worthwhile.

Initially, she'd made allowances to cover tradesmen's expenses, for, although she could take care of the painting and most of the finishing touches, the kitchen had been in serious need of a complete overhaul and the acquisition of new electrical appliances. The bathroom and laundry also required new fittings. Electrical wiring replaced, the plumbing checked...

In many ways, it had been a mission. But now, twelve months down the track, she could honestly say she was pleased with the result, aware that the money spent had added measurably to the property's market value.

Lisane spent the afternoon completing the remaining architraves, then she cleaned up, took her laptop out to the small table and chair set beneath a magnificent jacaranda tree and caught up on work she needed to review in preparation for the following day.

Dinner was a mixed salad and smoked salmon, a bowl of fresh fruit, and she had just finished dispensing with the dishes when her cellphone rang.

She quickly dried her hands and picked up.

'Lisane…Solene.'

It wasn't seven already, surely? 'I was going to call you.' A quick glance at her watch assured it was a few minutes past the hour. 'How are all the wedding preparations?'

Her sister gave a faintly hollow laugh. 'We're contemplating an elopement.'

Lisane crossed into the lounge and sank into a comfortable chair. 'That bad, hmm?'

'Like you wouldn't believe.'

It didn't take three guesses to determine the source. 'Jean-Claude's beloved *maman*?'

'Uh-huh. Two weeks before the wedding she wants to change floral arrangements for the church…again.'

Two months ago it had been orchids, only to be discarded last month for cream roses.

'It gets worse,' Solene lamented. 'She thinks ivory would complement my gown, rather than pale pink, for the flower-girl, when the dressmaker has already finished the dress.' Solene gave a heartfelt groan in despair. 'I'm about ready to scream.'

Oh, dear. 'You've tried diplomacy?'

A significantly eloquent sigh echoed down the line. 'Been there, done that.'

Jean-Claude's mother had taken both Lisane and Solene beneath her maternal wing when they lost their own mother a few years ago, wistfully looking upon them as the daughters she'd never had. A kindly woman, with good intentions. Except for one slight flaw…she liked to be in control.

'It's your wedding,' Lisane pointed out gently.

'Hah!'

'Jean-Claude—'

'Issued an ultimatum this afternoon.'

'And?'

There was a few seconds' silence. 'Tears, apologies, more tears.'

She could imagine just how it went, and how distressed her sister had been. Wedding preparations should be pleasurable and exciting…not fraught with nervous tension.

'Two more weeks, Solene, then you can relax.'

'You think?'

'Definitely.'

'Your dress is gorgeous.'

They'd shared images via email, decided on colour, and as they were the same height and dress size it had been a simple matter for Solene to take Lisane's place with fittings.

'Can't wait to see you.'

Solene's faintly wistful response brought a slight lump to Lisane's throat. 'Me, too.' Weekly phone calls and email contact didn't cut it. 'Saturday.' She relayed her flight details, then ended the call.

* * *

Monday soon proved to be one of those days when whatever could go wrong...*did.*

Lisane woke late, saw the red digits blinking on her digital alarm, cursed the electrical fault through the night and hit the floor running to complete the fastest shower on record. Once dressed, she filched a cereal bar from its packet, collected her briefcase, laptop, and unlocked her garage.

She could still make it into the city on time *if* the traffic flow was unhindered by roadworks...

Lisane slid in behind the wheel of her VW Golf, ignited the engine, reversed out onto the street, navigated it, only to groan out loud minutes later as she saw the long stream of vehicles stretching as far as the eye could see.

When at last the endless convoy began to inch forward, no one seemed inclined to allow her to ease into the flow of traffic. Desperate measures were called for, and minutes later she made it amidst a cacophony of irate car horns accompanied by a few graphic hand gestures and mouthed blasphemy.

Why would the city council choose peak-hour traffic to conduct road repairs? Although, to be fair, this particular stretch bore heavy traffic all through the day and into the night.

She extracted her cellphone, activated the loudspeaker function and called work, notified her superior she'd be late, then continued the crawl-like pace into the central city.

Arriving late involved some serious catch-up time, and she examined the day's agenda, liaised with the police prosecutor, went through case notes, consulted with her client prior to his appearance in court—and, despite her cleverly structured questioning of the witness, the magistrate deemed in conclusion that there was sufficient evidence for the case to be heard in a higher court before a judge and jury at a future date.

It wasn't the result her client had hoped for, but, given his prior conviction and the strength of the witness's testimony, she could only reiterate fact and arrange a debriefing consultation.

Lunch was a chicken and salad sandwich followed by fresh fruit eaten at her desk, after which she made several phone calls and outlined pertinent points on her case notes prior to a late-afternoon consultation with a solicitor and his client, involving documented injuries incurred in an accident, which should conclude in a reasonable financial settlement for the client.

It was after five when Lisane saved all data to disk, closed down her laptop and pushed paperwork into her briefcase.

Home sounded good. She'd shower, don comfortable clothes, eat, then put in a few hours reviewing documentation in regard to a consultation scheduled for the following day.

An hour later she checked the contents of her refrigerator, decided she wasn't in the mood for food just yet and crossed to the small second bedroom which housed a desk, bookshelves filled with law books, her sewing machine and a dressmaker's dummy bedecked in a partly finished gown.

She could already 'see' the completed garment, the total picture with stiletto heels and evening bag, and her fingers began to itch as she viewed the soft drape of silk chiffon.

It wouldn't take much...

Within minutes she was attaching the requisite tacking, and she soon became lost to everything but the artistry of creation as she fed the chiffon carefully through the machine.

The thin spaghetti straps required a steady hand, and she measured the length, then fitted both.

There was immense satisfaction in the knowledge that only the fine hand-stitching remained, and she switched off the machine then stretched her arms high to ease the slight kink in her shoulders.

Food seemed a sensible option, and she fixed a tuna salad, filched bottled water from the refrigerator and ate while scanning the day's newspaper headlines.

It was after nine when she opened her briefcase and began reading documentation.

At some stage the burr of her cellphone intruded, and she picked up to discover Zac on the line.

'Hi.'

His soft chuckle curled round her nerve-ends and tugged a little. 'You sound distracted. Bad day?'

'It could have been better.'

There was a slight pause. 'Want to talk about it?'

What was the point? 'Not really.'

She could almost see the way his deep brown eyes darkened, the hard acceptance beneath a degree of cynicism. Criminal law dealt on occasion with the under-belly of society, people who possessed few if any scruples and some who committed unspeakable acts.

'All we can do is our best.'

Lisane gave a slight grimace. 'And when the best isn't good enough?'

'For whom? The client whose prior record makes him a threat to the community?'

It wasn't about winning, but representing the law within the parameters of a legal system designed to seek justice for all.

Her lips curved into a faint smile. 'OK, now you've made me feel better...how was your day?'

'I could come tell you in person.'

She was tempted. Seriously tempted. Terrific sex, and afterwards strong, warm arms to cradle her close. For a moment the image was overwhelming, and she queried lightly, 'Are you waiting for an invitation?'

'No.'

A bubble of laughter escaped her throat at the faint mockery in his voice, and she voiced teasingly, 'See you in fifteen.'

Fourteen, Lisane determined as headlights threw a sweeping beam across the front of her cottage, followed seconds later by the faint snick of a car door closing.

Lisane met him on the front porch, her eyes wide and faintly luminous in the dimmed light as he framed her face.

His mouth brushed hers, felt her lips part in welcome, and he angled his head and went in deep, savouring the taste and the scent of her. Wanting, needing her warmth, her touch.

Dammit, all of her.

He was aware of her arms reaching to encircle his neck, and felt her fingers weave into the thickness of his hair, sensed their soothing movement against his scalp and he feathered a light path down the length of her spine to cup her bottom, bringing her against the thick hardness of his desire.

He could take her now, dispense with her clothes, his

own…the effect she had on him was a sorcery both sweet and carnal.

For a moment he'd neglected to remember where they were, clearly visible in the dim porch light to anyone who chanced a look.

Zac eased back a little, and reluctantly relinquished her mouth as he leant his forehead against her own.

She was incapable of saying a word as he shaped her shoulders, then he let his hands slide down her arms to thread his fingers through her own.

'Let's take this indoors, hmm?'

The cottage design was simple. A wide hallway separated the lounge on one side from the main bedroom opposite. From there the hallway opened into a large living area, with two small bedrooms to the left. The kitchen, bathroom and utility room stretched across the rear of the cottage.

Silently she turned at his direction and together they entered the hallway and closed the door behind them.

Zac lifted a hand and trailed fingers down her cheek. 'Are you done with work for the night?'

It would be easy to say *yes*, only for honesty to win out. 'Not quite.'

His thumb pressed against the centre of her lower lip, and his smile held a tinge of amusement as he released her. 'I'll go make coffee.'

Lisane watched him turn towards the kitchen, and she let her gaze linger on the wide expanse of shoulder, aware of the powerful musculature beneath the fine chambray shirt. The taut waist and the tight butt moulded by figure-fitting black jeans.

Just looking at him made her heart rhythm accelerate

to a faster beat. And that was only part of it! Her nerves flared and took on a life of their own, almost *humming* with the anticipation of his touch…his possession.

To be so attuned to him scared her a little. It was as if he was a part of her, attached but not bound.

There were times when she could tell what he was thinking, predict how he would react in a given situation.

Then just as she thought she could read him, he would surprise her…as he did now.

Coffee?

He'd disappear calmly into the kitchen and do coffee, when she could have sworn he'd sweep an arm beneath her knees and carry her into the bedroom?

Sure, she could follow him, wind her arms round his neck, pull his face down to hers…and invite him to continue from where he'd left off.

It was what she *wanted* to do.

Instead she settled down, found her place in the documentation and continued reading, pausing occasionally to make notes.

Minutes later Zac placed a mug of steaming coffee on the desk, then he crossed to the bookcase, retrieved a book and trailed light fingers across her shoulders.

'I'll take this into the lounge. Join me when you're done.'

Lisane lifted her head, caught his warm smile…and felt her bones begin to melt.

The anticipation, the promise of how the evening would end, sent heat curling deep in her belly, and a faint tinge of pink coloured her cheeks as she caught the teasing quality evident in his dark gaze.

'Go,' she directed with mock severity, and heard his husky chuckle as he left the room.

Dammit, how could she possibly focus on *work* when all she could think of was *him*?

Fifteen minutes later she closed the bulky file and slid it into her briefcase. Then she stood, stretched her arms high in order to ease the faint kink at the base of her neck, collected her empty coffee mug and returned it to the kitchen before entering the lounge.

Zac looked up, closed the book he'd been reading and extended his hand without offering so much as a word.

Lisane crossed to his side and let him pull her down onto his lap.

His hand shaped the back of her head as he eased her cheek into the curve of his shoulder. 'Tired?'

It was so good to feel the solid thud of his heart and have his fingers begin a soothing massage at her nape.

Restful…not. How could she relax when her entire body was incredibly attuned to *his*?

The exclusive subtle scent of his aftershave teased her senses, as did the clean smell of his skin, his clothes. But it was more than the shape and form of him. She admired his sharp mind and his degree of integrity, adored his sense of humour and his ability to relax away from the strictures of his profession.

Yet on another level his legal expertise in the court-room held her in awe, exposing as it did a steel-like ruthlessness that showed no mercy. A quality that put him ahead of his contemporaries and earned immeasurable respect.

A man one coveted as a friend, and had every reason to fear as an enemy.

'Difficult case?'

Lisane lifted her head and met eyes that were dark and slumberous. 'Just a lot of information to absorb.'

Zac inclined his head in agreement. 'In order to cover any unexpected contingencies.'

Even in the most open-and-closed case, one needed to be prepared for the element of surprise by opposing counsel.

'Anything you want to run by me?'

One minor detail kept sticking in her mind, and she voiced it, instinct rather than purported fact providing the slight niggle of disquiet.

She knew all the angles, and had explored each and every one of them, consulted her superior…yet still it refused to gel.

'Instinct should never be ignored.' Zac's eyes narrowed slightly. 'Where are you tempted to go with this?'

It sounded illogical, even as she relayed her thoughts, yet his slight indication of agreement gave a sense of satisfaction.

'It's possible.'

Lisane examined his features carefully. 'But not probable.'

'Always be prepared to expect the unexpected.'

It was a mantra every law student learnt by heart, and she gave him a lopsided smile. 'Point taken.'

His fingers threaded through the silky length of her hair, shaped her head and brought it close to his own.

The touch of his mouth was warm against her softly parted lips, and she was unable to prevent a husky murmur of approval as he slipped a hand beneath the hem of her T-shirt and sought a silk-encased breast, teasing the firm flesh as he unerringly found its hardening peak.

His mouth firmed over hers, taking her deep as his tongue tangled with her own, seeking to conquer in a manner that tore the breath from her throat.

Lisane wound her arms around his neck and held on, savouring his touch, his possession, as she met and matched his own.

There was no sense of time or place. Only the desire to assuage a mutual need.

His clothes, hers, became a frustrating irritation and she didn't protest as he tugged her T-shirt over her head, then freed the clasp on her bra.

Her hands were equally busy as she undid the buttons on his shirt, then reached for the fastener on his jeans.

With one fluid movement Zac rose to his feet with her in his arms, heard her bubbling laughter, stilled it with his mouth, and carried her through to the main bedroom.

'Witch.' The huskily voiced imprecation held amused resignation as he tumbled them both down onto her bed.

'And that makes you…what?' she teased, then gasped as he removed his jeans, shucked off his briefs and dispensed with the remainder of her clothing.

'Let's find out, shall we?'

His erection was a potent force, and she soothed the silky head with an exploratory touch, heard the breath hiss through his teeth, then she brushed the taut skin with a few finger-pads, lightly, in a deliberate tease that brought a husky groan from his lips.

Control…he had it. Yet she was fascinated to discover what it would take to break it.

How far would he allow her to go?

Seconds later it was her turn to gasp as he sought the satiny folds at the entrance to her femininity and latched on to the highly sensitised nub, initiating a deliberate stroking movement that sent her wild.

Soon it wasn't enough, and she was barely aware of

urging his possession as sensation spiralled, sending her high…so high it was almost more than she could bear.

'Now.' Was that her voice *begging* for release? The part of her brain that engaged rationale insisted it had to be.

'Not yet.'

Oh, dear heaven. *Yes.* Otherwise she'd go insane with need.

Except he wasn't done. And she almost wept as he brought her to fever pitch…with his hands, his mouth in an oral supplication that blew her away, so far out of her mind she barely stifled an exultant scream as he entered her in one powerful thrust.

Her vaginal muscles contracted, tightly sheathing him as she stretched to accommodate him. When he began to move, she met and matched his rhythm as shameless, pulsating emotion took them to an electrifying high, held them there, then tipped them over into a magically sensual nirvana that was erotic and exquisitely primitive.

Treacherous, Lisane reflected later as she lay in Zac's arms on the edge of sleep.

Because she never wanted it to end.

An inner voice silently demanded, 'Does it have to?'

Sadly, she didn't have an answer.

CHAPTER THREE

THE day's workload commanded all of Lisane's attention, and it was mid-afternoon before news of a colleague's promotion reached her ears.

Well-deserved, given Sue's attention to detail and unrelenting dedication to each case she handled.

'Celebration time. Champagne on me. Tomorrow night?' came through via inter-office email, and over the next hour responses indicated a resounding 'yes', followed by Sue's instructions re time and place.

The thought of a girls' night out was a pleasurable one, and Lisane spent Tuesday evening making notations from various law books. Gradually, with steady persistence, she was gathering sufficient information to present a strong case. Together with covering every contingency opposing counsel might draw from.

Even so, there was that edge, the knowledge she may have slipped up on one unexpected but important detail.

It kept her up late, and resulted in pertinent dialogue with her superior next day.

Consequently it was a relief to slip behind the wheel of her car and juggle peak hour traffic clogging the arterial roads leading from the city.

She reached the cottage with an hour in which to shower, dress and be on the road again.

Basic black was 'go anywhere' attire, and Lisane fixed her hair into a careless knot, applied blusher and lipgloss, then slid her feet into stilettos, collected her purse, her keys, and locked the front door before slipping in behind the wheel of her silver Golf.

Traffic flow into the city was steady, and she parked beneath the inner-city hotel, then took the lift up to the Atrium lounge.

Three of her associates were comfortably settled with drinks before them, and no sooner had Lisane greeted them than the final member of their coterie arrived.

It was lovely to relax and unwind away from the office. To talk without the constant constraints of work, and they took their time before crossing into the restaurant.

Champagne was the celebratory toast of choice, and Sue's promotion was given due merit before a waiter delivered their starters.

Fine food and drink, and good company. Who could ask for anything more of an evening spent with friends?

The amazing thing in being the fabulous five, as they regarded themselves, was the friendship they shared in and out of the office. There was no element of envy, jealousy or the desire for one-upmanship…just five young women who got along.

'Oh, my. Look who's just walked in.'

Someone of note, obviously, Lisane deduced as she discreetly turned her head, only to feel her stomach twist at the sight of Allegra in the company of her parents.

Dressed to kill in a red cut-away cocktail gown that ventured into the almost-too-much-skin territory, Allegra resembled a catwalk model…confident, faintly aloof, and stunning.

'Wow.'

Sue's hushed comment didn't come close, and the questions followed in tandem.

'No male partner?'

'Maybe he's joining them?'

'The question is…*who*?'

Speculative conjecture at its best…and discretion, given it was no secret Allegra had her eye on Zac Winstone.

More than an eye, Lisane accorded silently. The female barrister was in for the kill, and didn't care who knew it!

'Uh-oh, she's just picked up her cellphone.'

'She's smiling.'

'The woman's a bitch. In and out of the courtroom.'

'OK, girls, let's move it along, shall we?'

Sue lifted her champagne flute. 'Sure. Here's to women doing it for themselves.'

'Ah…you might like to rephrase that.'

Amelie grinned. 'Just checking you're on the ball.'

'Wicked.'

'But fun.'

Truly a girls' night out, Lisane decided with a degree of humour. Memorable, in that their jobs dealt with serious issues within the parameters of the law. Where evil intent superceded good, and justice needed to be seen to be done. Not always successfully.

Making it work was the challenge. Examining legal precedents in order to close any slight loopholes opposing counsel might offer. And above all, attempting to do one's best for the client…whether guilty or innocent.

'What are your thoughts on the Marshall case?'

There was a collective groan. 'Forbidden territory. Nothing, but *nothing* to do with work is going to escape our lips tonight.'

There was a pause while the waiter delivered their mains, and Sue barely waited until he was out of earshot before voicing,

'OK, so let's have an update on the men in our lives.'

The theme was familiar, Lisane mused. Lack of dedication to the relationship, little if any commitment, and emphasis on sex. Two young women in their group were content with the status quo, while one appeared misty-eyed and vowed she wanted the ring, marriage and family.

'Lisane?'

'Pass.'

'Not good enough. Answer the question.' Sue's teasing mockery brought some light laughter, and Lisane entered into the spirit of the game.

'Sorry, counsellor. Privileged information.'

'Damn.'

'Don't look, but a serious hunk of a guy is being led towards Allegra's table.'

Lisane controlled the desire to check. Common sense reassured her that it couldn't be Zac. But just for a few seconds the possibility didn't seem beyond the realm of reality. The Winstone and Fabrisi families were legal and social equals, dedicated to charitable causes, and were frequently seen in each other's company.

Surely Zac would have told her if he intended to join Allegra and her parents this evening…wouldn't he?

Allegra had developed manipulation into an art form, and possessed few, if any, scruples where Zac was concerned.

'Wonder who he is?'

'Family friend?' Sue ventured. 'The parents are greeting him like a long-lost son.'

The waiter cleared their plates and took an order for dessert...sinful choices in the name of celebration, and warranting some serious time in the gym to compensate.

Coffee followed, and they lingered a while, then took care of the bill and made their way to the powder-room.

Lisane was the last to leave, and just as she opened the door it swung in, causing a hasty few steps back to avoid a collision.

The last person she wanted to see up close was Allegra...but there was no avoiding a confrontation. One Lisane opted to make very brief.

'Allegra.'

'He's my cousin, darling.' Words spoken without preamble, and the woman's smile held a brilliance that was totally at variance with the cool glitter in her eyes. 'On a brief visit from Perth.'

'How nice for you.' She stepped around Allegra in a bid to leave the powder-room, only to have her passage blocked.

'He's serious eye-candy, and does service as a social handbag.'

Lisane held the young woman's gaze and successfully masked her disquiet. 'My friends are waiting for me.'

'Another minute or two won't matter.' Allegra smoothed a hand over one slender hip, then she speared a lacquered nail in the air a few inches from Lisane's face. 'Take note. Zac is mine.'

It took two to fight, and she wasn't about to go there. 'If that's true,' she managed evenly, 'why is he with me?'

Allegra's eyes became ice. 'You must know Zac will never marry you.'

She needed an exit line, fast! 'Did it occur to you we might be content with the relationship,' she waited a deliberate beat, then added quietly, 'the way it is?'

'Not for long.' The woman's triumph was tainted with evil satisfaction. 'Any time soon his ring will be on my finger.'

'Really?' How could she sound so calm, when inside her nerves were shredding? She held Allegra's gaze as she took a determined step forward, silently challenging the woman to step aside.

For a moment it didn't appear as if Allegra was going to move, then she lifted one eyebrow in a gesture of disdain and shifted slightly.

Lisane stilled the urge to rush out the door, choosing a measured, unhurried pace, and braced her shoulders against the nervous tension feathering icily down her spine.

'We were about to initiate a rescue mission,' Sue declared quietly as Lisane joined the group of four young women lingering a few feet distant. 'Are you OK?'

'Fine.' She managed a warm smile. 'Let's go, shall we?'

It wasn't difficult to keep up a carefree façade as they took the lift down to the car park, and she kept the smile in place until she slid in behind the wheel of her car.

Allegra's taunts echoed inside her head, and she almost wished she'd told the woman to get a life...except common sense had silently warned of the possibility of professional repercussions.

Allegra Fabrisi held a degree of power...a word here and there, an unfair criticism, and it could result in the speculative attention of Lisane's peers.

Roll on Saturday!

Three weeks' absence in Sydney would provide a welcome breathing space. There were the final planning stages, the wedding itself and a lovely break in which to visit the beach, check out the shopping malls, and just relax.

Lisane collected the sack of groceries from the seat of her car and carried them indoors.

The dinner menu she'd planned for Friday evening was relatively simple, and she toed off her stilettos, then quickly assembled ingredients and began preparations.

An evening meal timed for seven enabled her to cook, then shower and change and set the table.

She made it with a few minutes to spare, and she slid the herb bread into the oven as the doorbell rang.

Zac's familiar tall frame filled the aperture, and the mere sight of him sent the beat of her heart into overdrive.

'Hi.'

He'd discarded a professional business suit for black tailored trousers, a white chambray collarless shirt and a black butter-soft leather jacket.

Wow seemed an inadequate description.

'Come through,' she managed steadily, and she stood aside so he could precede her down the hallway.

With considerable ease he paused to drop an overnight bag in her bedroom, shrugged out of his jacket, then he gathered her in against him and took possession of her mouth in a leisurely kiss.

Oh, my, was all she could think when he released her.

He'd brought wine, which he took into the kitchen, uncorked and let breathe while he admired the finishing touches she'd made to the room.

'Would you like a drink?'

Zac turned towards her. 'Just wine with dinner.'

Lisane checked the herb bread, saw it was beginning to crisp, and enquired about his day.

'Fact-gathering, validating authenticity, a conference call.' And one intriguing brief he had yet to decide whether to accept. 'You?'

'Nothing out of the ordinary.' Just a pile of paperwork she'd needed to shift before day's end, notations for ongoing cases ensuring the colleague taking over her workload for the next three weeks was *au fait* with current files.

Last night she'd packed her bag ready for the flight to Sydney. As bridesmaid, she'd also assembled games and prizes for Solene's bridal shower party, and the hen-party. All she needed to do in the morning was add last-minute essentials before Zac drove her to the airport.

The food with its delicate sauce was a hit, and she took pleasure in Zac's compliment.

She was far from a domestic goddess, but she liked making her home attractive, cooking good food and presenting it well. It seemed to be a family trait, for Solene read cookbooks as others read…books.

Dessert comprised a fresh fruit salad jazzed up with wine and accompanied by whipped cream drizzled with crystallized sugar, and afterwards they took coffee in the lounge.

It was comfortable having him here like this. Her territory, with its easy familiarity.

She was going to miss him, miss *this*, being with him, sleeping with him…forget the *sleep* part, making love with him.

For her it was *love*, not simply the act of sharing physical sex. Had he guessed how it was for her? In a way she hoped not, for it would only increase her vulnerability level.

Tonight was special. She'd set the scene with fine food, and soon…soon he'd take her hand and lead the way to her bedroom.

It was there they'd indulge all the senses, and make love long into the night. Her imagination took flight, creating images which heated the blood and set her pulse racing to an increased beat, until the wanting became need.

He knew. Had to, and the warmth of his smile held sensual promise as he rose to his feet.

His kiss possessed warmth, then heat, and she leant into him, absorbing his strength as she kissed him back with hungry passion.

A hunger Zac returned in kind as they moved towards the bedroom, shedding clothes along the way.

Naked, he cupped her bottom and lifted her high against him, then he lowered his head and took the peak of her breast into his mouth, nipping the hardened aureole with his teeth until she reached the brink between pleasure and pain.

Lisane retaliated with a love bite to the sensitive curve at the edge of his neck, felt his body tense, then he shifted his attention to her mouth in a possession that shredded every nerve-cell in her body.

Just as she thought she might need to communicate a need to breathe, he positioned her to accept his hardened length and surged into her moist heat, filling her as he released her mouth and buried his lips in the hollow at the base of her throat.

She was with him, part of him, body and soul, and she began to move, slowly at first, then with increasing abandon until she became almost a wild thing in his arms.

It wasn't enough, for there was so much more, and together they fell onto the bed in a tangle of limbs and laughter, to love each other again and again through the night until exhaustion overcame passion and they drifted to sleep in each other's arms.

The alarm sounded loud, too loud, and Lisane groaned, hit the *off* button, glimpsed at the darkened room and buried her head beneath the pillow.

It couldn't be five already.

'One hour to check-in time,' Zac drawled as he reached for the bedside lamp. 'Shower, dress, coffee, then hit the road.'

How much sleep had she had?

Not enough, she decided as a hand whipped away the pillow and tossed back the bedcovers.

'OK, OK,' she muttered. 'I'm out of here.'

The shower did much to waken her, and Zac's presence in the shower stall ensured she didn't linger over-long... although the temptation to savour his tautly muscled body was hard to resist.

Except it wasn't an option, given the time constraint, and almost as if he knew he took possession of her mouth in a brief, hard kiss, then released her.

'Go,' he said huskily. 'Or you won't make the flight.'

It took only minutes to towel herself dry, then she pulled on a robe and made for the kitchen, where the aroma of freshly brewed coffee greeted her.

She filled two mugs, added sugar, then sipped hers with

appreciation. It was hot, too hot, and she decided to dress while it cooled.

Zac was in the process of dressing when she entered the bedroom. She quickly collected fresh underwear, donned it, then pulled on jeans, a cotton top, stepped into jogging shoes and applied minimum make-up, fixed her hair, then she shrugged into a tailored jacket, placed toiletries and make-up into her bag and fastened it. All done.

They had a smooth run through to the airport, and Lisane checked in her bag as a voice on the Tannoy announced last call for boarding on her flight.

It was better this way, she decided as Zac caught her close for a brief hard kiss. Then she went through the security barrier, turning briefly to wave at him before disappearing down the long passageway leading to her flight departure bay.

Three weeks was a long time. Too long, she despaired, equally torn between wanting to stay and needing to leave.

Although she'd get to see him next weekend when he flew in for Solene's wedding.

The one-hour forty-minute flight was uneventful, except there was the familiar pull of *home* as she caught sight of Sydney Harbour, the famed bridge and nearby opera house.

Disembarking was achieved with minimum ease, and there, waiting just inside the Arrivals lounge, were her sister and fiancé.

Hugs, laughter, and more hugs as they greeted each other before lining up at the luggage carousel.

There was so much to say, such excitement, that Lisane and Solene barely drew breath during the drive to suburban Manly on the northern side of the city.

Daylight saving had not long come into effect, which meant Sydney time was an hour ahead of Brisbane.

'All the girls will be here around two for the bridal shower.'

Hadn't she checked the list, in-flight, that Solene had emailed detailing the lead-up to the wedding?

Saturday afternoon, bridal shower.

Sunday, barbecue with Jean-Claude's parents.

Monday, dress fittings.

Tuesday, last-minute shopping.

Wednesday…what was Wednesday?

Thursday, wedding rehearsal.

Friday, collect all wedding gear and run a final check of everything.

As the bride's sister and only bridesmaid, Lisane was in charge of ensuring everything ran as smoothly as possible.

A priority was to unpack and change, eat lunch on the run while checking there was sufficient food and drink for the afternoon, the novelty games she'd organised as entertainment, gift prizes…and text-message Zac.

Jean-Claude left minutes before the first guest arrived, and it became a fun-filled few hours with some twenty young women and Jean-Claude's mother present.

There was some teasing and much laughter as Solene received some lovely gifts, and Jean-Claude's mother lingered to help clean up after the last guest departed.

'Alain is so looking forward to seeing you again,' Chantelle confided. 'He's been at a bit of a loss since you moved away to Brisbane.'

She gave Chantelle a warm hug. 'It'll be lovely to catch up with you all. How is Henri?'

'He's well, dear. I'm hoping you and Alain will spend some time together.'

Lisane felt an edge of tension begin to make itself known. Alain was the youngest son, and perhaps his mother's favoured son...one she had so hoped Lisane would marry.

'I have a partner,' she said gently, aware Chantelle knew of Zac's existence in her life. 'You'll meet him when he flies in for the wedding.'

'Yes, but you're not engaged or committed to him, are you?'

There was no sting intended in the words, and none taken, but they served to remind her neither Chantelle nor Alain had accepted she'd moved on.

'Sorry,' Solene intimated after Chantelle left. 'I meant to warn you.'

'It's OK.' What else could she say?

Dinner was a convivial meal, and afterwards they spent time reviewing the guest list, the table seating at the reception venue, then clarified a few minor details Solene wanted Lisane to check, so it was late when they decided to head to bed.

'Tomorrow,' Solene bade with a weary smile, 'we talk about *you*. I want to hear first-hand all about the hunk in your life.'

What to tell? Lisane contemplated over breakfast next morning when her sister quizzed her about Zac.

'He's special.' And how!

'You love him.' It was a statement, not a query, and one she couldn't deny.

'Does he love you?' Solene persisted gently as she refreshed their tea and coffee.

Did he? She couldn't be sure. Affection, without doubt, and passion. Or was it merely lust? 'I hope so.'

'Has he asked you to move in with him?'

Sleeping over wasn't the same as living together. Would she, if he asked her? In a heartbeat. 'We prefer our independence.'

'Darling, this is Solene, your sister, remember? We don't keep secrets from each other.'

A soul-searching heart-to-heart? 'He hasn't asked,' she responded lightly. 'But if he did, the answer is yes.'

The phone rang, and Solene took the call…which successfully diverted the conversation.

'Chantelle,' Solene informed, 'suggesting we go over before the guests arrive this afternoon for some family time. Apparently she's planned a surprise.'

And what a surprise it turned out to be!

Stretched high beneath Jean-Claude's parents' covered terrace was a banner proclaiming 'Welcome home, Lisane!'

There were hugs and kisses, a celebratory cake…and Alain.

Lisane didn't know whether to laugh or cry, and somehow managed both…but not for the reasons Chantelle, Henri or Alain imagined.

Accept it in the spirit in which it's meant, she thought, and she did, joining in the gaiety with spontaneous enjoyment.

Alain, however, was something else.

He was a friend, a good one of long standing. But that was all. Throughout the afternoon she endeavoured to indicate that, except he chose not to notice.

Wherever she moved, he ensured he was not far from her side. He'd touch her arm, put a light arm loosely over her shoulder. Top up her drink, check she had sufficient to eat.

To everyone else it appeared to be simple friendship, but she knew she wasn't mistaken in thinking that, as far as Alain was concerned, there was more to it than that. And there wasn't much she could do about it.

At least, not here, not now.

The last thing she wanted to do was hurt his feelings, or upset Chantelle.

There was an awkward moment when her cellphone rang and she took a call from Zac, choosing to move indoors for a degree of privacy.

The sound of his voice curled through her body and made the blood in her veins sing.

'Working hard?' she managed lightly, aware he was deep in preparations for a case due to begin in court the next day.

'Taking a break. And you?'

'Attending a barbecue hosted by Jean-Claude's parents.'

'Have fun.'

Wish you were here. 'Will do. I'll text-message you tomorrow.'

'Sleep well,' Zac bade, and ended the call.

Not without you, she added silently, longing for his touch, the feel of him beneath her hands, her lips.

When she re-emerged Alain caught hold of her hand, and brushed his lips to her temple. 'Please,' she protested quietly.

'I've missed you so much.'

'Nothing has changed, Alain. Don't do this.'

'Let me take you to dinner tomorrow night.'

'I'm sorry.' She gently disentangled her hand and mingled with the guests, helped Chantelle organised coffee, and afterwards joined her in the kitchen as they cleaned up.

It was after eleven when Solene and Jean-Claude indicated the need to leave, and Lisane gave a silent sigh of relief the evening had come to an end.

The following few days were hectic, with visits to the dressmaker for fittings, checking with the florist, the cake decorator, ensuring there were sufficient sugared almonds...and a moment of blind panic when Solene discovered there was a hitch with her specially designed wedding ring, and it would be a rush to have it finished on time.

Lisane calmed her sister down, spoke firmly with the jeweller...and repeated the process a day later when the wedding caterer enlightened them that the warehouse wouldn't be able to supply the exact napkins Solene had chosen for the tables.

Wednesday evening's hen-party provided some light relief, in that Lisane had chosen a theme and invited several of Solene's girlfriends to participate in the fun and games...all of which involved accentuating Solene's final few days as a single woman.

'If you've organised a male stripper, I'll kill you,' Solene vowed as Lisane announced the main event.

'Something infinitely more tasteful.'

Jean-Claude, disguised as a pirate, to spirit Solene away for the night. Except first he had a part to play...which he did very well, and it was only when Solene began to yell for help that he revealed his identity. After which he scooped his wife-to-be into his arms and carried her out to the waiting limousine, whose trunk held a bag with a change of clothes.

The most solemn pre-wedding event was the wedding rehearsal, scheduled for Thursday evening at the church.

Jean-Claude had chosen Alain to be his best man, which meant Lisane, as bridesmaid, would be his partner for the day and the official part of the evening.

The immediate family gathered and went through their practised steps without a hitch at the minister's direction.

Afterwards they all went on to a restaurant to celebrate the rehearsal in anticipation of the day itself.

Two evenings from now Solene and Jean-Claude would be married, the wedding party would be in full swing… with Zac at Lisane's side.

She was almost counting the hours!

CHAPTER FOUR

SATURDAY dawned bright and clear, with the promise of mild early-summer sunshine. Tree leaves glistened with droplets of moisture from an overnight rain-shower, and there was a freshness in the air that boded well for a lovely day.

In keeping with tradition Jean-Claude had spent the night at his parents' home, and Lisane slipped a robe over her nightshirt and padded into the kitchen.

Ten minutes later she knocked on Solene's bedroom door and placed the tray of food she'd prepared on the bedside pedestal.

'I smell coffee.'

'Breakfast,' Lisane announced with a laughing smile as her sister slid up in the bed and sleepily examined the tray.

Juice, eggs benedict, bacon, croissants, jam, and steaming black coffee.

'Yum.'

'There's enough for two.' She sank down onto the edge of the bed, picked up a hot, crisp croissant, then bit into it with a blissful expression.

'This is the bride and bridesmaid thing?'

Lisane took another bite. 'Sisterly.' She motioned to

the tray. 'Eat up. From here on in the day is going to be a hectic rush.'

'So says the bridesmaid—'

'Who's been a bridesmaid or three, and knows the score.'

Solene sipped her juice and wrinkled her nose. 'Is this the part where we discuss vitally important things like—?'

'The birds and the bees, and preparing oneself for the new husband?' she queried, tongue-in-cheek, and watched her sister break into unrestrained laughter.

'A bit late for that, isn't it?'

'Well,' Lisane said primly. 'I aim to do my best.'

'Thanks,' Solene said gently. 'I'm so glad you're here to share the day with me. It wouldn't be the same without you.'

'Same goes.'

The eggs benedict were divine, even if she said so herself, and the coffee was to die for.

'The florist is delivering—'

'At nine,' Lisane reassured. 'Jean-Claude has the rings. Zac is taking a cab from the airport and should be here around eleven.'

'The photographer is due at one, Chantelle is dropping off Henri at two and taking Zac back to the house. He'll go to the church with Jean-Claude and Alain. The limousines are booked to arrive at two-thirty.'

Solene lifted a hand and Lisane gave it a high-five.

'Piece of cake.'

Well, almost.

The hairdresser was late…the result of a flat tyre. The make-up artist went to the right street in the wrong suburb and rang in a panic for directions.

'Tell me again,' Solene said in a controlled voice. 'This *is* supposed to be the happiest day of my life?'

Lisane attempted to soothe. 'Everything will be fine.'

'Hah!'

The phone rang for the umpteenth time, and Lisane took the call. It was Chantelle, concerned the flowers to decorate the church had yet to arrive.

Lisane sorted it out, relayed the florist's van was due any minute. The doorbell rang, and she let in the make-up artist.

A short while later she opened the door to find Zac standing in the aperture.

'Hi.'

He took in the silk robe, rollers in her hair, caught the slightly frazzled expression and reached for her, enjoying for a brief second the surprised look in her eyes before he captured her mouth in a slow-burning kiss that promised much.

When he lifted his head she could only look at him in total bemusement, and his lips curved into a warm smile.

'Better.'

'I have to...' She gestured helplessly towards the lounge, and he pressed a thumb-pad to her lips.

'I know.' He picked up a suit-bag and hooked it over one shoulder, then collected his overnight bag. 'Show me where to stow these. Then tell me what I can do.'

He followed her down the hallway and deposited his gear, then he cupped her head and kissed her again.

'Much better.'

He looked so good. Felt so good. It was so utterly tempting to move back into his arms.

Except there was a wedding to prepare for, a bride to calm, and they all needed to eat.

'Lunch,' Lisane offered, distracted. 'I made sandwiches early this morning. They're on platters in the refrigerator.'

She gestured in the general direction of the kitchen. 'I'll make coffee. Or there's bottled water—'

'Go.' Zac shrugged out of his jacket and tossed it on the bed. 'I'll take care of it.'

They took a fifteen-minute lunch break, and from then on in everything seemed to progress smoothly.

The make-up artist and the hairdresser worked in tandem, creating magic, then it was time to dress.

The photographer and his assistant arrived ahead of time, so too did Henri, courtesy of Chantelle, who collected Zac, and before long it was time to leave for the church.

Solene had chosen a simple gown in the palest silk chiffon *café au lait*, with a fitted strapless bodice and a full-length skirt that flared in soft folds from the hipline. Instead of a veil, she draped a long, soft scarf in matching silk chiffon over her hair. The effect was stunning, and in her hand she carried a beautiful budded red rose.

Lisane's gown was identical in style, in a deeper coffee colour.

'You make a beautiful bride.' Lisane gave Solene a careful hug. 'Love you heaps.'

'Thanks. You, too.' Solene blinked rapidly. 'Oh, hell, I wasn't going to do this.'

'No tears allowed.' She offered a soft grin. 'Think mascara and foundation touch-ups, arriving late at the church.'

Solene's lips trembled a little, then she turned towards Henri. 'Let's go do this, shall we?'

Jean-Claude's father took her arm and touched light fingers to Solene's cheek. 'It is a great honour to escort you into the care of my son.'

Lisane followed her sister to the limousine, ensuring her gown was safely tucked in before she left the chauffeur to close the door, then she slid into the second bridal car.

It was the most poignant wedding she'd attended, for many reasons, the foremost being Solene and Jean-Claude's obvious love for each other. There was a touch of sadness that her parents weren't able to witness the occasion, and an emotional few minutes when Solene and Jean-Claude said their personal vows.

Alain took his role as best man very seriously... although perhaps that should be amended to Alain enjoying his role as her partner a little too well.

Although why shouldn't he slip an arm around the back of her waist or take hold of her hand as they stood with Solene and Jean-Claude during the photographic session featuring family and guests?

The closeness was solely for the benefit of the photographer and the bridal photos. So why did she harbour an uncomfortable feeling Alain was silently staking a claim?

Was it because of Zac's presence among the guests?

Don't be silly, she silently chastised. She was just being acutely sensitive, and blamed the feeling on an over-active imagination.

Although the feeling increased as they joined Solene and Jean-Claude in the limousine, in which they were driven to a prearranged destination for bridal shots.

It was more than an hour before they returned to the reception venue, where the numerous guests mixed and mingled in the large lounge area. Waiters were in evidence offering trays of canapés and drinks.

Lisane skimmed the room, and saw Zac in conversation with Chantelle and Henri. Immaculately attired, he stood out from every other male among the fellow guests. It wasn't so much the cut of his clothes, but the man himself.

He gave the impression of being very relaxed and laid-back, but beneath the calm exterior was a razor-sharp mind and a compelling ability to analyse the minds of others. It made him a powerful adversary in the court-room, and a man only a fool would choose to cross.

She began weaving her way through the numerous guests, pausing every now and then to converse with a friend, an acquaintance.

'Ah, there you are,' Chantelle greeted with a smile. 'We were just explaining to Zac how Henri and I regard you as part of our family.'

'You've both been very kind,' Lisane said with genuine sincerity. 'Solene looked beautiful, don't you think?'

Zac reached for her hand and laced his fingers through her own, then brought them to his lips. 'So do you.' His eyes held hers, and she couldn't look away.

Oh, my. She could feel the heat flare deep inside and send tiny flames licking through her veins. There was the anticipation, the promise of how the night would end.

She was supremely conscious of him, the innate sensuality he managed to exude without any effort at all…and its effect.

His fingers tightened fractionally on hers, and it was all she could do to control the piercing sweetness suffusing her body.

Everything faded from the periphery of her vision, and for a moment she lost sight of time and place.

Almost as if he knew, he brushed a thumb-pad against the veins at her wrist, and she offered a slow smile that undoubtedly didn't fool him in the slightest.

'Ah, here's Alain.'

Lisane heard the relief evident in Chantelle's voice and turned slightly to accommodate his presence.

'The *maître d'* wants to seat the bridal party and begin serving the first course.'

Was there an element of disapproval in Alain's voice?

'Of course,' she said at once, and turned towards Zac. 'I won't have much of a chance to catch up with you until later.'

He trailed light fingers down her cheek. 'Enjoy.'

The food and champagne went down well…a little too well for Alain, and the toasts and speeches were given in an amusing vein, which brought laughter from the guests when Jean-Claude mentioned some of the highlights of courting Solene.

The cutting of the cake became a celebratory moment, and afterwards the DJ set up his equipment.

There were friends among the guests, people Lisane had known all her life. With Zac by her side, his hand linked with hers, it was almost possible to sense the silent conjecture his presence generated as she effected introductions.

'You're a hit, especially among the women,' Lisane declared with sparkling humour, and sensed his amusement.

'I'm duly flattered.'

The bridal waltz began and they watched Jean-Claude lead Solene onto the floor, then circle it to a slow, haunting waltz.

Alain crossed to her side and took her hand. 'We're next.'

Together they followed the bridal pair's lead, and were soon joined by Chantelle and Henri, then the majority of the guests.

'Zac seems to be quite a catch.'

Lisane felt Alain's hand tighten on hers as he pulled her in close. 'He's a nice man.'

What a tame description for someone of Zac's calibre! Yet what could she say? *He knocked me for six from the first moment I saw him?* That really would go down well, not to mention be hurtful.

'Very obviously wealthy.'

He sounded vaguely bitter, and, unless she was mistaken, jealous. Something for which she'd never given him cause during their friendship.

She looked at him carefully. 'I don't judge people by their wealth or lack of it.'

'Prominent barrister,' Alain continued. 'Attractive. And undoubtedly inventive between the sheets.'

Her eyes clouded a little. 'Stop right there,' she warned quietly. 'Or I'll walk off the floor.'

Alain lifted one eyebrow. 'At your sister's wedding? I doubt it.'

'Watch me.'

'My turn, I think?' Zac's indolent voice intervened, and there was something in the depths of his eyes that encouraged Alain to relinquish his hold.

Zac drew her in, and his gaze narrowed at the rapid-beating pulse at the base of her throat, the faint convulsive movement in her throat.

'Problems?'

'Nothing I can't handle.'

Except it wasn't the time or the place, and it saddened her Alain was using alcohol as a prop to quietly vent his feelings.

'He doesn't want to let go.'

She lifted her face to his. 'No.' It bothered her he hadn't managed to move on and make a life of his own. 'We grew up together. He wanted me to have the same feelings for him as Solene has for Jean-Claude.' She paused. 'Except to me,' she said quietly, 'he's always been the brother I never had.'

'His mother isn't helping the situation.' He made it a statement rather than a query. Chantelle had managed to sprinkle none too subtle hints into their conversation during the afternoon drive to and from her home.

Lisane managed a faint smile. 'You noticed, huh?'

The edges of his mouth twitched a little. 'You could say that.'

'Permissible evidence.'

Zac controlled the husky chuckle threatening to emerge from his throat as he splayed the hand resting at the back of her waist and drew her close against him. 'You might care to rephrase that.'

He saw the moment it hit her, and he delighted in the faint colour tinging her cheeks. 'It's become a little warm in here, don't you think?'

The light teasing quality in his voice was the polar opposite to the hard-hitting, merciless tone he employed in the court-room.

'I think you should behave,' she reproved with mock humour.

'Will you say that in a few hours' time?'

The mere thought momentarily trapped the air in her lungs and attacked the fragile tenure of her control.

'Anticipation is good for the soul,' Lisane offered primly, and heard his soft laughter.

'I shall take pleasure in proving you wrong.'

Imagining just how he'd achieve that caused her to almost miss a step.

'Perhaps we should circulate a little,' she managed, and wasn't sure whether to feel relieved or faintly peeved when he complied by leading her from the dance floor.

A prickling sensation niggled the back of her neck, almost as if someone was watching her every move. Alain? She didn't want to risk a skimming glance among the guests to check.

His disquiet…jealousy, she amended, was unexpected. Or was she simply being incredibly naive to hope he'd accept another man in her life?

Knowing she had a partner was one thing…being confronted with his physical presence was another.

Oh, give it up, she silently counselled. Hadn't she moved to another city in another state to start over so any relationship she formed wouldn't be in his face?

It was Solene and Jean-Claude's day. A beautiful wedding, followed by a lovely, relaxed, fun evening.

Any minute soon the bride and groom would bid their guests goodnight and leave for their hotel.

Almost on cue the DJ halted the music, and Henri, as master of ceremonies, took the microphone and announced Solene and Jean-Claude's departure.

It took a while, and Lisane was among the last to hug them both. 'Love you,' she bade as she attempted to hold on to her emotions.

'Right back at you.'

'See you tomorrow at the airport.'

Then they escaped into the waiting limousine.

Why did *happy* feel so sad? It didn't make sense!

Soon most of the guests had left, the gifts were loaded into a security van and Zac used his cellphone to summon a taxi.

Lisane bore Alain's narrowed gaze as she bade his parents 'goodnight', then she slipped into the taxi at Zac's side.

It had been an emotion-filled day, and one she'd relive many times as she examined photos and replayed the DVD.

Zac caught hold of her hand and lifted it to his lips. 'Tired?'

She looked at him, glimpsed the passion evident in those dark eyes, and smiled. 'If I was to say *yes*?'

'I'd promise to do all the work, then let you sleep.'

Desire, raw and primitive flooded her veins, and she aimed for a light-hearted response. 'Sounds like a plan.'

The night was dark with a pinprick of stars, and the only illumination was street-lights. Traffic was minimal, and the passage to Solene and Jean-Claude's Manly home was achieved in a short space of time.

Zac paid the driver while Lisane used her key to open the front door. The hall light sprang on, revealing some of the detritus of the day looking strangely out of place in Solene's normally immaculately kept home.

It wouldn't take long to set straight, and she began picking up, only to have Zac move to her side.

'Leave it until morning.'

His hands closed over her shoulders as he turned her round to face him, then he lowered his head and sought the sensitive curve at the edge of her neck, lingered there, then trailed up to settle at her temple.

Heat uncoiled from deep within and suffused her body, awakening each and every sensual pleasure point as she leant in against him.

Hands crept up and held his head fast as she slanted her

mouth against his, tasting his lips with the tip of her tongue as if she was beginning a tantalising sensual journey.

He possessed a beautifully shaped mouth, and she explored it at leisure, examining soft and hard tissue, the hard porcelain-like teeth, his tongue…delighting when it furled and began to slow-dance with her own.

It became more, so much more until the touching of mouths was no longer enough.

Lisane had lost awareness of where they were, and she told herself she didn't care. 'You're wearing too many clothes,' she managed, discovering somehow he'd shrugged out of his suit jacket and loosened his tie.

'So,' he said in a low and husky voice, 'take them off.'

Her fingers were deft in freeing his shirt buttons, and she undid the belt at his waist and loosened the top button of his trousers.

Zac toed off his shoes as they dealt with each other's zip fastening.

She loved the feel of him…the strength of his shoulders, the satiny skin covering taut musculature, and his narrow waist. Lean hips, tight buttocks, and the size and strength of his erection.

He found the slim satin edges of her thong and slid a finger beneath each seam at her hips and slipped them free, then he traced a path across her bikini line, tantalising in a way which had her responding in kind.

The only illumination came from the hall light, which cast a dimmed glow in the darkness of night.

Her fingers sought him, and she traced the hard length of his penis with a delicate touch, exploring the stretched foreskin with fascination, enjoying its smooth silkiness as it swelled beneath her feather-light finger-pad.

His body tensed, and she heard his husky groan as she brought him to the edge of control, then it was her turn to gasp as he sought her moist feminine heat and unerringly found the acutely sensitised clitoris.

Orgasm so strong it sprang in a rapidly spiralling coil through her body, and she gave an involuntary cry as he sent her to the brink, held her there, then fastened his mouth over hers as she fell.

The need to have him inside her was overpowering. In one fluid movement she straddled him, and felt his hands shift to cup her bottom.

'Patience, hmm?'

She heard his voice, and felt him move as he transferred them both down onto the bed.

Zac used his arms to support his weight as he began a slow tasting down the edge of her throat, savoured the sensitive hollow, then trailed to the soft fullness of her breast.

Lisane cried out as he explored the sensitive peak then took it into his mouth and suckled until she groaned with the intense pleasure before trailing to its twin and rendering a similar supplication.

The muscles in her belly quivered slightly as he moved lower, and she whimpered when he reached the highly sensitised heat and brought her to orgasm.

Just as she thought she could stand it no longer he positioned himself and entered her in one long thrust, filling her as she stretched to accommodate him.

It was almost more than she could bear, and she arched her body, then joined him in a sexual rhythm that took them both to the edge, held them there, then released them in a mutual sensual free-fall.

Wow. Lisane closed her eyes as the ecstasy diminished, not wanting it to leave the afterglow of sensational sex.

Lovemaking, she substituted. For her it had been more, so much more than just sex.

She felt Zac's lips brush her mouth, and she felt her own part beneath his.

It would be so easy to say *I love you.* And she almost did. Except she knew she'd die if she detected so much as a moment's hesitation in his response.

Zac eased himself from the bed, and moments later she heard the shower running, then he returned to gather her into his arms.

There was a dreamlike quality in standing beneath the shower-spray as he gently soaped her skin, and when he was done she took the soap tablet from his hand and returned the favour, loving the way his body tensed beneath her ministrations.

Afterwards, towelled dry, he carried her back to bed and curled her close in against him.

Lisane struggled through the veils of consciousness as the aroma of fresh coffee teased her nostrils. And there was the smell of food…was that bacon? Eggs? Toast?

'Come on, sleepyhead,' a familiar male voice teased huskily. 'Breakfast.'

She lifted her head from the pillow and looked at her wrist, only to realise she wasn't wearing a watch. 'What time is it?'

'Just a little after nine.'

Nine? That meant they only had an hour before they had to leave for the airport.

She took in Zac's tall frame attired in dress jeans and a chambray shirt and groaned out loud. 'You should have woken me.'

His smile almost melted her bones. 'I just did.'

'Before.'

'You were sleeping so peacefully it seemed a shame to disturb you.'

She sat up, realised she wasn't wearing a stitch and pulled the sheet high, only to hear his husky laughter.

'Come on, imp.' He reached for her robe and tossed it within reach. 'You can get dressed after you've eaten.'

It was only then they managed to catch up on each other's week…snatches of exchanged information as they ate, then cleared the dishes, and by the time she dressed, did something with her hair and added moisturiser and lip-gloss, it was time to leave.

'I wish you didn't have to go.'

Zac collected his overnight bag and hooked his suit-bag over one shoulder as she picked up the keys to Solene's car.

'Unfortunately I have to be in court first up tomorrow, and I have transcripts I need to read in order to put the fin-ishing touches to my notes.'

Lisane knew the drill, appreciated its importance, and understood only too well. Except it didn't lessen the ache close to her heart at the thought of not seeing him for another two weeks.

Hell, two weeks seemed a lifetime!

Traffic was relatively easy on a Sunday morning, and they entered the airport terminal to find Chantelle, Henri and Alain waiting for them. Zac joined the appropriate queue and returned with his boarding pass just as Solene and Jean-Claude entered through the automatic doors.

They didn't have long together, only sufficient time for a few hugs and minimum conversation before the last call for Zac's flight was announced over the Tannoy.

Lisane felt her mouth tremble slightly as Zac lowered his head to hers, and nothing prepared her for the passion as his mouth possessed hers in a kiss that reached right into the heart and soul of her and branded her his own.

When he lifted his head his eyes gleamed dark, their expression enigmatic as they speared hers. 'I'll call you.'

He inclined his head towards Solene and Jean-Claude, Chantelle and Henri, Alain, then he turned and went through Security.

'Oh, my,' Solene murmured minutes later as she leaned in close to bid Lisane goodbye. 'That was something else. Take care, little sister.'

'Have a great holiday.'

'Bet your life on it.'

'That was the second call,' Jean-Claude warned, and after a quick hug they passed through into the security area.

'Would you like to come back to the house for lunch, Lisane?'

She glanced towards Alain and his parents, and tempered her refusal with a smile. 'I'd love to, but I have plans.'

'To catch up on some sleep?' Alain suggested.

Lisane ignored the faint edge in his voice and responded evenly, 'I'm sure we're all a bit tired from the wedding.' She met Chantelle's concerned gaze. 'Perhaps another time?'

'Of course, dear. We'll be in touch.'

She could have lingered a while. Probably should have, she reflected with some remorse as she drove out of the parking building and headed towards the city.

CHAPTER FIVE

LISANE spent the morning outdoors tending the garden beds along Solene's driveway, plucking out weeds and loosening the soil surrounding the hardy natives with their red and green foliage, the sturdy proteas and the clumps of busy-lizzies.

She examined the small expanse of lawn front and back of the house, decided it could do with some grooming, and retrieved the mower.

Sunshine, fresh air and achieving a neat garden was immensely satisfying, and the sun was edging high in the sky when she stowed the garden equipment in the garage.

A shower and change of clothes featured high on her list of priorities, and she had just locked the rear door when the front doorbell pealed.

Who? A salesman? Delivery guy?

Lisane checked the peep-hole, saw it was Jean-Claude's mother, and opened the door.

'Lisane.'

Chantelle greeted her with an affectionate smile. 'I was passing on my way to lunch with friends and thought I'd stop by and invite you to share dinner with us tonight.'

A kind woman who meant well, and whose invitation

she could hardly refuse. 'Love to. What time would you like me to be there?'

'Seven, sweetheart. I have some photos of the wedding. It'll be lovely to relax and catch up.'

Which reminded her to check her digital camera and run off some prints. 'I'll look forward to it.' She'd take a bottle of wine and collect flowers from the florist.

Which she took care of later in the afternoon.

Choosing what to wear to dinner didn't pose a problem, and she took pleasure in the pencil-slim black skirt and fitted blouse, dressed it with a tasteful drop pendant, added a few bracelets, put the finishing touches to her hair and make-up, then she slid her feet into stilettos and collected her bag.

Jean-Claude's parents resided in nearby Allambie Heights, and they both greeted her with a smattering of French and effusive warmth as they drew her into their home.

They were kind, well-meaning people of whom she was very fond…too well-meaning, she determined when Alain arrived minutes later.

She offered a polite smile as he crossed the room and brushed his lips to her cheek.

He was a pleasant man. Someone who would make a wonderful husband and father. So why hadn't she been able to love him as he deserved to be loved?

Was it so wrong to want the mesmeric hunger of primitive passion? To know a desire so strong it was almost shocking in its intensity?

And, having discovered both, to be aware that anything less could never be enough?

On the surface the ensuing few hours proved very

pleasant. A superb cook, Chantelle had excelled herself in presenting a gourmet meal of remembered favourite dishes from the days when Lisane and Solene had been frequent visitors.

On reflection, there were a number of 'remember when's sprinkled through the dinner conversation. Reminiscences that brought easy laughter, during which it was almost impossible not to experience a feeling of *déjà vu*.

'We miss you so much,' Chantelle offered with genuine sincerity. 'In another year or two, praise be, there will be a baby. It would be good for Solene to have you close.'

Lisane had a mental image of her sister pregnant with Jean-Claude's child, the babe itself, and felt the pull of familial loyalty. To share the day-to-day progress and rejoice in every small step would be incredible. Yet to do so would mean relocating to Sydney…and where would that leave her with Zac?

'Brisbane is only a one-hour forty-minute flight away.' Her warm smile was genuine. 'I'll visit often.'

'Ah, but if you were home, it would be better.'

'*Chérie,*' Henri chastised gently. 'Lisane has her own life, is this not so?' He didn't wait for an answer. 'Besides, who knows what the future will hold?'

'There is something you do not share with us?'

She suddenly became the focus of three pairs of eyes.

'Zac and I are very happy together,' she offered quietly.

It was almost possible to read Chantelle's mind: but my son has offered you *marriage*.

Did the official marriage certificate matter so much in the twenty-first century? If there were children, yes. But wasn't it possible to co-exist in a relationship with an agreement of mutual commitment?

For how long? A silent voice taunted.

Did she *want* permanence? To raise a family…grow old with him?

Her heart knew the answer. She just didn't want to go there right now.

'Then I am very pleased for you.'

But disappointed, Lisane added silently. 'Thank you.' She wanted to say more, but couldn't bring herself to voice the words.

'Coffee, *chérie*.' Henri's suggestion brought his wife to her feet.

'Of course.'

'Let me help you.' Lisane followed Chantelle into the kitchen, and took down cups and saucers while Chantelle fixed the coffee machine.

'It was a lovely meal, as always,' she complimented gently as they worked together with the ease of familiarity.

'You are most welcome. You know that.'

Yes, she did, and the knowledge brought a sense of sadness at having upset Chantelle's dearest wish to unite the younger Deveraux sister in marriage with her youngest son.

How could she explain to Alain's mother that, while she valued Alain's friendship, it wasn't possible to love to order? Nor was it fair for Chantelle to encourage him to hang in there on the off-chance Lisane might have a change of heart.

The coffee was done, and Chantelle loaded the tray. 'Let's go join the men, shall we?'

It was after ten when Lisane indicated a need to leave, and she thanked her hosts as Alain walked her out to the car.

She deactivated the alarm and turned towards him with a smile. 'Take care.'

'Always. And you.'

He lowered his head and brushed his lips to her cheek, then he found her mouth in a kiss with intent to seduce.

Don't, she silently begged. Don't do this. To me. To yourself.

She attempted to free herself, and he reluctantly let her go.

'Alain—'

'Old times' sake, Lisane?'

'Not fair.'

'Because I want to be with you?'

She should walk away...and almost did. 'We've already done this.' Her voice was quiet, steady. 'Nothing has changed.'

'So let's not do it again?'

'Please.' She crossed round to the driver's side, slid in behind the wheel and ignited the engine.

At the first set of lights she took the opportunity to switch on her cellphone, heard the familiar beep alert, checked messagebank and had time to read *Call me. Z.*

It didn't take long to reach Solene's Manly home, and she activated speed dial as soon as she stepped indoors.

Zac answered on the second ring, and the sound of his low-pitched drawl sent tiny curls of sensation spiralling deep within.

'Hi.' Her voice sounded husky to her own ears... choked, she amended as she summoned his image to mind without any effort at all.

'Missing me?'

Oh, yeah...in spades. 'A little,' she allowed, and heard his soft chuckle.

'Remind me to make up for it.'

Lisane settled down into a chair. 'Promises, promises. Where are you?'

'In bed.'

'Now, there's a provocative thought.' Extremely evocative, given he didn't wear a stitch beneath the sheets. All that smooth, tanned skin stretched sleek over powerful musculature.

She could almost sense his male scent, the clean smell of soap lingering on his skin from a recent shower…and felt her bones begin to melt.

'How was your day?'

Lisane relayed it in brief detail, adding, 'I spent the evening with Jean-Claude's parents.' Honesty compelled her to include, 'Alain was there.'

'Naturally.'

It was easy to slip into teasing mode. 'That bothers you?'

'Should it?'

'And here I was, afraid you might be jealous.'

'He has my sympathy.'

The evocative factor moved up a notch. She wanted so badly to be with him, it was almost a physical pain.

'No response, Lisane?'

'You want flippant…or deeply serious?'

'The latter might lead to something too hard to handle.'

A light laugh escaped her lips. 'Titillating phone sex, Zac?'

'A very inadequate substitute.' There was humour in his voice.

Wasn't that the truth! 'How's the case going?'

'Opposing counsel has built a strong defence.'

He would be exploring every angle, attempting to gain any edge. 'Too strong?'

'Difficult,' Zac conceded.

'You predict he'll walk?'

'Not if I can help it.'

His expertise in the criminal-law field was well-known, and lauded by his contemporaries in the justice system. A reputation that had gained him a few enemies over time.

'Don't work too hard.' The light caution held genuine concern, and she could sense his answering smile.

'Sweet dreams. I'll call in a few days.'

Lisane heard the faint click as he cut the connection, and she did likewise, taking time to reflect on their conversation as she checked Security before entering her room.

Sleep came easily…too easily, for Lisane woke as dawn was breaking, caught the reality, and closed her eyes in the hope of slipping back into a subconscious lulled by erotic imaginings too highly sensual to want to let go.

Except it wasn't going to happen, and, after a few minutes spent reviewing her plans for the day, she swept the bedcovers aside and stood to her feet.

Whoa. Not such a good idea. Her head wasn't sure if it belonged on her body, and there was a war going on in her stomach.

Something she'd eaten last night?

The escargot? Chicken fricassée? The delicious torte?

Whatever, it wasn't going to stay down.

OK, she reasoned several minutes later after brushing her teeth and rinsing her mouth out. Somewhere, somehow, she'd developed a stomach bug. Twenty-four hours of bland food, plenty of water, and she'd be fine.

Dry toast and an apple proved to be a good strategy, and she busied herself sorting the various boxes of wedding gifts delivered soon after nine. Something which brought vivid memories of the wedding itself.

Then it was time to change and drive into the city to meet lifelong friends Alyse, Karen and Gigi for lunch.

Smart casual wear would suffice, and she stepped into dress jeans, added a fashionable cotton top, then slid her feet into stilettos.

A restaurant at Darling Harbour overlooking the water was their venue of choice, and she was first to arrive.

Sunlight kissed the smooth water's surface, giving it a dappled effect with shadows cast from nearby high-rise hotel, office and apartment buildings.

A favoured area of many, Darling Harbour featured several restaurants and a large shopping complex, with easy access from the inner city.

Admired and frequented by day and by night, it drew patrons and tourists alike.

Lisane followed the *maître d'* to their reserved table, accepted a glass of iced water, and withheld perusing the menu until she was joined by her friends.

'Hey,' a warm feminine voice greeted minutes later, and was doubly echoed as Alyse, Karen and Gigi moved in close to exchange fond hugs in greeting. 'We have an hour…well, forty-five minutes.' They each took a seat and checked out the menu. 'Let's order, shall we?'

Lisane chose something light, and it was wonderful to relax in the company of good friends, to gossip and catch up, to laugh a little.

'OK, *give*,' Alyse begged as the waiter delivered their meal. 'I want to know more about that gorgeous spunky partner of yours.' She offered an impish grin. 'And does he have a brother? A cousin? *Any* male relative who looks and acts like such fabulous eye-candy?'

'An uncle, if you fancy the over-forty male. And there's a cousin or two.'

'Yes, please. Name, phone number.'

Lisane offered a mischievous smile. 'Only a slight problem there.'

Alyse leant forward. 'No problem is insurmountable.'

'The cousins reside in America.' There was a collective audible groan. 'And the uncle lives in London.'

'Oh, well, there goes the master plan.' Alyse's eyes twinkled with devilish fun. 'Moving right along…when can we expect to see a ring on your finger?'

Here we go. The third degree, as only long-time friends can conduct an interrogation! 'You'll be among the first to know.'

'Tight as a clam,' Karen offered. 'Well, that's OK. Just make sure you issue an invite for the big day.'

Why confide the possibility that it may not happen?

Lisane reached into her bag and extracted a slender packet. 'I've brought some photos.'

The best of the best, which Alyse, Karen and Gigi exclaimed over with enthusiasm, from Solene's dress, the flowers, cake, to the groom's brother.

'Did I detect a little one-upmanship going on with Alain?'

A slight understatement, and thankfully out of sight and hearing of most of the guests.

'Did you know he talks about you all the time?' Gigi offered quietly.

'The man needs to move on.' Karen cast Gigi a faint frown.

Lisane picked up on the subtext. Gigi was perfect for Alain. 'Go for it.' Her enthusiasm was genuine, and glimpsed

Gigi's slightly anguished expression. 'I mean it. If you want my blessing…it's yours.'

'There's no chance—'

'None at all,' she said gently.

Alyse checked her watch. 'Five minutes, girls.' She turned to Lisane. 'We're doing dinner and the movies tomorrow evening. Join us.'

'Done. Tell me what time and where, and I'll be there.'

'I'll SMS you.'

They had the waiter bring the bill, settled it, then walked out onto the quay, said 'goodbye', and Lisane elected to browse the shops awhile before heading for the northern suburbs.

Dinner comprised a salad and fresh fruit, after which she slotted in a DVD, watched it, then collected the new suspense novel she'd bought and retired to bed.

The sun was casting bright strips of light through the wooden shutters masking the bedroom window when Lisane came awake and aware she'd slept in.

Eight-thirty? For heaven's sake, why so late?

There were a number of things she wanted to do with the day…so rise and shine, dress, have breakfast and make a start.

She slid out of bed, stood to her feet…and felt her stomach execute a few vicious rolls, necessitating a speedy path to the bathroom.

Again? Maybe the stomach bug was alive and well and determined to stay on for another day.

OK, so she'd deal with it, try for another bland breakfast, and hope for the best.

A suspicious niggle had her doing the maths…and she

came to the conclusion there was no chance. Besides, she was on the Pill…admittedly low dosage, but it hadn't failed her before. So why should she imagine it might do so now?

She made a deal with herself. If the symptoms persisted, she'd purchase a pregnancy-testing kit. It would be easy enough to dispense with if it wasn't needed.

But what if…? No, she wouldn't go there.

Busy. She'd plan the next few days allowing the minimum time in which to think.

It worked mostly because she bought fabric and used Solene's sewing machine to make two casual cotton tops and a tailored skirt suitable for the office.

The cinemaplex Alyse nominated formed part of a large shopping complex with several restaurants and cafe's available for in-house and outdoor dining, and they chose a pavement café for a light meal before buying tickets for the highly awarded film which had scooped the Oscar pool.

There could be no doubt why the film was such a success, for the acting, direction and cinematography were excellent.

Lisane declined extending the evening by sharing coffee, and took Karen's gentle teasing,

'We know. You want to rush off and call Zac. Go for it, girl. If I had a hunk like him waiting for me on the other end of a phone, I wouldn't hang around either.'

Except when she reached the house and checked, there were no messages on her cellphone.

No, no, *no*. Not again, Lisane groaned as she hit the ground running. Two more mornings of this didn't bode well.

There was nothing else for it but to retrieve the pregnancy-testing kit and do the test, and her fingers shook as she extracted the relevant equipment.

The instructions were clear, and she took a deep breath, uttered a silent prayer…and waited for the result.

It was crazy not to want to look, and she did a silent count to ten before she checked…then she leant back against the tiled wall and slid down to sit on the floor.

Pregnant. She was *pregnant*.

Dear lord in heaven…what was she going to do?

OK, so the test didn't offer a one hundred per cent certainty. What if it was wrong?

There was only one way to find out for sure, and she checked the time, the local doctor's surgery hours, saw she had an hour before she could dial the listed number…and showered, dressed, then had breakfast.

Ten more minutes.

The longest minutes in the known universe before she keyed in the number, pleaded urgency and managed to secure a mid-morning appointment.

It was impossible to stay still, and after half an hour of pacing the floor she tied back her hair, added lip-gloss, collected her bag and drove to the medical centre.

With half an hour to spare, she bought the day's newspaper, crossed to a nearby café, ordered a cup of tea and filled in time leafing through the pages.

Overseas section, local news, social column…

A newsprint photo looked incredibly familiar, and she took a closer look.

Allegra Fabrisi? Featured in a Sydney newspaper?

Lisane skimmed the newsprint, and almost reeled with shock.

Allegra Fabrisi, barrister and daughter of eminent Brisbane judge Leo Fabrisi, is expected to announce her engagement soon to a prominent Brisbane barrister and member of the wealthy Winstone family.

Did hearts stop?

For a moment she felt as if she couldn't breathe.

Dear God. *Zac?*

Had to be. Unless…

No, not even Allegra would resort to initiating a false statement…surely?

Get a grip. There was only one way to handle this. She needed to speak with Zac.

So do it, why don't you? a tiny voice prompted.

Except he'd be in court and beyond contact except in a dire emergency. And somehow an SMS wouldn't cut it.

Instead she put a call through to his chambers and left a message for him to contact her that evening.

Lisane wasn't conscious of how long she sat there, or of the people walking by, the sound of traffic, or the occasional blast of a car horn.

All these months had she just been a convenient bed-partner? A fill-in for the woman destined to be Zac's wife? The many nights of lovemaking, the sharing of primitive passion…was it all faked on his part?

Yet none of it seemed to equate with the man she thought she knew so well.

Lisane closed her eyes, then opened them again.

Time. What was the time?

A quick glance at her watch revealed she was due in the

doctor's surgery *now*, and she caught up her bag and crossed into the medical centre.

Half an hour later she retraced her steps and ordered more tea. Hot and sweet in the hope it would soothe her shattered nerves.

Seven weeks pregnant.

It didn't seem possible. Except the doctor had explained precisely how the low-dose Pill was rendered ineffective for the month if there was more than a thirty-six-hour gap between dosage. Narrowing it down, with some pertinent prompting, she was able to pinpoint it to a gastric attack during late August.

'I take it this isn't a planned pregnancy?'

The doctor's words reiterated themselves several times inside her head, and she didn't know whether to laugh or cry.

She was pregnant to a man who was about to become engaged to another woman.

Oh, *hell*. What was she going to do?

Worse, who could she confide in?

No one, except her sister, and Solene wasn't due back in Sydney until Saturday.

The rest of the day passed in a blur as she examined her options, and, although termination was one of them, she knew deep down she'd never be able to bring herself to do it.

Single-motherhood.

Something which would mean relocation from Brisbane.

A slightly hysterical laugh rose in her throat at the thought of flaunting her pregnant belly in the court corridors frequented by both Zac and Allegra.

Not funny!

There was, of course, the slim chance Allegra had deliberately orchestrated the reference to the Winstone family, and it wasn't Zac.

Sure, and pigs might fly.

Lisane forced herself to eat an evening meal and viewed television vacantly as she waited for Zac to call.

When the phone rang at seven she snatched it up and voiced a faintly breathless 'hello'…only to discover it was Alain, not Zac, and she curbed her impatience with effort.

'I want to apologise for last night. I was way out of line.'

Please. I don't need this right now. 'Alain—'

'I thought maybe we could go somewhere,' he intercepted quickly. 'Share a coffee, take in a movie. As friends,' he added. 'Nothing more.'

'Thanks, but—'

'No thanks?'

'I think I'm coming down with something.' Something due to hang around for another seven months…before emerging to become a lifetime commitment!

'Take care.'

'I'll be fine.' Sure, she acceded with a degree of cynicism. She was anything but *fine*.

She couldn't settle, and after channel-surfing she switched off the television and picked up a novel…only to discard it after fruitlessly reading pages without absorbing a word.

Zac…where the hell are you?

OK, she'd wait half an hour, then she'd call *him*.

Except when she did, the call went straight to his messagebank.

Lisane woke several times during the night, checked the time, then her cellphone, and finally slid into a deep sleep from which the insistent burr of the cellphone early next morning had her fumbling for the phone.

'Did I wake you?' Zac's husky voice held amusement as she struggled into a sitting position.

'I slept in.'

'You sound surprised. Late night?'

'In a manner of speaking. You?'

'Dinner with family and friends.'

Lisane closed her eyes, then opened them again. 'Of whom Allegra was one?'

'Yes.'

So it was true. 'Should I congratulate you?'

There was a second's silence. 'Congratulations are a little premature. The news isn't official.'

Almost on cue her stomach roiled, and she barely had time to offer, 'I'll call you back,' before dashing from the bed into the bathroom.

Dear heaven. *This* was morning sickness?

Saturday arrived. With unhurried movements Lisane cleaned up as usual, then dressed in jeans and a top before entering the kitchen to prepare breakfast.

Afterwards she cleaned the house, then shopped to re-stock Solene's pantry in preparation for her sister's return.

Activities which occupied her hands, but did little or nothing to detract from the host of chaotic thoughts and images swirling inside her brain.

The first and foremost being...*how could he?*

Several times she castigated herself for being a fool. Hadn't all the signs been evident?

Yet she'd gone with her heart instead of listening to her head. *Fool.*

Lisane left for the airport mid-afternoon, thankful that Solene and Jean-Claude's flight was on time, and their enthusiastic, laughter-filled reunion did much to lighten Lisane's mood.

Everything was wonderful…Hayman Island, the accommodation, food, swimming.

'We're going back for our first wedding anniversary,' Solene determined as she leant back against her husband's chest.

Lisane kept her smile in place and fought back the threat of tears. Damn, this was hard! She was on an emotional see-saw that swung every which way but loose.

By evening she felt as if her face would crack from the strain of keeping a smile in place, and she nursed a headache that seemed to worsen by the hour until she pleaded the need for an early night.

Sunday brought little improvement, with a busy morning preparing food for a celebratory lunch Solene and Jean-Claude were hosting for family and friends arranged to view the opening of their wedding gifts.

It was a casual meal, buffet-style, held outdoors in the back garden, and fun and laughter, mixing and mingling, made for an enjoyable hour before the main gift-opening event.

Lisane was appointed to write each gift item against the prepared list of invited guests, and it was almost six when the last person departed.

'Let's vote to skip dinner in favour of eating leftovers,' Solene suggested, and received a unanimous *yes*.

Within minutes they'd each filled a plate and sat eating picnic-style at the kitchen table.

'If you don't mind,' Jean-Claude began as he finished his meal, 'I'll go transfer our holiday photos onto the laptop and print them.' He leant forward and brushed his lips to Solene's cheek. 'You girls can exchange girl-talk.'

CHAPTER SIX

'OK, WHAT'S up?'

Oh, heavens. Sisterly inquisition, with no leading preliminary! 'What makes you think something's wrong?' Calm, rational words that merely brought forth a narrowed look.

'Because you're pale, dark-eyed…and I can read you like a book.'

So much for bright conversation, light laughter and affectionate warmth. 'I caught a stomach bug.' Could a tiny foetus loosely fit that description? She barely resisted the impulse to place a protective hand over her stomach and murmur an apology.

'How long have you had it?'

Oh, around two months. Except her knowledge extended to only a few days. 'Since mid-week.' Truth by omission. The question was whether Solene would accept it without further enquiry.

Fat chance.

'Everything OK between you and Zac?'

Just brilliant. 'I understand he's about to become engaged.'

Her sister's eyes sharpened. 'And you know this… *because*?'

'There was an announcement in the daily newspaper.'

Solene's expression resembled a mother hen fussing over a lonely chick. 'Let me see the news-clipping.'

Lisane retrieved it and placed the slip of newsprint in Solene's outstretched hand, watching as she skimmed the brief announcement before carefully putting it to one side.

'You've checked the Brisbane-based papers?'

Every page, each article. 'Yes.'

'And?'

'The announcement is identical.'

'Unusual, don't you think? Given the Winstone and Fabrisi families are in the top echelon of Brisbane society? One would expect to see a photo of the happy couple, some journalistic detail and an indication of when the wedding will take place.'

Hadn't she puzzled over the same thing? Examining every angle until it had almost driven her mad?

'You haven't considered Allegra could be responsible?'

Oh, yes. Every minute of every day…let's not even count the nights! She wasn't conscious of biting the edge of her lip until there was the faint sting of pain.

Solene offered a thoughtful look tinged with an edge of cynicism. 'What does she have to lose? If confronted with the announcement all she has to do is provide a suitable statement citing misinterpretation of the spoken word and blame the journalist.'

That much made perfect sense. Allegra possessed the ability to twist the English language every which way…in the court-room, and out of it.

'What was Zac's reaction?'

Lisane endeavoured to hide the pain encompassing her body. Dammit, why did it have to hurt so much? 'I need to call him.'

'And you *haven't*?'

Lisane's silence succeeded in edging her sister's speculation up a notch.

'OK. *Give*. The whole story. And don't leave anything out.'

Two sisters who knew each other a little too well for either one to be fooled by the other.

What was the point in prevaricating? 'I'm pregnant.' There, she'd said it.

Solene dispensed with the niceties, and got straight to the point. 'How long have you known?'

It seemed like a lifetime. 'Five days.'

'You've had the pregnancy confirmed?'

The doctor's visit was indelibly imprinted on her brain, and his diagnosis had haunted her ever since. 'Yes.'

'You have to tell Zac,' her sister said quietly.

Lisane rolled her eyes, unsure whether to laugh or cry. 'You think?'

Solene frowned. 'Don't be facetious.'

Delaying it wouldn't gain a thing. Hadn't she lain awake at night composing numerous words to convey the news? Only to discard each and every one of them.

She could just imagine how that would go, especially if she caught him at an inconvenient time. And when wouldn't it be an inconvenient time? During the day was impossible…he'd be caught up in chambers, in court, consulting with a client and his solicitor. Important stuff that shouldn't be interrupted, except in an emergency situation.

Did enlightening he was going to become a parent fall under *emergency*? Somehow she didn't think so.

Evenings? He was in the middle of an important case. He'd be examining court transcripts, searching for an edge, preparing notes…

'You're not considering a termination?'

Lisane lifted a hand, then let it fall helplessly to her side. 'You think I haven't agonised over this?' she demanded wretchedly. A child was a precious gift. One she could never willingly destroy.

Yet the solution brought up the question of parental rights, reaching an agreement to share the responsibility of raising a child. It was more than financial obligation…the physicality of sharing in the child's upbringing raised numerous questions.

The most glaring one being how she could bear to agree to her child being nurtured by Allegra as Zac's wife in a custody agreement.

If in fact the proposed marriage was a reality.

She closed her eyes against the painful image, and aimed for a semblance of calm as for the hundredth time she reflected on the passion evident in Zac's kiss minutes before he boarded the flight to Brisbane.

Could he have faked it?

Surely not. Unless he'd faked everything about their relationship, and she'd been just a convenient body willing to share herself with him…for as long as it lasted.

Was that all she was to him?

Had Allegra been right in intimating approval of him 'having a little sexual freedom' before settling into marriage…with her?

'Hey, stop with the agony, already.' Solene reached

forward and enveloped her in a sisterly hug. 'It's Sunday evening. SMS his cellphone and ask him to call.'

Why did it feel such a leap of faith? Wanting to hear his voice, yet dreading what he might have to say.

'Don't think,' her sister bade gently. 'Just do it.'

Hesitation wouldn't solve a thing, and with a sense of fatalism she caught up her cellphone and keyed in a brief message, checked and then sent it.

'I'll make a cup of tea.'

The panacea for all ills in a time of need, Lisane reflected silently, and felt her stomach execute a slow twist as the minutes ticked by…and her cellphone didn't ring.

'Maybe he doesn't have it with him.'

Sure, as if that was likely. He *always* carried it, and had messagebank activated if he wasn't able to take a call.

Lisane accepted the tea, refused anything to eat and tried to ignore the nerves knotting inside her stomach.

Logic rationalised Zac would eventually check his cellphone, and when he did he might consider it was too late to call.

Oh, *hell*…why did life have to suddenly become so complicated?

'Want to watch a movie on DVD?'

She caught her sister's caring expression, the underlying commiseration, and knew if she didn't *do* something she'd end up in tears. Hormones swinging every which way but loose!

'I'll probably fall asleep. Around nine my body shuts down like a light.' Too true, and right on cue the tiredness began to envelop her like a shroud. 'If you don't mind, I'll catch an early night.' She stood to her feet and trailed gentle fingers down Solene's cheek. 'Thanks for being there.'

'Always.'

The guest bedroom was only a few steps down the hallway, and Lisane quietly closed the door behind her, then began discarding her clothes.

Minutes later she sat propped up in bed and reached for a book filled with mischief, mayhem and gripping suspense in the hope she'd become immersed in the characters, the plot.

It worked to a degree, and each time her mind wandered she dragged it back to the printed word. Until the page became a blur and the book slid from her fingers.

Turn the light off and go to *sleep*, for heaven's sake, an inner voice dictated, and she reached for the bedside lamp in silent obedience…only to hear the definitive burr of her cellphone.

For a few heart-stopping seconds she couldn't move, then fear the call would end before she picked up galvanised her into action.

Recognition of the caller ID increased her nervous tension, and her 'hello' sounded breathless even to her own ears.

'Lisane.' His deep drawl tugged her heartstrings, and there was little she could do about the pain skittering through her body. 'I've just accessed my phone.'

It took resolve to keep her voice light. 'You've been working?'

'A dinner break which lasted longer than anticipated.'

She just stopped herself from asking *with whom*? 'How's the case going?'

'Reasonably well.'

'That's good.'

Coward. Cut the niceties…and tell him!

The words spilt out. 'I wanted to offer my congratulations.' She waited a beat, then offered quietly. 'Perhaps you should check last Tuesday's paper. Page five, right-hand column.' Without cohesive thought she cut the connection.

There, she'd done it.

Only to have her cellphone give its distinctive burr mere seconds later. Except she didn't pick up.

Over the next several minutes it rang on two more occasions. With resolve she activated messagebank and switched off the cellphone.

It was late. Too late to be considered a reasonable hour for anyone to place a call to the house-line. And dammit, she refused to check for any messages to her cellphone.

Morning would be soon enough.

Lisane fell asleep soon after her head touched the pillow. Something which came as a surprise when she woke next morning, for somehow she'd expected to lay awake agonising over hanging up on Zac's call…worse, choosing not to pick up when he rang back.

It was still early. The house was quiet, although she could hear birds twittering in the trees outside her window. Somewhere a door slammed, a car engine fired, and in the distance a dog barked. Soon to be joined by other dogs in tandem.

She resisted the temptation to turn on her cellphone and check for messages, discarding it on a 'need-to-know' basis. Later, when she was dressed and had settled her stomach with tea and toast…maybe then.

Sunshine filtered through the curtains, fingering the room with warmth, and minutes later she tossed back the bedcovers and cautiously swung her feet to the floor.

So far, so good. Maybe if she moved slowly the desire to heave would be averted.

Sure! Three steps and she had to break into a run to reach the *en suite*. Six-to-eight more weeks of this, and she'd be a wreck. The thought she might be in the minority of women who suffered thus through the entire pregnancy brought her out in a sweat!

A shower helped, and she put on jeans and a top, pulled her hair into a loose knot at her nape, then she emerged from her room and made her way to the kitchen.

The aroma of freshly brewed coffee teased her taste-buds and accelerated a craving for her usual morning caffeine fix. Tea just didn't seem a satisfactory substi-tute!

Solene was stacking toast onto a plate with one hand while the other dipped a teabag into a cup of hot water. Bacon sizzled in the pan, almost perfectly crisp and ready to serve.

'Hi.' Lisane breathed in with appreciation. 'Smells great.'

Her sister turned and shook her head in dismay. 'You're not supposed to be here.'

Lisane arched an eyebrow. 'Where else should I be?'

'In your room. I was going to bring you breakfast in bed.' Solene gestured towards the table. 'Go sit down.'

Solene in older-sister mode was quite something!

She effected a mock salute. 'Yes, ma'am.' And did what she was told.

'Jean-Claude?'

'He left early to meet Alain. They're taking the boat out for the day.'

A plate of bacon and eggs was placed in front of Lisane. 'Eat!'

'Thanks,' she said gratefully. 'My turn to cook tomorrow.'

Solene pulled out a chair opposite, took a sip of ruinously black coffee, then nursed the cup in both hands.

Lisane picked up cutlery and cut into a strip of bacon, added some egg and forked the morsel into her mouth. Ambrosia.

'Are you OK?'

Now, there was a telling question! She cut straight to the chase. 'Zac rang. We spoke. I hung up on him.'

Her sister's eyes sharpened a little. 'I'm interested in the *we spoke* part between "Zac rang" and "I hung up on him".'

'Basically the conversation was limited.' On reflection, she hadn't really given him a chance. But then the jury was out as to whether he deserved it or not. 'I suggested he check the newspaper...I offered the date, page number and appropriate column.'

She cut a small square of toast and added bacon and egg, ate it and followed it with a mouthful of tea.

'One assumes he rang back?'

'A few times.'

'*And?*'

'I let messagebank take any further calls, then turned off the cellphone.'

Pensive doubt clouded her sister's gaze. 'You've checked for messages.'

A statement, not a query. Lisane rolled her eyes. 'Not yet.'

'Don't you think you should?'

'I will. Eventually.'

Solene leant forward slightly. 'Do you really think that's the best way to handle the situation?'

The clear ringing tone of the land-line provided an intrusion, and Lisane carefully replaced her cutlery. 'If that's Zac, tell him I'm in the shower.'

Coward. She needed to know…yet she didn't want to hear what he had to say. Which was a conundrum, and at variance with common sense.

'Please.'

Solene shook her head in slight exasperation, crossed to pick up the receiver, and relayed the customary greeting while Lisane watched and listened to her sister handle Zac's queries as if nothing were amiss.

Damn, but she was good!

The conversation didn't go over-long, and Lisane waited until her sister cut the connection.

'Thanks.' The word was heartfelt, and earned her a wry smile.

'He wants you to return his call.'

Butterflies began beating their wings inside her stomach…or at least, that was what it felt like!

'Go check your cellphone for messages.'

She could do that. Should have done it as soon as she woke. Except morning sickness had intervened, and afterwards the need for food seemed more important.

Oh, for heaven's sake! Whatever SMS message Zac had sent her was *there*. To delay checking what he'd said was ridiculous!

Minutes later she switched between three printed texts on the small screen.

Pick up.

Call me.

We need to talk.

Lisane silently handed the slim phone to her sister, who skimmed the text and handed it back.

'You can't delay calling him.'

She met Solene's gaze…eyes as blue as her own, and filled with concern.

'But first,' she ventured quietly, and tried to still the way her stomach began to churn, 'I need a plan.'

'Which you've already given some thought?'

How could she not have done? Her mind had been tortured with various scenarios since confirmation of her pregnancy.

The one constant was her decision to keep the child.

'The only solution,' Lisane began with quiet resolve, 'is to end the relationship, give in my notice and relocate.'

'You think Zac will accept that?'

She gave a slight shrug. 'We're just…friends and lovers. No commitment given or expected.'

Except it was more than that. Much more. For her.

No man, other than Zac, had the power to make her *feel* so much. He was her light, the very air she breathed. Everything.

Love?

Did love play untold havoc with your emotions? Or was it just pregnancy hormones?

How was she to know for sure?

Solene leaned forward and caught both Lisane's hands in her own. 'It's not like you to run away from anything.'

'No?' She barely kept the scepticism from her voice. 'What about when the heat became unbearable with Alain?'

'You left…after you had the courage to tell him how you felt.'

She was unable to prevent a faint wryness in her tone. 'Alain has a different perspective.'

'He loved you. Still does.'

It made her heart ache she couldn't love him the same way.

'I can't see Zac not wanting to share in his child's life.'

She didn't know his stance on children. The subject hadn't arisen. 'It's better I relocate.'

She could lease out her cottage … her mind raced ahead with alternatives, weighing up options.

'Leaving Brisbane is *Plan B*,' Solene assured.

'And what do you perceive as *Plan A*?' Even as she launched the question, she already knew the answer. 'Something permanent?' For a moment she felt as if she couldn't breathe. *'Marriage?* Because it would be the *right* thing to do?' She shook her head in silent negation. 'Don't even go there.'

'OK, let's return to *Plan B*,' Solene ventured with ease. 'If you decide to relocate, why not Sydney, where I can be on hand with some back-up? You could stay here until you get settled in a new job and find a place of your own.'

She felt as if she was going to cry. 'You're a sweetheart, and I appreciate the offer.'

'Why do I get the feeling there's a *but* in there?'

Did ambivalence fall into the pregnancy hormonal basket? Along with contrariness and indecision?

Her sister's concern was palpable. 'Promise me you won't make any decisions until you've talked to Zac.'

As if she wanted to do that any time soon! Yet putting it off wasn't going to help.

'Let's go shopping. Lunch is on me.' People, shops, coffee—*tea*, she silently corrected—and bright conversation. Maybe they'd even fit in a facial and manicure… anything as a distraction from her dilemma.

'OK. Why not aim for the best?' Solene swung easily into the mood with a teasing smile. 'Double Bay?'

'It's a date.' Lisane collected her cellphone and sought the privacy of her bedroom in which to make the call.

Zac answered on the third ring, and the sound of his voice succeeded in twisting her stomach into an impossible knot.

'You have some explaining to do.'

Pent-up anger held tightly in check was evident, and she retaliated in kind.

'So do you.'

'Allegra.'

'Uh-huh.' Chameleon, witch and superb actress.

'A journalistic misunderstanding.'

Sure, and piglets fly! Strike one for the very clever attorney.

She didn't know whether to laugh or cry…because it didn't change a thing.

'Why don't you catch the next flight home?'

The huskiness in his voice did strange things to her equilibrium, and she clenched her fingers against the urge to say *yes*.

She could almost feel the warmth of his arms, the touch of his mouth against her own. The sweet sorcery that was theirs alone. Her body craved his with a need that shook her slim frame.

He'd captured her heart, but she had to think with her head.

Oh, dear lord, why did it have to be so difficult? 'I've decided to base myself in Sydney.'

There was a moment's silence. 'Perhaps you'd care to run that by me again.' His voice was too quiet, and so controlled it sent shivers down her spine.

'It's a decision I'm entitled to make,' she reminded with polite civility. Difficult, when she was weeping inside, and there was a need to sit down before she slid ignominiously to the floor.

'Accept it's over, Zac.' She cut the connection before he could offer a further word, and the finality of her action was almost more than she could bear.

For what seemed an age she sat frozen in silence. Waiting for *what*…Zac to call back? Oh, *please*, give it a break. It's done. Over.

So get on with it, why don't you?

Splash your face with cold water, change your clothes, apply make-up, then go try to enjoy the day.

Actions she completed on autopilot, and she practised a bright smile as she joined Solene, who took one look and wisely refrained from offering a word.

'Let's hit the shops.'

They did, checking out the window displays in exclusive Double Bay, entering selective boutiques to examine and try on a variety of clothing, beautiful Manolo Blahnik shoes too ruinously expensive for their individual budgets…but fun to let their imaginations soar with boundless possibilities should they ever have the resources to indulge in such luxuries.

'Lunch,' Lisane determined as they exited from yet another boutique. 'I'm starving.'

That was another thing she was beginning to discover about the effects of early pregnancy…food. The taste, texture, and particularly its aroma appeared to have heightened and changed.

The restaurant Lisane chose was upmarket, mostly filled with the 'in' crowd. Society matrons meeting to nibble at small portions of fine food and exchange gossip, partners sharing a business lunch, and the occasional roue holding court with the woman *de jour*.

The temptation to check her cellphone for messages was difficult to resist.

'Do you want to talk about it?'

The waiter had poured iced water into their glasses, taken their order, and there was that pleasant anticipatory lull of a shared meal in good company.

Lisane didn't pretend to misunderstand. 'Not particularly.' She took a sip of water, then replaced the glass onto the table.

Reality began to hit, with all its ramifications, despite her belief in having made the only decision she considered feasible.

Handing in her resignation was one thing...citing a family crisis would ensure she worked out minimum notice. Which meant she'd be in the court stream and likely to see Zac, even in passing.

Would they acknowledge each other?

Oh, come on ... get a grip! *You* ended the relationship, remember?

It was the sensible thing to do.

Wasn't it?

So why did it have to hurt so much?

The waiter delivered their meal, smoked salmon curled over a potato-salad stack and topped with a generous rocket salad. Eaten at leisure and washed down with iced water, it made for a pleasant meal.

Look at the big picture, a silent voice intruded. Sydney, having Solene's support, a new job...and a beautiful child. A part of Zac that would be unquestionably hers for the rest of her life.

And his.

Something she was morally bound to tell him, and she should have...except it hadn't seemed appropriate to convey news of his impending fatherhood over the phone.

Oh, why not tell it like it is? At the last minute, she'd chickened out.

How could she say… *By the way, I'm pregnant. What are we going to do about it?*

Lisane closed her eyes briefly, then opened them again.

This time last week her life had been good. Now it was topsy-turvy with a number of complications.

'Would you prefer coffee or tea?'

They lingered a while, taking the opportunity to catch up on the more prosaic aspects of their lives before continuing a leisurely browse among several boutiques lining both sides of the street.

It was after five when Solene pulled into the driveway behind Jean-Claude's four-wheel drive.

Fresh salad and a baguette rested on the kitchen servery, and Jean-Claude and Alain could be seen out back readying the barbecue.

'Good to see you making yourselves useful,' Solene teased as she lifted her face for her husband's lingering kiss.

Lisane dampened down the tiny spiral of emotion, and moved to Alain's side. 'I gather it was a satisfactory fishing jaunt.'

'Very. We managed to cover a lot.'

'Brotherly companionship, huh?'

His steady gaze held a quality she didn't want to examine. 'You could say that.'

Jean-Claude wouldn't have confided her predicament in Alain, surely?

'I'll go change,' she managed quietly. 'A dress and heels aren't exactly back-yard barbecue wear.'

Jeans and a top, she decided as she reached her room,

and she quickly effected the change before slipping her feet into sandals.

When she emerged it was to find Alain waiting for her in the kitchen, and his expression held a degree of purpose that made her heart sink a little.

'Alain, please.'

'Just…hear me out.'

Please don't do this, she begged silently.

'I can offer you marriage. Be a father to your child in every way, including adoption.'

This was the man with whom she'd shared her childhood, friend, confidant…someone she could trust with her life.

'I appreciate it,' she said gently. 'Really. But you deserve someone who loves you.'

He took hold of her hands. 'Whatever you offered me would be enough.'

No, it wouldn't. Not when my heart and soul belong to someone else. My child. How could I lie with you at night and pretend you were another? You'd know. You couldn't help but know.

Words she couldn't say. Wouldn't, because it would hurt him more than he needed to be hurt.

'I care for you.' She removed her hands from his grasp. 'Too much to take advantage.'

He opened his mouth to speak, and she pressed a finger to his lips. 'So, let me thank you from the bottom of my heart. And promise, should I ever need your help I'll ask you for it.' She laid the palm of her hand over his cheek. 'Let's go outside and join the others, shall we?'

Alain didn't move. 'You won't,' he managed in a voice that mirrored his dejection. 'You're so independent, you'll go it alone rather than ask anyone for help.'

Especially me. He didn't add the last two words, but they were implied, and Lisane felt incredibly sad.

He'd make a wonderful honorary uncle. But she couldn't tell him that.

Life wasn't fair. *Love* was unfair.

'Let's go eat.'

The alfresco meal was relaxed, the fish succulent, and it was almost like old times when the four of them had shared so much.

Jean-Claude put on a few CDs, kept the music low, and when it grew dark he switched on a string of coloured lights.

This is how it could be, Lisane thought fleetingly. Family and, in the future, children. The link tying them together.

Except she wasn't part of that link.

Being with Zac had introduced her to an emotion so powerful it had become all-encompassing, primitive…like nothing else she'd previously experienced, or ever would again.

On Friday she'd take a morning flight to Brisbane and use the weekend to contact leasing agents, draft a letter of resignation…and make contact with Zac.

Even thinking about the how and when of that contact set her nerves on edge. She could, probably should have told him about her pregnancy over the phone. At least she wouldn't now be a quivering wreck at imparting the news.

'OK?'

Lisane turned and slid an arm around her sister's shoulders. 'Fine. Thanks for today, it was great to have your company.'

'Maybe tomorrow we'll take in a movie?'

She managed a smile. 'Sounds good.'

The music, the cool night breeze provided a peaceful air, and an unaccustomed weariness began to descend.

Was early pregnancy supposed to sap energy levels with clockwork regularity?

A ringing sound came from indoors, and Jean-Claude rose to his feet. 'I'll get it.'

The barbecue had long been cleaned, the dishes dispensed with, and any time soon they'd turn off the lights and retreat indoors.

It wasn't late, not long after nine unless she was mistaken, and she turned towards her sister.

'Would you like me to make tea and coffee?'

'We'll do it together.'

They rose to their feet and had only taken a few steps when Jean-Claude appeared in the doorway. His features were solemn, and his customary smile was absent.

'What's wrong?' The question fell from her sister's lips.

'Lisane. There's someone to see you.'

What? *Who?*

Then Jean-Claude stood aside, and she almost died at the sight of Zac's tall frame filling the aperture.

CHAPTER SEVEN

ZAC...*here*?

Yet there could be no mistaking the man moving towards her.

Everything seemed to have lapsed into silence. Lisane didn't hear the music, and Solene, Jean-Claude and Alain stood on the periphery of her vision as her world closed in on one man.

'What are you doing here?'

Had she just said those words? She bore no recollection of voicing them.

Zac noted her pallor, assessed the way her eyes had dilated into huge dark pools, the faint quivering of her mouth...and experienced a degree of satisfaction.

The desire to haul her in close and kiss her senseless was paramount. Except it wasn't the time or the place.

'We need to talk.' He let his gaze rove from Solene to Jean-Claude before settling on Lisane's pale features. 'We can do it here, or elsewhere. Choose.'

Alain moved forward a step, only to pause at the look Zac cast him in silent warning.

Zac's gaze speared hers, watching and divining each

fleeting emotion on her expressive features. 'Your call, Lisane.'

It was no contest. *Here* wasn't really an option. 'I'll collect my bag.' Was that her voice? It sounded almost fragile.

It didn't take long to drag a brush through her hair, apply lip-gloss and check her bag.

His hire car was parked on the street, and he unlocked the passenger door, saw her seated, then he crossed round to slide in behind the wheel.

Zac didn't offer a word as he ignited the engine and sent the car purring towards the intersection, then he headed towards the city, handling the traffic with ease.

The silence stretched interminably, and she turned her attention to the passing nightscape, idly noting the flashing coloured neon atop distant tall city buildings.

The car slowed and pulled in to the kerb adjacent to a group of shops, and indicated an Italian restaurant.

With smooth ease he slid from behind the wheel and waited until she emerged before locking the car.

'I didn't eat on the flight.'

The restaurant was well-patronised, and within minutes they were seated and handed a menu.

'Would you like something?' Zac queried as a waiter hovered close by.

'Just tea,' she accepted quietly while Zac perused the menu and gave their order.

She waited until the waiter left before speaking. 'It would have been easier to pick up the phone.'

He leant back in his chair and regarded her with deliberate appraisal.

A well-known technique designed to unsettle an opponent. For a crazy few seconds she wrestled with the feeling that was his intention, and she held his gaze, silently daring him to break it.

'Of late the phone hasn't been our best form of communication.'

His drawl held a degree of irony she chose to ignore.

The waiter delivered her tea, set down a glass of wine for Zac, then retreated out of sight.

'What made you think you could dismiss me so easily?'

Straight to the point. Well, she could play the same game.

'The shoe is on the other foot, surely?' she offered coolly, and saw the edge of his mouth tilt a little.

He didn't pretend to misunderstand. 'Allegra's ill-timed announcement to the Press.'

'Perfectly timed,' Lisane corrected. 'And deliberately designed to set the cat among the pigeons.'

An eyebrow slanted in silent query. 'Your trust in me is so tenuous?'

Was it? A week ago she'd have said *no*…but now she wasn't so sure. 'Allegra covets being Mrs Zac Winstone,' she managed with stark honesty. 'It's what her parents want.' Her pause was imperceptible. 'And yours.'

His eyes didn't leave hers, and his silence stretched until her nerves screamed in silent protest.

'They've said as much?'

Oh, his mother was too clever to put it into words, when implication worked just as well. 'No.'

'Allegra?'

In spades. 'You could say that.'

'It didn't occur to you if I wanted to marry Allegra I'd have done so by now?'

In my more rational moments.

'Or that Allegra appears to derive enjoyment in manipulating certain situations?'

Wasn't that the truth!

Her eyes sparked blue fire. 'What would you have had me say, Zac?' She was on a roll. 'It's OK with me to share you with another mistress?'

His eyes lightened with a degree of humour, and she stood quickly to her feet. 'Oh, to hell with it. This conversation isn't going anywhere.'

She turned away from him…felt the room begin to spin, then blackness descended and there was nothing.

Lisane gradually became aware of voices, and there was something cool covering her forehead. A sense of awareness rose through her level of consciousness, and her eyelids fluttered open.

Zac leant in close, his features creased with concern, and she saw two waiters hovering within touching distance.

Realisation hit…the restaurant, their argument. She'd stood too quickly…

'Lisane.'

'I'm fine.' Reassurance which didn't quite cut it.

'Sure you are.' Zac's expression darkened as he caught hold of her hands. 'I'll get you to a doctor.'

Lisane met the concern evident, and weathered it. 'I don't need a doctor to tell me what I already know.'

His eyes held hers, assessing, only to narrow fractionally. 'You're ill?'

'Not exactly.'

He went still, and she saw something sharpen in the depths of his eyes. 'You're pregnant?'

Given a choice, she'd have chosen a better time, another place. 'Yes.' She closed her eyes, then opened them again.

She made to rise to her feet, only to have Zac still her movements.

'Not so fast.' He pulled her cup and saucer close. 'Drink some tea.'

Hot, sweet, it had a soothing effect, and she watched in silence as he waved away the meal he'd ordered.

'Eat,' she protested as the waiter hovered.

A slightly hysterical laugh rose and died in her throat as Zac gave the food a cursory glance, then redirected his attention to her.

'How long have you known?'

She closed her eyes, then opened them again. 'Four days.' Days when she'd practised what she was going to say. Words that had seemed so rational for the path she'd chosen to take.

'Tell me,' Zac began carefully. 'When was I supposed to learn about my impending fatherhood?'

He was too controlled, too quiet. Like the lull before the storm.

'Or was it not part of your plan?'

Her chin lifted in silent defiance. 'How can you ask that?' Eyes as deep as sapphires blazed with anger. 'You think I should remain in Brisbane and prove an embarrassment to the Winstone family? Not to mention myself?'

'Why *embarrassment*?'

'Think of the consequences to your career, social status, and the Winstone name.'

'That's the basis for your decision?'

'Yes, dammit!'

'You don't perceive me supporting you or having an active part in our child's life?'

'My life, my child, my responsibility.'

'Our child. Our responsibility,' Zac corrected with deceptive quiet. 'We'll get married.'

For a moment she couldn't speak. 'Marriage wasn't part of our arrangement.'

'It is now.'

'I don't see marriage as *the* solution.'

'You'd deprive a child of its father? The right to feel safe and secure within a relationship with two parents, the possibility of a sibling or two? Grandparents? Consigned to the care of a nanny while you work? Having to share custody? Is that what you want for our child?'

He was good. Too good. He'd also fight tooth and nail to gain equal parenting time. With the power to make her life extremely difficult if she chose to oppose him.

'We've been together for almost a year. The only thing we haven't shared is living quarters. Why not legally formalise the relationship?'

'For the sake of the child.'

'For our future as a family.'

What about love? she agonised silently.

Didn't he realise she would never have entered their relationship if she didn't *love* him?

Yet the *l* word hadn't passed her lips…even when she'd been caught up in the depths of passion.

Zac desired her. Of that she had no doubt. But desire, emotional and physical, was a hunger of the senses. A sexual and sensual expression related to need.

Love was something else. The merging of twin souls, attuned in every way. The forever, once-in-a-lifetime kind.

A relationship could be broken.

Marriage was meant to be a lifetime commitment.

It was something she wanted. For the right reasons.

Not as a matter of convenience, because it appeared to be the right thing to do.

Was it asking too much to want the whole deal?

Would she be a fool to query if Zac would have suggested marriage had she not been pregnant with his child?

Don't go there.

Besides, you already know the answer. Why have him put it in words…words you don't really want to hear?

'Believe I'm not going away any time soon.' His voice held the deceptive silkiness of underlying determination.

Zac summoned the waiter for the bill, paid it, then he rose to his feet. 'Shall we leave?'

Lisane reached for her cellphone as they hit the pavement. 'I'll call a cab.'

He gave her a look that would have withered an adversary on the spot. 'You think I'll let you do that?'

'Why, when you're staying in a city hotel?'

'Jean-Claude offered me a bed for the night,' he relayed smoothly.

'Which you accepted.'

'You object?'

Her eyes sparked blue fire as they clashed with his. 'As long as you understand you won't be sharing mine.'

Zac unlocked the car and held open the passenger door. 'Get in, Lisane.'

The drive to Solene's home in suburban Manly was achieved in total silence, for there didn't seem to be a thing she could think of to say that wouldn't contain an element of conflict.

The house was in darkness as Zac drew the car to a halt adjacent to the pavement, and once indoors Lisane quietly turned towards the hallway…only to come to an abrupt halt as firm hands closed over her shoulders.

She barely had time to gasp a faint protest before his mouth took possession of her own in a kiss that plundered at will, conquering with the sweep of his tongue as he demanded her response.

Hungry and frankly sensual, he wove his own brand of magic until a tiny groan in capitulation sounded low in her throat, and in one simple movement she wound her arms round his neck and arched her body into the hardness of his own.

Zac slid a hand down her back to cup her bottom as he held her firmly in place, then he angled his mouth and went in deep.

Lisane had no idea how long it lasted, only that it wasn't enough. Not nearly enough as the desire for skin on skin became paramount. And need. Fast-burning need that sent her up in flames.

So much so, she whimpered in protest as he began to withdraw, easing her down with the soft brush of his lips against her own, the light, soothing movement of his hand up her back, and the gentle squeeze to the nape of her neck.

All it would take was a word, the slightest gesture, and they'd share the same room, the same bed.

She was tempted, so badly tempted it took tremendous strength of will to step back from him. The dimmed light made it almost impossible to discern his expression, and her mouth shook a little as she forced a whispered 'goodnight'.

Fingers lightly trailed a gentle path down one cheek. 'Sleep well.' He paused fractionally, then added with a tinge of humour, 'If you can.'

Zac watched her walk down the hallway to her room,

saw her close the door behind her, and the pencil-line of light shine beneath her door.

Frustration ran through every muscle in his body, and he fought against the desire to follow her. The image of her beautiful, silken skin laid bare tightened his erection to an uncomfortable level, and he wanted nothing more than to kiss every inch of her with tantalising slowness until she begged for his possession.

Instead he contemplated the benefits of a cold shower, only to dismiss it as he moved quietly to the room opposite the woman whose body he craved.

He wanted, *needed* to be with her. Lie with her, hold her. Convince her that marriage to him was the only solution.

His solution, he differentiated a long time later as he lay staring at the ceiling.

It would work. He'd make it work.

Because there was no other course he could conceive or accept.

CHAPTER EIGHT

LISANE drifted through the veils of wakefulness, content and secure on a subconscious level that when she opened her eyes it would be to face the familiar routine of her usual weekday.

Rise and shine, shower, eat breakfast, dress, then drive into the city to the court house.

The alarm hadn't sounded, she decided drowsily, so she had time to settle deeper beneath the covers and lapse back into sleep.

Except something brushed across her cheek, and she gave an inaudible groan as she turned her head to one side.

'Lisane.'

Zac?

Zac had stayed over...or was it the reverse?

Mmm, nice. She could think of nothing better than to wake in his arms and bury her lips against his warm, muscular chest, feel the touch of his hand as he trailed his fingers over her hip to trace the length of her thigh, then seek the moist heat beneath the soft, curling hair at the sensitive apex.

Early-morning sex. A great way to begin the day.

She reached out a hand, and found nothing except the coolness of an empty space in her bed.

The reality brought her fully awake and aware. Her lips parted in a soundless gasp as Zac sank down onto the edge of her bed.

He was fully dressed in a business suit, buttoned shirt and tie, clean-shaven with a Blackberry in one hand and an overnight bag at his feet.

'What are you doing here?'

He took in her tumbled hair, clear skin and examined the way her pupils dilated beneath his gaze.

'Saying goodbye before I leave for the airport.'

It was impossible not to feel a tinge of remorse. 'There was no need for you to make the trip.'

'We've already done that.'

The tiny lines fanning out from the outer corners of his eyes seemed a little deeper, so too the groove slashing each cheek. Loss of sleep? Or maybe he'd stayed up late reappraising transcripts and making notes prior to his appearance in court today.

He indicated a tray resting on the bedside pedestal. 'Solene sent in tea and toast.'

If she didn't move, she'd be fine. It was the readjustment of her body from horizontal to a vertical position that seemed to provide the necessity to rush very quickly to the bathroom.

'Thanks. I'll have it later.' After you've gone, she added silently, caught the slight quizzical twist at the edge of his mouth and knew he'd read her mind.

'I'd like you to reschedule your return flight.'

'Solene and I have plans for the rest of the week,' she managed evenly.

'Your sister is happy to change them.'

Of course she is. Anything to ease me into what she perceives as a happy-ever-after solution. 'I'll be back on Friday.'

It was a minor victory, and possibly a foolish one as Zac rose to his feet, collected his overnight bag and made for the door. 'I'll be in touch. Take care.'

Then he was out of sight, and she heard the faint murmur of voices, a door click shut, followed soon after by the sound of a car engine.

Lisane felt a strange sense of loss…which didn't make any sense. She was relieved to be rid of his disturbing presence…wasn't she?

Yet his forceful image remained in the forefront of her mind, *there*…his male scent beneath the subtle tones of his cologne almost a tangible entity, and a vivid reminder of the man himself. The extent of his power.

His marriage proposal should have thrilled her. It was what she'd secretly hoped for, yet never expected.

So why hadn't she accepted it with a joyful heart?

Because it was merely an expedient arrangement…one he'd initiated because of the child she carried.

Zac's child. A Winstone heir.

One he had every intention of claiming as his own. A child who shouldn't, by any sense of the word, have the slightest whiff of illegitimacy associated with its name.

'You're crazy,' Solene verbalised later that morning as they wandered around the Rocks area. 'What are you trying to prove?'

Sisterly honesty was nothing if not brutally blunt.

'You love him.' Solene ticked one finger off another. 'You almost *live* with him. He's one gorgeous hunk of a man. He comes from a prominent family. He's in a prestigious profession. And he's obscenely wealthy.' She lifted both hands in the air in a gesture of unaccustomed temperament. *'Hello!'*

'So I should accept his proposal with due gratitude, and be content to live my life wondering if marriage would have been offered if I hadn't fallen pregnant?'

'Oh, for heaven's sake. Get a grip on reality, why don't you?' Solene paused and turned to face her. 'You think he boarded a flight just to come talk to you in person if he didn't care?'

Lisane cast her sister a cynical glance. 'Or maybe he was just ticked off because I hung up on him and refused to take his calls?'

Solene stabbed the air in emphasis. 'Answer me this. When he discovered you were pregnant, why didn't he simply offer financial support and leave you holding the baby…literally?'

'Because it's a Winstone heir?'

'Is that what you think?'

'Dammit, I don't know what to think any more!'

'It seems to me you're bent on shooting yourself in the foot!'

'OK, so I'm a fool to want it all.' This time it was she who threw her hands up in a gesture that was part anger, part despair. 'Do you blame me for that?'

'It's what we all want,' Solene ventured quietly. 'But don't lose something worth having, just because it doesn't quite fit your expectation of perfection.' She gestured towards a nearby restaurant. 'Shall we go eat?'

Food. She seemed to be fixated on food, discovering by trial and error that some of her favoured dishes no longer suited her palate.

Consequently she deliberated over the menu, chose

something safe, then she sank back in her chair and took an appreciative sip of iced water.

'Truce?'

'Done,' Solene agreed.

Together they spent a lovely afternoon browsing the various shops, examining the crafts displayed, stopped by for flavoured ice, then they joined the stream of traffic departing the inner city for the northern suburbs.

Dinner was eaten alfresco in the cooling evening air, and afterwards they retreated indoors to watch a movie on DVD.

Zac didn't call, but then Lisane hadn't expected him to, and Solene and Jean-Claude didn't mention his name. There was a text message on her cellphone next morning, keyed in brief SMS shorthand, to which she responded in kind.

A method of communication which continued over the next few days. Days when direct calls were inadvertently missed, messages left and responses sent.

Deliberate tactics, or happenstance?

Lisane kept a smile in place and the talk light as Solene drove her to the airport on Friday morning. It was hard saying goodbye, and she felt slightly bereft as she boarded her flight.

Now that she was alone there was little she could do to still the increase in nervous tension as she drew closer to Brisbane.

She had an agenda. A list. Things to do which would ensure she kept busy until Zac called her at seven.

Busy was good. It wouldn't allow her too much time in which to think.

Three weeks' absence meant the cottage would need a clean, and somewhere in there she'd need to get in fresh food. Unpack.

Not necessarily in that order, she reflected as she disembarked at the domestic terminal and headed for the luggage carousel.

The long line of taxis made for an easy exit, and the traffic seemed less dense than its Sydney counterpart. Suburban Milton looked endearingly familiar, the cottage even more so, and she changed into cargo trousers, pulled on a T-shirt and began systematically dealing with a host of chores.

It was almost six when she unpacked the last item of food and stowed it in the refrigerator. Everything was done, except for sorting through her mail…something she'd aim to do before Zac arrived. But first, she needed to shower and change.

Zac hadn't specifically mentioned dinner. Would they eat in or out?

Lisane chose dress jeans, pulled on a singlet top and added a cropped blouse, applied light make-up and left her hair loose.

If he'd made a restaurant reservation that required more sophisticated wear, it would only take a few minutes for her to change.

She entered the lounge and switched on the television, watched for a while, then she checked the time. Seven-fifteen. Maybe he was held up in traffic.

At seven-thirty her cellphone beeped with an incoming SMS relaying an unexpected delay, and it was almost eight when a sweep of car headlights hit the front of the cottage.

Lisane had the door open before he set foot on the porch, and a tumble of words rose to the surface that failed to find voice as he anchored her face between his hands and bestowed a brief, hard kiss.

An action which temporarily robbed her of the ability to speak. Then he curled an arm over her shoulders and drew her indoors.

'Have you eaten?'

Such a prosaic question, when food was not uppermost in her mind. 'Not yet.'

'Grab your house-keys, and we'll go find somewhere close by.'

She opened her mouth, only to have him press it closed. 'Later.'

He chose a Park Avenue restaurant only a short distance away, and she waited until they were seated before querying,

'Are you going to tell me what held you up?'

An apt choice of words, Zac accorded. Except it was *who*, not what.

A gun pointed at his head, an outstretched hand, a harsh voice demanding money at a light-controlled intersection had come out without warning, and in hindsight only because he had the window wound down.

He'd had nowhere to go, trapped by cars front, back and either side. So he'd carefully reached into his jacket pocket and handed over a spare billfold filled with several hundred dollars in notes.

Then the youth had sprinted away, dodging between cars until he disappeared down a side street out of sight.

The traffic lights changed, the cars began to move, and Zac had followed through until he could pull into the nearest kerb. He had rung the police on his cellphone, then drove to the nearest police station and gave his statement.

There was the question as to whether he had been a deliberate target or simply the victim of a random act.

His field of expertise, his chosen profession lent the former a possibility the police had refused to discount.

'A slight altercation demanding my time.' Truth by omission. He perused the menu and suggested she do the same.

'You had a good flight?'

They exchanged pleasantries as they ate, polite and somewhat innocuous, given there was much to discuss.

Lisane waited until the waiter served dessert and took their order for tea and coffee before venturing carefully, 'Will you begin, or shall I?'

Zac leant back in his chair and regarded her thoughtfully. 'Cut to the chase?'

She knew the law as well as he did, and how the system worked. As father of their child, any court would grant him reasonable access and custody rights. That was a given.

Add Zac's financial status was far superior to her own…and she had no choice but to deal with it.

'I suggest we compromise.'

Her eyes sharpened a little. 'In what way?'

Zac reached for his stemmed glass and savoured the last measure of wine before subjecting her to a steady appraisal.

'We share the same residence for a month. As a prelude to marriage.'

Lisane was silent for a few timeless seconds. Was she being very cleverly manipulated…or did he really *care*?

Did it matter?

A few weeks ago she'd have agreed in a heartbeat. So what was so different now?

Don't answer that!

The waiter delivered their tea and coffee, offered a smile and departed silently.

'It's reasonable for me to want to care for you, support you through the pregnancy, the birth.'

'Don't regard me as an obligation.'

Zac wanted to shake her. Did she really think he'd give her a snowflake's chance in hell of walking away from him?

'Did I imply that?'

Being with him was what she wanted...wasn't it?

What price stubborn pride?

And what, in the name of heaven, was she afraid of?

They were going to be forever linked together because of their child. A joint united parental front was better than two separated parents living in different cities, different states.

Think of the child. Its stability and security.

'Yes.' She held his gaze with unblinking solemnity. 'I'll move in with you.'

Was he pleased? Relieved? She couldn't be sure.

'You won't regret it.'

But would *he*? she wondered.

Only time would tell.

It was after ten when Zac entered the quiet suburban Milton street and brought the Jaguar to a halt in the cottage driveway.

Nervous tension curled through her belly as he followed her indoors.

What in the name of heaven was the matter with her?

They'd been lovers for almost a year. Dammit, she'd agreed to marry him! Why *now* did she feel hesitant at the thought of sharing a bed with him? It was crazy.

Lisane made her way to the kitchen and filched bottled water from the refrigerator.

'Would you like a drink?'

She felt rather than heard him move in close behind her.

'The only thing I want—' He reached forward and plucked the plastic bottle from her hand and placed it on the bench, then he turned her round to face him '—is you.'

He cupped each cheek, then he angled his head and went in slow, brushing her lips with his own, savouring their soft fullness, felt their slight trembling and shifted a hand to hold fast her nape.

Zac took his time, wanting, needing her response, and when it came he shifted his body in close against her own and held her there, making her shockingly aware of his erection, its hard length, its power, and the anticipation of the pleasure he could gift her.

It wasn't enough, not nearly enough. He needed to touch her, caress the silken softness of her skin, and he pulled the top free from the waistband of her jeans, then slid a hand to cover one lace-covered breast. Teasing its soft fullness with the light brush of his fingers…and felt rather than heard the soft moan deep in her throat.

Her hands crept up over his shoulders and slid into the thickness of his hair as she held his head in place, and he went in deep, taking them both to a place where there was nothing else but passion…the heady desire of witching, shameless need.

With one smooth movement Zac lifted her up against him, parting her thighs so they straddled his hips, and a soft, husky sound emerged as she buried her mouth against his throat.

He carried her into the main bedroom and slid her body slowly down his own, then with infinite care he removed her top, and unclipped her bra, letting her breasts spill free.

Beautiful, their delicate peaks hard with desire as they anticipated the touch of his hands, the benediction of his mouth.

Lisane's fingers worked the buttons on his shirt, then clutched a handful of soft cotton, wrenched it free and let her mouth bestow random kisses over the tightly muscled skin at his chest.

His body jerked as she took one male nipple between her teeth and rolled it, creating a pleasure that verged towards the edge of pain.

He wanted her naked, and needy...for him, only him.

There was no reason for words, just the touch of skin on skin, the leisurely tasting that edged the passionate tension to a mesmeric, electrifying climax as he sent her high, held her there, then he entered her in one long, careful thrust that took them both to the brink, where sheer primeval sensation became a glorious rapture so intense it was almost impossible to bear.

Afterwards Zac rolled onto his back, carrying her to rest on top of him, and she buried her face into the curve of his neck, exulting in the closeness, the faint muskiness of his skin mingling with the scent of recent sex.

His hand soothed a gentle path over her spine, curved over the soft swell of her bottom, then eased up to settle at her nape.

Soon he'd shift her to lie curled in against him and they would sleep...but for now he wanted the post-coital closeness, the lingering aftermath of very good sex.

CHAPTER NINE

'I WENT grocery shopping yesterday,' Lisane protested over breakfast next morning, and wondered precisely *why*, when her shift into Zac's apartment was imminent. Common sense didn't appear to be uppermost in her mind of late.

Zac cast her an amused look as he drank the last of his coffee. 'Why not box and gift them to the city homeless shelter?'

She had no problem with that. She did, however, protest at his suggestion to call in professional packers.

'Why,' he queried reasonably, 'when it can be done in a fraction of the time and with minimum ease at your direction?'

She had household linens and towels, books, ornaments...*furniture*.

'Because I need to sort out what to take, and what can be stored.'

He stood to his feet and began clearing their breakfast dishes. 'A decision on removalists and storage can be made later.'

Zac made it sound easy. A small truck dispensed by professional packers would transport all her personal effects in one move. Whereas even with two cars it would take two or more trips.

She was, she decided ruefully, merely being pernickety. Why choose the difficult path when there was a simple one?

'OK.' Lisane gave a slight shrug in capitulation. 'Let's get it done.'

Wealth equated with power, and all it took was for Zac to make a phone call to arrange to have a husband-and-wife team arrive in an hour.

They were good, careful, very efficient, and in what seemed a very short time everything she needed to take had been packed, loaded into the enclosed truck and was ready for delivery.

Lisane ran a security check, then she collected her keys and followed Zac onto the porch.

'You leave first, and I'll follow,' he indicated as she crossed to the garage.

Why should it feel different from any other occasion when she'd driven to Zac's apartment? she pondered as she drove away from the cottage.

Except this time she wouldn't be coming back…at least not in the usual sense.

This move was a large step towards permanency.

With a view to marriage.

It was what she wanted. But not in the order it was happening.

And not, she reflected sadly as she entered the inner city, as a result of *duty* because of the child she carried.

Oh, for heaven's sake…we've been there, done that, so let's not do it again.

As Zac indicated, the transition from her cottage to his

apartment was effected with minimum effort, and within a short space of time her clothes were neatly displayed in the large walk-in wardrobe in the main bedroom, and everything else placed in drawers.

Dinner was something they sent out for and ate alfresco on the terrace as they watched the city come alive with streetlights and coloured neon while the sun disappeared beneath the horizon.

From this height everything looked so peaceful…a tranquil nightscape that never failed to entrance, despite the knowledge the city's underbelly held crime and violence.

An inevitable dark side Zac dealt with in the courtroom on an ongoing basis…as did she, to a lesser degree.

Winners and losers, Lisane contemplated. Aware that the guilty sometimes got off, while the occasional innocent was deemed guilty.

'I have something for you.'

Lisane turned towards Zac, whose profile was slightly shadowed in the reflected light spilling onto the terrace from indoors, making it difficult to gauge his expression.

She watched as he withdrew a small jeweller's box and placed it on the glass-topped table.

A protest left her lips as he opened the box, then she gave an audible gasp.

Something was an exquisite diamond solitaire that shot prisms of red and blue fire as he transferred it from the box to her finger.

'I can't accept this.'

'It's the appropriate symbolic gift.' There was a degree of humour evident in his voice.

Lisane's eyes widened with a measure of shocked pleasure. 'Anything much *less* would have been adequate.'

'No,' he responded with teasing indolence. 'It wouldn't.'

A slight frown creased her forehead. 'Zac—'

'We mutually agreed on a period of engagement, did we not?'

'Yes,' she allowed. 'But—'

'No *buts*.'

She wanted to say he was going too fast, and that a ring was too much, too soon.

'Tomorrow we're lunching with my parents,' Zac continued. 'I've also organised for an announcement notice to appear in tomorrow's newspapers.'

Oh, my.

'No comment?'

Stop the world, I want to get off, came vividly to mind! 'Do they know about the baby?'

'They're very excited about the prospect of a grandchild.'

Tomorrow *is* going to be fun. Her stomach was already staging a silent protest of its own by twisting into a nervous knot.

'Why don't you go phone Solene?'

A sisterly exchange offering a mix of congratulations— *you're doing the right thing*—commiseration—*his parents are part of the package*—and common sense—*thank heaven you've come to your senses*?

'She's on your side,' Lisane offered, and saw one eyebrow lift in a gesture of musing cynicism.

'And that's a bad thing?'

'Yes.'

Zac gave a husky laugh. 'Let's agree to disagree, hmm?'

Lisane rose to her feet without a further word, and

gasped out loud as he pulled her down onto his lap, then fastened his mouth on her own in a kiss that stole her breath.

'I'm going to run a bath.' He released her onto her feet and shaped her slender frame. 'Come join me when you're done.'

Heat surged through her body at the mere thought of sharing his ablutions, the soft, fragrant bubbles and the slow drift of his hands on her body.

'The bath water might have cooled by then.'

'You think?'

His faint chuckle sounded softly in her ear as she retreated indoors.

Conversation with her sister was of necessity a little one-sided, given Solene and Jean-Claude were dining with his parents.

Consequently Solene's responses were restricted to 'uh-huh', 'that's great', *'really?'*, and lastly the promise to call back at a more suitable time.

Lisane cut the connection, her expression thoughtful as she moved through the luxurious apartment towards the main bedroom.

She found her eyes drawn to the ring on her hand, and she examined its purpose while endeavouring to find a balance between sheer joy and unwanted reflection.

Why the feelings of ambivalence?

A faint groan in self-castigation emerged from her throat.

It was like riding an emotional see-saw…and more than time she got off and grounded herself firmly in reality.

Zac was in the process of shedding his clothes when she entered their bedroom, and he took one look at her guarded expression, detected the warring emotions and kept his voice light.

'Not the most convenient time to talk?'

Lisane threw him a quick glance, and felt her heart execute a backward flip at the sight of the muscular symmetry of his honed body, the sleek flex of sinew apparent with every move. 'She'll call back.'

His gaze pierced hers as he unbuttoned his jeans, slid them down over his thighs and stepped out of them. Without a further word he crossed to her side and swept an arm beneath her knees, then lifted her lightly against his chest.

'What do you think you're doing?'

She missed his teasing smile as he walked towards the *en suite*.

'Zac?' Dear lord, he did intend dumping her fully clothed into the bath?

'Don't!' The plea escaped as a scandalous shriek as he held her suspended over the gently steaming bubbles. 'Please,' she added in desperation, and didn't know whether to laugh or cry as he eased her down onto her feet.

'Fool.' She curled her hand into a fist and aimed it at his shoulder, heard his soft laugh and repeated the action, only to have his mouth settle over her own in a warm, evocative kiss.

It was all too easy to link her hands together behind his neck and sink in against him. To savour the warmth of his embrace and anticipate the heat as he gently released her from her clothes.

No protest emerged from her lips as he swung her into his arms and stepped into the bath, then settled her down to sit in front of him.

The water temperature was just right, and she closed her eyes as she leant back within the cradle of his arms. A powerful thigh lay either side of her own, and a soundless sigh of pleasure remained locked in her throat as he soaped a sponge and began lightly smoothing it over her skin.

'Is it working?'

Lisane didn't pretend to misunderstand. 'You know it is.'

Right at this moment there was no need for words. They were perfectly in tune, twin halves of a whole, and nothing outside this marble-tiled steam-filled room mattered…only them, the stirring emotions beneath the slow, caressing drift of hands, the gently seeking fingers, the touch of his lips against her temple, her ear, her soft, vulnerable nape.

It was almost possible to believe the impossible…that he adored and cherished her.

She turned slightly in his arms and angled her mouth into his, then traced its contours with the tip of her tongue, ventured in and began exploring his mouth's texture.

Zac allowed her free rein, then he took control and went in deep, his possession frankly sensual…until it wasn't enough. Not nearly enough.

In one careful move he repositioned her to sit facing him, and he cradled her close as he sought the sensitive hollow at the edge of her neck, then trailed low to tantalise the soft fullness of her breast.

With an achingly slow touch he shaped her body with his hands, then he tested the weight of each breast before sliding up to cup her face.

His kiss was so incredibly gentle, she felt boneless and wholly his as need spiralled from deep within, heating her blood to fever pitch.

More, she wanted, *needed* more, and the breath became trapped in her throat as he trailed an exquisite path to the apex of her thighs, initiating an exploration of her labia before seeking the sensitive clitoris.

Lisane cried out at his touch, almost begging his fulfilment as he drove her high…so high she arched up against
him, then held back a low moan as he caught the peak of
one swollen breast in his mouth and began to suckle.

When she thought she could stand it no longer, he positioned her carefully and surged in deep, felt rather than
heard her satisfied sigh.

Then it became her ride, her body which controlled the
action…and it was he who held on, his voice a low,
guttural groan as she took him high until he bucked
beneath her in a primitive climax he ensured she shared.

Post-coital pleasure lingered a while, and Lisane rose
from the bath, filched a towel from its rack, then she stood
still as Zac took it from her nerveless fingers and began
blotting the moisture from her body.

Afterwards she returned the favour, conscious of his warm
appraisal of her ministrations until she was done, then he
curved an arm around her waist and led her into the bedroom.

Sleep came easily, and Lisane woke next morning to the
tantalising smell of freshly brewed coffee, bacon, eggs
and toast.

'Rise and shine,' a masculine drawl bade with amusement, and she lifted her head to see Zac attired in a towelling robe, tray in hand.

Rising wasn't a problem. It was shining which needed
some work!

'Tea and toast is supposed to do the trick.' He handed her
both, then crossed round to the other side of the bed, placed
the tray in a strategic position, then slid between the sheets.

She took a careful sip of tea, and followed it with a bite
of toast. 'Don't take it personally if I suddenly cut and run.'

Maybe this time…maybe not, Lisane decided minutes

later as she threw on a robe and made a hurried dash into the *en suite*.

Man, she hoped this morning habit would soon change!

'Anything I can do?'

She sponged her face, and kept her back to him. 'This is one experience I'd prefer not to share.'

'Tough.'

Toothbrush, toothpaste, and within a few minutes she was done. When she turned he was still there, leaning against the doorway.

His appraisal was anything but swift, and she met his steady gaze with equanimity. 'I'm fine.'

He straightened as she drew close and stood to one side so she could pass. 'Debatable.'

'I can sleep in another room if this bothers you.'

'Not a chance in hell,' Zac stated quietly, and she threw him a dark glance.

If he dared say 'we're in this together', so help her, she'd hit him.

Breakfast in bed, or eaten out on the terrace?

The terrace won, and they sat in companionable silence, enjoying the sun's warmth as it fingered the cityscape.

Peaceful, Lisane reflected, without the rush of weekday traffic clogging the streets and the cacophony of protesting horn-blasts.

Soon she'd dress and… Her mind came to a screeching halt as reality hit. She wasn't going anywhere. She was here to stay.

And today, she remembered, they were lunching with Zac's parents.

Could she plead a malaise and opt out?

Coward, she remonstrated silently.

Felicity and Max Winstone were nice people.

Lisane was engaged to their son.

Lunch, she decided, would be a pleasant occasion... *wouldn't it*?

Choosing what to wear posed a difficult decision. Smart casual or the whole deal? And if the latter, should she opt for the tailored office suit or something softly feminine?

She dithered, a victim of increasing nervous tension, then muttered an unladylike oath beneath her breath and selected a soft draped skirt in varying brown hues, added a toning knitted top and a filmy fitted over-blouse, slid her feet into stilettos, then tied her hair back with a chiffon scarf.

The result was elegant boho chic, and, she hoped, *right*.

A pulse beat quickly at the base of her throat as Zac's Jaguar turned into the established tree-lined street in one of the city's most prestigious suburbs.

'You're very quiet.'

'I'm reserving sparkling conversation for your parents.'

'You have no need to be nervous.'

Are you kidding? *Lunch* was a whole different ballgame from a social function meet-and-greet.

OK, you can do this, she bade silently as Zac eased the car into the driveway of a gracious mansion set well back from the road and came to a smooth halt outside the main entrance.

The large double doors stood open, and Max and Felicity Winstone appeared in the doorway, then traversed the few steps down to the car.

Smiling, Lisane saw at once, and giving every appearance of delighted happiness.

It was, she decided minutes later, going to be all right

as she recovered from the congratulatory hugs…and the general bonhomie as they were seated in the lounge.

Max brought out champagne, and they toasted the occasion, the baby, and enquired about a wedding date.

'Soon,' Zac concurred smoothly, and incurred his mother's faint frown.

'Darling, these things take time to arrange.'

'No guest list, no media.' His voice was firm. 'Just immediate family and a celebrant.'

'But—'

'No, mother. The only decision is location.' He took hold of Lisane's hand and raised it to his lips. 'We're considering holding the ceremony in the garden at Sovereign Islands.'

They were? Since when had she agreed to a wedding *soon*?

And how soon was *soon*?

'The Gold Coast?'

'Is that a problem?'

Felicity recovered quickly. 'No, of course not. Perhaps we could host a party for you in Brisbane following the honeymoon?'

Lisane almost felt sorry for his socially conscious parent, and she turned towards Zac. 'That would be lovely, don't you think?'

She caught the faint gleam of amusement apparent before he focused attention on his mother. 'Thank you.'

Lunch was a pleasant meal eaten in the formal dining room, and afterwards Lisane offered to help clear the table…something Felicity appeared to welcome.

'We'll just stack everything on the servery,' Zac's mother declared as Lisane followed her into a large, beautifully appointed kitchen. 'I'll deal with them later.'

'It wouldn't take long,' she suggested, and received a warm smile.

'Why not? It'll give us the chance to chat.'

Depending on the subject chosen, *chat* might not be such a good idea!

'For years we thought Zac would choose the daughter of one of our dear friends.'

Uh-oh, here comes the punchline…*Allegra*.

Should she pretend to understand, or go for silence? Silence, definitely.

'Except it didn't happen,' Felicity continued. 'Zac is very much his own man.' She offered a warm smile. 'Max and I are happy to welcome you into the family.'

You are? 'Thank you.'

Felicity began rinsing plates and transferring them into the dishwasher. 'The babe is a wonderful bonus.'

Really? 'I'm glad you think so.'

'I'd like to share in your pregnancy, if I may?'

Share as in…how?

'Help set up a nursery. Take you shopping. Fun things we can do together.'

What could she say, other than…'Thank you'?

Felicity closed the dishwasher door and dried her hands. 'Let's join the men, shall we?'

It became a pleasant afternoon, as Felicity led them on a tour of her garden, a subject which revealed a mutual empathy with gardening, the sowing of seeds, favoured flowers and shrubs.

Max Winstone had indulged his wife's green fingers with a small glasshouse filled with beautiful orchids, which Lisane admired with genuine pleasure.

Afterwards Felicity served afternoon tea out on the

terrace, and it was almost five before Zac indicated their intention to leave.

'We'll see you Friday evening,' Felicity bade as they reached the front entrance. 'The Fabrisis' cocktail party.'

You have to be kidding.

'You hadn't forgotten?'

Could they forget…*please*?

'We intend spending the weekend at the coast.'

We do?

'We'll put in an appearance,' Zac indicated.

Oh, *good*. The cat among the pigeons? Wasn't that going to be fun!

'Not quite what you expected?'

The query came as Zac eased the car through the gates and entered the tree-lined street.

She wanted to say 'the jury is still out', except that wouldn't have been fair. She'd hold on to any reservations until after Friday evening.

'It has been a lovely afternoon.'

'Which you're relieved to have done with.'

She looked at his profile, saw the strong jawline, the sculptured facial bone structure. 'Will you hold it against me if I say "yes"?'

'Not at all. I felt much the same when I met Solene and Jean-Claude.'

'Impossible. You're the quintessential male, in no doubt as to who and what you are.'

A smile split his mouth to reveal even white teeth. 'Merely a façade.'

'Fool.'

He entered the inner city and turned his attention to negotiating traffic. 'Feel like taking in a movie tonight?'

'The cinemaplex or DVD at home?'

'Your choice.'

'DVD,' she said without hesitation. 'Microwave popcorn, and an icy soda.'

'Done.'

CHAPTER TEN

LIVING with Zac lent a permanency to their relationship. The advantages were many, not the least of which being sharing so much more of his life on every level.

Lisane adored the apartment, and relished its close proximity to the inner city, for it meant she could walk to and from work each day and not have to deal with battling peak-hour traffic.

Mostly they ate in, meals which Lisane prepared, and afterwards they inevitably caught up on an overload of work.

Zac often left the apartment an hour, sometimes two, before she did in the morning…and they rarely arrived home at the same time each evening.

Twice he came to bed long after she was asleep, and she stirred at the soft drift of his hand, exulting in a leisurely, tactile lovemaking before curling in against him to sleep until morning.

Friday dawned with overcast skies and light drizzling rain. A preliminary warning as to how the evening would fare?

Lisane spent the day agonising over what to wear… whether she should go all-out in the glamour stakes, or stick with the classic little black dress.

Allegra, she knew, would excel in the latest designer wear, so why even attempt to compete?

Yet it was her first social occasion as Zac's fiancée, and, although she'd graced his arm at many soirées in the past, tonight would be different.

Even the thought set the butterflies in her stomach batting their wings in protest as she rode the lift to the penthouse apartment.

An hour. She had an hour to shower, fix her hair and make-up, then dress.

Lisane had only just entered the main bedroom when she heard Zac enter the apartment, and she slipped off her stilettos and began stripping off her outer clothes.

'Hi.'

The bright greeting didn't fool him in the slightest, and he crossed the room to her side, cupped her face between both hands, then angled his mouth against her own.

'What was that for?' she queried breathlessly as he released her, and his dark eyes gleamed with humour.

'Because I felt like it?'

'Distraction therapy.'

His soft laughter curled round her nerve-ends and tugged a little as he removed his jacket and loosened his tie.

She slipped off her tights, selected fresh underwear and disappeared into the *en suite*.

Seconds later she adjusted the temperature dial at the top edge of 'warm' and stepped beneath the stream of water.

Ten minutes to shower and wash her hair, ten minutes to shape it with the hair-drier, a similar amount of time to—

The glass door slid open and Zac stepped in beside her.

'You can't,' Lisane began as he took the soap from her hand. 'We don't have—'

'Time? Yes we do.'

He was so incredibly gentle it made her want to cry, and when he was done he collected the container of shampoo and began massaging the scented liquid into her scalp, rinsed it, then he shaped her shoulders and let one hand drift down her body, exploring each curve, the indentation of her navel, before seeking the feminine heart of her.

Skilled fingers found and stroked the sensitive nub with a touch that sent waves of sensation escalating through her body, and he caught her husky groan with his mouth in an explicit oral supplication.

She instinctively reached for him, only to have her hand imprisoned in his own.

'You can have your way with me later,' he promised, smiling as she began to protest, and he dropped a light kiss to the tip of her nose. 'Now go.'

Her body still sang from his touch as she filched a towel and used it to dry herself, before wrapping it sarong-wise round her slender form while using another to dry her hair.

Zac emerged from the shower and dried himself, then hitched the towel around his hips and disappeared into the bedroom.

It would be pleasant, Lisane decided, if they were simply dining out, instead of attending a Fabrisi cocktail party.

Something clenched inside her stomach at the thought of the evening ahead. The only positive was Zac would be at her side, and after a few nerve-racking hours spent smiling and engaging in scintillating conversation they intended driving to the Gold Coast for the weekend.

She conjured an image of his beautiful Sovereign

Islands home, their overnight bags ready to be stowed in the boot of his car…and determined to keep that image in the forefront of her mind.

The classic black dress, Lisane decided, and donned a black bra and thong. The dress was fully lined, negating the need for a slip, and she extracted new sheer black tights, pulled them on, then she slid her arms into her robe and began styling her hair with the hair-drier.

Painstaking care with her make-up brought the desired result, and she entered the bedroom to find Zac clad in black tailored trousers, pristine dress shirt, and in the process of adjusting his tie.

It took only minutes to step into her dress, close the zip fastening, then slip her feet into black stilettos.

Zac shrugged into his suit jacket as she collected her evening bag, and minutes later they rode the lift down to the underground car park.

'You look gorgeous,' he complimented, and she offered him a quirky smile in response.

'Thanks. Same goes.'

A gross understatement, she acknowledged as she slid into the passenger seat. For *he* could steal any feminine heart with effortless ease.

Was he aware of the effect he had on most women? Oh, tell it like it is…*all* women from sixteen to sixty!

He possessed the presence, the power and a primitive sensuality that promised much.

A considerable understatement, Lisane allowed silently, wondering just how many women there had been who could attest to his ability to deliver.

Focus, she commanded silently as the Jaguar joined the stream of traffic vacating the city.

Suburban Ascot encompassed prime real estate with splendid views of the city, and the Fabrisi mansion featured a stately heritage-listed property whose original owner featured high within Australian government circles.

No expense had been spared in its preservation, and it offered a glimpse into a previous century while retaining an innate graciousness their hosts took great care to maintain.

Nerves were hell and damnation, Lisane allowed as she circled the large formal lounge at Zac's side, and her eyes widened slightly as they settled on their hosts' daughter.

Tall, her sable hair beautifully groomed, Allegra looked stunning in a black fitted gown whose design hugged her toned curves to perfection.

Oh, my. This was the moment Lisane had been dreading. A face-off between the new fiancée and the woman who had assumed Zac's ring would be hers.

Perhaps it was appropriate they were both dressed in black?

Don't go there!

Did Zac have any idea of the situation he'd created?

Was it her imagination, or did the buzz of conversation suddenly become still as the guests surreptitiously observed Allegra cross the room?

Zac placed an arm along the back of her waist, and she killed the desire to lean in against him.

'Darlings.' Allegra's smile was a brilliant facsimile that didn't quite reach her eyes. 'I understand congratulations are in order.' She leaned in close and brushed her lips to the edge of Zac's mouth, lingered a few seconds too long as she pressed a hand to his chest, before she turned towards Lisane to bestow an air-kiss. 'How wonderful for you both.'

Polite was the only way to go. 'Thank you.'

'Do enjoy yourselves.' The megawatt smile was a mite overdone. 'We'll catch up again later.'

Hopefully not. Although somehow she had the feeling it was inevitable as she watched Allegra work the guests with consummate charm.

Mixing and mingling was an art form, with the exchange of air-kisses, the occasional European press of a cheek to each side of the face, a handshake, the light touch of a hand to the arm…combining greetings and small talk.

Max and Felicity Winstone arrived late with offered apologies.

'We were only a block away when the car developed a punctured tyre,' Felicity explained. 'Of all the times for it to happen.' She leaned in close and dropped a light kiss to Lisane's cheek. 'How are you, my dear?'

Max followed suit, and Lisane was grateful for the public gesture of familial solidarity.

Charmaine and Leo Fabrisi proved generous hosts, with uniformed staff presenting numerous trays of canapés and exotic-looking finger food, while waiters proffered champagne.

No special occasion, just a gathering of friends, she perceived. One of many such invitation-only evenings considered *de rigeur* on the social calendar of the favoured few.

Lisane and Zac's engagement brought voiced congratulations, and after a while her facial muscles began to ache from maintaining a constant smile.

'When is the wedding?' proved to be the most oft-asked query, and Lisane simply deferred to Zac, whose 'soon' answer brought the inevitable 'you haven't set a date yet?' response.

She would have given almost anything to drink something alcoholic to dull the edges...for, quite frankly, mineral water just didn't do it!

It was almost as if some instinctive warning mechanism had moved on to alert.

Fool, she chastised silently. Such an acute degree of sensitivity is ridiculous!

What could possibly occur in a large room filled with people...and Zac at her side?

Except a visit to the guest powder-room?

Beautifully decorated, she noted, with two individual stalls to accommodate female guests. And the only logical place Allegra could possibly stage a confrontation.

Lisane turned to face the elegantly clad young woman, and felt her heart sink.

'Allegra,' she acknowledged.

'You must think you're very clever.' The warm smile and the polite, friendly tone of voice were remarkably absent.

Oh, dear...the gloves were very definitely off. 'Is there a point to this?'

'What did you offer to get the ring, Lisane?' Allegra's eyes resembled flint as they narrowed with speculation. 'Bedroom tricks?'

She kept her gaze even. 'Why not love?'

The other woman laughed, although there was no humour in the sound. 'Oh, please. Don't insult me.'

'Are you done?'

Allegra's eyes glittered. 'Pretty little ring, darling.' Her head tilted slightly. 'Although I'd have chosen something...*more*.'

Calm. Polite. She could do both. 'It's the gift itself that's important, don't you think?'

Allegra's hands curled, and for a wild moment Lisane thought Allegra might hit her.

'Hope you don't have any secrets a close scrutiny might reveal. I doubt Zac would appreciate the media attention.' She turned and swayed towards the door, only to pause and look back over her shoulder. 'Don't count on making it to the altar.'

Where was a smart comeback when you wanted one?

The door closed behind Allegra before Lisane could think of a pithy response.

Well, now, wasn't that *fun*?

She needed a moment to compose herself before joining the guests, and she practised a smile, checked it in the mirror, only to discard it as totally fake.

Think warm and fuzzy.

A newborn baby, small and perfect, with Zac's dark hair and smile.

Better.

Just to be sure she added a touch of blusher to her cheeks and applied lip-gloss before re-entering the large lounge.

Zac was deep in conversation with an associate, and she made her way towards him.

As she reached his side he caught her hand and threaded his fingers through her own, then he absently brushed a thumb over the delicate veins inside her wrist.

'Ready, darling?'

Darling? Zac had never called her anything other than her name. Yet it appeared they were about to leave, and for that alone he deserved a stunning smile.

'Whenever suits you.'

His gaze narrowed thoughtfully as it skimmed her

features, noting the slight pallor beneath the expertly applied cosmetics, the faint shadows in those beautiful blue eyes.

Allegra?

Without doubt.

Leaving took a while as they paused to speak with his parents, before seeking their hosts, and Lisane gave a small sigh of relief as she slid into the front seat of the Jaguar.

Sovereign Islands lay a fifty-minute drive south, and they bypassed the city route and chose the gateway bridge which linked directly with the major motorway south.

The night sky was a dark indigo with a sprinkling of distant stars and a sickle moon.

It was good to lean back against the head-rest and let the tension ease from her body as she viewed the passing and opposing traffic.

'Did Allegra threaten you?'

No preliminaries, just straight to the point! Lisane didn't pretend to misunderstand. 'The word is open to interpretation.'

'As in?'

'I can assure you there are no skeletons in my family closet which could prove an embarrassment to the Winstone dynasty,' she revealed drily.

He spared her a swift dark glance and a muscle bunched at the edge of his jaw. Allegra could be a bitch, and he could well imagine her stinging verbal attack.

'I handled it.' And she had. Although she'd have given her eye-teeth to have come up with a cutting parting remark!

Lisane closed her eyes in a pretence of sleep, only for it to become a reality, and she came awake to the touch of

Zac's lips brushing her cheek…and the visual knowledge the car was stationary in the lit garage of his Sovereign Islands home.

'We're here.' An obvious statement, if ever there was one.

Zac slid out from behind the wheel, gathered their overnight bags from the trunk and led the way into the house.

A beautiful home, Lisane acknowledged with pleasure as she followed him into the main lobby.

High plastered ceilings, ivory-painted walls, with matching ivory marble tiles covering the ground floor. Modern furniture, floor-to-ceiling tinted glass along the eastern side of the house to catch the view out over the water. Formal and informal lounges, a formal and informal dining room, spacious kitchen, guest retreat and utility-rooms comprised the lower floor, with a wide curved staircase leading from the main lobby to the upstairs suites.

She had fallen in love with the place at first sight, its design and style, the magnificent view, the pool and the serenity it offered after the rush of city life.

'I'll take these upstairs.'

Lisane turned towards him with a smile. 'I'll go make a cup of tea. Will you have coffee?'

'Thanks.'

She had it ready by the time he entered the kitchen, and they took it out onto the covered terrace, where there was nothing except the water, the sky and the faint moving starboard light of a cruiser moving languidly on the bay.

The peace and tranquillity soothed her soul, and she slid off her stilettos and leant back in the comfortable lounger.

'We could take the boat out tomorrow.'

Lisane turned towards him and admired his profile in the dimmed light. Angles and planes, strong facial bone structure and a broad, loose-limbed frame possessed of whipcord strength.

'We could stop off at Couran Cove for lunch and relax there for a few hours.'

'Sounds great.' The day, the cocktail party, the drive…it was beginning to catch up with her, and she fought against the tendency to slip into a light doze.

What was it with the evening tiredness?

'Come on, sleepyhead,' Zac bade with amusement as he rose to his feet, stacked their cups together, then extended his hand…which she took and collected her shoes as she entered the house at his side.

'Go on up to bed. I'll take these through to the kitchen, then follow you.'

It was bliss to remove her outer clothes and peel off her tights, then she crossed the room to the *en suite* and began cleansing off her make-up before brushing her teeth.

Lisane reached for a covered elastic band to secure her hair, only to have Zac appear behind her and still her hands.

'Leave it loose.'

He stood head and shoulders above her, her hair so pale in contrast to his own, and she appeared positively petite in comparison to his broad frame.

A warm melting sensation crept through her body as he lifted the hair at her nape and brushed his lips to the sensitive curve beneath one earlobe.

His hands skimmed over her shoulders and deftly unfastened her bra, then slid the straps down over her arms.

All that separated her from nudity was a black silk thong, and she could almost feel her eyes dilate as he reached forward and cupped her breasts in his hands, gently shaping them until she felt the peaks harden beneath his touch.

'Zac…' It wasn't a protest, just a helpless wisp of a sigh as she watched her body bloom beneath his hands.

She could almost swear the surface of her skin tinged the palest pink as blood fed sensitive nerve-endings, and her eyes darkened to the deepest sapphire.

'This isn't fair.' The faint groan left her lips, and she felt the latent sensuality in the brush of his mouth along the edge of her shoulder, the hard ridge of his arousal as he drew her back against him.

One hand slid over her ribcage to her stomach, then splayed low as it inched beneath the thong and sought the intimate folds protecting her femininity.

Moist heat greeted his questing fingers, and she arched back against him as he leisurely stroked her, gradually increasing the intensity until she went wild in the throes of acute sensation.

Ohmigod. Was that wanton female depicted via mirrored image *her*?

She looked almost unrecognisable, her lips parted in the aftermath of ecstasy…and her eyes. Dear heaven, her eyes…

Lisane bowed her head and let her eyelids drift closed. Not in shame…but it was almost too much to witness. A secret part of herself she'd never seen, never realised existed.

'This is what I see each time we make love,' Zac said huskily. 'A beautiful young woman who is so caught up in passion it consumes her body, her soul.' He took hold of her shoulders and turned her to face him, then he tilted her chin so she had to look at him.

'My woman,' he said quietly. 'The mother of my child. Soon to be my wife.'

She lifted her arms up and clasped her hands together

behind his neck, then urged his head down towards her own and she angled her mouth into the warm heat of his in a kiss that offered him her heart...everything she was.

It would be so easy to say she loved him...would love him for as long as she lived.

Except the words remained locked in her throat as he swept an arm beneath her knees and carried her to their large bed, laid her there and dispensed with his clothes, aware she watched every move before he joined her.

Their lovemaking was leisurely, a long, sweet tasting that inched the sensuality high until only the physical coupling would suffice, and she cried out as he entered her in one long thrust, then clung as she enclosed him, becoming lost as he took her high, so high the muscular spasm of multiple orgasms shook her slender frame.

Afterwards he held her close, and she drifted to sleep in his arms.

Breakfast was something they cooked together and shared out on the terrace. There was no hurry to do anything, and they read the Saturday-morning papers, then Lisane tidied the kitchen while Zac went down the jetty to inspect the cruiser.

It was a beautiful summer's day, the skies blue with barely a drift of cloud and the sun warm with the promise of fine weather.

Lisane packed cold drinks into the cooler, added fruit, then she collected a hat, sun-screen cream, and was ready when Zac returned indoors.

Shorts and a top was suitable wear, with a sweater draped over her shoulders, its sleeves loosely knotted beneath her throat. Joggers on her feet, sunglasses pushed high on her head.

Zac wore similar apparel, and she looked silently askance as he collected the cooler.

'No problems. Let's go.'

The sea was smooth, with only the slightest breeze to ripple its surface as Zac headed out towards the open harbour, *en route* to Couran Cove.

They passed so many mansions sited on the seven linked islands comprising suburban Sovereign Islands. Almost every island was built on, magnificent multi-million-dollar homes on various canal- and bay-front land. Prestigious, expensive and luxurious, there were boats and cruisers moored at almost every jetty.

Palm trees lined the streets, and residential gardens bore flower borders, topiary and sculptured fountains, beautiful bird-baths, scrupulously maintained by an army of professional gardeners and landscapers.

Zac headed the cruiser towards open waters and made steady speed to a tourist island almost forty-five minutes distant.

The air was fresh with a brisk ocean breeze, and as they drew close a string of villas was apparent set against the background of rainforest.

Private craft were moored at the jetties, and a number of tourists were on a day trip to enjoy what the island offered.

Lisane found it fun to ride the island 'train' around the various carriageways where bush-chalets nestled in seclusion, and she took Zac up on his suggestion to lunch at the oceanfront restaurant.

Through the plate-glass windows lay the numerous sand-hills, spinifex, and the Pacific Ocean, whose blue waters stretched far out to the horizon as they sparkled and dappled beneath the midday sun.

Fine food, a relaxed ambience... Pleasant, she determined, to share time with him without needing to rush anywhere.

Here, dressed in casual attire, he didn't look the hard-hitting criminal lawyer of high repute who possessed a verbal repertoire second to none.

Lisane saw him lift an enquiring eyebrow, and her mouth curved into a musing smile.

'I'm trying to decide who you might be if you weren't *you*.'

His faint laughter curled round her heart.

'And what have you come up with?'

She tilted her head to one side, and her eyes assumed a slightly wicked sparkle. 'Nothing seems to fit.'

He finished his coffee, withdrew his wallet and paid the bill. 'Shall we leave?'

They rode the 'train' part-way and chose to tread the winding track through the lush rainforest to the harbour.

'Thanks,' Lisane said with sincerity as they boarded the cruiser.

'For what, specifically?' Zac queried as he started up the engine and began easing the craft away from the jetty.

'The weekend,' she elaborated simply. 'Today.'

'It's a pleasure.'

It was almost five when he secured the cruiser at Sovereign Islands, and Lisane went on up to the house while he shut everything down.

A shower was a priority, for there was salt-spray in her hair, on her skin, and she needed to wash off the sun-screen cream.

Zac entered the *en suite* as she emerged from it, and she pulled on dress jeans, added a knitted top, then she secured her damp hair into a pony-tail. Moisturiser, lip-gloss, and she was done.

'Want to eat in or go out?'

Zac strolled into the bedroom with a towel hitched at his hips.

He was something else. Strongly muscled torso, admirable breadth of shoulders, and possessed of an intrinsic sensual sexuality that melted her bones every time she looked at him.

'In,' she said at once. 'I'll cook.'

He pulled on underwear and stepped into jeans. 'There's steak in the refrigerator. I'll set up the barbecue.' He reached for a polo shirt and dragged it on. 'You fix a salad.'

Just as they were about to eat there was a light shower of rain, which meant transferring their meal indoors.

Afterwards Zac slotted a DVD into the player and settled down onto the sofa with Lisane curled close against him.

A romantic comedy, it had laugh-out-loud moments, and the last thing she remembered watching was a stay-at-home dad trying to cope with a toddler, a rebellious four-year-old and a dog which had somehow slipped into the house and was creating mayhem.

She was unaware of Zac lifting her into his arms and carrying her to bed, and she barely stirred when he carefully divested her of her clothes and slid her into bed.

It was morning when Lisane woke, and late, she determined with a swift glance at the bedside clock, and she rose gingerly into a sitting position, then patted her stomach and bade it *behave*.

Minutes later she cautiously slid from the bed and made it into the *en suite* without having to break into a run.

Could this be the beginning of the end of morning sickness? If so…yahoo and hallelujah!

It was impossible to suppress a grin as she dressed in jeans and a cropped top, and it became a delighted smile as she went downstairs to the kitchen, collected a bowl and added muesli and fruit, then carried it out onto the terrace.

Zac was seated at the outdoor table, coffee in hand, and he glanced up as she approached.

'Hi.'

'You should have woken me.'

The warmth of his smile sent spirals of sensation curling through her body as he reached forward and drew out a chair for her. 'Why?'

'It's too nice a day to spend any of it in bed.'

'I thought we might drive into Surfer's Paradise and take a walk along the beach.'

Lisane wrinkled her nose at him. 'You're indulging me.'

'You don't want to be indulged?'

'You're kidding me?'

Bliss, absolute bliss, she decided an hour later as they trod the sandy foreshore adjacent to the esplanade, where high-rise apartments dominated the skyline.

Fresh air carrying the tang of the sea on a soft breeze beneath the summer sun. What could be more inviting?

Walking hand-in-hand with a lover as they strolled along the broadwalk?

Relaxing over a café latte at a pavement café and watching the people walk by?

All of that, and more, Lisane decided as she became lost to introspection of the deep and meaningful kind.

She had earned Zac's respect and affection. He would,

she knew, ensure she was well cared-for and gift uncon-
ditional love to their child.

It was enough.

Wishing for the moon and the stars in the love stakes
was the stuff of dreams, not reality.

He was insisting on marriage, permanence.

It was what she wanted…so what was the problem?

'Pleasant thoughts?'

Zac's musing drawl intruded on her self-analysis, and
she offered him a slow, sweet smile.

'Yes.'

'Do you intend to share?'

Her smile widened. 'No.' Her eyes assumed a mischievous gleam. 'You might get a swelled head.'

The edge of his mouth twitched a little. 'Let's move
on and have lunch.' He withdrew a note from his wallet
and signalled the waitress, paid for their coffee, then he
rose to his feet and caught hold of her hand as they walked
to the car.

Tedder Avenue at Main Beach was a perfect choice, and
she gave him a delighted smile as he eased the Jaguar into
a parking space.

'You really know how to indulge a woman.'

'Taking you to lunch?'

She waited a beat. 'That, too.'

Zac trailed light fingers along the edge of her jaw. 'An
admission, Lisane?'

He had to know the effect he had on her. All it took was
a look, the touch of his hand…and she melted.

I love you.

Her lips parted as the words rose from her throat and
lingered unvoiced on the tip of her tongue.

For a heart-stopping moment it seemed as if the world stood still, and she couldn't move.

Her eyes seemed locked with his, and she felt her mouth tremble as he traced their outline.

She lost all sense of time and place, and her pupils dilated as he angled his mouth to her own in a kiss that was little more than a light brush of his lips before he raised his head.

'Food, hmm?'

There was a teasing quality to the afternoon, an anticipation of something magical just beyond her reach. A promise she chose not to analyse or examine too closely for fear it might only exist in her imagination.

They concluded a magnificent day with dinner at an Italian restaurant overlooking the nearby marina, and it was close to midnight when they reached Sovereign Islands.

Early tomorrow morning they'd drive to the Brisbane city apartment, change into the obligatory business suits, and join their working colleagues.

But tonight…they had what remained of the night, and a leisurely loving that became a sensual supplication of the senses.

CHAPTER ELEVEN

THE morning sun held the pleasant warmth of an early summer, with barely a few wisps of soft white cloud drifting beneath the clear blue sky.

It held the promise of a beautiful day, Lisane predicted as she entered the court-house and took the lift to a suite of offices on an upper floor.

The weekend at the Gold Coast had been relaxing and a lovely break after a hectic week, both work-wise and socially.

Now, however, it was back to work with a vengeance, with the usual investigative process involving phone calls, consultations and one minor paperwork snafu which required correction.

The new girl was still finding her feet, for which Lisane made allowances. Tact and diplomacy worked well, but this was the second time the identical mistake had occurred. Which led to a suspicion the lauded praise listed in her CV might not be entirely accurate.

Consequently it was a relief to take a lunch break at her favoured café, and she bought a magazine at the news-stand *en route*, ordered, then chose a pavement table.

Herbal tea, divine food, fresh air and sunshine…who could ask for anything more?

An interesting magazine article held her attention for its hard-hitting exposure, and she glanced up as a man pulled out a vacant chair at her table.

'You don't mind if I share?'

There were a few empty tables, and a slight frown creased her forehead. She kept her voice light. 'There are other tables.'

Middle-aged, perhaps close to fifty, short cropped hair, attired in well-worn jeans and T-shirt, he didn't appear to pose much of a threat.

'What man would choose to sit alone when he can share time with a beautiful young woman?'

She couldn't help feeling mildly irritated as he rested both arms on the edge of the table, and she merely offered a polite smile before returning her attention to the magazine.

'Nice day.'

Conversation? She really didn't want to do conversation!

'Don't want to be interrupted, do you?'

Oh, heavens. 'Not particularly,' she managed quietly.

'Your life is on track.' He indicated the expensive ring on her finger. 'Nice.'

The hair on the back of her neck began to prickle as instinct provided caution.

'My son's life is ruined because of your fancy man.'

Stand up and leave. Now.

His eyes dulled and became hard. 'Don't move.' He moved one hand sufficiently for her to see a switch-blade resting beneath it. 'Saw your picture in the paper.' His lips parted slightly. 'Been watching out. Figured it was just a matter of time before I got you on your own.'

There was traffic, people walking by. She wasn't alone. There were police on patrol in the mall. A security guard on duty outside a nearby bank. Maybe she could attract their attention…

'I'd be able to hurt you and disappear in the crowd before either one of them got here.'

True, but if he thought she was just going to react like a frightened wimp, he had it wrong. 'A judge would have convicted your son on evidence—'

'Dug up by your devious lawyer boyfriend.'

Keep talking, a silent voice bade. 'Tell me about your son's case.'

'Don't start with the psycho-babble. I know all the angles.'

No, you don't. But she couldn't say that. 'Did your son's representative lodge an appeal?'

'Didn't work.'

Just as she'd thought. 'I'm sorry I can't help you.'

'You think I don't know what you're up to? Keep talking, try to get me onside in the hope I'll let you go?' His mouth thinned. 'Forget it.'

'How long will it take before our presence draws the waiter's attention? Tables are filling,' she pointed out, thankful it was true.

'You haven't finished your lunch.'

Lisane looked at the food remaining on her plate. Like she was hungry? Although the teapot held more than one cup. Maybe…

With slow movements she reached for the teapot and refilled her cup, then she lifted it with both hands and took an appreciative sip.

Don't hesitate. *Now*.

In one swift action she tossed the contents of her cup in his face, rose to her feet and ran.

She was vaguely aware of his startled yelp, followed seconds later by something sharp hitting her shoulder. Someone shouted, a table crashed and she fell to the pavement.

Most ungainly and inconvenient. She tried to stand... and couldn't quite make it.

Why, for heaven's sake?

There were people moving around her, a woman crouched down beside her. 'Just sit quietly. Someone is ringing for an ambulance.'

Why an ambulance?

It was then she saw the blood. And glimpsed the switch-blade embedded in her upper arm. Almost on cue she became aware of the pain.

How could she feel slightly dazed, yet be acutely aware of her immediate surroundings? It didn't make sense.

Her tights were ruined. One stiletto was scuffed. And as for her jacket...

She tried to check her watch and almost blacked out at the pain.

OK, so she wouldn't be going in to work this afternoon. She should phone in...

'An ambulance is on its way. You're going to be fine.'

There was one burning question. 'Did they get him?'

An answer in the affirmative meant her action hadn't been in vain.

From then on in everything happened quickly. The police arrived, followed minutes later by the ambulance.

An injection worked effectively and the pain began to subside a little as details were recorded.

By the time she reached hospital sedation had kicked in and she was feeling drowsy.

The last thing she remembered was being wheeled into Theatre...

Lisane could hear low, muted voices, and someone was doing something to her arm.

Where was she?

Submerged in her subconscious, or emerging into reality?

Her eyelids drifted open and she discovered she was in a room with pale cream walls, a television set mounted high, and there was a nurse intent on taking her blood pressure.

'Good girl. You're awake.'

In slow motion it all came flooding back. Lunch, man, the attack, police, ambulance.

Hospital, she was in hospital.

Her arm felt cumbersome swathed in a bandage and resting in a protective sling.

'I'm pregnant.' Somehow that seemed more important than anything else.

'Baby's fine, dear.'

Well, of course it is. Her arm had nothing to do with the tiny foetus in her womb.

For some reason that made her smile.

'Lisane.'

She recognised the voice and turned her head to see Zac standing close to her bed.

His features appeared relaxed, but there was something apparent in the depths of those dark eyes she chose not to examine too closely.

'How long have you been here?'

He had instant recall of the initial phone call transferred to his chambers. How he'd left instructions to postpone the afternoon's schedule before taking the lift down to his car and driving at speed to the hospital. Agonising at just how bad it could have been, and barely able to contain his rage that it had happened at all.

He'd demanded the best surgeon, a private suite... pacing up and down the corridor until the surgeon emerged from Theatre with news. Waiting impatiently while she was in Recovery before she was transferred to this suite.

Aware just how shaken up he was beneath the calm, cool exterior he managed to exude with seeming ease.

Zac bent down and brushed his lips to her cheek. 'A while.' He took hold of her hand and enfolded it in his own. 'How do you feel?'

Her eyes widened a little. How *did* she feel?

Thirsty. Not quite with-it. A little pain, some discomfort.

Safe, she decided, now that he was here.

'OK,' she managed cautiously, and swivelled her head towards the nurse. 'What's the damage?'

'The blade touched the bone, but didn't splinter it, and you have a deep flesh wound.' The nurse checked the drip, wrote something on the file, then attached it to the base of the bed, offered Zac a curt nod and left the room.

Lisane swallowed the sudden lump in her throat, and aimed for some light humour. 'It could have been worse.'

Just how much worse was something she preferred not to contemplate.

Zac pulled up a chair and sank into it, his expression carefully enigmatic as he leant towards her.

'I guess you want chapter and verse,' she offered before he had a chance to say a word.

'When you feel up to it.'

'I'm not exactly at death's door.'

The fact she could have been almost brought him undone. Even now his gut twisted painfully at the thought of how close he'd come to losing her.

'You don't need to stay,' she managed quietly.

He caught her hand and carried it to his lips. 'Trying to get rid of me?'

'Didn't you have an important meeting scheduled for this afternoon?'

'Postponed until further notice.'

'But you—'

He pressed her lips closed, and his mouth curved into a faint smile. 'Quit while you're ahead, hmm?'

Too much. He was way too much for her to cope with right now, and she felt her eyelids flutter a little as she fought the tendency to close them.

No doubt due to the after-effects of the anaesthetic, she decided drowsily as she slipped into a light doze.

When Lisane woke the room was bathed in electric light and the curtains at the window were closed.

What time was it?

From habit she checked her wrist, and found it bare. Her ring was also missing…

'I have them.'

Zac rose from the chair and extracted an envelope from the breast pocket of his jacket.

'You're still here?'

What a silly question…of course he was here, she could see him, couldn't she?

He lifted her left hand and slid the beautiful solitaire in place, then he attached her watch.

This close he had a strange effect on her breathing, and she was suddenly aware of the subtle tones of his cologne, the sensual pull as he leant in.

At that moment he turned his head and caught the expression evident in her eyes, and for a millisecond he didn't say a word, then he lifted both hands and cupped her face.

His lips grazed hers, lingered, then opened to meet her own as he savoured the sweetness of her mouth.

Lisane wanted to hold him there, to deepen the kiss to something more. Except he monitored the pace, kept it relatively light, then gently broke free.

'Where were we?' she managed breathlessly, and heard his soft laugh.

'Before you fell asleep?' he teased. 'Or just now?'

It delighted him to see the soft tinge of colour creep over her cheeks. He lifted a hand and brushed a tendril of hair back from the edge of her neck, then buried his lips in the sensitive curve.

Every nerve-cell came sensually alive as piercing sweetness surged through her body, and her mouth trembled slightly as Zac lifted his head.

A husky imprecation sounded low in his throat, and his eyes locked with hers.

'I'll alert the nurse you're awake. She suggested you might like something light to eat.'

Food. Now that she thought about it, she did feel hungry, and she ate the soup, the small omelette, and enjoyed the small dish of cantaloup and yoghurt.

'Better?'

Lisane inclined her head as the nurse reappeared and

topped up the painkiller in her drip, checked her vital signs, then disappeared.

'I've seen the police report.'

She knew the procedure. The police department would send someone in to take her formal statement, followed by a routine chain of events which would finally end in the court-room.

'When can I come home?'

Not the Milton cottage. Zac's apartment.

Since when had she begun to think of it as *home*?

'Tomorrow, all being well.' His eyes darkened fractionally. 'You won't return to work for at least a week. Understood?'

The injury was to her left arm. 'I'm sure I could manage.' Heavens, she could take and make phone calls, use her right hand for the laptop, and arrange client appointments.

'No.'

'Zac—'

His eyes hardened. 'It's not negotiable, Lisane.'

'You can't—'

'I could have lost you.'

There was something in his voice, barely beneath the surface of his control, that halted anything else she might have said.

'So,' he added with gentle silkiness, 'bear with me on this.'

Why did she suddenly feel as if she was on the verge of taking hold of something just beyond her grasp?

The air between them was suddenly electric as everything in the room faded. There was only the man, a heightened awareness, and something raw and primitive existent that almost tore the breath from her body.

It was then the nurse entered the room, and she took one look at the patient and pursed her lips.

'Mr Winstone, your fiancée needs to rest.' There was mild reproof evident in her voice. 'I suggest you take a meal break. Visiting hours conclude at eight.'

For a moment there appeared to be a silent battle of wills, which, despite the Winstone influence and wealth, the nurse intended to win.

'You're right, of course,' Zac conceded. He leant forward and cupped Lisane's cheek in the palm of his hand, then traced her mouth with his thumb. 'I'll be back in an hour. Is there anything you need?'

'A brush for my hair. Toothbrush and toothpaste.' She paused. 'Some fresh clothes to change into for tomorrow.'

'Done.'

Lisane leant back against the nest of pillows when he left and mentally replayed the past few minutes, examining not so much his words, but their implication.

He'd sounded as if he cared. A lot.

Maybe she'd take courage in both hands and ask him.

Again, maybe not.

The nurse returned, removed the drip, checked her temperature and blood pressure, and handed out two painkillers.

For a while she channel-surfed the in-room television until drowsiness overcame her and she slipped into a deep sleep, unaware of Zac's return, or how long he stayed with her.

Pain woke her through the night, and from then on she dozed and woke at regular intervals until dawn when the early-morning hospital routine kicked in.

Discharge was granted later in the day, and she was dressed and waiting when Zac walked into her suite.

His gaze skimmed her features, noted the shadows beneath her eyes, and dropped a light kiss on her cheek.

'How's the pain factor?' He brushed a hand down the length of her spine and let it rest at her waist. 'The nurse reported you had a disturbed night.'

'Bearable.' She refused to own up to anything more. Not that he was fooled in the slightest.

'I don't think another twenty-four hours here would do any harm.'

'Please. I'm taking painkillers.' She lifted a hand in an expressive gesture. 'Hospital, or at home…what's the difference?'

They drew abreast of a bank of lifts. 'As long as you understand one false move and I'll have you back here before you can turn around.'

The warning brought a faint smile as they rode the lift down to ground level. 'OK. Point taken.'

'I could have called a cab.' Lisane kept the protest light as they passed through Reception to where his Jaguar was parked illegally immediately outside the hospital entrance.

He shot her a piercing look. 'You think I would have agreed to that?' He used a modem to disarm the car's security system and opened the passenger door.

She slid into the seat and unconsciously held her breath as he leant in to fasten her seat belt.

Why did she feel so vulnerable around him? It was like being on an emotional roller coaster…crazy. Worse, it seemed, since pregnancy hormones had kicked in.

Maybe silence was a safer option, she mused as Zac eased the powerful car into the stream of traffic and headed towards the inner city.

Entering the penthouse apartment was heaven, for she

loved its spacious rooms, the clean lines of the design and decor, with its panoramic view over the city, the meandering river to the hills way in the distance.

An apartment high in the sky, part of the city, yet removed from it with the benefit of restaurants, shops, all within walking distance, parks, entertainment.

Lisane crossed the lounge to the expanse of floor-to-ceiling tinted armoured glass and drank in the cityscape, doubting she could ever tire of the view or take it for granted.

'Lost in thought, or simply admiring the view?'

She turned her head slightly as Zac came to stand beside her. 'Both, I guess.'

He placed an arm along the back of her waist. 'Want to share?'

What would his reaction be if she said *I love you*?

Even one second's hesitation in his response would tear her apart.

Did the all-consuming, everlasting kind of love exist in real life? Or were there degrees of love where two people could successfully co-exist on different emotional levels?

Was it too much to hope Zac might feel the same way about her...as she did for him?

Did it really matter?

In her heart of hearts, the answer had to be *yes*.

She needed to be wanted for herself, not because she was carrying his child.

The fact he intended to make a life with her should be enough. There were those who would consider her insane to want it all, when she had so much.

Except this apartment, his Gold Coast mansion, everything he owned...they were only material possessions.

It was the man himself, his values and beliefs that mattered. And above all, his love.

At what point did a man and a woman declare their love for each other? Not the empty, meaningless words uttered in a moment of passion. The genuine, emotion-filled expression of true, everlasting love.

Who, she wondered a trifle sadly, possessed sufficient courage to lay bare their heart...*first*?

Zac's hand slowly traversed her spine and came to rest at her nape. 'You're very quiet.'

Because I'm terrified and afraid...and so incredibly emotionally mixed-up, it's crazy!

Steps, Lisane reflected.

Isn't life all about taking steps?

Even small steps result in progress...in one direction or another. And how was she going to know in which direction she was going unless...?

'Do you have any idea what I went through when I heard you'd been injured?' Zac queried huskily as he carefully turned her within the circle of his arms.

She looked at him, and became mesmerised by the darkness evident in his eyes.

'Your child is safe.'

Something moved in those dark depths, and she couldn't look away. 'You think the child you carry is my only concern?'

Isn't it?

A soft imprecation emerged, pithy, emotive and emitted with restrained vengeance.

Her eyes widened at the silent anger evident in his expression, and for a wild moment she thought he might physically shake her.

Tears welled, shimmered and threatened to spill beneath his intent gaze.

'It would have been easier if…' she began, and faltered to a halt, unable to say the words.

'You miscarried? For whom? You?' Zac demanded in a harsh, almost ravaged voice.

No, she longed to scream. *You.*

'You can't deny the pregnancy has caused complications.'

'How so?'

Oh, heavens, why hadn't she just shut her mouth? 'We shared a pleasant relationship,' she began unevenly. 'A mistaken pregnancy wasn't meant to form part of it.'

'You regard the conception of our child as a mistake?'

Oh, hell. She should know better than to parry words with the maestro of verbiage. 'Unexpected and un-planned,' she clarified.

'But not unwanted.'

How could it be otherwise? A child in Zac's image. A darling little dark-haired boy with big dark eyes and a gorgeous smile.

'No.'

Was she so steeped in tradition? Did it really matter if the conception of a child came before marriage?

Not if *love* was the main criteria.

Yet she didn't even know if what he felt for her was anything other than fondness and affection.

Was either emotion a strong enough foundation for marriage?

Sadly, she didn't know.

'What do you think will change when we marry?'

When not *if*. Lisane noted the difference. 'Marriage should be for ever.'

'You perceive ours won't last?'

He was good at this. Too good. 'How can it?' she said simply.

'Perhaps you'd care to explain your reasons why?'

'Dammit, we're not in a court-room!'

'No,' he agreed with brooding savagery. 'Otherwise I'd verbally tear you to pieces.'

'So what's stopping you?'

Zac cupped her face and bent his head down to hers. 'This.' Then his mouth was on hers in a possession that transcended anything he'd bestowed on her before.

Riveting and evocative, it was raw, primitive and passionate. Taking more than she could give in a ravishment so shamelessly intense, she uttered a faint moan in protest.

Lisane felt the moment he sensed it, and she gave a choked sigh as his mouth softened into a slow, sensual supplication that fragmented her senses and wreaked havoc with her emotions.

A tear spilt down her cheek, touched his mouth and was followed by another.

She closed her hand into a fist and hit his shoulder in a punitive effort as he slowly eased to a gentle, evocative tasting until her lips trembled beneath his own.

When he lifted his head she could only look at him with dark eyes bruised with emotion, and he pressed his lips against each eyelid in turn.

'*You*,' he vowed quietly. 'Only you.'

Lisane opened her eyes and met his own. Then almost died at the expression evident. Naked passion…and something more, so much more.

'The knowledge you carry our child is a wonderful gift. For both of us. One I would never deny,' he added gently.

'But it is you who matter to me more than anyone or anything in this world. You're the love of my life. Everything.'

Zac watched her face transform as the impact of his words registered. The joy, *love* evident in her beautiful blue eyes…for him.

'Without you,' he said gently, 'there is no light, no warmth. Nothing.'

He'd never said, not once…

'How could you not know?' His voice was husky with emotion. 'Every time we made love…it was with my heart, my soul. All that I am.' He paused imperceptibly. 'For you. Only you.'

A faint smile tilted the edges of her mouth. 'And I thought it was just good sex,' she teased, and gasped as he caught her lower lip between his teeth, nipped a little, then released it.

'Minx.' He laughed softly.

Her eyes gleamed and almost danced with mischief. 'Hmm, maybe I will marry you, after all.'

His eyes held hers, no longer light, but strangely serious. *'Because?'*

Her expression sobered. 'I love you.' The words came from the depths of her heart. 'I always have. From the very beginning,' she said quietly, adding, 'Otherwise I wouldn't be with you.'

Zac rested his forehead against her own. 'Thank you.'

His warm breath teased the loose hair at her temple, and he gently tucked the wayward lock behind her ear.

'Tomorrow we'll go down to the coast for a few days.'

She moved her head to look at him. 'Tomorrow? But you have a busy schedule. Aren't you due in court on Friday?'

His smile almost undid her. 'Postponed and rescheduled.'

'Oh.'

'There's more.'

'As in?'

'A wedding.'

'Whose?'

He pressed a light kiss to the tip of her nose. 'Ours.'

She couldn't think of a suitable word, and he touched a finger to her lips.

'This weekend.'

'But you can't—'

'An intimate family wedding in the garden of our Gold Coast home.'

'It isn't possible to arrange—'

'My parents, Solene and Jean-Claude.'

A very private ceremony. 'Really?' No fuss, no media, just immediate family and a celebrant.

'Really.'

Her eyes lightened to a brilliant cerulean blue. 'Saturday?'

'Uh-huh.'

Oh, my.

'Everything is organised.'

'I think maybe I should sit down.'

His soft laughter sent warmth fizzing through her veins, and she laid her head into the curve of his shoulder, exulting in his clean male scent beneath the subtle tones of his cologne.

'Go do that,' Zac bade as he gently put her at arm's length. 'Connect with Solene while I put a meal together.' He glimpsed the unasked question on the edges of her lips. 'And no, I didn't enlighten her about the assault.'

That meant she could keep it light and downplay the details.

'Half an hour, OK?' He trailed light fingers down her cheek, and his smile almost melted her bones. 'We eat, then you get to rest in bed.' He touched a finger to her parted mouth. 'Doctor's orders.'

Did happiness transcend physical pain? It seemed that way, for her wounded arm was the last thing on her mind as she talked with Solene, whose excitement almost matched her own.

The wedding arrangements took precedence as they discussed apparel, flowers, the ceremony itself, exchanging ideas.

'There's just one other thing,' Lisane added, and gave a brief outline of the assault.

'My God.' Solene's dismayed concern hit home. 'Are you all right? This happened *yesterday*. And you're only telling me *now*. Put Zac on the phone.'

'He's in the kitchen—'

'Preparing dinner? Which means you can't. Put him on the phone.'

'There's no need to fuss—'

'You're my baby sister. I can fuss all I like, and I will until I get some answers.' There was a second's silence. 'If I don't get them, I'm on the next flight. Bank on it.'

Lisane walked into the kitchen, caught Zac's raised eyebrow and offered him the hand-held phone. 'Solene.'

He calmly answered the questions Solene obviously shot at him in rapid succession, and from what Lisane could tell he easily dealt with each and every one of her sister's concerns before he solemnly handed back the phone.

'OK. I'm convinced. Just be warned I want all the details at the weekend.'

'Got it.'

'Now go eat, and take care.'

'Yes, ma'am.'

'I'm so happy for you.' Solene sounded as if she was close to tears. 'Love you heaps.'

'Same goes.'

Lisane cut the connection, and watched as Zac served pasta onto two plates, added the sauce, and took herbed bread from the oven.

'Go take a seat.'

It was a delicious meal, and she said so, then attempted to kill the tendency to yawn as tiredness began to descend. The pain in her arm had moved up from a persistent niggle to a nagging ache.

'Let's get you settled in bed,' Zac declared as he noted her pale features and dilated eyes.

'I can manage.' A useless protest he ignored as he carefully divested her of her clothes, gave her bathroom time, then saw her nestled against a bank of pillows in their large bed.

He operated a module which automatically opened cabinet doors exposing a television set, switched it on, then handed her the remote.

'I'll be back in a few minutes.'

He returned in five minutes with tea and painkillers, ensured she took the latter, then he stretched out beside her and locked his hands behind his head.

'Thanks.'

His eyes met hers, and he had to wonder if she had any idea what she did to him, or the power she held with her loving smile.

It was the smile that melted his heart every time, for it seemed to come from deep inside, radiating to her eyes, almost liquidising those lovely blue depths with an emotion so expressive it was all he could do not to pull her into his arms and kiss her senseless.

More, much more. To slowly bare her skin, and embrace every inch of her with his lips, to succour and tease, take her to the edge of sensual fulfilment, then hold and join her in a glorious mutual climax before sharing the free-fall.

To think he might have lost her…

His eyes hardened, and his heart turned to stone. The man who assaulted her would pay, and pay dearly. If the switch-blade had entered her body mere inches to the right, he'd be making arrangements for her funeral, not their wedding.

'You don't need to stay with me.'

Zac slowly turned his head towards her and reached for her hand. In seeming slow motion he brought it to his lips, and she almost died at the expression evident in those dark eyes.

'Yes,' he managed quietly. 'I do.'

Everything she'd ever wanted, hoped and longed for was right here.

Love. The enduring, everlasting kind.

A gift so infinitely precious, it was beyond price.

Emotion filled her until it became almost more than she could bear, and her mouth shook a little as moisture welled in her eyes.

Dammit, she wasn't going to cry.

'Don't,' Zac chastised gently, and she managed a trembling smile.

'I didn't think it was possible to be so happy.'

His eyes held hers. 'Believe that's not going to change.'

He'd make sure of it.

All the days of his life.

It was a while before he sensed her breathing begin to deepen, and long after she fell asleep he eased himself from the bed, shed his clothes, then carefully slipped in between the covers to lie at her side.

She needed to rest, and he wasn't going anywhere soon.

EPILOGUE

'READY?'

'Yes,' Lisane said simply.

Within minutes she'd descend the curved staircase at Solene's side and walk outdoors into the garden, where Zac stood waiting for her in the presence of his parents, Jean-Claude and the celebrant.

'You look beautiful,' Solene complimented with genuine sincerity as she leant in close and touched Lisane's cheek with her own. 'There are so many wishes…' she trailed gently. 'I'll settle on one. May you be as happy for the rest of your life as you are today.'

'You're going to make me cry if you say anything more.'

'Don't you dare,' her sister admonished.

The past few days had passed with a dreamlike quality, Lisane reflected, for Zac had organised everything with admirable ease.

Within an hour of their entering his Sovereign Islands home on Wednesday morning, a bridal consultant had arrived with a large folder of dress designs and material swatches, from which Lisane chose a simple gown in ivory silk. Ivory roses were the flowers of choice for the bridal bouquet and floral decorations. Everything was co-ordi-nated, from a private caterer to the wedding cake.

It had seemed an impossible challenge, but an emi-nently successful one, Lisane concluded as she admired the result with awe.

The weather was perfect, clear skies, warm early-summer sunshine, with barely the slightest breeze drifting in from the sea.

'Let's go do this, shall we?'

It took only minutes to descend the stairs and cross the marble-tiled floor to where the floor-to-ceiling glass doors stood open to reveal a manicured lawn, garden borders and miniature topiary.

A roll of cream carpet led to a rose-decorated arbour, where Zac stood waiting for her.

He was something else, his tall, broad-shouldered frame attired in an impeccably tailored dark suit.

Almost by instinct he turned towards her, and she felt as if her heart stood still for a few telling seconds before it kicked in to pulse at a rapid beat.

Clearly evident were the extent of Zac's emotions as she slowly trod the carpet towards him. It made her want to smile, laugh and cry…all at the same time.

'Wow.'

Solene encapsulated it in one softly spoken word.

Was it possible to walk on air? It certainly felt as if her feet didn't touch the ground.

The smile won out, lighting up her features and lending her eyes a luminous quality as she reached his side and interlinked her fingers with his own.

Without thought to anyone else, Zac lowered his head and laid his mouth gently against her own, savoured, then reluctantly withdrew to smile at the faint tinge of colour accenting her cheeks.

It was a beautiful ceremony. Those present endorsed and applauded it.

Although throughout Lisane's total focus was Zac, the look of love he made no attempt to hide, and the manner in which he promised to cherish and protect her all the days of his life as he placed a circlet of diamonds on the finger of her left hand.

Words she repeated to him in a clear, unwavering voice as she took his left hand and slid on a gold band.

Laughter, smiles and hugs were gifted and exchanged against the backdrop of sparkling ocean waters and blue sky.

There were photographs and celebratory champagne, which Lisane declined in favour of an innocuous mix, finger food, followed later by a sumptuous meal indoors.

Max and Felicity Winstone appeared genuinely delighted with their daughter-in-law, and the prospect of becoming grandparents.

Something for which Lisane was immensely grateful, and she said as much soon after they farewelled their four guests at the end of the evening.

Zac curved an arm around her waist as he led the way upstairs.

'Two sets of parents, the fathers respected associates and close friends, whose wives contrived a private dream.' He brushed a light kiss to her cheek. 'Allegra and I grew up in each other's shadow, friends but never lovers.'

Not for the want of trying on Allegra's part, Lisane thought quietly.

Except that was in the past, and she held the future in her hands.

There was only now, and all the tomorrows she'd share with the man who was the love of her life.

In slightly less than seven months there would be a child…a precious gift, uniquely theirs.

Life, she accorded with a satisfied sigh, was better than good.

It was a very special miracle.

'Tired?'

They reached the upper floor and turned towards their bedroom.

'It's been a wonderful day,' Lisane offered gently. 'Thank you.'

Zac lifted a hand and trailed light fingers down the edge of her jaw. 'We have the night.'

She turned her cheek into the palm of his hand. It was fun to tease a little, and she tilted her face towards his own. 'Mmm, is that an invitation or a promise?'

'Both.'

Her soft laughter captivated him, and in one fluid movement he lifted her into his arms and carried her to their suite.

'Caveman tactics, huh?'

He took the pins from her hair, and let the light weight fall onto her shoulders.

'Need,' Zac said softly. 'For you. Only you.'

Her eyes shimmered a little as she offered a tremulous smile. 'Me, too.'

Simple words from the depths of her heart.

The Greek Tycoon's
Virgin Wife

Helen Bianchin

CHAPTER ONE

XANDRO EASED THE Bentley GT into the centre lane as traffic crawled through one intersection after another in a general exodus of Sydney's inner city.

Streetlights vied with neon signs as the sun sank low on the horizon, streaking the western sky a brilliant red that subtly altered in hue as dusk descended and changed day into night.

It had been a tough day, with two high-powered meetings, a conference call, and numerous demands on his time.

He could do with a massage to ease the tension…except there wasn't time. In less than an hour he was due to attend a prestigious charity dinner.

Alone.

He was acquainted with several women, any one of whom would drop everything to share the evening with him, willingly providing scintillating conversation laced with coquetry and an invitation to share a bed.

But he hadn't risen through the business ranks to head a financial empire by indulging in endless pleasure.

An enviable quality inherited from his father?

If so, it had to be one of a very few. A wry smile tugged his mouth. Yannis Caramanis had been best-known as a hard-nosed son-of-a-bitch, ruthless to the point of mercilessness, and rich as Croesus. Husband to no less than four wives, the first of whom had borne him a child…Alexandro Cristoforo Caramanis.

A son destined to be an only child, for Yannis refused to consider an heir and a spare, thus creating rivalry, jealousy, dissent and the rupture of an empire he'd striven so hard to build.

Subsequent wives had coveted his father's wealth and what it could do to gild a life of endless pleasure and social status. Until the gilt wore off and they were discarded for the next beautiful young thing. Arm candy. Very serious arm candy whom Yannis ensured were each gifted no more than their due via water-tight pre-nuptial agreements.

Xandro rolled his shoulders, eased the Bentley forward through a set of traffic lights and took the New South Head road to suburban Vaucluse.

The soft, intrusive burr of his BlackBerry brought a muttered imprecation, and he extracted the unit, checked caller ID, let it go to messagebank and switched the unit to mute.

Success brought responsibilities…too many, he mused, for modern technology ensured he was constantly available, twenty-four by seven.

And while he relished the cut and thrust of high-powered business…excelled in it, he allowed wryly…there were other challenges in life he needed to explore.

One in particular.

Marriage.

Family.

One woman who was honest and without artifice, who'd occupy his bed, make his house a home, be a charming hostess, and provide him with children.

Someone who had little illusion about love, and was

prepared to view marriage as a business proposition without the complication of emotion.

Affection, the exultation of the sexual act…but *love?* What was it?

He'd loved his mother with a child's love, only to have it taken away from him. As to his stepmothers…each of them had had only one goal in mind. Yannis' money, the gifts and the lifestyle. A child was a nuisance and better served to be tucked away in an expensive-boarding school with term breaks spent at various exclusive holiday camps overseas.

He learnt very early to succeed in order to gain his father's attention. Consequently he excelled at everything.

And when Yannis had settled him into a lowly position within the Caramanis empire, he fought hard to prove his worth. So hard, there was no time for social frivolities.

The effort had earned him Yannis' pride, a stake in his father's empire, multimillionaire status…and the attention of women.

Some more clever than most, and one in particular who had almost convinced him to put his ring on her finger.

Almost.

Except a precautionary investigation had revealed details that ordinarily wouldn't have come to light.

A practice he continued to employ whenever he decided to become close to a woman. Calculated, perhaps…but it eliminated any nasty surprises.

Xandro managed a wry smile as he eased the Bentley into a street lined with exclusive real estate.

His home was a mansion situated high on a hill and bearing splendid views over the harbour. Purchased five years ago, he'd had it remodelled and refurbished, installed a live-in couple to manage the house and grounds…a luxury residence where he slept, worked and entertained.

Xandro Caramanis.

The man who had everything.

A worthy successor to his father.

Hard, ruthless…coveted by women, but attached to none. Isn't that how the tabloids depicted him?

A little over half an hour later, showered, shaved and attired in an evening suit, Xandro slid into the Bentley and headed towards the city.

Traffic had eased somewhat, making for a relatively smooth run to the inner-city hotel where tonight's fundraising event was being held.

Valet parking, deferential recognition as he bypassed the lift and took the sweeping staircase to the mezzanine floor where fellow guests mingled and sipped champagne.

Pre-dinner drinks provided an excellent opportunity for committee members to work the room, ensuring guests were informed of the next upcoming event on the social calendar.

Muted music filtered through strategically placed speakers, providing a non-intrusive background for easy conversation.

The evening held the promise of yet another successful fundraising event, from which in this instance disadvantaged children would benefit.

Xandro let his gaze idly skim the room, observing his fellow guests in an unobtrusive manner, greeted and acknowledged several within his immediate vicinity…came full circle, then returned to linger on one young woman's features.

Fine facial bone structure, a pretty mouth… He liked the way she held her head, the expressive movement of her hands. Ash-blonde hair swept high on her head in a style that made his fingers itch to release the pins holding its length in place.

Refined elegance from the top of her head to the tips of her delicate feet.

And slightly nervous, he detected idly, beneath the practised smile…and wondered why, when she was so well versed with the social scene.

Ilana…daughter of society maven Liliana and the late Henri Girard.

Attractive, slender and petite, in her late twenties, she possessed an aloof persona in the company of men…a quality that had earned her an *ice maiden* tag. With reason, or so rumour abounded…although the only known fact was her hastily cancelled nuptials to Grant Baxter on the eve of their wedding.

Two years on, she mixed and mingled with the city's social glitterati in the company of her widowed mother.

Many men had attempted to date her, but to Xandro's knowledge none had succeeded.

Impeccable background, charming manners and well versed in the social graces, Ilana Girard would, he'd decided, make an eminently suitable wife.

All that remained was to implement a starting point, begin the courtship…and put forward his proposal.

Xandro's eyes narrowed slightly as Liliana Girard separated from her daughter's side and began moving towards him.

'Xandro. How lovely to see you here.'

'Liliana.' He took her outstretched hands in his, then lowered his head and lightly brushed his lips to her cheek.

'If you're alone this evening, perhaps you would care to join Ilana and me?'

Xandro inclined his head in silent acquiescence.

'Thank you.'

He allowed Liliana to precede him, his gaze becoming deliberately enigmatic as he saw the moment Ilana sensed his approach. The imperceptible stillness in her stance, the slight lift of her head, like a fragile gazelle scenting danger.

Then the moment was gone, replaced by a practised smile as he drew close.

People-watching was an art-form, body language an acquired skill...both at which he was incredibly adept. 'Xandro,' Ilana managed with cool politeness, and silently damned the way her pulse kicked in to a faster beat.

There was something about him, an indefinable quality that raised the hairs at the back of her neck in silent warning...of what?

Tall, for even in four-inch stilettos she had to lift her head to look at him.

Attractive, Ilana accorded silently, in a leonine way, for the lighting accentuated his broad sculptured facial features, strong jaw-line and the enigmatic expression in his dark eyes.

His tailoring was impeccable and individually crafted, downplaying rather than emphasising his impressive breadth of shoulder.

Intensely masculine, he bore an aura of power that was un-contrived, yet only a fool would fail to detect the ruthlessness lurking beneath the surface.

'Ilana.'

He made no attempt to touch her...so why did she harbour the instinctive feeling he was merely biding his time? It didn't make sense.

'I believe you're sharing our table this evening.' She was well versed in the art of social conversation and could converse in fluent Italian and French, thanks to a year spent in each country studying couture.

Yet in this man's presence she had to consciously strive to

present a certain façade. Aware, in some deep recess of her mind, that he saw straight through it.

His gaze remained steady. 'Is that a problem?'

What would he do if she said…*yes?*

A polite smile curved her mouth. 'It'll be a pleasure to have you join us.' And knew she lied.

'One of the committee members has just signalled me,' Liliana posed. 'I won't be long.'

For a moment Ilana felt bereft, and incredibly vulnerable. She could escape with good reason…excuse herself and drift towards another group of guests. Except it would be a cop-out, and a fruitless one, for she doubted such a move would fool Xandro in the slightest.

It was inevitable they'd cross paths. The Caramanis empire was a known benefactor of several charities, and gala events such as this evening's fundraiser ensured Xandro's presence, usually with a stunning female in tow.

Yet this was the third time in recent weeks he'd attended an evening function without a partner.

So who's counting? a silent imp taunted…and she stilled the soft oath that rose and died in her throat.

The thought he might deliberately seek her out was laugh-able. She was his polar opposite, and besides, she was done with men. Had been for more than two years, and once bitten…

A faint shiver slithered down the length of her spine as memory provided a vivid replay of that fateful night when her hopes and dreams had been so cruelly shattered.

She'd survived and moved on, losing herself in her career to the extent it consumed her life. There was little she wanted or needed. No unfulfilled dreams.

'Darling.' The soft feminine voice was pure feline, and

matched the tall, willowy blonde who drifted close to Xandro's side. 'I didn't expect to see you tonight.'

'Danika,' Xandro acknowledged with a polite smile that failed to reach his eyes.

The Austrian-born model trod the international fashion catwalks and was much sought-after by designers, despite her behind-the-scene tantrums. A nightmare to work with, she possessed a magical ability to model clothes that put her among the élite.

'You've met Ilana?'

Brilliant blue eyes spared her a perfunctory look. 'Should I have?'

The deliberate put-down was softened with an ingenious tilt of that exquisitely painted mouth.

'Ilana is a fashion designer.'

'Really?'

Bored disinterest couldn't have been better feigned. This was party time, and the glamorous model had only one goal in mind...Xandro Caramanis.

Who could blame her? The man was the catch of the decade!

'I'm not familiar with your name. Ilana...*who?*'

'Girard,' Xandro informed silkily.

Ilana decided there was never going to be a better moment. '*Arabelle* label.' She waited a beat. 'You're wearing one.' So too was she, a gorgeous, figure-hugging halter-neck design in deep pink slipper-satin.

Danika's eyes narrowed fractionally. 'It was sold as an original.'

'Gifted,' Ilana corrected, and saw the model lift a dismissive hand.

'My agent deals with the minor details.'

'She follows your instructions.' It was part of the deal, part of the play Danika employed. Designers adored her panache, and turned a blind eye to any contretemps. The gift of one of their original designs meant little in the big scheme of things.

It was all about marketing…recognition…sales.

Danika placed a lacquered nail to the lapel of Xandro's evening suit and offered a seductive smile. 'I'll ensure we share the same table.'

With an unhurried movement he removed the model's hand. 'No.'

Just…*no?*

Succinct, and almost crushing…if one tended to be easily hurt.

Ilana caught a glimpse of ice in Danika's startling blue eyes as the model's lips formed a deliberate pout. 'Poor darling, you'll miss out on some fun. I'm available if you change your mind.' Danika wriggled her fingers in a silent farewell before melting into the crowd.

It was as well the ballroom doors opened and guests were encouraged to take their seats.

Although seconds later Ilana wasn't so sure as Xandro captured her elbow and led her into the vast room set with well over a hundred tables.

His fingers were warm on her bare skin, his touch electrifying as heat rose deep inside and threatened to affect her equilibrium.

It wasn't a feeling she coveted, and she fought an instinctive need to withdraw from him. 'There's a reason for such seeming togetherness?' she demanded quietly, and saw one eyebrow slant in musing humour.

'I enjoy your company?'

She looked at him carefully. 'It would help if you enlighten me as to what game you're playing.'

'Would you believe…none?'

'Should I be flattered?' she queried sweetly, and heard his faint husky chuckle.

'You're not?'

'I'd hate to shatter your world,' Ilana relayed in droll tones as a pretty young thing personally directed them towards a prestige table close to the stage.

Name cards designated seat placings, and it came as no surprise to find Xandro's name card placed next to her own.

How difficult could it be to converse, smile and play the social game?

Pretend, a tiny voice prompted. You're good at it.

'What would you like to drink?'

There was bottled wine on the table, but lunch had been a non-event, and alcohol in any form would go straight to her head.

'Just water, thanks.'

Xandro poured iced water into her goblet, then filled his own. 'To good fortune.' He touched the rim of his goblet to hers in a mocking salute.

The table filled, Liliana joined them and, introductions completed, the evening began with the usual opening speech by the nominated-charity president.

The lights dimmed, and waiters began serving food to the guests as the guest speaker took the podium.

She was supremely conscious of the man at her side…the exclusive tones of his cologne, the clean smell of freshly laundered clothing mingling with the barely detectable essence of male.

There was something dangerous about him that threatened the carefully built armour she'd painstakingly erected in her need for self-preservation.

It made her wary, almost as if she had to gather all her wits together and be on constant alert in his presence.

For heaven's sake, an inner voice silently expostulated. Xandro Caramanis is nothing to you.

What's more, you don't want him to be.

So get over it!

Yet the feeling persisted, making it difficult for her to relax.

Ilana ate mechanically, forking morsels of delectable food into her mouth without really tasting a thing.

It didn't help to be aware her apparent coupling with Xandro garnered interested speculation. Or that Xandro was the focus of Danika's attention.

Was he bent on publicly denouncing whatever relationship he'd enjoyed with the glamorous model?

'No.'

His quietly spoken negation momentarily startled her, and she didn't pretend to misunderstand as she met his inscrutable gaze.

'Really?' She arched an expressive eyebrow.

'No.'

The reiteration held an inflexibility she couldn't ignore, and she hated the tense knot tightening in her stomach.

She wanted to demand *what are you doing?* Except the words remained unuttered as she deliberately turned her attention to a neighbouring dining companion and engaged him in meaningless social niceties.

Yet Xandro's presence was inescapable, and it irked her unbearably that he had the power to unsettle her nervous system to the extent she became conscious of each movement, every breath she took.

Did he know?

Dear God, she fervently hoped not!

The dinner seemed to take forever, concluding with coffee and a worthy if wordy speech by the nominated-charity chairperson.

Muted music filtered through strategically placed speakers, providing a reason for guests to move freely among the tables, converse…and for many it signalled an end to a pleasant evening.

Any minute soon Liliana would rise to her feet, thank fellow table guests for their patronage, bid them good night…and Ilana would be free of Xandro's disturbing presence.

Except her relief was short-lived, as Xandro expressed his intention to escort them to the lobby.

'It isn't necessary.'

'On the contrary.' He cupped her elbow, exerting slight pressure as she surreptitiously endeavoured to put some distance between them.

Don't, she wanted to protest.

'I'm considering setting up an auction to benefit the Leukaemia Foundation, and I'd appreciate Liliana's advice.'

Her mother showed genuine delight. 'How generous of you. Of course I'll be only too pleased to help in any way I can.'

'Good,' Xandro concurred smoothly. 'With that in mind, perhaps you'll both accept an invitation to dine with me in order to discuss details? Shall we say Thursday of next week?'

'Thank you.'

Liliana would, Ilana knew, rearrange her social schedule in the blink of an eye to accommodate Xandro Caramanis.

They reached the lobby, and Xandro signalled the concierge to have his car and her own brought up from valet parking.

Within minutes a silver Bentley GT slid to a halt outside the main entrance.

'Seven o'clock,' Xandro indicated, withdrawing a card from his billfold and penning a few lines on the reverse side. 'My home.'

With an economy of movement he passed a tip to the

bellboy, then he slid in behind the wheel and eased the sleek car out into the flow of traffic.

Seconds later Ilana's dark blue BMW slid to a halt, and Liliana waited only until Ilana cleared the hotel vicinity before voicing,

'What a lovely invitation, darling. And quite a coup to have Xandro request my help.'

What could she say, other than…'So it would seem'?

'You have reservations?'

Several. Although she refused to settle on any *one.*

'You must go, of course.'

'*We,* darling. As in both of us.'

Ilana brought the car to a halt at an intersection. '*Maman,* no,' she said gently.

Liliana offered a pensive look. 'You won't change your mind?'

Not any time this century, she silently vowed. The less she came into contact with Xandro Caramanis the better!

CHAPTER TWO

PREPARATIONS FOR THE current Fashion Design Awards ensured Ilana spent most of the weekend in the workroom as she checked and re-checked the selection of garments both she and her partner, Micki, had chosen to enter in the various sections.

The judging process comprised examination of the fabric, stitching and finishing by a panel of experts who provided a grading in advance of the final catwalk judging.

Which meant ensuring every detail was perfect…or as near to perfect as it was possible to get.

Winning in any category added to a designer's status, lifting interest and sales. Although for Ilana, the focus was on fashioning quality fabric into faultlessly assembled stylish garments.

As a child she'd adored dressing her dolls, and with Liliana's help she had made patterns and cut and fashioned her own range of dolls' clothes, progressing to designing and making her own outfits.

A degree in fashion design followed by an apprenticeship with one of Australia's top designers had eventually provided the opportunity to work overseas for a few years…Paris, Milan and London, before she returned to Sydney, where she'd set up her own workroom.

Diligence and hard work had seen her acquire recognition among her peers, with the *Arabelle* label rated highly among the social set.

While Ilana possessed the talent and expertise with design, needle and thread, it was her childhood friend, Micki Taylor, whose business nous completed their successful partnership.

Micki's flair for selecting the right accessories was faultless, for she had the ability to put together a successful fashion showing that lifted it above the rest.

Ilana loved the creative aspect of transforming a vision into reality. To be able to look at a fabric and visualise the finished garment was a gift…one she didn't regard lightly. Colour, fabric, style. She lived to make it work and come alive. Infinitely special to the woman who bought it. Any accolades and awards were a bonus.

The week leading up to the design-awards night involved long hours double-checking everything was covered, including back-up plans should a contracted model call in sick…or any one of several things that could go wrong.

Days when she seemed to only take time out to eat and sleep, she reflected wearily as she entered her apartment early Tuesday evening after a fraught day.

The thought of a long soak in a bubble bath and a decent meal was tempting, except it wasn't going to happen.

Instead she only had time for a quick shower, a change into a cocktail dress in *café-au-lait* lace, the application of make-up and fixing her hair into a simple knot before driving to Double Bay to attend the evening's gallery showing with Liliana.

A prestigious affair, invitation-only, it heralded the grand opening of new premises in three adjoining villas whose interiors had been gutted and converted into a spacious gallery owned by an established family known in the art world for discovering and fostering artists.

Cars lined the wide, tree-lined street in suburban Double Bay, and Ilana circled the block twice before finding a space.

Two security guards flanked the gallery entrance, one of whom checked her name off the invitation list whilst the other indicated the foyer.

'Darling.' The family's eldest son took her hand and leaned in close to brush his cheek against her own. 'Welcome.'

'Jean-Paul.'

Jean preceded each male name in the family…Jean-Marc, the patriarch, his two sons, Jean-Paul and Jean-Pierre.

People mingled in groups sipping champagne and accepting proffered canapés from uniformed staff. Muted music emitted from concealed speakers, a suitable background to the guests' conversation.

A waitress offered a tray laden with flutes of champagne and orange juice. As much as she needed the lift of champagne, she selected the latter. There were trays of canapes making the rounds and she accepted a napkin, added a few bite-size morsels and sampled each of them in relatively quick succession.

'There you are, darling.' Liliana appeared at her side, and Ilana leant forward as they pressed cheeks.

'The architect and interior decorators have done well,' she offered quietly, and caught her mother's warm smile.

'I agree.' Liliana indicated the wide glass-panelled walls, the planned lay-out. 'It's quite something.'

Ilana cast a quick glance at the mingling guests. 'A good crowd.'

'Who would refuse Jean-Marc's invitation?'

The effusive family patriarch was something of a legend

in the art field, possessed of a shrewd mind and an almost un-failing instinct for the success of an artist's work.

Many of his patrons had made a small fortune from his advice, and the opening of new premises was a *cause célèbre*.

'Come take a look,' Liliana bade as she drew Ilana forward.

'You've seen something you like.'

Her mother chuckled. 'How can you tell?'

She offered an answering laugh. 'The gleam in your eyes.'

'I'll aim for solemn interest in the hope Jean-Marc will ne-gotiate the price.'

Together they moved slowly, pausing to speak to a friend, smile at an acquaintance, until Liliana stopped in front of an exquisite landscape, all trees and sky and almost *alive*. A lifelike vision in oils, each detail seemingly applied with a master's stroke.

'You're going to buy it.' A statement, rather than a query, and Ilana could picture the perfect location in her mother's home.

'Yes,' Liliana conceded with a faint smile. 'The formal dining room.'

The colours would blend beautifully, and she said so.

'My thoughts, exactly.' Liliana glanced up as Jean-Paul appeared at her side.

'Is that a *yes*, Liliana?'

'Definitely.' Her mother waited a bit. 'With a little ne-gotiation.'

'I'm sure my father will be amenable.'

A promised five-per-cent discount was offered on the in-vitation for each purchase…whether Liliana could bargain further was debatable.

A discreet *reserved* sticker was attached…to be replaced with *sold* when the purchase became a done deal.

There were other paintings, beautifully showcased, featuring many categories…some impossibly bold, extrovert in the extreme with great slashes of colour and without any definition.

Traditional, a young child's face with huge sad eyes and a single tear. An incredible seascape, with wild, turbulent, white-tipped angry waves depicted in such detail one could almost sense the salt-spray stinging the skin.

A modern piece depicting the agony of war in a riveting portrayal too close to home.

Emotion, sadness, joy. They were all exigent, portrayed on canvas.

Ilana exchanged an empty flute for one filled with champagne, and filched another three canapés from a proffered tray.

'I should go talk with Jean-Marc.'

'Sure. Catch you soon.' She'd wander a little, savour the light, fizzing bubbles, and maybe something would catch her eye.

It did, but not in the way she wanted it to. The painting held a haunting quality, dark and far too stark for anyone's peace of mind.

'Interesting,' a deep, familiar male voice offered, and she stood still, wondering why her self-defence mechanism had failed to alert Xandro Caramanis' presence.

Then it kicked in with a vengeance, and sensation scudded down her spine, sending little licks of flame from somewhere deep inside. They touched her central nervous system and sped rapidly through her body, warming her skin.

'Tell me,' Xandro drawled, 'what you see.'

He was standing close, within touching distance, and she had the feeling if she leaned back fractionally her shoulders would bump against his chest.

It would be so easy to take a slight step forward…but then he'd know, and she couldn't bear him to guess the effect he had on her.

'Too much.'

Why hadn't she expected him to be here tonight? Xandro Caramanis represented serious money…very serious money.

Naturally he would have received a coveted invitation.

He moved to her side. 'A painful memory, do you think? Or a warning?'

'Perhaps both?'

'Not exactly comfortable viewing.'

'No.'

His height and breadth of shoulder made her think of a warrior…and wondered if the male body beneath the fine tailoring hid powerful musculature.

Somehow artificial enhancement and Xandro Caramanis just didn't mesh.

The thought did nothing for her peace of mind.

She should excuse herself and move away. To remain attempting idle conversation didn't appeal. Besides, she didn't need the added tension.

Ilana turned slightly towards him, and immediately wished she hadn't.

His facial features were compelling, with arresting bone sculpture, an intensely sexual mouth and dark eyes that saw too much.

'You look tired.'

'How kind of you to care,' she managed with intended facetiousness.

'Does it bother you that I might?'

'Not in the least.'

His soft laughter was barely audible. 'Have dinner with me.'

She thought of the banana she'd hastily peeled and eaten as she rode the lift down to the basement car park, and the few gulps of bottled water, followed by orange juice, champagne and exotic canapés. Hardly an adequate meal.

Where was the harm in light, careless banter in a room filled with guests? 'Will it damage your ego if I refuse?'

His mouth curved into a musing smile. 'I'll accept a raincheck.'

'I wasn't aware I'd requested one.'

'Next week,' Xandro continued as if she hadn't spoken.

'I'll be in touch.'

'When you've checked your social diary?'

He regarded her steadily. 'Name an evening.'

Instinct warned she was treading dangerous territory. He possessed a waiting, watching quality that made him impossible to read. 'And you'll set aside any previous obligations?'

'Yes.'

Her stomach executed a backward flip, trembled a little, then didn't rest easy.

He didn't move, didn't touch her...but she felt as if he did. Everything faded from her vision, and the noise, the filtered music grew silent.

The air between them seemed electric, and for a moment she could have sworn time stood still.

How long did they remain there in silence? Seconds, a minute? *Two?*

Then she saw his features relax, his mouth curved a little at the edges, and she became aware his attention had shifted slightly.

'Liliana.'

The sound of his voice brought the large room and its milling occupants into focus, and she felt the tension begin to ebb from her body as she slowly turned towards her mother.

What just happened here?

Nothing.

Something. She sensed it...felt it.

'Xandro.' Liliana's smile was genuine. 'Have you seen anything you like?'

You're wrong.

Oh, for heaven's sake. Get over it. He's playing a game... and you're *it*.

The challenge.

Like he has so few in his life, he needs to hunt the unattainable?

'Yes. Something I intend to reserve for myself.'

He was talking about a painting...wasn't he?

Or had the flute of champagne addled her brain and she was the only one who imagined a hidden meaning?

Coffee, hot, strong and sweet. Preferably black. It might clear her head...and keep her awake. Which she didn't want, when she desperately needed a reasonable night's sleep.

She could excuse herself and leave. Liliana knew how hectic the past few weeks had been, and how many more long hours she still needed to put in before awards night.

Yet stubborn pride stiffened her spine, and she indicated the far end of the spacious gallery. 'There's something I want to have another look at.'

Ilana had the instinctive feeling she didn't fool him in the slightest as she offered a dismissive smile before turning to thread her way through the guests.

She ensured she maintained a leisurely pace, and pretended a genuine interest. She smiled, pausing every now and then to exchange pleasantries with an acquaintance.

Talking the talk, she reflected a trifle wryly. Working the room. Accepting good wishes for the upcoming design awards.

How long had she been here? Two hours...a little more?

It was almost ten when she caught Liliana's attention and indicated her intention to leave.

One of the bouncers stepped forward as she exited the main entrance. 'Is your car parked close by, miss?'

'Not far from my own.' The male voice was far too familiar. 'We'll walk together.'

She didn't want his company, didn't need to suffer his disturbing presence. 'I'll be fine.'

Touch me and I'll *hit* you, Ilana vowed silently as she stepped out briskly. If he'd deliberately timed his exit to coincide with her own...

She made no attempt at conversation, and it irked unbearably he chose silence, when she so badly wanted the opportunity to snub him.

How long did it take to reach her car? Minutes...five at the most, and she breathed a faint sigh of relief as she deactivated the alarm and reached for the door, only to have her hand collide with his own.

Warm, hard, strong beneath her fingers, and she snatched her hand back as if she'd been burned by a flame.

'Thank you.' Two polite, succinct, stilted words as he pulled open the door for her to slide in behind the wheel.

Xandro leant forward and placed a business card on the dashboard. 'My private cellphone number.'

An invitation to call him?

Offer her business card in exchange for his?

As if!

Ilana slid a key into the ignition and fired the engine as he closed the door, aware as she drove away the mild headache she'd harboured for the past half-hour had turned into a full-blown migraine.

Great. That was all she needed.

Too little sleep, too much tension…

It was a relief to reach her apartment, undress, remove her make-up and pop a couple of painkillers.

Tomorrow, she reflected as she hit the pillow, was another day.

CHAPTER THREE

ORDERED CHAOS REIGNED in the workroom.

Fingers flew, soft and not-so-soft curses registered beneath the music flowing from one of the city's popular radio stations, the steam iron hissed in harmony with the rain hitting the tin roof.

Ilana checked schedules, confirmed the agency supplying the models, and ensured the van-hire firm had the pick-up time right.

It would all come together on the night…it always did, she allowed wryly. But today…well, the day before awards night meant blood, sweat and a few tears.

'Delivery boy out front.'

A frown creased Ilana's forehead. Delivery? All the deliveries were in for the day.

Micki's assistant went out the front and returned with a generous bouquet of pink and cream tightly budded roses.

Liliana?

Ilana detached the card from the Cellophane.

Xandro. There was no mistaking the name written by a male hand…following a personalised message: *Good luck.*

'Wow. *Nice.* Who?' demanded Micki.

Thinking quickly on her feet, she pocketed the card and

managed a smile. 'Good-luck wishes for tomorrow night.' She moved to the tiny alcove that served as a minuscule kitchen and withdrew a vase from the storage cupboard.

It was a kind gesture…if only simple kindness were his motivation. Somehow she doubted anything about Xandro Caramanis could be *simple*.

There was little time to even *think* as Saturday dawned and team *Arabelle* went into action with preparations for the evening's awards.

Practice didn't make perfect, for it failed to factor in the many variables that could cause a hitch or three, or more.

An hour before the first model was due to hit the catwalk saw the backstage dressing room filled to capacity with racks of clothes, anxious designers, a fraught seamstress or two, hair and make-up assistants lobbying for room in front of inadequate mirrors. Not to mention cellphones pealing and chirping every few minutes.

Bedlam didn't begin to cover it.

And it would get worse.

There was hardly room to move, and too many bodies in too small a space made for short tempers…successfully muted by background music piped into the large hotel ballroom seating over a thousand guests.

Organisation and co-ordination were the order of the night. Each designer had a list detailing each category and order of appearance.

'Sorry I'm late.'

Ilana heard the voice, vaguely recognised it, turned…and felt her heart sink.

Danika was the replacement model?

Oh, my.

OK, so they'd handle it.

But not too well, Ilana determined as she sought to batten down a sense of frustration at Danika's continuing contretemps.

'These shoes aren't right.'

'That belt…are you out of your mind?'

Swept-up hairstyle, when Danika insisted on wearing it loose.

'Definitely not that *faux* jewellery…get me something else.'

Muted grumbles from various designers were enhanced by eye-rolling and unladylike muttered oaths.

Out the front, everything was fine.

Backstage, it was something else.

'If she makes one more complaint,' Micki threatened as Danika took the catwalk, 'Just *one* more, I'll have her for breakfast.'

'On cinnamon toast, or dipped in eggs Benedict?' Ilana queried with wry cynicism.

'Preferably drowned in my coffee.'

'Espresso or chai latte?'

Micki rolled her eyes. 'You're a riot.'

'An hour, and it'll all be over,' she reminded.

Minutes later Micki handed the model bangles and earrings, which received an expressive sigh in resignation.

'Not until the fat lady sings,' Micki assured as Danika disappeared out onto the stage.

Applause could be heard above the music.

One by one the models returned, effected a quick change and readied themselves for the next category.

Cocktail wear, then evening wear.

Ilana had created a stunning gown in red, with a finely pleated bodice, a draped full-length skirt with a side-split reaching almost to the hip.

To give due credit, Danika showcased it with incredible panache.

'I'll take this instead of my fee.'

'It's an original and part of a collection.' And not intended as barter.

'Precisely why I'll have it.'

'Impossible.' Micki stepped forward and slid down the hidden zip fastening. 'The gown is to feature in next season's showing.'

Danika offered a supercilious glare. 'Make another.'

Deep breaths...one, two... 'Then it won't be an original,' Ilana said calmly.

'Tough.'

Bridal-wear became the final category, and *Arabelle* opted for the traditional, with exquisite lace, a demure neckline, and tiny covered buttons from nape to tailbone. A soft, flowing full-length skirt overlayed with lace moved like a dream with every step the model took.

The finale awaited the final judging...emotion and tension ran high among the assembled designers as to which one of them would win in each given category.

Meanwhile the models hovered, ready to don the winning garment.

This was the moment everyone had been waiting for, and the organisers played up the drama, building the excitement as the judging numbers were handed in.

Then the winning categories were announced...from the beginning, and the model reappeared on stage with the designer to generous applause.

The suspense was killing, and Ilana clutched Micki's hand as the evening-wear category was announced.

Arabelle won with the red gown.

And *Arabelle* took out the bridal category.

It was an incredible moment as Ilana and Micki went up on stage and stood together, wearing their signature black leggings and blousson tops and stiletto-heeled boots as Danika paraded the catwalk.

The presentation, the short speech. Elation, joy, nerves and relief.

Then it was time for the whole congratulatory thing as photographers' cameras flashed in split-second unison.

'Darling, I'm so very proud of you.' Liliana hugged her tight. Others followed, until Ilana thought her head might spin.

'Congratulations.'

The male voice was a familiar one, and she felt the thud of an increased pulse-beat as she turned slowly to meet Xandro's steady gaze.

His presence was unexpected. Tonight's event wasn't something a heterosexual male would consider attending alone in normal circumstances.

Several questions raced through her brain. Could he be joining Danika later? Perhaps going on to a nightclub?

Or was he with someone else?

He didn't lack for female partners, that was for sure!

Oh, for heaven's sake…stop it! What if he is with someone else? As if you care!

So why this slight jolt of wishful *longing?* Almost as if some deeply hidden imp was bent on teasing her subconscious with what it might be like with this man.

'Thanks.'

He emanated leashed strength and a degree of latent sensuality. It was a lethal combination, and much too much for any feminine peace of mind.

Beneath the sophisticated façade lay the heart and soul of a modern-day warrior. Ruthless, forceful and all-powerful. Only a fool would attempt to toy with him.

It was easy to see why women fell at his feet.

Fascination, the thrill of the chase…and the instinctive knowledge he knew precisely how to touch, with his hands, his mouth, to gift the ultimate pleasure. And take it for his own.

Flame and heat, searing, exultant at its zenith. But afterwards…what then?

'Are you done?' His barely audible voice held a faintly teasing quality, and she wondered with sudden shock just how long she'd stood there looking at him.

Please God, surely it was only seconds?

Soft warmth flooded her cheeks as she battled for composure, and she glimpsed his faint smile an instant before he lowered his head and brushed his mouth against her own.

His lips were warm, and she felt the teasing sweep of his tongue as it lightly caressed the shape of her mouth in a kiss that tore the breath from her throat. For it held the hint of *more,* so much more.

All she needed to do was tease the edge of his tongue with her own in silent invitation.

Except she didn't. *Couldn't.*

A faint tremor shook her body, and she prayed fervently he didn't sense it.

Ilana was unprepared for the way his mouth hardened against her own as he cupped her face with his hands and went in deep, conveying evocative intimacy with practised ease.

It rocked her senses, and she was aware of a quickened pulse-beat, the seemingly loud thudding of her heart as she became lost in a sensual pool so intense there was only the man and the sensations he aroused.

Worse was her own unbidden response…something which surprised and devastated, given no man, not even her ex-fiancé, had managed to reach so deep into her emotions.

Almost as if he knew, he lightened his touch, withdrawing a little until he lifted his head.

For a moment she could only look at him, her eyes wide and impossibly dark as she caught something in his expression she was unable to define.

Then it was over as he released her, and she tried valiantly to assure herself it meant little.

Just a kiss, when celebratory hugs and kisses were being gifted in abundance.

And knew she lied.

His kiss struck a chord and stirred emotions in a place where she'd locked and thrown away the key.

A strangled sound escaped her throat, and for a moment she couldn't tear her eyes from his.

Please, an inner voice decried. *I don't want this.*

There was nothing she could read in his dark gaze, and she managed a faint smile as her attention was caught by another well-wisher.

Except his touch lingered, and she felt as if she was acting on autopilot long after he withdrew from sight. Why had he kissed her like that?

To impress her?

Or was he merely playing a game with her in order to make Danika jealous?

The latter thought brought a surge of anger and fostered a sense of deep resentment. There was no way she'd allow herself to be used as a pawn by any man…especially Xandro Caramanis!

What was more, she'd tell him so.

Arabelle's win brought an invitation to participate in a charity fundraiser, requests to view her summer designs and firm bookings for months ahead.

'I'll go backstage and help the girls load our clothes into the van,' Micki indicated quietly, and Ilana inclined her head.

'I'll come with you.'

The atmosphere was lighter, the models had changed into their own gear and most had left, together with the hair-stylists and make-up girls.

Camaraderie reigned, and, if there was disappointment from the designers who didn't place, it didn't show.

Ilana and Micki's assistants had everything in hand. Shoes, accessories, *faux* jewellery were all individually boxed. Garments restored to their dress-bags, and it was only a matter of shifting them out to the van for transporting back to the workroom.

'A word before I leave.'

Ilana summoned a smile as she turned to face Danika. 'Thanks for filling in,' she reiterated, and the model's shoulders lifted in a dismissive gesture.

'It's what I do.'

And not the purpose of the conversation, if the model's venomous glare was any indication.

'Hands off Xandro.'

Her gaze was remarkably steady. 'They were never on him.' True. His hands had been on *her*.

If looks could kill, she'd drop dead on the floor.

With an elegant flounce Danika swivelled towards the exit and swiftly moved out of sight.

It was no secret the model had the hots for the Greek-born tycoon. Along with many of the city's socialites.

Except Ilana Girard…the one young woman from whom Danika had nothing to fear.

The irony of it brought forth a wry smile.

'We're done.' Micki lifted a hand and Ilana met it mid-air.

'Now let's *party!*' She named a bar within walking distance, linked arms with Ilana and headed towards the exit. 'Liliana will be there, of course.' She waited a beat. 'And Xandro.'

Ilana's heart gave a sudden jolt, then settled into a faster beat. 'Why *Xandro?*'

Micki lifted up a hand and ticked off a finger as she listed a few reasons. 'Because he kissed you like a man determined to have *more* of you. He happened to be deep in conversation with your mother when I extended the invitation. And it's high time you started dating again.'

'You took it on yourself to arrange my life?'

'Just the night,' her friend and partner assured with a wicked grin. 'What follows is none of my business.'

'Nothing, absolutely *nothing* is going to happen.'

'Uh-huh.'

Ilana shot her a dark glance. 'I'm not interested.'

'Ah,' Micki allowed quietly. 'But *he* is.'

'I very much doubt it was more than a challenge.' Her voice held wry humour. 'Kiss the ice maiden and see if you can make her melt.'

'And did you? Melt?'

In an ignominious puddle. Not that she'd admit it to anyone. 'He's practised in the art of kissing.'

'No toe-curling, gut-wrenching, off-the-planet reaction?'

In spades, and then some.

She managed a light shrug. 'Not really.'

Team *Arabelle* were already seated when Ilana and Micki walked into the trendy bar, and there was champagne on ice, finger food spread out on the table.

Xandro rose to his feet, indicated a seat next to his own, and before Ilana could refuse Micki took the chair opposite, leaving no choice.

There were champagne toasts, much light-hearted laughter...and her stomach executed a painful somersault as Xandro touched his flute to her own and held it there a few seconds too long. His eyes were dark, unreadable, and she felt suddenly out of her depth.

He was seated too close, his thigh only a few centimetres from her own, and she was far too aware of his potent masculinity.

Ambivalent feelings coursed through her veins, teasing her with what could be...if only she had the courage to reach out for it.

Followed by the fear of opening her vulnerable heart to a man who might destroy her.

It was far wiser to refrain from having anything to do with *any* man...Xandro Caramanis in particular.

At midnight the girls began making a move to end the evening, and together they converged on the pavement, caught up in 'good-night' hugs.

'I'll drive you home.'

Ilana spared Xandro a fixed glance and shook her head. 'I'll take a cab.'

'No, you won't.'

Was it her imagination, or did everyone suddenly disperse with discreet speed? Even Liliana.

'Don't be ridiculous.'

Xandro took her hand in his. 'My car is parked close by.'

'Are you always so bossy?'

'Let's just go with I gave Liliana my word to see you safely home.'

Ilana found herself seated in a luxury vehicle before she had time to think about it. The result of a little too much champagne, or clever manipulation?

Music filtered softly through the car's speaker system, and

she leaned back against the head-rest and closed her eyes as she reflected on the evening...the clothes, the models, the judging. Winning.

And Xandro's kiss.

Wow...was the word that came readily to mind.

What would he be like as a lover?

Not that she intended to find out.

Hell, she dared not go there. Instinct warned she'd never survive with her emotions intact.

Besides, how could she ever forget Grant Baxter's dire threat after she'd opted out of their wedding?

I'll kill you if you date another man.

For two years she hadn't wanted to get close to any male of the species.

She assured herself nothing had changed.

Except it had. And she didn't know what to do about it.

CHAPTER FOUR

'WAKE UP, SLEEPYHEAD.'

Ilana turned her head and looked at Xandro's strong features beneath the lit bricked apron adjoining the entrance to her apartment building.

'I wasn't asleep.'

His teeth shone white as he smiled. 'Pleasant thoughts?'

'Thanks,' she offered belatedly as she released the seat belt and reached for the door-clasp.

'You're welcome.'

She couldn't move as he captured her face and leant in close for a brief evocative kiss.

Then he let her go, and she scrambled from the seat with undue haste. Otherwise she'd have been tempted to stay, wind her arms around his neck, and sink in against him as she returned the salutation.

And that would never do.

He waited until she passed security and entered the lift, then he fired the engine and eased the Bentley onto the street.

It had been a great night, Ilana determined as she entered her apartment. Terrific celebration. Winning took it off the Richter scale.

Tomorrow—*today,* she corrected as a last waking thought, was Sunday, and there was no need to set the alarm for some unearthly hour before dawn.

A caffeine hit followed by a hot shower helped a little, so too did something to eat, followed by a couple of painkillers and more hot strong coffee.

The apartment had been just a place to sleep for more than a week in the rundown to awards night, and Ilana gathered clothes, ran the washing machine and took care of a few essential household chores before changing into designer jeans and a loose top and heading for the workroom.

The sun's rays fingered warmth as she trod the pavement, and she slid sunglasses into place from atop her head to shade the midday glare.

Cafés were filled with the Sunday-brunch crowd, and cars tracked the oceanfront road in search of parking.

A light breeze drifted in from the sea, feathering the fringes of numerous beach umbrellas dotted on the sandy foreshore.

For many the weekend invited relaxation, stretching out on the sand for the day to gain a tan, cooling off in the water, wandering across the road for sustenance in any one of several cafés.

Tantalising aromas teased the air, tempting her with the promise of a late lunch when she was done restoring order to the workroom.

Ilana unlocked the door, set down her bag, cellphone, and went to work clearing the detritus. There was a need to update her appointment book, check dates, asterisk possible openings and pencil in contact numbers.

Next came a close examination of garments that had graced the catwalk the previous evening. Some would require spot cleaning, others put aside for the dry-cleaner, and she needed to scrutinise hems for any minuscule damage.

In general, models were careful, but occasionally in the rush of a quick-change it was possible for a lacquered nail to catch in a seam, a hemline.

It took a while, and she breathed a faint sigh of relief that only two garments required minimum repairs, and she'd assembled those needing the dry-cleaner.

Ilana crossed to the refrigerator and filched bottled water, unscrewed the top and took several long swallows before capping it.

Almost done.

For a moment she indulged in a mental review of the previous evening, visualising each garment in each category…only to pause with a frown.

The red evening gown. It wasn't among the collection of garments returned to the workroom.

A tight ball of tension curled inside her stomach.

She had to be wrong…but she knew with sickening certainty she wasn't.

Danika. It had to be.

What she wanted to do was call the model and breathe fire and brimstone!

Damn. She needed the complication like a hole in the head!

Instead, she had little recourse but to contact Danika's agency, explain, request return of the gown and offer another in its place.

At that moment her cellphone pealed, and she picked up, offered her usual greeting…and received silence.

She checked the battery level, saw it was fine, then heard the call disconnect.

Within minutes it rang again, with the same result, and

when she activated the call-back feature it registered a private number, denying access.

Weird. Unless the caller was close to an out-of-range area and the cellphone was cracking up.

Ilana had the model agency she used on speed-dial, and an answering machine picked up.

It was Sunday…what did she expect? A further call to the manager's cellphone went straight to message-bank.

A muttered oath spilled from her lips. Defeated and angry, she had little option but to lock up, go have lunch, then return to her apartment.

She chose a café, ordered, and picked up the leading city newspaper from a selection the café offered its clientele.

The waiter delivered a chai latte, and she barely had time to take more than a sip when her cellphone pealed.

'Should I warn him you're a frigid little bitch?'

The call disconnected before she had a chance to respond, and she closed her eyes, then opened them again in an effort to control the surge of shocked anger rising from deep within.

Grant?

Emerging out of the woodwork after nearly two years?

An icy shiver shook her slender frame. Why? And why *now?* Unless…

No, it wasn't possible anything she'd done or said had stirred the dark beast that lurked beneath her ex-fiancé's surface charm.

Her mind went into overdrive as she replayed his words.

Then it clicked.

The photographers at the Fashion Design Awards. Surely one of them hadn't captured the moment Xandro touched her mouth with his own?

Ilana flipped pages until she reached the social section, and she quickly scanned the featured prints, honed in on one of them and felt the breath catch in her throat.

If the photo didn't spell it out, the caption certainly did, followed by printed text speculating Xandro Caramanis and Ilana Girard were an item, given they'd been seen together several times over the past few weeks.

Hell. The omnipotent innuendo of the Press.

Did they realise what they'd done?

An item?

Together?

She wanted to curl her hands into fists and *hit* something. Or someone!

Could she demand a correction?

Sure, and pigs might fly! The newspaper editor would fall about laughing.

He had no conception of the effect that particular photo, caption and text would have on her life, or any knowledge her ex-fiancé was a practised chameleon capable of extreme rage.

A waiter delivered her food, and she looked at the Caesar salad, then forced herself to fork a few mouthfuls before pushing the plate to one side, her appetite gone.

Ilana paid her bill and walked towards her apartment building. Nervous tension tightened the muscles in her stomach to a painful degree, and it wasn't until she was safely inside that the tension began to ease a little.

The light was blinking on her answering machine, and she hit the play-back function, pen in hand.

A message from Liliana, one from Micki, a few congratulatory calls, then Grant's voice—

'I'm watching you.'

Her landline was ex-directory, and it unnerved her Grant had managed to access it.

Anger meshed with very real fear as she retrieved Xandro's card and dialled his cellphone.

He picked up on the third ring. 'Ilana.'

Her fingers tightened on the phone. 'Do you have any idea what problems the newspaper photograph and idle social supposition has caused?' Her voice was tight, controlled and angry. 'Or its ramifications?'

'I'll be there in ten minutes.'

'You can't—'

'Ten minutes, Ilana.'

The call disconnected, and she hit *redial,* heard it ring, then it went direct to message-bank.

A very unladylike oath fell from her lips.

Damn him!

If he arrived at her apartment building and Grant was watching…

Without thought she collected her bag and keys, then took the lift down to the lobby.

She was a mass of nerves by the time Xandro's Bentley swept into the entrance, and she had to consciously force her feet to walk at a normal pace, when every nerve-end suggested she run.

Calm, she must remain calm, she told herself as she reached the car, opened the door and slid into the passenger seat.

'Please. Can we get away from here?'

Xandro wanted to demand an answer, and he would… soon. But for now he did as she asked, and drove until he reached Double Bay, then he cut the engine.

'Let's go.'

'I don't want—'

'We'll relax, eat, and you can tell me what's worrying you.'

She flung him a cautious look. 'I've already eaten.'

He crossed round to her side of the car and opened the door. 'Maybe you'll be tempted by an entrée.'

Minutes later they entered a charming restaurant where the *maître d'* greeted Xandro with the deference of a valued patron, seated them, then sent the wine steward to their table.

Ilana declined in favour of chilled water, and Xandro joined her before perusing the menu and ordering for both of them.

The waiter retreated, and Xandro regarded her carefully, noting the agitated way the pulse beat at the base of her throat. The barely controlled anxiety emanating from her slender frame.

'The photograph in today's newspaper,' he prompted.

Where did she begin? And how much did she explain?

Enough…just enough to have him understand.

'My ex-fiancé made certain…threats, when I cancelled the wedding.'

'And you're concerned the photograph will reach his attention?'

Ilana hesitated a fraction too long, and his eyes narrowed. 'It already has?'

'Yes.'

'Problems?'

She drew in a deep breath, then released it slowly as she inclined her head.

He regarded her carefully. 'As in?'

'Please…just accept my word for it.'

'Do you consider yourself to be in any danger?'

She didn't know whether to laugh or cry.

Did abusive phone calls come under that heading?

Threats…as long as they remained verbal, were nuisance value.

Yet if Grant acted on any of them, then the answer had to be *yes*.

Except who knew for certain? How could she judge?

What good would it do to explain her ex-fiancé was mentally unbalanced?

It wouldn't change a thing, for the photograph constituted damage already done.

The waiter delivered their order, and Ilana toyed with the food on her plate while Xandro ate with enjoyment.

'I want to spend time with you.'

Her heart seemed to stop, then race to a quicker beat. 'I don't think that's a good idea.'

'Because of your ex-fiancé's threats?'

She wanted to cry out that he didn't understand...except somehow she suspected he knew too well.

'Perhaps I've lost all trust in the male of the species?'

'You're sufficiently intelligent to know all men are not the same.'

'They all want the same thing.'

'Sex? There's a vast difference between sex for the sake of it, and lovemaking.'

'Really?'

His eyes speared her own. 'A man who ignores gifting a woman pleasure whilst seeking his own displays carelessness.'

'Who could doubt your vast experience?'

His soft laughter did strange things to her equilibrium, and for a wild moment she mentally envisaged what it might be like to take Xandro as a lover.

Akin to inviting emotional nirvana...with only one end.

It wouldn't last, of course. How could it? But oh, what a journey!

'I have tickets for dinner and a show Tuesday evening. I'd like for you to join me. Shall we say six-thirty?'

Xandro was asking her out?

'I don't think—'

'Six-thirty,' he insisted as he signalled for the bill.

Independence had her reaching for her wallet, only to have Xandro voice a determined refusal.

Ilana sat in silence as he sent the Bentley along the arterial road leading to Bondi.

A date with Xandro? If Grant should see them together, it would only increase his anger and incite heaven only knew what reaction.

She had to refuse. There was no other way, and she said so as he brought the car to a halt outside the entrance to her apartment building.

'I'll meet you in the city, if you prefer.' He paused fractionally. 'And I won't accept *no* for an answer.' He named a restaurant. 'Six forty-five.'

He leant towards her and touched his mouth to hers in a brief, erotic exploration, then he lifted his head. 'Take care.'

Sleep didn't come easily, and Ilana woke next morning with a headache which painkillers diminished but didn't banish.

At the workroom every peal of the phone tightened her nerve-ends, and by midday she felt like a wrung-out dishrag.

'What's going on?'

She glanced up from the appointment book, met Micki's look of concern and summoned a rueful smile.

'Headache. You know how it is.'

Micki shook her head. *'Give.'*

'Seriously. Excitement, and not enough sleep.'

The door buzzer sounded, and Micki answered it, returning with yet another floral tribute to join several delivered through the morning.

'For you.'

Gorgeous cream and yellow roses, with a card bearing the message 'Until tomorrow evening. Xandro.'

They were beautiful, and served to remind her to call him from home this evening to cancel out of his invitation.

The phone rang, Micki picked up and held up a hand as she mouthed silently—'Danika's agency.'

It took a while, firm words were said, and Ilana anticipated the result. 'Impasse?'

'Danika notified them the gown was a gift in lieu of her usual fee.'

'And?'

'Her word against ours.'

Which meant the red evening gown had to be withdrawn from the next season's showing and replaced with an equally noteworthy gown.

Calls continued through the afternoon, among them two hang-ups and one from Xandro, which Ilana declined to take, earning her a puzzled frown from Micki.

'Are you crazy?' her partner demanded quietly as she replaced the receiver.

Right now she didn't need the complication of any man in her life…least of all Xandro Caramanis. 'I don't want to get involved.' Dared not, if she was to retain any peace of mind.

She withstood Micki's concerned scrutiny for a few long seconds, glimpsed her friend's momentary indecision and sensed her faint sigh.

'Darling, he's a gorgeous, sexy hunk of manhood.' She effected an expressive eye-roll. 'A woman only has to *look* at him and *melt*.'

'You think?' she managed with a wry smile.

'You *don't?*'

'No.' And knew it to be a blatant lie.

A better friend she'd search hard to find. They'd shared much, and would inevitably share more as the years progressed. The real reason for opting out of her marriage to Grant Baxter at the eleventh hour was the exception, and it said much that Micki accepted the subject was off-limits.

'For what it's worth, I don't think he's going to give you much choice.'

Impossible. She was in control. She could choose.

Yet even as the reaffirming words occurred, they were followed by doubt.

Xandro Caramanis hadn't reached his late-thirties having achieved such an exceptionally high level of success without employing a degree of manipulative power. He wheeled and dealed with elemental ruthlessness, tearing down companies and rebuilding them.

The man commanded a veritable empire.

So what?

Her emotions had been torn apart, and she'd rebuilt her life. She was self-sufficient, strong.

A survivor.

Following her disastrous wedding eve she'd made a personal vow never to place her trust in a man again.

So why in the name of heaven was she now besieged with conflicting doubts?

Because of one man's mouth on her own? Stirring buried emotions into life again and making her long for the impossible.

It wasn't fair. None of it was fair.

'Let's go with upbeat and funky music for next season's

showing,' Micki suggested. 'I'll put a few tracks together and you can say *yea* or *nay.*'

'Accessories,' Ilana began briskly as she focused on business, 'are your specialty.'

'I'm already on it. Vamp it up? The catwalk visual is a whole different story.'

'Agreed. We need to fine-tune the garment running order to suit the model running order.'

'The bookings are complete and confirmed.'

'A standby?' Essential to cover any last-minute no-show. 'Done.'

Ilana sank back in her chair. 'Make-up and hair organised?'

Micki offered a smile that bore cynical humour. 'On target to show, entertain and *sell.*'

'As of today.'

'Oh, yeah. Between now and *the* day, anything can happen.'

And frequently did. Fifteen minutes on the catwalk equated to several thousand hours behind the scenes, with the day itself becoming a nightmare of gigantic proportion as tempers frayed over delays, missteps, tantrums, wardrobe malfunctions…to name a few!

Each of which were forgotten when the showing was accorded a success, sales soared…and following on the heels of euphoria was the need to put strategies together for the next season's showing…

The mad, mad world of fashion design, Ilana reflected musingly.

Work proved busy, with calls from clients requesting consultations, a charity organisation requesting *Arabelle* conduct a showing…and another call from Xandro, which she again declined to accept.

It was something of a relief when she recognised Liliana's number, and a smile curved her lips as she took the call.

'Darling, why don't you join me for dinner this evening? I'll cook. Just the two of us.'

They'd catch up, laugh a little, relax, and the food would be divine. 'Love to. Six-thirty? I'll bring the wine.'

Liliana's spacious apartment overlooked the water at Watson's Bay, and Ilana felt the tension of the past week begin to subside as she greeted her mother warmly.

A redolent aroma drifted from the kitchen, and she breathed it in, offering an appreciative compliment.

Coq au vin, glazed vegetables and a delicious torte for dessert, together with a glass of fine chardonnay and followed by coffee.

Together they discussed forthcoming social engagements, and those of note occurring over the past few weeks. Not the least of which featured the Fashion Design Awards.

Liliana was an astute woman, and a very caring mother. Xandro Caramanis didn't receive a mention, nor the photograph which had appeared in the Sunday newspaper.

'I imagine you've been extremely busy,' Liliana ventured. 'You're sleeping well?'

Subtle, Maman. Very subtle. 'I'm fine.' And knew she lied.

She wasn't fine. How could she be when Grant's shadow blighted her at too frequent intervals?

It was late when she left, and the night sky held the threat of rain, which soon became a reality as she traversed the main arterial route towards Bondi Beach.

Traffic was sparse, and the electronic swish of the windscreen wipers had a vaguely hypnotic effect. Upbeat music helped, and the CD was playing the last track when she sent the BMW down into the basement car park of her apartment building.

It had been a very pleasant evening, great company, fine food and good conversation.

Ilana slid from behind the wheel, closed the car door, pressed the remote locking mechanism and headed for the lift.

CHAPTER FIVE

THERE WAS NOTHING quite like being woken from a deep sleep at the crack of dawn by the persistent ring of a cellphone, and Ilana filched the unit from her bedside table in an automatic movement, activated it and offered a husky 'Hello', only to be greeted by silence, followed interminable minutes later by the distinct click as the caller disconnected.

Wrong number?

When it rang again an hour later she automatically picked up…to silence.

Two hang-ups couldn't be dismissed as coincidence.

She keyed in the combination of symbols and digits that activated caller ID…only to receive a recording stating the call was from a private number and unable to be identified.

Grant.

It was a simple option to switch both landline and cellphone to messagebank, thus allowing her to screen incoming calls.

She checked the time, groaned at the early hour and endeavoured to summon sleep…without success.

With a muttered imprecation she slid out of bed, pulled on her robe and went into the kitchen to make coffee.

It was during the short walk to the workroom that she remembered she hadn't called Xandro and cancelled their date tonight.

So go, why don't you? Behaving like a wimp was only pandering to Grant's threats.

A decision she was inclined to change several times during the day.

Except determined resolve saw her shower and change into a glamorous evening trouser-suit and drive into the city.

Xandro greeted her as she entered the restaurant, and her eyes widened when he brushed his mouth fleetingly to her own.

'Beautiful.'

The compliment pleased her, and she offered a tentative smile as he signalled the *maître d'* to show them to their table.

So they'd talk a little, sip a glass of wine, eat, take in the show...then she'd get into her car and drive home.

How difficult could it be?

So remarkably easy, she began to relax and enjoy his company. He had the ability to make a woman feel comfortable...or did he sense her inner turmoil and merely seek to ease it?

Ilana refused to analyse the reason. Later, maybe, when she was alone. But for now she was content to live in the moment.

To pretend for the space of a few hours the evening was what it appeared to be.

A waiter took their order, and Xandro kept the conversation light, aware if he pushed a little too hard Ilana would withdraw into herself and any progress he might have made so far would be lost.

And he didn't intend to lose.

Their food arrived, and they began to eat.

'You spent time overseas. France and Italy, I believe?' he posed, and saw her expression lighten. 'Was it all study?'

'Intense.' Ilana smiled in reflection. 'Really intense. The temperament of the European fashionista is legend.' A faint bubble of laughter escaped from her lips. 'But we managed to squeeze in some fun, explore a little. I learnt a great deal.' Paris...the exotic eclectic, the women young and old with their inherent sense of style. Milan...the city, the people. Her sojourn in Tuscany...who could forget?

Those had been the carefree days, a time when she'd trusted freely and been fortunate not to have that trust violated in any way.

'As students we shared accommodation and food,' she relayed, unaware how her eyes sparkled and her features lightened in memory. 'At weekends we hired a car and explored the countryside, bought food and ate picnic-style.'

Xandro felt a surge of protectiveness for the young girl she'd been, her love of life and all it had held.

There was a strong desire to gift that back to her.

He could, once she'd learnt to trust him.

He wanted her.

In his bed, his life. As his wife.

Yet if he suggested marriage *now,* she'd run a mile.

He wheeled and dealed on a daily basis in a business world where cut-throat decisions were the norm.

But this was different...personal.

The theatre was within walking distance, and the show proved to be excellent entertainment, with a balance of wit and pathos, glorious costumes and clever dialogue.

Ilana enjoyed the evening, and said as much as they joined the general exodus of patrons.

She was conscious of Xandro's hand at the back of her waist, and his close proximity.

'Where are you parked?'

He saw her into her car, then leant in close. 'We'll stop off at Double Bay for coffee, and afterwards I'll follow you home.' He named a popular café, then trailed light fingers down her cheek. 'I'll be right behind you.'

And he was, catching up within minutes as they headed towards Double Bay.

It was one of the 'in' scenes for the social set, and she wondered why she hadn't insisted on going directly home. Yet a part of her didn't want the evening to end.

Just for a while he made her think of the unattainable.

Was that such a bad thing?

Ilana opted for tea while Xandro ordered coffee, and afterwards she had little recall of their conversation...only the awareness they appeared to share.

The uncanniness of it shook her a little. To be so in tune with a man, especially one of Xandro's calibre, wasn't something she envisaged, and she had difficulty accepting his interest was genuine. And if it was, where it might lead.

It was almost midnight when they left, and she turned towards him with a few polite words in thanks as they reached her car...only to have him capture her head and move his mouth over her own in a kiss that succeeded in obliterating all rational thought from her mind.

How long did it last? Seconds, minutes? She couldn't even begin to hazard a guess.

All she knew was the need not to have it end.

Xandro gently eased back, teasing her lower lip with tiny nibbled kisses, before releasing her. The urge to touch her, make love, was barely controlled, and he took considerable strength of will to take hold of her keys, disarm the alarm, then see her seated behind the wheel.

'I'll see you at the cocktail party tomorrow night.'

She could only nod in silent acquiescence as she fired the engine and eased the BMW out into the traffic.

The streets were relatively quiet, and she was conscious of Xandro's Bentley following as she headed towards Bondi.

She paused fractionally as she reached her apartment building, flashed her lights in signatory thanks, then used her security card to access the underground car-park.

The electronic gate lifted, and she swept the BMW down into the concrete cavern, then eased it into her nominated space.

Two separate bars of neon lighting were out, which was unusual. One, maybe…but two? And she was willing to swear both had been working a few hours ago when she left.

A faint sound had the hairs along the back of her neck standing up in instinctive alarm.

The next instant hard hands closed over her shoulders and a forceful shove sent her crashing into the rear of a parked car.

'Bitch.'

A hand connected with the side of her face before she had a chance to recover her balance.

Grant…*here?*

One look into his face revealed he was stirred up by alcohol or drugs, or both, and bent on inflicting pain.

Don't take your eyes from him, don't think…

Pain pulsed over her cheekbone, along her jaw, and she ignored it as she waited, watchful of his next move.

There was a small can of capsicum spray in her bag. A personal alarm attached to her keyring. She wore knee-high boots with killer heels. All of them were practical weapons…

'What does it take for you to listen to me, bitch?'

Don't allow him to goad you into saying anything.

Ilana saw the moment he meant to strike, and she used his forward momentum to put him on the hard concrete.

The heel of her boot crunched on bone and sinew, and he screamed, rolling away from her as he nursed his injured hand.

A stream of obscenities reverberated around the concrete cavern, and she used his momentary incapacity to extract the capsicum spray from her bag as she covered the few metres to the lift.

Adrenalin pumped through her veins, temporarily negating fear as she jabbed the call-button.

Please, please, don't let it be stopped on a high floor.

Mercifully the doors slid open within seconds, and she stepped inside, slid her security key into the slot and punched in her floor code.

It wasn't until she entered her apartment, locked and bolted the door and set the security alarm, that reaction set in.

Her hands began trembling of their own accord, and parts of her body hurt.

Dear lord in heaven.

A long hot shower helped, and she towelled her hair, then blow-dried it. Habit ensured she completed her nightly routine, and afterwards she crept into bed, dimmed the lights and sat watching figures on the television screen in the hope the movie would occupy her mind.

She must have eventually fallen asleep, for when she woke the morning sun was fingering filtered light into her bedroom, and she checked the time, slid out of bed and the breath hissed from her throat as bruised muscles complained in earnest.

Ilana dressed in comfortable clothes, ate breakfast and took the lift down to the basement car park, aware her stomach curled with nervous tension as she walked to her car. Foolish, for it was morning, the sun shone, the basement was well lit and common sense dictated Grant was long gone.

The day settled down into a normal pattern, and twice

during the afternoon Ilana picked up the phone and pressed Liliana's number on speed-dial, only to cancel before the call could connect.

The thought of attending a cocktail party this evening held no appeal.

She didn't want to go. Make that she *really* didn't want to appear in public tonight. The past few days had been fraught, and she was still endeavouring to make sense of Grant's re-appearance in her life.

A verbal attack she could deal with. But violence was something else entirely.

Grant's words echoed and re-echoed inside her brain. *Stay away from him.*

Yet every step she took, every social function she attended included Xandro's presence. Avoiding him was almost impossible.

Worse, was the disturbing effect he had on her composure. As to her reaction…let's not go there.

Crazy. It didn't make sense.

Dammit. Why had her life become so complicated?

A few weeks ago everything had seemed so…*normal*. She'd spent long working hours, enjoyed some time with a few trusted friends and accompanied Liliana to social events.

Yet all that had changed, and little of it for the better.

Now she had half an hour in which to shower, do something with her hair, carefully camouflage an emerging bruise beneath make-up and choose something to wear before she needed to meet Liliana in the downstairs lobby.

Figure-hugging black lace with three-quarter sleeves and matching black stiletto heels would suffice, and she wound her hair into a simple knot atop her head.

Her mother's Lexus was parked out the front of the apartment-building entrance as she emerged from the lift at ground level, and she slid into the passenger seat, leant forward to brush her lips to Liliana's cheek in greeting, and somehow managed to maintain a light, innocuous conversation during the brief drive to Rose Bay.

Cars lined the curved driveway of their hosts' waterfront mansion, and here it was impossible to dispel the familiar onset of nerves as she accompanied Liliana into their hosts' sumptuous lounge, a customary warm smile in place as she greeted familiar faces.

Xandro stood deep in conversation with a fellow guest, his tall, broad frame instantly recognisable. Almost as if he sensed her appearance he lifted his head and his dark eyes seared her own in the few seconds before she glanced away.

A uniformed waiter proffered a tray bearing flutes of champagne, and Ilana accepted one and sipped its contents in the hope it might help steady her nerves.

An hour, then she'd plead a headache and call a cab. Liliana would express concern, but understand.

Meanwhile she'd mingle and endeavour to appear as if she was enjoying a pleasurable evening.

Not exactly easy when her face ached, it hurt to smile and engaging in conversation employed far too many of her facial muscles.

Lack of sleep, the maximum painkiller dosage, coupled with a fraught day spent in the workroom…and it was a wonder she was still standing.

Champagne, she soon perceived, wasn't the answer, and she discarded her partly filled flute in favour of iced water.

'Ilana.'

Xandro's deep drawl sent her pulse thudding to a faster beat, and she assembled a slight smile as she turned towards the dark-haired man whose physical presence had the power to shred her nerves.

His eyes narrowed fractionally as he took in her pale features, the deep green of her eyes and the skilful but heavier than usual application of make-up. Different, but not unattractive, than the natural look she normally chose.

'Are you OK?'

Oh, heavens. 'Fine.'

His expression didn't change, although she was prepared to swear she caught a sudden stillness in those dark eyes. 'What happened?'

It was apparent something had. Whether she'd confide in him was another thing.

'I don't want to play with you,' she managed, and saw his eyes harden.

'You think what we share is a game?'

'I have no place in your personal life.'

'Yes, you do.'

She felt the colour leech from her face, only to have it return in a warm flood.

With a deliberate movement he caught hold of her hand and threaded his fingers through her own.

Ilana was immediately aware of her betraying pulse-beat as it rapidly went into overdrive at his touch, and the faint slide of his thumb over the veins at her wrist merely added to her humiliation.

She wanted to wrench her hand free and almost did, except she aimed for a more surreptitious approach...and dug her nails into his knuckles. With no tangible effect whatsoever.

'Don't,' she managed quietly, and saw one eyebrow lift in quizzical query.

'Hold your hand?'

She attempted to tug it free, only to fail miserably.

Her eyes were bright…too bright, as she fought against the threat of tears. 'Please don't do this.'

He loosened his hold, but didn't release her, and she had the feeling his fingers would tighten if she attempted to pull away.

'You've received another threat from your ex-fiancé.'

It was a statement, not a query, and Ilana couldn't quite meet his gaze. 'What makes you think that?'

'I'd say it was a given.'

She should never have come here tonight. Yet it was easier to attend than offer excuses neither her mother nor Xandro were likely to accept.

'Are you going to tell me about it?'

'No.'

'You don't have to handle this on your own.'

Ilana looked at him carefully. 'Enlisting anyone's help will only worsen the situation. Believe me.'

The headache she'd been harbouring all day seemed to have erupted into something quite severe with the noise factor and her own accelerated nervous tension.

Ilana scanned the room with a sense of desperation. Liliana…where was she?

'Your mother is deep in conversation in the far-right corner of the room.'

Xandro's voice held a quietness she didn't dare examine as he released her hand, and without a backward glance she began threading her way in Liliana's direction.

The headache she'd intended to fabricate had become a reality, and there was no need for pretence as she relayed the need to leave.

'Oh, sweetheart,' Liliana commiserated. 'I'm so sorry. Do you want me to—'

'No,' Ilana said quickly. 'Stay. I'll call a cab.'

'I'll drive you home.'

Xandro had the tread of a cat, and she closed her eyes, then opened them again. 'It isn't necessary.'

'Thank you,' Liliana said with innate charm. 'How kind.'

She had a choice…argue and refuse, or leave silently. In deference to her mother, their hosts and guests, she chose the latter, only to retrieve her cellphone when they were merely ten paces down the driveway.

The night air held the slight chill of early summer, and she was barely aware of the shadowed shrubbery.

'What are you doing?'

'Calling a cab.'

'No, you're not.'

'Go to hell.'

Dark, almost black eyes blazed at her temerity, and in that instant time seemed to stand still.

Everything faded as she became startlingly aware of him, the almost primitive sensation electrifying the air…and the pounding beat of her heart.

In seeming slow motion he drew her close and fastened his mouth over her own in a kiss that took hold of her anger and tamed it.

The movement pulled at her bruised cheek muscles, and a whimper of pain rose and died in her throat. Then there was nothing else but the man, his strength and the taste of him as she became caught up in the possession of his libidinous mouth, the sensuous thrust of his tongue and its silent promise.

How long did it last? Seconds? *Minutes?*

Emotional meltdown, she perceived hazily as he released her, and for a few perilous seconds she thought she might subside in a heap as she fought for some measure of composure.

'Shall we start over?'

Dear lord in heaven. Start *where?*

'I can't believe you've suddenly lost your voice.'

There was amusement apparent, and it rankled. 'I'm endeavouring to find the words,' she managed with a degree of cynicism, and waited a beat. 'To damn you with no praise.'

'You're paraphrasing.'

Ilana flung him a dark look which was mostly lost in the moonlit night. 'Believe it's intentional.'

He deactivated the car alarm and walked a few paces to where the Bentley was parked, opened the passenger door and stood to one side. 'Get in, Ilana.'

She didn't move. 'Doesn't it register with you that I don't want to?'

'You have nothing to fear from me.' His voice was quiet, too quiet. Almost as if he knew...

And he couldn't. No one did. Except Liliana.

'I'd prefer to take a cab.'

Xandro didn't say a word, and after a few timeless minutes she reluctantly took the necessary steps to his car.

How long would it take to reach her Bondi beach apartment? Too long, she perceived as Xandro slid in behind the wheel and fired the engine.

Her lips tingled from the pressure of his own, and she could still taste him, *feel* him. Her jaw hurt, so did her cheekbone. A wave of fragility captured her senses, and for some strange reason she felt close to tears.

Don't, she silently besieged. To have even one tear escape would be the final humiliation.

Think happy thoughts. Sun-kissed days, cloudless skies, rose gardens and the drift of multicoloured petals. Kittens gambolling in the grass in a tangle of soft fur…*anything* other than dark memories and the man at her side.

It worked, mostly, combined with the scene beyond the windscreen, the neon lights, traffic, the minutes disappearing as the distance grew shorter to her destination.

Xandro didn't offer so much as a word, for which she was inordinately grateful, and she breathed an inaudible sigh of relief as the Bentley slid to a smooth halt immediately adjacent to the entrance to her apartment building.

Ilana released her seat belt and reached for the door-clasp in a quick co-ordinated movement, a brief word of thanks escaping her lips as she did so.

She'd only moved a few steps when she heard the almost silent click of a car door followed by the faint beep of the alarm as Xandro moved to join her.

'I'll see you to your apartment.'

'No.' She wanted him gone, to enter the lift and know within minutes she'd be safely inside her private sanctuary…and alone.

She punched in the security code which released the outer doors, and moved quickly into the lobby…but not quickly enough, for he was there at her side.

The lift was operated by a security key, and she stood resolutely still.

He lifted a hand and traced the damp rivulet down her cheek, and his eyes narrowed at the fleeting shadow of pain in her own.

The single tear moved him, as did the proud tilt of her head.

'Please. Just…go.'

For a moment she thought he meant to ignore her directive, then he gestured towards the lift. 'Summon it. When you're inside, I'll leave.'

She hesitated, unsure whether he would do as he said, then she reached out and punched the call-button.

Seconds later the melodious ping heralded the lift's arrival, and she moved quickly inside the electronic cubicle.

The momentary fear shadowing her eyes for an instant before the doors slid closed stayed with him as he exited the external doors…and long after he sent the sleek Bentley purring through the suburban streets to Vaucluse.

Ilana secured the triple lock and slid the latch-bolt in place, then she crossed the spacious lounge to the kitchen. All the lights blazed in welcome, a precaution she took whenever she envisaged returning home after dark.

A cup of tea, some painkillers and a change into night-wear…in reverse order, she decided as she crossed into her bedroom.

It felt good to cleanse off her make-up…not so good to see the darkening bruise covering her cheekbone. There were vivid marks on each upper arm, and she'd camouflaged those, too, then chosen a long-sleeved top to cover them.

She added a robe and padded out to the kitchen, switched on the electric kettle and filched a teabag from its canister and dropped it into a mug, then she shook out two painkillers and swallowed them down with water.

Minutes later she carried the steaming mug into the lounge and used the remote module to switch on the television.

It was a relief to settle down on a comfortable cushioned sofa, and she curled her legs beneath her as she channel-surfed.

Something white on the floor caught her eye just inside the front door. An envelope? From whom?

She crossed the room, checked it bore her printed name and address, and wondered why it had been pushed beneath her door when all mail was consigned into individually numbered locked boxes in the lobby.

A single piece of paper, Ilana determined as she extracted and unfolded it. Bearing four words.

'Get rid of him.'

Unsigned. But then, only Grant would send her such a note.

An involuntary shiver shook her slender frame, and several queries flooded her brain. The apartment-building security was tight, and one of the main reasons she'd bought into it. That Grant had managed to breach it was a concern.

For two years she hadn't dated…hell, she wasn't dating *now*. Was she?

Sharing dinner with Xandro, spending time with him at a social function or three, having him drive her home…they were acquaintances, part of the same social circle, friends.

So what was a kiss or two?

Except it was more than that.

Worse, there was a part of her that wanted it to be *much* more.

Dared she discount Grant's threats and accept whatever Xandro offered?

As far as she could see, either way led to heartbreak…hers.

The tea in her mug grew cold as she stared sightlessly at the television screen, and at some stage she switched it off, double-checked the front door locks were secure, then she tipped the tea down the sink and went to bed.

Sleep didn't come easily, and twice through the night she woke from a pervasive nightmare that left her trembling, so much so she switched on the bedside lamp and read until her eyes began to close.

On the edge of sleep it was Xandro Caramanis's darkly powerful image which filled her mind.

CHAPTER SIX

ILANA ROSE EARLY and made hot strong coffee, added sugar, then she settled down into a comfortable cushioned chair close to the wide glass doors leading onto a small terrace overlooking the bay.

It was a lovely early-summer day, the sun shone and glistened on the dappled ocean water, and already beach-lovers were walking on the sand along the shoreline. Soon sun umbrellas would dot the foreshore, their bright colours providing a visual kaleidoscope.

Ilana adored the casual atmosphere, the views from her beachfront apartment, and the proximity to a bustling, ever-changing esplanade.

Half an hour, then she'd change and walk the short distance to work.

Creating a design to replace the red evening gown wasn't an easy task, for it had to top the winning Fashion Design Award entry.

Ilana sketched and discarded, assembled ideas at her desk, and it was late afternoon before she had a design she felt did justice to the colour and fabric she'd chosen.

At midday she took a break to retrieve her laptop from the apartment.

Whilst there she checked the answering machine and saw it held several recorded messages…most of which bore long silences followed by a hang-up.

Persistent, pathetic…but with the desired stomach-churning effect the anonymous caller sought.

Although *anonymous* was a misnomer.

The nuisance calls, cleverly made from a public phone or a private unlisted number to ensure nothing registered on her caller ID, led directly to Grant…of this she was certain.

Proving it was another thing.

Meanwhile she'd take each day as it came, and deal with whatever her ex-fiancé chose to throw at her.

A few years ago she'd been a carefree young woman planning a future with a man she'd thought to love.

Except it was a fallacy, as she had eventually discovered to her cost.

A slight shiver slithered along her spine as she took the lift down to the lobby. Any thought involving Grant upped her nervous tension, and sent her imagination into overdrive.

The morning had been long and fraught, and she stopped at a café for a packaged salad sandwich and takeaway latte.

Ilana had only moved a few metres along the pavement when she had the instinctive feeling she was being watched.

She kept walking, resolutely refusing to glance back over her shoulder or indicate in any way something or someone had disturbed her.

Grant? She fervently hoped not. Harassment via phone calls she could handle. Stalking was something else.

The prickling at the base of her neck remained, and there was a sense of relief on reaching the workroom.

The afternoon hours swiftly took a downward turn.

A seamstress went home sick, a machine became uncharacteristically recalcitrant with every correction Ilana tried. She pleaded with it, swore, pleaded again…then she threw up her hands and called the technician.

She was tired, felt a mess, probably looked like one and, worse, she was as jumpy as a cat on hot coals. Each ring of the phone caused her stomach to knot, and she had Micki answer all calls, choosing only to speak to legitimate business contacts and Liliana.

All she wanted was for the day to end so she could go home. She even fantasised about a steaming bubble-bath and a cold drink, preferably something mildly alcoholic that would ease her nerves and loosen every muscle in her body.

Now, thanks to Xandro Caramanis, the media had latched on to her and subsequently brought Grant out of the woodwork. *I'm watching you.*

Had he been lying in wait outside her apartment this morning? Had he followed her to the workroom? Worse, was he sitting in a parked car on the street watching for the moment she locked up at day's end?

The thought he might be planning another subversive move was disturbing.

She could have easily stayed back, for there were sketches she needed to peruse, adjustments to make, and she wanted to drape and pin silk chiffon onto a mannequin to check if her visual image married with the fabric.

Instead she closed up and followed Micki and the two machinists out onto the pavement…only to pause at the sight of a silver Bentley parked at the kerb with Xandro leaning indolently against the passenger door.

'Ilana.' Xandro's voice was a lazy drawl that curled around her nerve-ends and tugged a little.

His business suit was fashioned from expensive fabric, the

fit perfection, downplaying rather than emphasising his impressive breadth of shoulder.

Intensely masculine, he bore an aura of power that appeared uncontrived.

And his mouth…*sin* personified, she reflected, vividly recalling the frank sensuality of its touch on her own. Bone-melting, and totally off the planet.

For a brief few minutes he'd made her forget who and where she was as he transported her to a place where there was no fear or insecurity. Only the promise of passion and the man who could gift it to her…if only she dared let him.

She was dimly aware Micki and the girls had moved out of sight.

'Hi.' Did her voice sound as calm as she meant it to be? She fervently hoped so. Displaying any form of vulnerability wasn't an option.

Xandro appeared relaxed, yet there was a waiting, almost watchful quality apparent. He straightened away from the car and moved to stand within touching distance.

She didn't want him close. He disturbed her, far more than she was comfortable with, and right now she was just holding herself together.

There was a line of parked cars on both sides of the street. Was it possible Grant might be sitting in one of them, watching…?

'I thought we could share a meal.'

But not together. Not tonight. 'I have plans.' Not exactly an untruth. 'Thanks, but—'

His eyes narrowed, and he took in her pale features, the slight furrowed frown and the dark green of her eyes.

'No thanks?'

'Xandro—'

'Indulge me.'

She lifted a hand and reefed back a stray lock of hair behind one ear. 'I can't.'

'You have to wash your hair?' He sounded mildly amused. 'Clean your apartment? Write to your Aunt Sally?'

'I don't have an Aunt Sally.'

'Should I be relieved?' One eyebrow slanted in silent query, and she quelled a sense of exasperation.

'Don't be ridiculous.'

Xandro watched the fleeting emotions she fought to hide, all too aware he didn't have the right to insist on an explanation. Something he intended to correct, very soon.

'Half an hour,' he reiterated quietly.

She knew she should refuse. If Grant happened to be watching, he'd see her walk away from Xandro Caramanis… and maybe Grant would perceive her action as a victory in his favour.

And *what?* Cease and desist from stalking her?

Sure, and cows flew over the moon!

There was a simple remedy…go to the police.

Yet what could they do, other than advise she take out a Restraining Order and file a report if Grant broke it?

Dammit. She was hungry, and half an hour…where was the harm? 'OK.'

There were several cafés to choose from along Campbell Parade, and Xandro ushered her into one of them, selected a table indoors, conferred over the menu, then he placed an order.

There was plenty of foot traffic, and the pavement tables began filling with patrons wanting to enjoy some down time, fresh air and the relaxing view of the beach before taking whatever mode of transport necessary to reach home.

'Tell me about your day.'

Ilana savoured the aroma of good coffee, and broke a tube of sugar into her latte. 'You really don't want to know.'

He copied her actions, and she noted the steadiness of his hands, the precise movement of his fingers as he tore the tube.

'Try me.'

Nice hands, she abstractly perceived. She'd enjoyed the feel of them cupping her nape, their gentleness when he'd framed her face.

Stop right there.

To dwell on how his touch affected her was nothing short of madness.

Ilana took an appreciative sip of fine coffee, felt the slight kick of caffeine hit her stomach, and regarded him carefully over the rim of her cup.

He did *enigmatic* very well. A little too well. Beneath his relaxed persona lay a very astute mind, and the known fact he was nobody's fool.

Light, she decided. Just keep it light. 'One staff member down. A sewing machine threw a hissy fit.' She effected a slight shrug. 'Too much to do in too little time.' She paused imperceptibly. 'Your turn.'

'The usual. An important meeting, a conference call.' Nothing he couldn't handle with one hand tied behind his back.

A waiter delivered two steaming bowls of risotto dredged with wild mushrooms, spinach, pine nuts and a liberal quantity of shaved Parmesan cheese.

It was delicious, and she ate with enjoyment, aware of his close proximity with every breath she took…even the way he held his flatware as he transferred food to his mouth.

Thinking about his mouth almost brought her undone, and she had to consciously school herself to focus on something else…anything, as long as it wasn't *him*.

Difficult, when he was seated opposite within touching distance.

It was a relief to finish eating, and she declined dessert in favour of more coffee as she began counting down the minutes before she could leave after having paid her share of the bill and offering a few polite words in thanks.

Except it didn't work out that way…and there was a part of her that wondered why on earth she thought it would.

Xandro shot her a searing look accompanied by a dangerously quiet 'No' as she laid notes on the table.

Her politely voiced 'Thanks' as they exited the café received an inclination of his head in acknowledgement.

She could turn and walk away, and he wouldn't stop her. She almost did…except her feet refused to follow the instruction from her brain.

'I have to catch up on work.' That much was true. And she felt the need for the security of her apartment.

'I'll drive you home.'

'It's not necessary. My apartment building is only two blocks down.'

He shot her a musing glance. 'I'm going in that direction.'

'Are you usually so…?' Words temporarily failed her.

'Determined? Yes, when it comes to getting what I want.'

'For the record,' she offered silkily, 'I dislike dictatorial men.'

His husky chuckle curled round her heartstrings and tugged a little. 'You want to stand here and argue some more?'

'What if I said I'd prefer not to see you again?'

His eyes lost their lazy gleam. 'I'd know you lied.'

Calm, measured words which almost tore the breath from her throat, and for a moment she felt acutely vulnerable.

Emotionally naked to a man who appeared to read her so well.

'You're wasting your time.' Her voice sounded ragged,

even to her own ears, and she gave a start as he caught hold of her hand and threaded his fingers through her own.

Without a word she walked at his side to the Bentley, slid into the passenger seat and fastened the seat belt as he crossed round to the driver's side.

In a few minutes she'd be home. And safe.

The drive was achieved in silence, and she had her security key in readiness as he drew the powerful car to a halt in the wide bricked apron adjacent to the main entrance to her apartment building.

She released the seat belt and reached for the door-clasp, a polite 'thanks' on the tip of her tongue, only to turn at the sound of his voice.

'You forgot something.'

Ilana looked at him in silent askance as he leant forward and brushed his mouth over the soft contours of her own.

Oh, dear God. She didn't want to feel like this.

To want, *need*...unwilling to trust. And afraid, very afraid of allowing any man, especially *this* man, to peel away the layers protecting her heart.

His hand closed over her arm, and a faint gasp escaped her lips as pain seared the tender flesh.

'What the devil?' His eyes narrowed as he caught the pain reflected in her own.

'It's fine.' Surely she could be forgiven for the slight prevarication? 'A bruise, that's all.'

He reached forward and gently pushed up her sleeve.

His expression didn't change, but she knew what he saw. The bruised finger marks on her flesh were quite distinct.

His eyes raked her face and he touched gentle fingers to her cheek where the slight swelling over her cheekbone seemed heightened somehow.

'Who did this to you?'

The outer doors swished open, and a tenant exited the lobby, casting the car and its occupants a cursory glance as he passed close by.

She reached for the door-clasp, only to still as Xandro's hand closed over her own.

'Your ex-fiancé?' His voice held a dangerous silkiness close to her ear, and she felt his warm breath stir faint tendrils of hair at her temple.

She wouldn't beg, or fabricate. 'You don't have the right to question me.'

The silence seemed to echo within the confines of the car's interior, electric, sibilant and almost frightening.

He removed his hand, released the door-clasp and leaned back a little. 'And if I did?'

'I don't deal in the hypothetical.'

She pushed open the door and slid to her feet, feeling a sense of relief to be free of him...only to have her stomach twist into a painful knot as he joined her before she'd taken a few steps.

He moved with the speed and fluid grace of a jungle cat, and at that moment it seemed to her he was almost as dangerous.

The soft chirrup of the car's automatic locking device succeeded in bringing her to a standstill, and she lifted her head to glare at him. 'Don't.'

Touch me, she added silently.

Or follow me into the building.

There was something in his stance, a quality she didn't care to define. One eyebrow lifted in silent query, and she was held suspended in his dark, probing gaze, wanting so much to turn and walk away from him, except her feet weren't responding to the dictates of her brain.

'It would be easier to tell me what happened.'

He didn't…*couldn't* know. Dammit, no one knew.

To provide Xandro with proof would be the height of foolishness.

'No,' she managed carefully. 'It wouldn't.'

Xandro regarded her in silence for several long seconds, noting her pale features, the slightly desperate plea in her voice…the anxiety she fought so hard to hide.

Did she realise the resources he had at his fingertips? The extent of his power?

'Your choice.'

Why did her nerves suddenly stir into jangling discord? It didn't make sense.

Take the initiative, a silent voice bade.

Bid him good night, turn and walk calmly to the entrance doors, key in your security code and cross to the lift.

If he stopped her, she'd deal with it.

Except he let her go, and she didn't look back as she progressed through security and summoned the lift.

It wasn't until she entered her apartment, secured the lock and set the alarm that she gave in to the reaction that threatened to consume her.

She was safe in her own haven. Alone, where no one could physically threaten her.

So why were her emotions every which way but loose? Pitching her to the edge of a mythical precipice where one false move could tip her into oblivion?

It didn't make sense.

Oh, give it a break! Do something…anything that will keep your mind occupied.

Within minutes she'd removed her outer clothes and pulled on an oversized T-shirt. Cleansing off make-up came next, then she brushed out her hair and twisted it into a single plait.

Better, she accorded, and padded into the room she'd set up as a home-office, booted up the computer and focused on the designs she was working on for next year's winter collection.

When she was done, she keyed in an email to Liliana with a diary of her day.

It was something they'd initiated when her father died. A daily diary via email. At first it was only meant to be temporary...but it had become a caring habit neither wanted to abandon.

At eleven Ilana switched off the lights and crept into bed, weary beyond belief, to fall asleep within minutes of her head touching the pillow.

The day began as any other, and became sufficiently busy to delay Ilana's efforts to add the finishing touches to the new evening gown. It was almost done when Micki and the girls closed down for the evening.

Fifteen more minutes should do it, then she'd leave.

It was a lovely evening, with the sun sinking low in the sky and a fresh breeze drifting in from the ocean as Ilana locked the workroom and took the few steps out to the pavement.

She'd stayed later than she intended, but there was a sense of satisfaction in knowing the newly designed evening gown would outshine the award-winning red which Danika had taken for her own.

Her lips curved into a faint smile, and she barely refrained from punching a fist in the air in silent jubilation.

She rang Micki, relayed the news and impulsively decided to relax over a chai latte in one of the nearby cafés instead of ordering the latte to go.

Just as she was about to leave she had the strangest feeling someone was watching her, and an edge of concern feathered its way down her spine.

It was early-evening dusk. She had nothing to fear, and her apartment building was not too far distant.

At that moment her cellphone rang, and she picked up without thinking to check caller ID. Then cursed herself for a fool as she heard Grant's familiar voice.

'Hey, bitch.'

She should have cut the connection, but she was beyond angry at his continual harassment. 'Afraid to show yourself in daylight?'

'How does it feel knowing I'm watching you?'

'You should get a life.'

'And spoil my fun?'

Ilana disconnected, and she hardly had time to draw breath when her cellphone chirped with an incoming text message that was short and graphically explicit.

She should leave and walk home. Except she refused to give Grant the satisfaction of seeing her cut and run.

Five minutes...ten should be long enough, and she deliberately waited them out, aware patrons were beginning to take up nearby tables.

OK, she was out of here. There were people present, and besides, she had a personal alarm with a strident sound guaranteed to wake the dead.

A fresh breeze sprang up, and she lifted a hand to push her hair away from her face.

It was then she heard a faint scuffle behind her, followed by a thud and a male grunt of pain, and she swung round to see Grant stumble as a man attempted to restrain him.

Except as she watched in horror Grant managed to break clear and sprint across the road with considerable speed.

'Who the hell are you?' Ilana demanded of the man Grant had barely eluded.

'He was about to accost you.' He turned to leave, and something about him didn't quite…fit.

'And you knew that…how?'

'By his suspicious actions, ma'am.'

The 'ma'am' did it. 'I don't believe you.'

He offered a negligible shrug. 'Car's parked upfront.'

Seconds later he indicated a dark-coloured sedan with tinted windows. 'Gotta go.'

Something about the car was familiar, and she suddenly remembered seeing it parked on the street the day before.

'I think you should tell me who you are.'

A police car slid to a halt at the kerb, and an officer leaned out of the window. 'You OK, miss?'

'This man was following me.'

The officer removed himself from the car and stood with his hand on his holster.

Handy things, pistols. They tended to lend a degree of caution. Add a uniform and authority, and the effect was impressive.

Questions were asked, an ID requested, followed by an explanation…and Ilana didn't like any of it.

A bodyguard?

Benjamin Jackson had been contracted by Xandro Caramanis to protect her?

The police officer slid back into the car and set it in motion.

'It appears I should thank you.'

'Just doing my job.'

'It might have helped, Benjamin,' she offered firmly, 'if you'd told me what that is.'

'Ben,' he corrected. 'The purpose is discretion.'

Anger darkened her eyes. 'Frightening the life out of me doesn't count?'

'That wasn't my intention.'

No, she didn't imagine it was.

Ben indicated the direction of her apartment building. 'I'll walk you back to your apartment.'

'I'm going out.'

He inclined his head. 'In that case, I'll see you safely to your car.'

He did, and she bade him good night, adding, 'Take the rest of the night off.'

It was meant to be a cynical comment, although he chose to take it seriously.

'I have my instructions, ma'am.'

'Ilana. My name is *Ilana*.'

She ignited the engine and sent the car up to street level, drove a few blocks, then pulled into the kerb and extracted her cellphone.

'Maman, do you have Xandro's address?'

If her mother was curious, she didn't express it.

'Of course, darling. Vaucluse.' Liliana cited the relevant street and number.

'Thanks.'

Five minutes later Ilana sent her BMW heading towards the eastern arterial route leading to Xandro's prestigious suburb.

She wanted to kill him. Well, maybe that was a bit too severe...*hit* him, at the very least. Not to mention verbally tear him to shreds.

Her mind seethed with everything she intended to say, and she wasn't too sure she could tone it down to anything resembling *succinct* or *civil*.

The quiet tree-lined street bore a mix of several beautiful homes, some new, others beautifully maintained set in manicured grounds.

Ilana sighted the appropriate number, parked, then she

crossed to the gated entry and identified herself via a sophisticated security system.

A large two-level home stood in sculptured grounds, its architectural lines blending superbly with surrounding scenery.

Within a matter of seconds the gate slid open and she quickly crossed the semicircular driveway to the main entrance.

As she reached it the door opened to reveal Xandro in the aperture.

'Ilana.'

He didn't seem in the least surprised to see her, and her anger went up a notch.

'How *dare* you?'

One eyebrow slanted in visible cynicism as he stood to one side and gestured towards the foyer. 'You want to have this discussion on my doorstep?'

She shot him a fulminating glare and stepped inside, hating his indolence…hating *him.*

The door closed, and she swung round to face him, her eyes blazing with pent-up fury as she raked his powerful frame.

'Who in *hell* gave you the right to interfere in my life?'

'Whatever happened to *hello?*' Xandro queried with mild amusement, gesturing to a room to his right.

She resembled a pocket-sized virago. All bristling fury and ready to lash out at him with the slightest provocation. He was almost inclined to test her control.

'You hired a *bodyguard,*' she expostulated. *'Why?'*

'Come inside, and I'll get you a drink.'

Her eyes blazed green fire. 'This is *not*—' she paused and attempted a deep, calming breath '—a social visit.'

'So I gather.'

She hadn't bothered to look at him…really *look* at him, for she was so consumed with anger it negated all else.

Now she did, and she became aware of his stance, the broad shoulders beneath his white shirt, with cuffs folded back revealing strong forearms, and there were a few top buttons undone, as if he'd wrenched off his tie in a bid to discard the day's directorial business image.

Tiny lines fanned out from eyes that resembled dark grey slate set in strong, masculine features.

There was strength apparent, not only of body but of the mind.

'You could have at least told me!'

'And your reaction would have been?'

She drew a deep breath, then released it. 'He frightened the bejesus out of me!'

'Grant Baxter?'

'Did you think I—' She stopped mid-sentence, and her eyes narrowed. 'Who?'

'You heard.'

Ilana felt the colour drain from her face.

How could he know?

Oh, for heaven's sake. *Get real.* How difficult could it be for a man of Xandro Caramanis's calibre to unearth information?

All it took was knowing who to call, how to delve deep enough. She'd been admitted into hospital…private, not public, following Grant's assault on the eve of her wedding. The hospital had records, there had been a police report, although she'd chosen not to press charges.

None of which were easily accessible…but not totally out of reach with the right contacts.

His eyes were dark, almost still as he watched fleeting emotions chase over her expressive features.

'There's a Privacy Act,' she managed darkly. 'You've contravened it. I could sue you.'

His shoulders lifted in a light shrug. 'Be my guest.'

She reacted without thinking, hardly aware of the swift upward movement of her hand until it connected with a resounding sound to the side of his face.

'Damn you!' Her hands curled into fists and she lashed out, hitting him where she could. His chest, a shoulder, his arm.

He didn't flinch, didn't move for several long seconds, then he caught hold of her wrists and held her easily.

'Let me go!'

'Enough.' His voice held a deadly softness she failed to heed. 'Stop it,' he cautioned quietly as she continued to struggle. 'You'll only hurt yourself.'

And she was hurt enough already. Angry…so very angry. With Grant. With Xandro.

Most of all, she didn't want to live like this. Always on the alert, conscious of any possibility…

Her breathing slowly steadied, together with her thudding heartbeat.

'Why?' she demanded.

Xandro didn't pretend to misunderstand. 'You required protection. I provided it.'

'Just like that?'

'Yes.'

His faint mockery caused her chin to tilt in defiance. 'Again…*why?*'

A slight smile curved his sensual mouth. 'I possess a caring heart?'

'I'm sure there's a legion of women out there who could attest to your—er—*caring.*'

'Not so many.'

'Really? You could have fooled me.'

For a moment she caught an amused gleam in those dark

eyes, and she was sorely tempted to hit out at him again. Would have, if she could have broken free of him.

'I came here to—'

'Vent?'

'Tell you to call off your bodyguard and stay out of my life!'

'Difficult.'

'*How?*' Ilana demanded. 'You pick up a phone and call him off.'

He had no intention of doing either.

'No.'

Her eyes resembled deep emerald, and sparked brilliant fire. 'Don't you get it?'

Xandro recalled his silent rage as he'd read the report tabling her injuries, and his immediate reaction. 'The bodyguard stays. So do I.'

She closed her eyes in an attempt to temper her anger, then opened them again. 'You can't do this.'

He regarded her steadily, and tamped down the urge to pull her close, hold her and let her absorb his strength. Assure he'd do everything in his power to keep her safe.

'You'll find I can.'

The very quietness in his voice momentarily unnerved her, and for a few heightened seconds she felt trapped by his gaze.

'I don't want any man in my life.'

'Tough.' Unequivocal, without negotiation.

Ilana opened her mouth in refute, only to close it again as she sought control. 'I'm done.' Her tone was tight, and her glare should have felled him on the spot.

Xandro released one hand, and retained a firm hold on the other. 'Shall we go eat?'

Ilana stared at him in disbelief. 'Here? With you? You're

out of your mind if you think—' She broke off. 'Dammit, there is no *we*.'

'Dinner,' he reiterated implacably.

'No.' She wanted out from here, away from this disturbing man and everything he stood for.

'A pleasant meal, a glass of wine.' His shoulders lifted in a slight shrug.

Sit opposite him in an intimate setting for two? Fork delicate morsels of food into her mouth whilst attempting conversation? Pretending all was normal and they were just friends?

'I don't think so.'

With that she tugged her hand free and crossed to the door.

As an exit line it worked well…although as she drove away she wasn't so sure.

A temporary victory, perhaps, in self-preservation?

Ilana made the drive to Bondi Beach with one eye on the rear-vision mirror. If she was being followed, it was hard to tell in the early-evening traffic.

She had a bad moment as she swept the BMW down into the basement car park, and she held the can of capsicum spray in her hand in readiness until she reached the safety of her apartment.

CHAPTER SEVEN

THE NEXT DAY saw a return to relative normality, with increased preparations for the fashion showing scheduled the following month.

A nationwide magazine wanted to do a feature. There was the need to study fashion being showcased on the catwalks in London and Milan, and check fabrics for next year's winter range.

There were no abusive phone calls from Grant, no hangups on her cellphone, landline, or messages left on her answering machine.

Had the episode with Xandro's hired bodyguard frightened him off? Or was he was merely biding his time?

Xandro made two calls, the first of which she declined to take, and the second wrought a polite refusal to his voiced invitation.

Ignoring him didn't work.

Whatever had made her think that it would?

A celebratory party held at the home of one of Liliana's closest friends saw a gathering of some of the city's social echelon.

It would be expected she'd choose something stunning to wear, and she didn't disappoint. Pale lilac georgette with a layered bodice and skirt, matching stilettos, and her hair piled high on her head drew several admiring glances.

It was inevitable Xandro would number among the guests, and Ilana found herself unconsciously looking for his familiar face as she mixed and mingled with fellow guests in the spacious lounge of their hosts' Point Piper home.

She smiled, indulged in meaningless social chatter, and assured herself she was having a great time.

Almost true, until she caught sight of Danika making a grand entrance...beautiful hair, skilfully applied make-up, sparkling diamonds at her ears, adorning her throat and wrist...wearing, of all things, the deliberately acquired *Arabelle* award-winning red gown.

Ilana barely avoided gritting her teeth. Although there was a part of her that had to concede the attractive model did the gown justice.

So maybe it's a *plus,* she consoled herself. Wasn't the object of any artistic creation a means to showcase the designer's talent?

A faint prickling sensation stirred the hairs at her nape, and she turned slightly and met Xandro's enigmatic gaze.

For a moment his eyes seemed dark, almost still, then a slow smile curved his mouth and she felt the slow burn of heat curl insidiously deep inside.

She hated that her body seemed at variance with her brain. Her life was all planned out. She didn't need or want to feel like this. Especially when every instinct she possessed warned she run from him as far and as fast as she could.

Hadn't she been hurt enough by Grant to be put off all men for life? Dammit, wasn't she *still* paying the price?

Why willingly tread that path again?

With idle fascination she watched Danika cross to Xandro's side, and she was unprepared for the sudden stab of pain piercing her heart as the model brushed her mouth to the edge of his.

Ilana immediately turned away, deliberately seeking conversation with an acquaintance near by.

Some of the guests spilled out onto a wide covered terrace, whose tinted glass walls and ceiling provided a fantastic view over the inner harbour to the city spires lit from inside, resembling tall sentinels against an inky sky.

Magical, Ilana accorded silently, enjoying the relative solitude.

'You seem to be developing a habit of avoiding my calls.'

Her personal antennae hadn't given advance warning of Xandro's presence. Then it kicked in, and she was willing to swear her body recognised his on some base level...otherwise why did the pulse begin hammering in her veins?

Not to mention the resultant warmth flooding her body as he moved in close.

Too close.

Ilana turned to face him, unable to tell much from his expression in the dimmed lighting. 'We have nothing to discuss.'

'Your ex-fiancé hasn't made contact?'

Xandro had no intention of telling her he'd stepped up her security by employing a second bodyguard to maintain surveillance on Grant.

A thorough investigation into Grant Baxter's background had revealed a tendency toward psychopathic behaviour way back in childhood, accelerating in his teenage years with an accusation of attempted rape at age nineteen, and one dismissal in the workforce for harassing a female employee.

'No phone calls, text messages, hang-ups.' She waited a beat. 'It didn't occur I might not want to speak to you? Or share your company?'

The corners of his mouth curved a little, and there was amusement evident. 'You make a refreshing change.'

She couldn't help herself. 'From clinging, simpering females who hang on to your every word?'

'That, too.'

'And here I was thinking you might be vulnerable to wicked women.'

His soft, husky laughter tugged at her nerve-ends, and a wry smile curved the edge of her mouth.

'Perhaps I should acquire a wife as protection.'

She recalled his dismissal of Danika, and tilted her head to one side. 'You think?'

'It might make for a relatively uncomplicated life.' His drawling voice held amusement, and she answered in kind.

'Somehow I don't see you as husband material.'

'Impossible I might want children?'

Ilana arched a deliberate eyebrow. 'To continue the Caramanis dynasty?'

'There would be worthwhile bonuses.'

'Bonuses' were something she didn't want to consider.

The mere thought of his powerful male body involved in physical intimacy momentarily undid her.

Ilana made to move away from him, only to have his head lower down to hers.

Firm fingers caught hold of her chin, tilting it as his mouth closed over hers in a kiss that stopped the breath in her throat.

Frankly sensual, he explored at leisure, tracing soft inner tissue, grazing her teeth, then probing her tongue, teasing it into an evocative dance with his own, promising much.

One hand slid to cup her nape, holding her head fast, and she began to respond, unable to help herself.

There was no sense of time or place…only the man and the effect his possession had on her body, her soul.

This—*this* was different from anything she'd previously experienced. The meshing of all the senses, transporting her to a place she hadn't imagined existed.

Almost as if he knew, he went in deep, taking her with him until there was only the man and the passion he evoked, inflaming her emotions until she felt she might shatter into a thousand pieces.

She became lost, so caught up with him that a soft protest sounded in her throat as he began to ease back a little, shifting his hands to cup her face, and his lips gently brushed hers before he released her.

For what seemed an age she could only look at him as she fought for a measure of composure.

His eyes were dark, so dark, as he pressed the pad of his thumb to the soft curve of her mouth.

Her mind reeled at the thought of how deeply her emotions were affected.

That hadn't been a kiss. It was possession.

What came next?

Nothing. Absolutely nothing.

Xandro caught the fleeting emotions evident…a degree of shocked surprise followed by a sense of fragility.

Ilana traced the inside of her mouth, tender from his touch, and she could still taste him, *feel* him.

Worse, she wanted more of him, his closeness, to savour some of the passion…

Whoa. Even *thinking* like this was madness. A madness she couldn't afford or condone.

'Would you find it so difficult?'

For a moment she just looked at him, then her face paled. He couldn't mean—

'To be my wife,' Xandro drawled as if he read her mind.

'That's a very bad joke.'

He made no attempt to touch her. 'No joke.'

She seemed to have lost the ability to string words together. 'I'm fine with my life just the way it is.'

'Very little would change. You have your work, I have mine.'

'You perceive a mutually agreeable proposition based on convenience?'

'Do you have a problem with that?'

This had gone on long enough. 'Was that what the kiss was all about?' Her eyes acquired a fiery sparkle as she quietly berated him. 'What comes next? Sex to determine if we're compatible?' She tilted her head as she injected scorn into her voice. 'If that's a marriage proposal, it sucks…big time.'

Ilana turned away from him and crossed the terrace to re-enter the spacious lounge, where she collected a flute of champagne from a proffered tray.

The chilled liquid held little appeal, and she discreetly discarded it, then she crossed to Liliana, indicated her intention to leave, sought out her hosts and bade them good night.

She had only taken a few steps down the path when Xandro joined her. 'I'll follow you home.'

'Don't be ridiculous.'

'It's not negotiable.'

For a brief moment she considered arguing with him. Instead she contented herself with spearing him with a baleful glare before she disarmed the alarm and slid in behind the wheel of her car.

Seconds later Ilana sent the BMW onto the street, and ignored the temptation to check her rear-vision mirror.

There was the temptation to take a circuitous route just for the hell of it, and she did detour via a few side-roads. Without success, for the only satisfaction she derived came from trying to elude him.

She was within a kilometre of her apartment when a passing car swerved in against her own, forcing her to the kerb with nowhere to go.

Ilana hit the brakes hard, felt the BMW rock on impact, heard the sound of screeching metal, and the airbag blew out as the car came to a sudden halt, followed the sound of a gunned engine and the screech of tyres.

Stunned shock kept her immobile for several seconds, and she heard voices…hard male voices, followed by an awareness someone was wrenching open the front passenger door.

Her seat belt was unclipped, and afterwards everything seemed to happen in quick succession.

Xandro was there, her hand somehow firmly clasped in his own, and she could hear him on his cellphone making calls. Soon there was the sound of sirens, and an ambulance pulled in, followed by a police car.

'I don't need an ambulance.'

Her protest went unheeded as she was helped onto a stretcher, transferred into the ambulance and taken to the nearest hospital.

She remembered assuring someone she was fine. After that everything became surreal. Questions, Accident and Emergency ward, a medical examination, X-rays.

And throughout it all Xandro remained at her side.

'I'm OK,' she recalled saying at one stage, only to have him give her a look that said more than any words could.

The end result was no broken or fractured bones. Only contusions, shock and the assurance she'd had a lucky escape. The

recommendation was overnight observation as a precautionary measure.

'I'd like to go home.'

The doctor exchanged a glance with Xandro. 'Miss Girard
is in your care?'

'Yes.'

'No,' Ilana refuted simultaneously, and glimpsed the
doctor's speculative look.

'The police are waiting in Reception to interview and take
statements from both of you.'

It took a while, and afterwards she swung her legs over the
edge of the bed.

'What do you think you're doing?'

'I'm going to dress and get out of here.'

Xandro moved with lithe ease. 'No, you're not.'

He swung her legs back onto the bed and eased her down
onto the bank of pillows.

She sent him a piercing glare. 'Says who?'

'You really want to argue?' He leant down and caged her
shoulders with his hands. 'Believe you're not going anywhere.'

'Since when did I give you permission to make any decisions for me?'

His eyes glittered with something she didn't care to define.
'Just—shut up,' he managed quietly. He didn't consider it
pertinent to relay he'd authorised a bodyguard to be posted
outside the door. 'Do you want me to contact your mother?'

'No,' she said quickly. 'Please don't. Liliana is due to board
an early-morning flight to Melbourne to visit her sister. There's
no reason for her to postpone. I'll tell her when she gets back.'

'You might need to re-think that.'

Her features paled as comprehension dawned. 'Someone
took photographs?'

'Yes.'

Even if a photograph didn't appear in newsprint, an account of the accident would. Xandro Caramanis was newsworthy, and the fact he was at the scene...

'*Hell.*'

Ilana closed her eyes against the sight of him, and felt the brush of his mouth on her own.

'Try to get some sleep.'

It was the last thing she remembered, and when she woke next it was morning, the nurses were doing their rounds and Xandro sat stretched out in a chair beside her bed.

Events of the previous night flashed before her eyes in graphic detail, and she carefully stretched her body, testing to feel where it hurt.

Stiffness where the seat belt had provided restraint, and her shoulder ached a little. But overall, not too bad. 'How do you feel?'

Ilana turned her head slightly and met Xandro's dark gaze, then said the first thing that came to mind. 'You're still here.'

'Did you think I wouldn't be?'

He'd relived the moment of impact countless times, the fuelled urgency to get her out of the car and away from danger. Together with the suspicion the crash scene had been no accident.

'I'll get dressed and leave.'

'After breakfast, when the doctor has seen you.'

Enough already. 'I've complied with medical advice,' she said firmly. 'Now, I'm out of here.' She pressed the buzzer for the nurse, only to be felled by hospital protocol.

Which didn't help at all, and the doctor's appearance while she reluctantly sampled food from her breakfast tray did little to appease.

It didn't take long to change into her clothing, which even she had to admit looked faintly incongruous at nine in the morning, and her attempt to order a cab at Reception was firmly dismissed by Xandro.

'No cab.'

'I can manage on my own.'

'But you won't.'

Ilana shot him a level look, and refrained from saying a word until Xandro slid the Bentley to a halt adjacent the entrance to her apartment building.

'There's no need—'

'Protesting won't alter a thing.' He slid out of the car, crossed round the front of it and opened her door.

Capitulation was the wisest course, and after a moment's hesitation she joined him.

She didn't say a word as they passed through security and rode the lift to her apartment. Inside, she turned towards him.

'Thanks.'

'Go pack a bag.'

'Excuse me?'

'You heard. Pack whatever you need for a few days. You're not staying here alone.' His tone brooked no argument, and she threw him a fulminating glare.

'No.'

He pushed hands into his trouser pockets and stood regarding her with dangerous calm. 'Someone made a serious attempt on your life last night.' His eyes seared her own. 'You'll be safer in my home than here.'

'What I want doesn't count?'

'In this instance…no. You want to pack? Or shall I?'

'You're the most infuriating man I've ever met!'

For a moment she seriously considered defying him,

except there was a compelling ruthlessness apparent that didn't bode well.

Given a choice, she'd prefer selecting what to pack, and she reluctantly retrieved a large backpack, tossed in a few changes of clothes and other essentials, closed the zip, then she collected her laptop, sketchbook and turned to face him.

'Satisfied?'

'For now.'

There was a sense of déjà vu in re-entering Xandro's elegant mansion. A few days ago she'd been consumed with anger and too focused on berating its owner to take much notice of her surroundings.

Now she was conscious of spaciousness, high ceilings, a wide gracious staircase curving towards an upper level, original oil paintings adorning walls and fine furniture.

A rectangular gallery at the head of the stairs led to several rooms, if the number of closed panelled doors was any indication, and Ilana followed Xandro along one side of the gallery to a pleasantly furnished suite with a queen-sized bed, mirrored dresser and chest of drawers. Neutral colours were offset by exotic silk bed-coverings, cushions and curtains. There was an *en suite* tiled floor to ceiling, with all the accoutrements, together with a folded pile of fluffy towels.

Xandro deposited her backpack and laptop onto a nearby chair. 'I'm sure you'll be comfortable here.'

'Thank you.'

He inclined his head in acknowledgement. 'We'll go down and I'll introduce you to my housekeeper. Judith and her husband, John, take care of the house and grounds.'

A pleasant woman with a friendly smile offered a warm greeting as they entered the kitchen, together with a man

Ilana recognised as the bodyguard who'd foiled one of Grant's attempts.

'Under no circumstances are you to go anywhere without Ben, or me, twenty-four-seven. Is that understood?'

She barely refrained from offering a salute. 'Yessir.'

Xandro's eyes darkened measurably. 'Don't try me on this.' The warning held a palpable threat only a fool would disregard.

'You have me at your mercy.'

'There's a remedy for sassy women.'

'I'm shaking in my shoes.'

'Take care, Ilana,' he offered in a dangerously silky voice.

'My dear, would you like some coffee? Or tea?' Judith intervened gently. 'Perhaps something to eat?'

'The study, Judith,' Xandro indicated. 'There are matters regarding the accident Ilana and I need to discuss.'

The BMW, insurance, police…they went through it together, questions which she was able to answer, the need for them both to go in to the police station to sign formal statements.

'There's one more thing,' Xandro indicated, and pushed the morning's newspaper across his desk. 'Read this.'

He'd opened it at the appropriate page, and Ilana leant forward to skim the contents.

Highly visible was a photograph of her on the ambulance stretcher with Xandro standing close by.

It wasn't so much the photograph, but the caption…

'Tycoon's fiancée in car accident.'

For a moment she felt as if she couldn't breathe, then she lifted her head and glared at him. *'Fiancée?* You're going to demand a retraction.'

'Not immediately.'

She felt like screaming in vexation. *'Why not?'*

Xandro sank back in his chair and regarded her silently, observing the fleeting emotions as realisation hit.

'You think it'll entice Grant to make another foolish move and be caught.'

It could work. Maybe. And if it did, Grant would be charged, sentenced, receive essential psychiatric treatment... and be out of her life.

'You've discussed this with the police?' she queried slowly.

'They're aware of my views.'

Ilana drew in a deep breath, then released it. 'What do you have in mind?'

He regarded her carefully. 'Allow it to appear our relationship has moved up a level.'

Her heart lurched, then skipped a beat. 'Specifically?'

He took his time in answering. 'The "engagement" stands. No one, not even Liliana, is to know otherwise. Your safety is of prime concern, and easier to manage if you're based here.'

She looked at him in disbelief. 'You're suggesting I move in with you?'

'That's a problem?'

Virtually *living* with him? Sharing his life? Suddenly there were butterflies fluttering in her stomach, beating wildly in protest.

'I'm not sure I like the idea.' Make that...not at all.

'The only person to fear is yourself.'

A statement filled with complexities, a few of which she chose not to examine too closely.

It didn't help he was right. Or that his suggestion made sense. What she needed, she decided, was an escape clause. Maybe more than one!

'I'll stay a couple of days.' A temporary concession, allowing her to reassess the situation midweek.

Two days. How difficult could it be? She had her laptop and sketchbook…she could hole up in her suite and only appear for meals.

'Good.' Xandro sat forward, and retrieved a business card. 'We'll get the formal police statements out of the way, then you can catch up on some rest after lunch.'

CHAPTER EIGHT

IT CAME IN the dark hours after midnight…a kaleidoscope of images that broke through the realms of a dream as it surged headlong into nightmare. Hauntingly real and so frightening she threshed helplessly in a semi-conscious need to fight, to protect herself.

The nebulous male figure assumed Grant's persona, his features becoming contorted with anger…the smell of alcohol a pungent entity as vile insulting words poured from his mouth and his hands became cruel, biting into her flesh, ripping at her clothes, forcing her to the floor. Her head rocked to one side from a stinging slap, and she cried out in sharp protest as she fought in desperation.

'Easy, now.'

The voice was different, distant, just beyond her subconscious grasp, and she reached for it, instinctively craving help.

'Ilana.'

The images faded as she came aware of a lit bedroom not her own, and her eyes dilated, starkly vulnerable with shadowed fear for a brief few seconds as she discovered she wasn't alone.

Seconds when she defensively backed up against the

bedhead in the bed until recognition hit...and the adrenalin dissipated as her heart slowly ceased thudding in her chest.

A nightmare. Dear God. It had just been a nightmare.

But so vivid she'd relived the reality from the moment Grant had appeared at her door on the eve of their wedding.

'I'm OK.'

Xandro bit back an oath.

The hell she was.

He'd come sharply awake at the sound of a faint feminine scream, heard it again and he'd hit the floor, pulled on jeans and quickly sprinted to the opposite side of the gallery, where he opened the door of her suite and felt the breath hiss between his teeth at the sight of her caught in the grip of a hideous nightmare.

At that particular moment he wanted to tear apart the man responsible for causing her so much grief.

'Does this happen often?'

Calm. Focus. She regulated her breathing, as she'd been taught to do, and forced herself to hold his gaze.

Until last night, she'd been doing fine. 'Usually something acts as a trigger.'

'Do you want to talk about it?'

A faint grimace twisted her lips. 'I've talked the talk with therapists, and moved beyond the road less travelled.' Her eyes were remarkably clear. 'I don't cry for me any more.'

It took time to rebuild trust. For some, it never happened.

'Can I get something to help you sleep?'

Ilana didn't want to sleep. Sometimes her subconscious mind took her right back to where the nightmare had left off.

'I'll read for a while. Maybe boot up my laptop.'

His presence disturbed her more than she wanted to admit. The jeans hung low on his hips, and he hadn't pulled on a shirt...clear evidence his impressive breadth of shoulder owed nothing to padded tailoring. Well-honed muscles flexed in chiselled perfection with every movement, and she could almost feel the warm heat emanating from his body.

Xandro took in her pale features, the too-wide eyes, and there was a part of him that wanted to lie down with her, pull her in and assure her ex-fiancé would never have the opportunity to hurt her again.

Instead he moved back a few paces. 'If you need anything, come get me.'

As if she'd do that.

Walk into his room, wake him, and say *please help me?*

Not in this lifetime.

She didn't offer a further word, and she watched as he walked from the room and closed the door quietly behind him.

Remaining in bed wasn't an option, and she retrieved her laptop, checked the batteries, then spent time keying in an email to Liliana. Xandro would have cable access, and she'd send it through in the morning.

There was a fashion magazine in her backpack, and she leafed through it until she'd read every word.

If she'd been home, she'd have padded out into the lounge, curled into a chair and channel-surfed until she found something interesting on television.

Anything not to lapse into sleep.

Except she could hardly wander at will in someone else's home.

How many hours until dawn? Three…four?

She reached for her watch, and groaned. Too many to stay awake.

Soon she found herself drifting, and she fought it as long as she could until sleep took her down, tossing her back into a scenario where the images returned to haunt her.

At some stage Ilana came sharply awake, her breathing as ragged as if she'd run a marathon, and she lay quietly in an attempt to orient herself with her surroundings.

Had she cried out? Please God, no.

She closed her eyes, then opened them again, grateful for the dimmed lighting illuminating the room.

Dammit, *do* something…anything.

She slipped out of bed and paced the floor, aware of a thirst that craved a cup of strong hot tea.

OK, so she'd go downstairs to the kitchen and make one. Who would object?

Minutes later the electric kettle was heating water and she reached into a glass-panelled cupboard to retrieve a mug… only to have the hairs at the back of her neck stand up.

Xandro spoke the instant she saw him. 'Unable to sleep?'

He had the tread of a jungle cat, for she hadn't heard a sound…and she should have. Strange house, different surroundings meant for a more finely tuned alert system.

She slowly released the pent-up breath she'd unconsciously held, and placed the mug down onto the counter.

'I didn't mean to wake you.'

He'd run a security check the instant the screen highlighted which room an intruder had breached, and this time he added a T-shirt to hastily pulled-on jeans before silently moving downstairs.

'Would you like some tea?'

She was a piece of work. Mussed hair from running her fingers through its length. Slender legs bare from mid-thigh down, and clad in a large cotton T-shirt bearing a cryptic message in Italian which translated to *Don't mess with me*. The literal version was more graphic.

There was little humour in being woken twice through the night by a woman not sharing his bed…and not likely to any time soon.

Any other woman would have slipped into exotic lingerie, applied minimum make-up, left her hair loose and spritzed perfume on tantalising pulse points.

'Hello…?'

Tea at four in the morning? What the hell…why not?

'Black, one sugar.'

Deft hands completed the request, and she slid the mug towards him.

'What now?' Xandro lifted the mug and swallowed a few mouthfuls. 'We discuss the art world, the state of the nation?'

'Feed me some details about your personal life,' Ilana suggested quietly. 'Family. Likes, dislikes. You've set the cat among the pigeons, and the media will bite.'

He kept it light, brief, downplaying his late father's obsession with work, the wives and mistresses who'd flattered Yannis and suffered his son.

'You're not going to reciprocate?' Xandro queried as she drained the last of her tea.

'Why? You already know most of it.'

A carefree childhood, stimulating travel abroad, a successful career…and a man who'd violated her trust.

'Grant Baxter. Where and how did you meet him?'

She really didn't want to go there. 'A veterinary surgery. My cat was sick. His dog had been injured in a fight and had to be put down.' She'd felt sorry for him, agreed to share coffee…and soon they were dating. 'He was kind, attentive, and I thought it was love. We got engaged, planned the wedding.' She paused to swallow a sudden lump which had risen in her throat. 'His male friends threw a party for him.

He got horribly drunk, turned up at my place around midnight and became angry when I wouldn't have sex.'

Angry didn't cover it.

'I had Liliana cancel everything,' she offered quietly, and saw his eyes darken.

'And chose not to press charges.'

Ilana recalled Grant's begging pleas. 'His mother had a bad heart.'

'Naturally, she still lives.' Xandro's voice assumed an inflexion she chose not to examine too closely.

Ilana offered a cynical smile. 'How did you guess?'

'While her son threatened you with more of the same if you dated another man.'

'Close.'

Xandro's eyes narrowed. 'That's it? All of it?'

She inclined her head and moved a pace to place her empty mug in the sink.

When she turned he was there, and she stood still as his hands cupped her face and brushed his lips to her forehead.

'Go try get some sleep, hmm?'

Then she was free, and she made her way towards the foyer, aware he joined her as she began to ascend the stairs.

When they reached the gallery he turned towards his suite, while she moved in the opposite direction.

Which was as it should be.

So why on the edge of sleep was it Xandro's image which invaded her mind?

Ilana woke to the insistent peal of her cellphone, registering as she picked up that sunlight was streaming through the window shutters.

'Darling, how are you?'

Liliana?

What was the time? *Nine?*

She struggled into a sitting position, felt the pull of bruised muscles, and endeavoured to push tumbled hair away from her face.

'I've just seen the morning's paper. Fortunately, Xandro had the presence of mind to call and assure me you were only kept in hospital overnight for observation.'

Ilana stifled a groan as realisation hit. Calling her mother early this morning had been a priority.

'Maman, I'm so sorry. I've just woken up.'

'Xandro explained.'

He did?

The last thing she'd wanted was for Liliana to read about the bogus engagement in the newspaper.

'I'm so very happy for you. Xandro is a wonderful man.'

Please don't. She hated deceiving her mother. Worse, she hated herself for acting out the part of a happy newly engaged daughter.

As soon as she disconnected the call she hit the shower and dressed in jeans and a sweater, caught her hair into a careless plait, and made her way downstairs.

Ilana entered the kitchen and found Xandro in the midst of pouring coffee while Judith broke eggs into a bowl.

His mouth curved into a warm smile as she crossed to the cabinet, retrieved a cup and placed it next to his own. 'Hi.'

'Hi yourself.' He lowered his head and touched his lips to her temple, caught her startled look and briefly captured her mouth with his own.

'Congratulations, my dear.' Judith beamed with genuine happiness. 'I'm delighted for you both.'

Role-playing, she discovered, wasn't too difficult as long as she smiled a lot, laughed a little and followed Xandro's lead.

Liliana's call was the first of several as the day progressed, and after lunch Ilana collected her laptop and sketchbook and sought the warmth of the enclosed terrace.

Work absorbed her attention, and she loved the creative aspect of design, capturing the vision on paper and transferring it to life with fabric and thread.

It was after five when she closed down the software programme, collected everything and went upstairs to her suite.

Her back and shoulder muscles ached, and she could feel the onset of a headache.

A leisurely hot shower would help, then she'd dress and go fix some garlic bread and prepare a salad to have with the steak Xandro intended to grill on the barbecue.

She shampooed her hair, then rinsed off and wound a towel sarong-wise round her slim curves and filched another to wind turban-style on top of her head.

As she emerged into the bedroom she heard the insistent peal of her cellphone, and she picked up...to silence, followed seconds later by heavy breathing, then the connection was cut.

Ilana's stomach muscles curled into a tight ball, and she switched to messagebank.

It didn't take much to deduce Grant had caught the engagement announcement in the newspaper.

How long before he made another move?

She really didn't want to have to live this way, always looking over her shoulder, expecting something to happen and never sure what it might be, or when.

It had to stop.

Jeans and a knitted top would suffice, and she applied

minimum make-up and left her hair damp and loose, slid her feet into flat shoes, then she went down to the kitchen to fix a salad.

Xandro joined her within minutes, and she was unprepared for the light brush of his lips to her cheek.

'Nice perfume. Subtle.'

'It's soap. And what was that?' Ilana looked at him with raised eyebrows, and caught his faint teasing smile.

'Practice. We'll be in the public eye tomorrow evening.'

Oh, what fun. 'I get to cling to your arm and gaze at you in pretend adoration.' She waited a beat. 'Where?'

'A dinner invitation with friends on their cruiser.'

'Are we talking casual or formal?'

'Formal. It's a large cruiser.'

OK, she could do that, but first she'd need to swing by the apartment and collect some clothes.

There was also work to consider, and she had no transport.

'Ben will drive you to and from work, and take you wherever you need to go.'

Mind-reading was also one of his talents?

One of many, she silently accorded. He was a sensualist who *knew* women and was well practised in all the moves.

As a lover he'd be dynamite.

Are you mad? Let's not go there!

Their evening meal was a casual affair eaten out on the covered terrace, and after they'd cleared up Ilana pleaded the need for an early night.

'I have something for you.'

Something was a beautiful solitaire diamond ring...a very expensive ring.

'No. I can't...' possibly wear it, she concluded silently, as he slid it onto her finger.

'Consider it essential window-dressing.'

'It's overkill.'

'It's what my fiancée would wear.'

'But I'm not. Your fiancée,' she added stoically, and he smiled, qualifying,

'You are for the time being.'

Ilana looked at the brilliant diamond in its exquisite setting. 'Thank you. It's beautiful.' She met his inscrutable gaze. 'I'll take good care of it, and return it when all this is over.'

'So thank me.'

She looked at him in silent askance as his hands closed over her shoulders and he lowered his head to her own, capturing her mouth in a kiss that reached in deep and tugged at her heart.

How long did it last? Surely not long?

Her mouth shook a little as he released her, and for a few seconds she couldn't move, caught in the thrall of a man who threatened to turn her personal world upside down. Worse. Someone who had the power to affect her more than any man she'd ever known.

If she let him.

It wasn't going to happen, for she couldn't withstand the emotional burn-out.

Xandro pressed a finger to the soft curve of her lower lip. 'You're thinking too much again.'

She murmured something that sounded slightly incoherent even to her own ears, and walked from the room when every instinct warned her to run.

CHAPTER NINE

ILANA ENTERED THE kitchen the following morning, greeted Judith, then assembled cereal and fruit into a bowl and took it out onto the covered terrace, where Xandro was draining the last of his coffee.

'Good morning.'

He rose to his feet and caught hold of her chin, lifting it so he could touch her mouth with his own in a kiss that lingered a little and left her feeling the need for more.

Which was crazy.

Slowly, steadily, he was invading her life, stirring emotions she didn't want disturbed.

Emotional safety was paramount in a need to protect her once-shattered heart. Over the past year she'd carefully assembled all the pieces back in place, allowing them to heal and mend, vowing no man would ever get the chance to shatter her heart again.

Now she found herself in a situation she couldn't wholly control, up close and almost personal with a man who disturbed her emotional equilibrium in a way that made her want to run and hide.

Except circumstance blocked any escape…even if it was only temporary.

It didn't help that his eyes held a teasing gleam as she broke away from him and took a seat at the table.

'We'll need to leave this evening around seven.'

She inclined her head in silent acknowledgement as Xandro rose to his feet and shrugged into his suit jacket.

'Have a great day.' She managed a brilliant smile that didn't fool him in the slightest, and she opened the daily newspaper and focused on scanning the pages as she ate.

Her cellphone rang just as she finished, and she checked caller ID, recognised the bodyguard's number and picked up.

'I'll be waiting out front whenever you want to leave for work.'

Ilana checked her watch. 'Five minutes?' All she needed to do was collect her bag and laptop.

Traffic was heavy, and it took a while to reach Bondi. Ben slid the four-wheel-drive into a parking space and cut the engine.

'There's no need for you to stay.'

'Xandro was most specific.' He handed her a card. 'My cellphone number. Call when you're ready to go collect clothes from your apartment.'

She opened her mouth to protest, only to close it again. 'Thanks.'

Ilana walked into the workroom to a chorus of voiced congratulations, hugs and the need to check out the diamond adorning her finger. Followed by questions...several of them, most of which she had no answer for.

'We're working out the details,' seemed to cover mostly everything and went towards satisfying a natural curiosity at the speed with which she'd supposedly agreed to marry one of the most eligible men in the country.

Work, fortunately, was all-consuming, and the morning

disappeared far too quickly. At midday she took a break, contacted Ben, and directed him to her apartment building.

'I'll walk.' She felt the need for some fresh air and sunshine.

'Uh-huh. We drive.'

Ilana rolled her eyes. 'Don't tell me…Xandro's instructions.'

'Got it in one.'

It seemed strange to have the bodyguard at her side, to wait and watch as he systematically checked the apartment's interior, then stand guard in the lounge while she riffled through clothes in the bedroom and tossed a generous selection into a capacious bag, added shoes, lingerie.

'Done.'

At that moment her cellphone rang, and her stomach clenched as she heard Grant's voice begin a torrent of abuse before she activated the *record* function.

When she checked, there were messages on her answering machine, three from friends wishing her well, two hangups and two from Grant.

'I'll alert Xandro.'

Ilana began to protest, then gave it up. Ben had orders he had no intention of waiving.

Together they took the lift down to the lobby.

'We'll head to Vaucluse. You can unpack, then I'll drive you to the workroom.'

'This is ridiculous.'

Ben merely smiled, unlocked the passenger door and stood waiting.

OK, so she wasn't going to win this one. With a sense of resignation she phoned Micki and relayed it would be at least another hour before she returned.

Something which made the afternoon almost a non-event,

work-wise, and she stayed back a while in order to finish an important assignment.

Consequently the traffic was even more chaotic than usual and it was after six when Ben drew the four-wheel-drive to a halt adjacent to Xandro's front door.

Three quarters of an hour to shower, dress, apply make-up and do something with her hair wasn't an impossible task. It just required multi-tasking.

Ilana chose an elegant evening gown in deep jade silk and added a pashmina embroidered with fine gold thread. Stiletto heels and designer evening bag completed the outfit, and she added a diamond pendant, ear-studs and thin diamond-studded bracelet.

Xandro looked resplendent and incredibly male in a formal evening suit, white shirt and black bow-tie as he watched her descend the stairs, and her heart gave a faint leap as she joined him.

No man had the right to emanate such an animalistic sense of power, or possess his elemental sensuality.

It was a dramatic mesh, and dangerous to a woman's peace of mind, for there was a sense of heat and passion evident beneath the surface…and the temptation to test what it would take to have him lose control.

If a woman was so inclined…and there could be no doubt many were.

A hollow laugh rose and died in her throat at the thought she was the one exception.

The Bentley was parked immediately outside the entrance, and she expressed surprise as Ben slid into the four-wheel-drive in readiness to follow them.

'An added precaution.' Xandro saw her seated and ignited the engine.

'Where are we boarding the cruiser?'

'A private marina, harbour-side.'

So how long did she have before *show-time,* where *pretend* was the game they were about to play?

Not long enough, she decided as Xandro eased the car into a parking space, and Ben drew to a halt alongside.

A security guard stood next to a steel gate checking guests' IDs against an invitation list before allowing them entry.

'Cruiser' was a misnomer, Ilana perceived as she viewed the large multimillion-dollar floating palace moored at the end of the jetty.

Brightly lit, multi-levelled and worth a fortune, it hosted some of the beautiful people numbering highly among the city's social élite.

She recognised an acclaimed Australian actor and his wife, three heads of industry and two parliamentarians. A television actress and her current lover, and an overseas model-turned-actress.

Almost thirty guests, including their hosts, mixed and mingled whilst sipping imported French champagne and nibbling exotic canapés.

'Darlings. Congratulations.'

The words were repeated again and again, accompanied by air kisses, the occasional gentle embrace...and Ilana smiled so much her face began to ache.

Xandro assumed the part of her lover with consummate ease, and he never left her side.

Protection...or merely ensuring she kept to the script.

His touch was a constant, and she felt his hand rest at the back of her waist, then trail a path to her nape and linger there a while before slipping low...too low, for the warmth of his palm was evident against the base of her spine.

It made it difficult to remain quiescent and attempt to ignore the way her blood seemed to heat in her veins.

Each and every nerve-end stretched as she sought control, and she was willing to swear each visible pulse hammered at a quickened beat.

This close she could inhale his clean male skin, the freshly laundered clothes and the subtle hint of very expensive cologne.

She didn't want to feel like this, and more than anything she wished it were possible to turn back the clock several weeks and have her life returned to when simplicity ruled and the only intrusions were work-related.

It was a relief when their hosts announced dinner would be served in the dining room.

Place-cards indicated preferential seating at a long oval table set with elegant chinaware, gold flatware and a variety of fine crystal goblets.

Ilana smiled a lot, conversed with guests seated close by and played it as if she were the happiest young woman in the country.

Which she should be…if the engagement were real and Xandro the love of her life.

His close proximity disturbed her more than she cared to admit, and there was little she could do to still the tiny curls of sensation beginning to spiral deep inside.

Almost as if he knew he slid a hand to her thigh and let it rest there for several long seconds before withdrawing it.

'Xandro, when can we expect the wedding?'

He spared Ilana an indulgent smile as he took hold of her hand and lifted it to his lips. 'Soon.'

'Speaks a man who has little knowledge of the planning involved,' Ilana declared with intended indulgence.

'A very private ceremony,' he enlightened.

A guest pursued, 'Ilana might want a traditional wedding.'

She'd almost had that, and vowed never to repeat it.

Oh, for heaven's sake…what was she thinking?

It was a game. Just a game.

'We need to consult our schedules.' That was sufficiently innocuous, and she laid her hand to his cheek. 'We're both busy people.'

He caught her wrist and held it as he pressed his lips to her palm.

It was evocative and sensual, as he meant it to be, and she silently damned him for playing his part a little too well.

Five different courses meant for a very leisurely meal, and she parried various subjects encompassing the movies, theatre, ballet and the current Cirque du Soleil showing in the city. Not to mention fashion…design, and she carefully avoided gossip and innuendo regarding recent contretemps on the two of the world's major catwalks.

Eventually the meal came to an end, and just as Ilana thought the evening was about to close their hosts led guests onto another level where a DJ spun CDs and encouraged everyone to dance.

Mostly everyone did, and Ilana made no protest as Xandro drew her close.

Slow dancing was seductive, and she allowed the music to weave its magic as he lowered his head and brushed his lips to her temple.

There was the temptation to move in close and meld her body against his own. Rest her cheek to the curve beneath his shoulder and have his arms slide down her back and cup her bottom intimately to his arousal.

And what if he isn't aroused? a vicious imp taunted.

But what if he is?

She told herself she didn't want to close the few centimetres that separated them to find out.

Why not?

Because then she wouldn't be able to face him, *knowing*.

It was easier to go with the moment, to slip into the part she was supposed to play.

And almost wish it were real.

Which hardly made any sense at all.

Soon they would leave, and the evening's charade would cease.

Only to begin again tomorrow, and for however long it would take to draw Grant out into the open and be caught.

'Time to leave, hmm?' Xandro gently widened the distance between them and threaded his fingers through her own.

'Midnight, and the pumpkin awaits?' she couldn't help teasing, and caught his warm smile.

'Something like that.'

Ben was waiting for them when they came off the jetty, and the four-wheel-drive followed at a discreet distance to Vaucluse.

The sound came out of nowhere, footsteps behind her, and she quickened her step, then broke into a run.

It was night, the streetlights were on, but no one could be seen. The apartment building was just up front, but the faster she ran the further away it seemed.

The footsteps were closing in on her, and any second now hard hands would grab her and pull her to the ground.

She didn't want to fight and struggle and be hurt again. A desperate cry emerged from her throat, begging for someone to help her…but no one was there.

'Ilana.'

She began to fight in earnest, thrashing against the hands that held her, trying to kick out, only to find her legs confined.

'Get away from me!'

She felt herself drawn against a hard, muscular chest and held there.

'Easy.' The voice was close to her ear, and she could feel warm breath against her cheek. 'You were having a nightmare.'

Oh, dear God...*no*.

Xandro saw the moment she realised where she was and with whom. Shock was reflected in eyes too large in a too-pale face, and he saw the faint tremor shake her slim form.

'I don't *believe* this.' Her voice shook as she pulled away from him, and she dragged back her hair in a defensive gesture, hating he should see her at her most vulnerable. Hadn't once been enough?

It was ages since she'd had the need for sedatives. Tomorrow she would go and pick up a prescription and get it filled.

Exhaustion pulled at her, at odds with the adrenalin still pumping through her veins.

'You want to go through it with me?'

'Therapy, Xandro?'

'Whatever works.'

'So I don't walk around the house and activate the infrared beams?'

A faint smile tugged at the edges of his mouth. 'That, too.'

His presence created a sense of security. For a crazy moment she wondered what it would be like to enjoy his protection, share his life, his bed...to wake in the night and know all she had to do was reach for him.

To love, and be loved.

Except it wasn't love he offered.

Was it the hour? The night? His closeness?

Playing *pretend* was dangerous.

It made her think too much. Want too much.

Crave for something she'd never had.

'I think you should go.' Was that her voice? So low and faintly husky with an emotion she couldn't begin to explain.

'Ask me to stay.'

She just looked at him, her eyes wide dark pools of shimmering emerald. For a long moment she wasn't capable of uttering a word. 'I can't,' she managed at last.

He regarded her carefully, his eyes so dark they were almost black. 'Because you're afraid?'

Not for the reason you think.

All he had to do was lean in close and cover her mouth with his own…and she'd be lost.

And if he did, she knew instinctively that she'd never quite be the same again.

Could he read her mind? Guess at the turmoil wreaking havoc with her emotions?

'Your call,' Xandro said gently.

She wasn't capable of saying a word. Her eyes were locked with his, unblinking, and she was unable to look away.

Minutes ticked slowly by as the room faded from her vision, and there was only the man, the electric tension and the sensation she was standing on the brink of a high cliff.

One step back and she'd be safe.

But if she stepped off…would she fly, or fall?

How was she ever going to know unless she took the risk?

He rose to his feet and looked down at her, and her heart went into serious overdrive.

Then he turned and walked towards the door.

In a matter of seconds he'd be gone, and she'd be alone… and more lonely than she'd ever felt in her life.

For a moment she couldn't say a word…then his hand rested on the door handle.

'Stay.' Oh, dear heaven. 'Please.' The last word was little more than a whisper.

Xandro stood still, his stance almost rigid. Then he turned to face her.

'Be sure. If I stay, there's no going back.'

She closed her eyes, then opened them again, suddenly aware of the rise and fall of her chest with each and every breath she took.

Her mind, her body…they seemed two separate entities.

'Stay.'

This was madness. What was she *doing?*

Xandro didn't move, he simply remained where he was and held her gaze, almost daring her to look away.

Then he slowly closed the distance between them, and when he reached the bed he held out his hand, watching as she looked at him in silent askance.

'Come here.'

He wanted her out of bed? Not in it?

For a few seconds she hesitated, then she placed her hand in his and let him pull her to her feet.

His eyes were dark, so very deep, and she lowered her lashes as he lifted a hand to her hair.

'Look at me.'

His fingers trailed to her cheek, then slid to cup her chin, and he traced the curve of her lower lip, pressed the soft centre and lowered his head down to hers.

The touch of his lips was light, fleeting, and had her wanting more…more than this teasing gentleness, and it was she who opened her mouth against his. She who sought the edge of his tongue with the tip of her own and began a tentative exploration, bestowing a slight nip to his lip, rolling it gently between her teeth before releasing it.

Xandro eased back a swathe of hair behind her ear and traced the thin scar at the base of her nape, the probable cause of which, her medical report had noted, was a chain having been wrenched from her neck.

He trailed his lips down the soft column of her throat and felt her breath catch as he sought the scar with his lips.

It was an evocative touch, light, so very light, then he slid his hands to cup her nape and angled his mouth over hers... and gently savoured the moist sweetness before taking possession in a manner that promised much.

One hand slid down her back, caressing her spine, before slipping to her waist and lingering there.

Ilana drank in the feel and male scent of him as she shaped his muscular shoulders, the hard biceps and the taut ribcage.

It wasn't enough. She wanted her hands on him, skin on skin, to explore and taste at will.

'Take it off.'

His voice held a huskiness that stirred her emotional heart, and she sought the hem of his T-shirt, then lifted it high and tugged it free with his help.

He was all warm skin and hard-toned muscle bound over powerful bone structure, with a sprinkling of dark springy chest hair arrowing down in a sparse line to where the waist-band of his jeans hung low over his hips.

She touched him, tentatively at first, trailing light fingers over his chest, circling one male nipple, then the other, exploring each nubbin until it hardened.

There was a need to taste him, and she leant in and laid her lips close to his heart, felt the strong, thudding beat beneath his ribcage, circled it with the tip of her tongue...then gently bit him.

She felt him tense, then his hands cupped her face and his

mouth captured hers in a kiss that took hold of her emotions and tossed them high.

His thumb-pad soothed the column of her throat, settling the faint sound within, then he drew back a little, tasting the soft fullness of her lower lip before slipping down to the base of her throat to linger at the hollow there.

A primitive sorcery began swirling through her body, touching each sensual pulse-beat and stirring it into wanton life.

Xandro's hands slid to shape her waist, gradually easing up the soft cotton fabric of her oversized T-shirt until it bunched together, and slid his hands beneath to touch bare skin.

With gentle care he tugged the T-shirt over her head and let it fall to the floor.

There was an instinctive need to cover her breasts, except he caught hold of her hands and held them away.

'Please.'

A faint smile teased his mouth at her apparent shyness. 'You're beautiful.'

He probably said that to every woman he managed to undress.

'Turn off the lamp.'

'No.' His refusal deepened her dark emerald eyes, and for a moment he glimpsed reticence...and something else. 'I want to see you,' he said gently. 'As you need to see me. So there is no doubt as to who you are with.'

She opened her mouth to protest, only to close it again, then offered, 'You're still wearing clothes.'

His eyes held a tinge of humour. 'You want to even the balance...or shall I?'

He caught her slight hesitation, lifted an eyebrow in musing indulgence, then he reached for the zip fastening and slipped out of the denim.

Fully aroused, he presented an awesome sight, and she

reached out a tentative hand to touch him, fascinated by the shape and texture, the silky covering, the engorged head of his penis.

'Slowly, *pedhaki mou,*' he warned gently as he caught hold of her hand and lifted it to his lips. 'Or it will be over before we've begun.'

He brushed light fingers over her breast, shaped it and teased the tender peak, watching as her eyes went dark. Then he lowered his head and used his mouth, drawing in one aroused peak and suckling until she cried out, then he shifted to render a similar treatment to its twin.

She became aware of his fingers trailing to her waist, circling her navel and exploring the small stud she wore there, before slipping down to the soft curling hair at the apex of her thighs.

A faint gasp whispered from her lips as he parted the delicate folds and began a highly sensitised stroking that had her pressing into his hand, wanting, needing more.

With gentle strokes he eased two fingers into the soft moistness, seeking the sensitive clitoris…and felt the sudden jolt of her body when he found it.

Sensation spiralled with a wild, mesmeric intensity, taking her high in a primitive trail over which she had no control, and she caught hold of him in order not to crumple into an ignominious heap at his feet.

Then she did cry out as he sank to his knees and traced an identical path with his mouth. Low, lower, until he reached the soft curling hairs…

No…*no*…he couldn't, *wouldn't*…but he did, and she clutched hold of his head in an effort to get him to cease the witching, sensuous invasion. Begging him in a voice she didn't recognise as her own as liquid fire shot through her body and she climaxed, shattering into a thousand pieces as he sent her high, so high she clung to him like a shameless wanton…unaware of anything except the exquisite sensation and the man who gifted it to her.

With infinite care he began a tracery of kisses over her abdomen to settle at her breast, then trailed to the hollow at the base of her throat, savoured it with his tongue, then captured her mouth in a long, drugging kiss as he swept her into his arms and took her down onto the bed.

Ilana linked her hands at his nape as he nudged a knee between her thighs, widening them apart as he positioned himself over her.

Say something.

Except it was too late, and she felt the intrusion, the tightness as moist tissues stretched to accommodate him, the hard, pulsing surge, the light barrier followed by the sting of pain… and became aware of Xandro's sudden stillness, followed by a vicious oath in a language she didn't understand.

She bit her lip to stop it trembling, her eyes huge dark pools as she caught the effort he made to retain control.

'Why didn't you tell me?'

Ilana turned her cheek against the pillow, and his fingers caught hold of her chin.

'Look at me.'

Her eyes shimmered with unshed tears. 'What difference would it have made?'

Xandro drew a deep breath, and his jaw muscles tensed. 'I would have been very careful not to hurt you.'

He began to withdraw, and heard her choked, 'Don't.'

'Ilana—'

'Don't stop.' It was so hard to say the words. 'Please,' she added, feeling utterly bereft.

For a long moment he remained still, then he lowered his

head to hers and took her mouth in a long, evocative kiss as he began to move, slowly, until he filled her completely.

It felt…good. Better than good.

'OK?'

She lifted a hand and brought his mouth down to hers, and it was she who kissed him, drawing his tongue into her mouth in an erotic dance that brought a groan deep in his throat.

Instinctively she lifted her hips, enticing something more, so much more, and he began to move. Slowly at first, small strokes that gradually lengthened and intensified as she caught his rhythm…and matched it. Exulting in the feel of him and the steadily spiralling sensation that made her cry out as he took her with him to the brink…then held her as she fell.

Afterwards he drew her in against him and cradled her close.

Her eyelids drifted closed, and her breathing steadied into a relaxed pattern…while the man at her side remained awake as she slept.

CHAPTER TEN

ILANA WOKE TO the persistent alarm summons from her cell-phone, groaned, then reached out to switch it off.

Seven already? It seemed as if she'd only been asleep for an hour or three.

The stretching movement brought the sudden awareness she wore nothing beneath the bedcovers.

Then she remembered.

The nightmare, Xandro...

Xandro.

She'd asked him to stay. And he had.

What was more... She closed her eyes against the images tumbling through her mind. Evocative, erotic and wholly primitive.

Dear heaven.

A slight sound had her eyes springing open again, and she threw a startled look as Xandro emerged from the *en suite*... naked, except for a towel hitched at his hips.

For a second her eyes locked with his, only to skitter away as he crossed the room to the bed.

He was too much...much too much.

'How do you feel?'

His voice held a quality she couldn't quite define, and she shook her head, unable to offer so much as a word.

She felt… *How did she feel?* she reflected a trifle wildly.

Acutely aware of his possession had to number high on the list.

'Look at me.'

He lowered his frame onto the edge of the bed, caught hold of her chin and he tilted her head towards him.

Soft colour tinged her cheeks, and her eyes seemed impossibly large.

He smelt of soap and clean male scent, and his hair was damp from his recent shower. This close he appeared all muscle and sinew and broad shoulders.

She remembered too well how it felt to have his arms hold her close, the touch of his mouth…oh, God, *everywhere.*

'Please. I need to go shower, get dressed…' She was dying here.

'Shut up,' Xandro berated gently, and, leaning in, he covered her mouth with his own, tracing its curve, then nipping the soft fullness so her lips involuntarily parted.

His hands cupped her face as he angled his head and began an evocative exploration that brought a tentative response before he eased back a little and examined her features.

'Better.' He caressed her throat with both thumbs, soothing the rapid-beating pulse at its base, his eyes dark and unreadable as he held her gaze.

'Let's—' she drew in a slightly ragged breath '—not do a post-mortem on last night.'

'Avoiding it won't make it go away.'

Honesty forced words from her mouth. 'It should never have happened.'

He tucked a fall of hair back behind her ear. 'You think not?'

She was equally damned whether she agreed or disagreed. 'I didn't expect you to be here,' she managed at last.

'You imagined I'd let you wake alone?'

Among the number of scattered thoughts filling her mind, waking alone wasn't one of them.

Uppermost was the most damning of all. 'We had unprotected sex.'

'I can vouch for a clean bill of health.'

A slightly hysterical laugh rose and died in her throat. She hadn't thought to ask.

Let's face it, she hadn't been *thinking* at all!

Implications rose to haunt her as she rapidly did the maths, then felt the tension begin to ebb with the knowledge a risk of conception was small.

'If you're worried about pregnancy…don't. If it happens, we'll deal with it.'

'There is no *we.*'

'Yes, there is.'

'No—'

'You want to argue?' There was a hint of something she couldn't define beneath the silky query, and her eyes blazed with green fire.

'Not at this precise moment, no.'

'Wise.'

'If you don't mind,' Ilana managed coolly, 'I'd like to go shower and dress.'

Xandro rose to his feet, and as soon as he left the room she caught up fresh underwear and made for the *en suite.*

Fool. The self-castigation served little purpose, and she stood beneath the shower as the hot water sluiced over her body. Then she picked up the soap and applied it vigorously, only to discover several tender places when she towelled herself dry.

What had she done?

Broken all her preconceived moralistic beliefs...so much for highly held principles!

She pulled on underwear, stepped into soft designer jeans and added a fashionable cotton-knit top, then she brushed her hair with vigorous strokes and let its length fall loosely onto her shoulders.

Her body still sang from his touch...and admit it, she felt *good.* Alive, in a way she hadn't imagined possible.

Minimum make-up accentuated a natural glow, and she slipped her feet into kitten heels, caught up her bag and laptop, then she drew in a deep breath and made her way downstairs.

Ilana entered the kitchen, greeted Judith, inclined her head towards Ben, and settled for yoghurt and fresh fruit, which she took out onto the glassed terrace.

Xandro glanced up as she joined him, and she took a seat opposite without so much as a word.

He lifted the silver pot and brought it close to her cup. 'Coffee?'

'Thank you.'

There was an inherent vitality evident, a sense of power beneath the sophisticated façade. All it took was a look and the blood began to heat in her veins, coursing through her body in a manner that heightened every pulse-beat, each sensory nerve-end.

The dictates of her brain were at variance with those of her intimate heart, and it took all her resolve to sit opposite him and calmly spoon food into her mouth.

It was a relief when he drained the last of his coffee and stood to his feet, and there was nothing she could do about the soft brush of his mouth to her temple.

'Take care.'

There were days when all went smoothly in the workroom, but today wasn't turning out to be one of them, Ilana determined with renewed frustration as ordered fabric didn't arrive when promised, and a client changed her mind about the size of covered buttons for what seemed the umpteenth time.

To compound things, there were three vicious calls from Grant to her cellphone…winding her up, in spite of her resolution not to let his threats get to her.

She would have given almost anything to walk along the beachfront, listen to music on her iPod and tune out the world for a while.

It would be difficult to elude Ben…but not impossible. Her mind sought possibilities, and her eyes gleamed as she latched on to one that might work.

'Micki, I need to go collect a prescription at the pharmacy.' She picked up her bag. 'Back in ten, OK?'

Micki lifted a hand in silent acknowledgement, and Ilana exited the workroom, smiled at Ben as he fell into step at her side.

Fifty metres separated them from the pharmacy, and she launched into an amusing anecdote as they covered the distance.

'You don't need to come in with me. I won't be long.'

Ben offered a smile and pretended an interest in the window display as she walked inside.

He would keep an eye on her, she knew, but if she was clever she'd gain the essential few minutes necessary to slip out the rear door, traverse the alley, then enter the side-alley leading back onto the main road. From there she could easily access the beach.

First she needed to appear to be examining something on one of the stands that would partially obscure her from Ben's view.

The plan she had in mind rested on one of the assistants

granting permission for her to slip out the back, and she picked a familiar face with the perfect excuse.

'Poor thing. Sure, go ahead, I'll close up behind you.'

Ilana felt a surge of elation as she made the back alley, and she sped quickly along the bitumen path until she connected with the side-alley leading onto the street.

Made it!

'Going somewhere?'

Elation turned into momentary despair as she turned towards a stern-faced Ben.

'A walk along the beach…alone.'

'Hardly a wise move.'

'Regard it as a lapse in common sense.' She searched his features in an effort to eke out some compassion. A disrupted night, too few hours sleep followed by a fraught day. 'Is it so terrible to want to escape for a while?'

'Foolish in the current circumstances. All you had to do was issue the request and I'd have walked along the beach with you.'

Except it wouldn't be the same. And she told him so.

'What's it to be? The workroom, beach or home?'

Home wasn't her home, and the beach had lost its appeal. 'The workroom.'

'I guess you're going to tell Xandro?' Ilana posed as they covered the distance to her place of work.

'It would be worth my job, my reputation, not to.'

So much for attempting a respite!

All told, it made for a frustrating day, and her stomach tightened as Ben slid the car through the gates guarding Xandro's mansion and brought it to a halt in the garage.

The space where the Bentley was usually parked was empty, and she felt a slight sense of relief as she entered the house ahead of Xandro.

How long did she have? Five—ten minutes?

Enough time to run a bath, and be incommunicado behind a closed door.

It would only delay the inevitable confrontation, but at least she'd gain some time alone.

With that in mind, Ilana filled the capacious tub, added foaming bath oil, then she stripped off her clothes, pinned up her hair and sank down into subtly scented bubbles.

Bliss, absolute bliss.

She let her eyelids drift down as the scented water worked its magic, indulging in a reflection of the day before inadvertently slipping back into the dark hours of the night...

'Tough day?'

Ilana's eyelids sprang open at the sound of Xandro's deep drawling voice, and she sank even lower in the water as she threw him a baleful glare. 'What are you doing here?'

He'd changed out of his business suit and donned casual chinos and a polo shirt. Looking, she determined a trifle ruefully, incredibly male and disgustingly fit. Cotton hugged muscular shoulders, outlined bunched biceps, lending him a powerful image.

Too powerful. She recalled a little too well how it felt to be held by him, the tactile gentleness of his touch. As to the sex...electrifying passion at its zenith.

'Don't you have something to tell me?'

She held his gaze and tried to determine his mood...only to fail miserably. 'I'm sure you've heard it from Ben in minute detail.'

He moved into the room. 'I'd like to hear it from you.'

She lifted a hand and indicated the bath. 'You have me at a disadvantage.'

'You chose the location.'

Her eyes sparked green fire. 'I didn't expect you to invade my privacy.'

'Your mistake.'

Xandro caught up a towel, unfolded it and held it out.

If he thought she'd calmly step out of the bath while he was there, he could think again!

'Go to hell.' She threw the soapy sponge at him and had a moment's satisfaction as it hit his chest.

With one fluid movement he reached forward and released the bath-plug, and she gave an angry cry as the water level began to subside.

'You…' Words temporarily failed her as she lunged for the towel and tugged it from his grasp, then rapidly covered herself.

It was too much. *He* was too much. And stupid hot tears sprang to her eyes. 'Go away. Please.'

The *please* got to him. For a few long seconds he stood looking at her. 'It'll keep.' Then he turned and left the room.

The thought of facing Xandro across the dinner table didn't sit well as she blotted the moisture from her body, then pulled on underwear.

Black tailored trousers and a white fitted blouse would suffice for an informal meal, and she caught her hair into a single plait, added lip-gloss, then moved lightly downstairs.

Xandro sent her a studied look as she entered the dining room, and she didn't offer so much as a word as she declined wine in favour of iced water.

Judith was a superb cook, the meal excellent, although Ilana barely did it justice.

She felt on edge and tense, and she longed for the meal to conclude so she could escape to her suite on the pretext of catching up with work.

'I want your word you won't try a stunt like that again.'

His words were clipped and inflexible, and she met his gaze with fearless disregard.

'I won't be treated like a recalcitrant child.'

'You're a responsible adult.' He waited a beat. 'What were you thinking?'

'So…bite me.'

'Cool it, Ilana. Trading insults won't achieve a thing.'

There was nothing like being direct! He read her a little too well, and it unnerved her more than she cared to admit.

With care, she placed her flatware onto her plate, folded her napkin, then she stood to her feet. 'You're quite right.' She was so polite, it was almost a travesty. 'Enjoy the rest of your meal.' She was cool, so very cool. 'Good night.'

It felt good to walk away with dignity…although she had the distinct feeling any victory might be short-lived.

How much longer before Grant stepped over the line? the silent query demanded as she ascended the stairs to the gallery.

She wanted out…out of this house, out of the farcical engagement, and away from Xandro.

Yet she was caught in a trap, one of her own making…with some help…and there was a need to see it through. Anything else was the height of foolishness if she was to resume a normal life without Grant's obsessive interference.

As always, Ilana found solace with her sketchpad, and she caught up her laptop, sat cross-legged on the large bed in the guest suite and set to work.

It was late when she put the laptop and sketchbook aside. She stretched her arms high, winced a little at the pull of stiff muscles, then she discarded her clothes, pulled on a cotton T-shirt and slipped beneath the bedcovers.

She slept dreamlessly and well, and woke to the sound of her alarm.

Time to rise, shine and begin another day.

Without thought she sat up and reached for the bedcovers…only to gasp at the sight of a familiar, tall, semi-naked male emerging from the *en suite*.

'What the hell?'

Xandro merely inclined his head. 'You're awake.'

Ilana glanced wildly at the space beside her, saw the imprint on the pillow next to her own, the tossed-back covers…

'You *slept* here?'

One eyebrow lifted in musing query. 'After last night you expected me not to?'

'That's unconscionable.' Soft pink coloured her cheeks and her eyes darkened to deep emerald. My God, he'd lain next to her all night and she hadn't been aware of his presence? How could she not have known? Surely she'd have sensed him?

Yet it had been the best night's sleep she'd had in a long time. Dreamless, almost as if her subconscious knew she was in a safe place with a man who guarded her safety with his presence through the night, and organised someone to watch over her during the day.

To sleep so easily said much for the fear she'd experienced since Grant had re-emerged into her life. Every waking moment had been caught up with anxiety…waiting for the moment her ex-fiancé might strike. The when and where of it.

Now, thanks to Xandro, she could acknowledge and deal with that fear, secure in the protection of a man she could almost dare to love.

If only he loved her in return.

And didn't that take the prize for wishful thinking! 'You can't sleep with me.'

'The operative word is *sleep*.' His voice was a low, husky drawl that sent her stomach muscles tightening into a hard ball. 'The bed is large. You can make a wall of pillows down its centre, if that'll ease your mind.'

'*Are you insane?*'

'Why so modest?'

'You know why, damn you!'

'The arrangement stays.'

'The hell it does.'

'Afraid, Ilana?' He paused imperceptibly. 'Of me…or yourself?'

'Next you'll offer your solemn word.'

His expression hardened measurably. 'You have it.' His voice was dangerously quiet. 'This suite or mine. Choose.'

His was larger, held two *en suites,* two walk-in wardrobes… *What was she thinking?*

'I don't have the time or the inclination to deal with it when I need to dress and get ready for work.'

'Then I'll make the choice for you,' he said silkily. 'Transfer everything into my suite.'

'Piglets will sprout wings and fly before I do such a thing!'

'In that case, I'll do it for you.'

'You can't—'

'Count on it.'

'*Why?*' The single cry was heartfelt, and she was sorely tempted to pick up a pillow and throw it at him. The only thing that stopped her was the threat of retribution in his dark eyes.

'I'll be there when the nightmare begins and you fight the bedclothes, before the darkness becomes so frightening you scream out for help.'

He saw it too well, knew first-hand how it was for her to be caught up in a rerun of Grant's rape attempt.

'You're taking the *caring* role a little too far.' Much too far.

'In your own words…"so bite me."'

With that he pulled on a silk robe and walked from the room.

For a few minutes Ilana didn't move, then she muttered something totally unladylike beneath her breath and hit the shower.

Xandro had already left for the city when she emerged downstairs, and she ate a light breakfast, collected her sketch-book and laptop, then left with Ben for the workroom.

Tension mounted as morning became afternoon, and Ilana was a mass of nerves by day's end. Liliana's call from Melbourne had elicited an 'are you all right, darling?' query, which earned a reassuring response.

The fabrications grew with each passing day, and there was a part of her that hated the subterfuge. Especially knowing they included her mother in the mix.

There were limitations, Ilana decided as Ben brought the vehicle to a halt in the garage.

She would *not* share the same room, the same bed, with Xandro. If he'd organised for her gear to be moved to his suite...she'd move it right back again.

Judith greeted her as she entered the foyer, her pleasant features softened with a warm smile.

'My dear, did you have a good day? Dinner will be delayed by half an hour. Xandro phoned to say he'll be late leaving the office. Incidentally, I've moved all your things into his suite. You might like to rearrange them.'

What could she say, except a slightly strangled 'Thanks?'

Vowing, as she ascended the stairs, to move every single item back to its original location.

It didn't take overlong, and she shed her clothes, took a leisurely shower, then dressed in capri pants and a knitted top, brushed out her hair and touched her mouth with lip-gloss before emerging into the bedroom...to find Xandro in the process of gathering an armful of clothes from the wardrobe.

'Leave them there.'

He looked at her, his eyes dark, almost still. 'You really want to do this the hard way?'

'I don't want to do it at all!'

'You want privacy…you'll have it. But we share a room.'

'Doesn't it matter what *I* want?'

'In this situation…no.'

'You are the most infuriating—'

'So you've already said.'

'Bastard.' The word held a degree of satisfaction, which he ignored as he strode towards the door.

'I'll only bring them back here again.'

'Then we'll have a very active evening.'

She barely refrained from throwing something at him, and plotted when she'd transfer everything…after dinner, when he secluded himself in his home office.

The plan worked, and she congratulated herself as she slid between the bedcovers and switched off the lamp. It was late, and she soon slipped into a deep sleep from which she awoke in the early dawn hours to discover the bed she slept in wasn't her own, nor was it her suite.

Worse, she wasn't alone, for Xandro occupied the other side of the bed separated by a line of pillows.

Some time in the night he'd collected her from her suite and brought her to his.

How dared he.

The temptation to pick up one of the pillows and hit him with it was strong.

Dark eyes sprang open and speared her own. 'Don't even think about it.'

His voice was husky, his hair tousled and he was in need of a shave.

'You have no idea what I had in mind.'

'If it involves body contact,' he warned, 'be aware you might not approve of the consequences.'

Ilana drew in a deep, calming breath and summoned a formidable glare. 'I don't like you very much.'

'Tough.'

At that moment her cellphone pealed, and she picked up.

'What's he like in bed, bitch?' The voice lowered to a salacious pitch. 'Which way do you like it?'

Ilana's fingers shook as she cut the connection, and her eyes became vaguely haunted.

'Grant?'

'Yes.' She couldn't bear to look at him, and without a further word she slid from the bed, crossed to the nearest *en suite* and quickly sluiced her face with cold water.

She felt sick in the stomach as she followed her normal morning routine, then she dressed, caught back her hair, applied minimum make-up and emerged into the bedroom.

'Do you want to tell me what he said?'

No. She shook her head. 'Just the usual filth.'

Xandro was freshly shaven and dressed in tailored trousers, a crisp white cotton shirt and in the process of fixing his tie.

His eyes narrowed as he took in her pale features. 'It's only a matter of time.'

Yes, but *when?*

'I don't feel like breakfast. I'll grab something at the deli later.'

He closed the distance between them and caught hold of her chin. 'Eat something here before you leave.'

'Is that an order?'

His mouth curved into a warm smile. 'A request, hmm?'

'I'll filch a tub of yoghurt from the refrigerator and take it with me.'

It was a compromise at best, and he touched a finger to her lips. 'I'll check in with you through the day.'

Then he released her, and she moved quickly downstairs, greeted Judith, collected the yoghurt, then followed Ben through to the garage.

The day followed a normal pattern, with a call from Liliana in Melbourne with an update on her sister's health, and two hang-ups which Ilana attributed to Grant.

It was more a matter of principle that Ilana transferred her belongings back to the guest suite on her return from work. Only to have Xandro move them back again.

He didn't say a word…but then, he didn't need to, and she lifted both hands in a gesture of surrender.

'OK, you win.'

Xandro accepted without argument her apparent need to pay close attention to the upcoming fashion showing, while he disappeared into his home office for hours each evening to liaise with various sponsors regarding the upcoming auction to raise funds for his favoured charity.

Ilana ensured she was already in bed when he joined her, and, although the line of pillows remained, it became more difficult to lie there beside him…so close, yet so distant.

All her senses were acutely attuned to him. And when she lay silent in the darkness it was impossible not to imagine what it would be like to have him reach for her, feel his mouth possess hers in a prelude to intimacy. She wanted to feel his hands on her, his mouth at her breast. Dear heaven…relive again the slow build to climactic orgasm and the joy of lovemaking.

With him. Only him.

So this was how it was to hunger for a lover's touch. To feel every nerve-end come alive until her body *sang* with anticipation. To want and need until it became all-consuming.

What would he do if she leaned across and trailed her fingers over one powerful shoulder? Traced the strong planes of his face and probed his mouth?

Would he tell her to stop…or haul her close?

She was too hesitant to make the move. Knowing she would die a thousand deaths if he rejected her.

CHAPTER ELEVEN

LILIANA'S RETURN FROM Melbourne helped bring together the final arrangements for Xandro's fundraising event.

No expense had been spared, with donations from various sponsors of jewellery, overseas trips, a car, imported champagne, a luxury cruise and a weekend at a health-spa resort.

A low profile didn't make a difference to the number of abusive calls from Grant…if anything the calls became more threatening and icily specific.

Living with Xandro had become more difficult with every passing day, for Ilana became increasingly aware of him. The sight of him stirred emotions she tried hard to keep buried, and it was almost as if all her fine body hairs recognised him on some base level, for she was willing to swear they rose up in silent acknowledgement each time he was within touching distance.

As to her pulse…it thudded into a quickened beat at the very thought of him. Reflecting on what they'd shared together sexually only made her long for what she knew she couldn't, *shouldn't* have if she was to retain a grasp on her emotional sanity.

Did he feel the same?

Somehow she doubted it.

On the evening the charity auction was held Ilana chose a stunning gown in a soft-coloured rose silk chiffon with a figure-hugging bodice and a skirt designed to swirl gently at her ankles. Fine crystal beads were sewn vertically on the bodice and fell in varying lengths down the skirt, creating a fine waterfall effect, and she wore matching stilettos, added a diamond pendant, ear-studs and bracelet.

'Beautiful,' Xandro complimented as they prepared to leave the house, and she subjected his tall frame to a sweeping appraisal.

He exuded potent masculinity and a ruthless sense of power…add impeccable tailoring in evening black, a crisp white dress-shirt and black bow-tie, and the result was devastating.

Every female heart among the guests would beat a little more quickly at the sight of him…including her own.

He bore the look that promised much, an inherent sensuality that wasn't contrived. For tonight he was hers.

So smile, she reminded silently, and give every appearance of being one of the happiest young women in the world while you schmooze with the guests. Remember…you're good at it.

The city hotel venue was spectacular, the decorative additions tasteful. Liliana's skilled touch was evident, and there wasn't an empty seat available…with names on a waiting list should there be a cancellation.

A successful evening was a given, and Ilana accorded due praise as Liliana checked the room with an eagle eye.

'It's fantastic.'

'I agree,' Xandro added with a warm smile. 'Let's hope the guests bid high.'

The Leukaemia Foundation would benefit greatly, especially the children. The effort put into the night's project had been enormous.

Ben was there, a discreet presence never more than a few feet away, and there was extra security checking the guests' IDs as they entered the grand ballroom.

It was doubtful Grant would attempt any form of attack in public. Subversive and underhand was more his style.

There were friends among the guests, acquaintances who'd come in support of a very worthy cause.

The social élite, Ilana reflected, were mostly genuine in their caring for such events, although there were those who rarely missed an opportunity to be seen and have their presence noted in the social pages. For some, most essentially women, *appearing* was an important feature in their lives.

Little expense had been spared in providing a delightful three-course meal accompanied by fine wine for the expensive ticket price, and by the time the meal concluded excitement for the auction had reached fever pitch.

There were, of course, the obligatory speeches, including one from Xandro, and he stressed the special needs of children stricken with the disease, together with the desire to provide assistance.

Brief, heartfelt, his words succeeded in drawing a groundswell of support as he thanked the sponsors, Liliana and the committee volunteers.

Professional slides of the various prizes were zoomed onto a screen set up behind the podium, then the auction began.

Figures escalated beyond expectations as guests entered into the spirited bidding, and in a planned directive the less expensive items were auctioned first, gradually leading up to the car as the grand prize.

The return flight to Dubai and seven-day accommodation package excelled, so too did a similar package to Paris. New York and Amsterdam followed closely, and several women attempted to outdo each other when it came to the items of jewellery.

The car, however, was knocked down to a prominent citizen at far above its market value.

When the bids were totalled, the sum raised reached several million dollars…an amount due to increase measurably from individual donations.

The evening was accorded an unequivocal success, and it afforded Ilana an eye-witness look at Xandro's philanthropic interests.

'You must be very pleased.'

His dark gaze met hers. 'Indeed.'

'The accolades are well deserved.'

His lips parted to show even white teeth. 'A compliment, Ilana?'

'Yes.' Her voice held a tinge of amusement. 'Just don't let it go to your head.'

'Remind me to take you to task.'

'I'm shaking.'

'As well you might.'

Coffee was served by attentive waiters, and it was a while before the witching hour of midnight brought the event to a close.

They were among the last to leave, and they saw Liliana to her car before crossing to Xandro's Bentley.

Ben accompanied them and slid into the four-wheel-drive as Xandro ignited the engine.

The drive to Vaucluse was uneventful, and once indoors Ilana crossed the foyer and made for the stairs, aware of Xandro's arm resting lightly along the back of her waist.

There was a sense of inevitability apparent as they gained the gallery and closed the distance to their suite.

All night she'd been aware of him and the acute sensitivity invading her body, bringing every nerve-end to shimmering life.

The feel of his mouth possessing her own, being held close in his arms, his touch, the sizzling heat...

Did he know how she felt? Could he sense it?

They entered the bedroom together, and she deposited her evening bag onto a nearby dresser as he shrugged out of his dinner jacket. With care she dispensed with her jewellery, and when she turned he was there, and he reached for her, drawing her close as his head descended to claim her mouth in a series of fleeting kisses.

'You're trying to seduce me.'

He smiled as he brushed his lips to the sensitive pulse at the base of her throat. 'Is it working?'

In spades. 'Hmm, maybe a little.'

A hand cupped her breast and a thumb circled its peak...an action which uncurled sensation deep inside and sent it spiralling through her body.

'An improvement?'

She could sense the humour in his voice...and it felt good to enter into light teasing play with him.

'Uh-huh.'

His mouth hovered above her own, and his breath was warm as it mingled with hers. 'How about this?'

She was gone from the moment his tongue slid between her lips, and a faint moan rose from her throat as he began exploring her mouth, the soft tissues, her teeth, the edge of her tongue...tantalising in a manner that had her responding without inhibition in an erotic tasting she didn't want to cease.

The blood sang in her veins, heating her body and bringing to life every sensitive pulse until she was sure he could hear their beat.

She wanted so much to be a part of him. To rejoice in what she shared in his arms…to place it among the memories she could retrieve during the many long, lonely nights ahead.

For soon it would end. Grant would surface, be caught and charged…and she would go home to her apartment and her former life.

Now why did that suddenly seem so not what she longed to do?

Except she couldn't stay. Dear heaven…even if he asked, how could she? To accept affection instead of love, knowing she didn't have his heart, his soul.

Xandro lifted his mouth from hers, and divined her expression. 'You think too much.'

'It's a female trait.'

He shaped her face and captured her mouth, searching deeply as she began to respond, uncaring how the evening would end.

She wanted the night and all they could gift each other. To wake in his arms and share the sweetness, the raw, primitive hunger with the power to liquefy her bones. Special, unique. An emotion that would live with her for the rest of her days.

There was no need for words…she told herself she didn't want them as she undid his tie, then released the buttons on his shirt and reached for the buckle fastening his trousers.

He toed off his shoes as she slid the zip fastening down, and he stepped out of his trousers and dispensed with his socks.

Unbidden, her teeth worried the fullness of her lower lip at the sight of his arousal, and her eyes locked with his, so dark with passion.

With care he gently turned her round and dealt with the long zip trailing her spine, then he eased the silk chiffon from her body.

All she wore beneath the gown was a silk thong brief, and

she slid out of her stilettos as he hooked his fingers beneath the silk straps at her hips and slipped them free.

Hands cupped her shoulders as he drew her back against him, and his lips traced the thin white scar at the base of her nape, then he gently caressed a path down the length of her spine before trailing up again.

His hands slid to shape her breasts, to tease and tantalise until the breath hitched in her throat.

With one fluid movement he swept an arm beneath her knees and carried her to the bed, then held her as he pulled back the covers before tumbling them both down onto percale sheets.

Ilana lay spellbound as he traced every inch of her skin with his mouth, pausing every now and then to nip a sensitive curve, a hidden crevice, until she ached with need.

'Please.' It was a broken cry in a voice she didn't recognise as her own.

His mouth took possession of hers as he gently eased his length into her moist intimate heart, felt the vaginal muscles contract around him as he surged in to the hilt.

She lifted her hips and wound her arms round his neck as he paused, and she huskily demanded, 'What are you waiting for?'

'You...to catch up.'

Then he began to move, slowly at first, then he slid into a quicker rhythm and she caught it, matched it and joined him on a mesmeric, pulsating ride that spiralled high...so high she cried out as her senses shattered.

Afterwards he curved her body in against his own and held her as she drifted towards sleep, and the last thing she remembered was the soothing trail of his fingers down her back.

Ilana must have slept, for she came awake to a steady heartbeat beneath her cheek, and she lay there without moving, exulting in the intimacy, the warm, tactile skin-on-skin contact.

The need to explore, to touch and discover each sensory pulse was uppermost. So too the desire to gift him erotic pleasure.

For a moment she wavered, tentatively hesitant to begin for fear he might brush away her hand.

Oh, for heaven's sake…what was the matter with her?

She rested her hand at the curve of his waist, then slowly traced a pattern over his ribcage, explored his male nipple with soft fingers before sliding up to his shoulder.

He didn't move, and his breathing didn't change.

Emboldened, she trailed the length of his arm, conducting a delicate tracery over muscle and sinew, then she let her hand slip to his hip, traversed his thigh…and drifted towards his groin.

'If you're intent on playing,' Xandro drawled, 'I suggest you stop now.'

'And if I don't?'

His warm breath teased the hair at her temple. 'Be very aware how it will end.'

'Promise or threat?'

'Both.'

His voice was a husky growl, and a soft answering chuckle emerged from her throat as she touched him, exulting in the strength of his arousal.

With a finger-light caress, she traced its length, tested the thick hardness and circled its base, then began easing gently upward until she reached the sensitive tip.

Filled with curiosity, and the desire to taste him as he'd savoured her, she pushed aside the covers and pressed her mouth to his male breast, teased a little before trailing gently towards his waist.

The hitch in his breath was a delightful reward as she

explored his navel with the tip of her tongue, and she shifted with tortuous slowness to hover over his smooth shaft.

She let her lips brush its length, then she conducted a teasing tracery with her tongue before resorting to the edges of her teeth as she bestowed a gentle nibbling that had his hands holding firm her head.

'Careful, *agape mou*. You're in danger of getting more than you bargained for.'

'Really?' It felt so good to have power over him. 'I'm not done.'

'Yes, you are.' With one swift move he shifted over her, positioned himself, and without any preliminaries he surged in deep, heard her gasp, then took her mouth in an oral possession that mirrored the physical act.

It was more, so much more than she believed possible. A primeval invasion, *pagan* and unrestrained as he took her with him, branding her his own as all her senses coalesced with his in explosive unison.

Oh, my.

She doubted she could move. She most assuredly didn't feel inclined to!

Could bones melt?

He was gentle in the aftermath, soothing her with his hands, his mouth, and she uttered a faint protest as he slid from the bed and swept her into his arms.

'What are you doing?'

He dropped a light kiss on her forehead as he entered the *en suite* and began filling the capacious bath. 'Bathing you.'

Sensual bliss, Ilana sighed as she lay in the cradle of Xandro's legs in deliciously warm, scented water as he gently soaped every inch, then just held her as she closed her eyes.

'Come on, sleepyhead.'

How many minutes had gone by? A few…or many?

She didn't really care as he lifted her from the bath, then towelled her dry before blotting the moisture from his body.

She slept curled up against him beneath the bedcovers, held within the circle of his arms, dreamless and complete.

CHAPTER TWELVE

EVERYTHING FOR THE Summer fashion showing was in place as Ilana checked the listings, conferred with Micki on a few last-minute adjustments, heard the fashionista deliver a brief introductory spiel, then announce the first category showing the *Arabelle* label.

All the work, planning and advance publicity had led to this moment, and Ilana crossed her fingers for luck as the music began and the first model took the catwalk.

The exclusive Double Bay venue was superb, the invited guests many, and Ilana sent up a silent prayer to the deity there would be no visible mishaps.

Smart casual led to tailored wear, followed by sophisticated afternoon and cocktail outfits. The *coup de grâce* was the evening-gown category, where each gown modelled gained much interest and applause.

Crystal-beaded chiffon designs, slinky, figure-hugging silk with varied necklines…strapless, spaghetti straps, halter and plunging V. Elegant evening trouser-suits with detailed beaded evening jackets. Slipper satin, lace and gorgeous crêpe georgette in block colours, classic black and soft, floaty florals.

As the model wearing the final gown disappeared backstage, from the podium the fashionista called for Ilana to take the catwalk, followed by the models.

She'd dressed in black…long leggings, knee-high stiletto-heeled boots, and a black top. With her blonde hair loose and flowing, she cut a dramatic figure, and she offered a dazzling smile as she strode down the carpeted walk, indicated each of the models in turn, then she returned to the stage and called on Micki to join her for the finale.

It was then Ilana saw Xandro standing at the rear of the room, and she lifted a hand in silent acknowledgement, caught his smile and felt warmth spear through her body.

'Success.' Micki's voice was barely audible above the applause, and Ilana uttered 'yes' in response as they reached the stage.

A final turn towards the audience, then together they disappeared backstage.

The collection required handling care, accessories stored, and the girls from the workroom took care of it as Ilana and Micki thanked the models, the behind-the-scenes staff.

'Go mix and mingle,' Micki instructed, and she gave Ilana a friendly push towards the side entrance. 'You deserve it.' A wicked gleam lit her dark eyes. 'And go kiss that gorgeous hunk of yours.'

'In public?' Ilana teased. 'For shame.'

She emerged to find Liliana waiting to envelop her in an enthusiastic hug.

'Well done, darling. I'm so proud of you.'

'Thanks to your unstinting support, since forever.'

'You have that without question.' Liliana moved aside as Xandro stepped forward.

'Incredible.' He cupped her shoulders and leant forward to

brush his lips to each cheek, then he captured her mouth with his own in a warm evocative kiss.

Dark eyes gleamed as he lifted his head, and for a moment she saw only him. Then the noise of feminine chatter and background music became evident.

'Thanks for coming.' She was utterly sincere. 'I didn't expect you to be here.'

Xandro caught her hand in his. 'I can't stay long. I have a scheduled meeting.'

She was just so pleased he'd put in an appearance, and she said so.

'My pleasure.' He lifted their joined hands and touched his lips to her knuckles. 'We'll go out to dinner and celebrate.'

'A date?' Together they'd attended social functions, playing an expected part. She lived temporarily in his house, occupied his bed and lent pretence to being his fiancée. But a date? 'Just us?'

Xandro's eyes gleamed with latent laughter. 'I'll make a booking.'

Ilana watched him leave, and witnessed the number of female eyes that followed his passage from the room.

Eye candy. Very serious eye candy.

If he was really *hers*...

Her heart jumped at the thought, and refused to settle into a normal beat.

He had her heart, her soul, freely given.

But did she have his?

Somehow the lines between pretence and reality had become blurred, and she no longer knew what was real.

Discounting his skill in the bedroom...what did she have?

Sufficient caring for her welfare to offer his protection…but was it only because his actions had contributed to Grant's reappearance in her life?

There were so many questions to which she didn't have the answers.

'Ilana.'

Her attention was caught by a society hostess, and for the next fifteen minutes or so she was in popular demand.

'Congratulations, darling. Love the gear.'

Danika, looking every inch the stunning model, beautifully attired, with skilfully applied make-up and perfectly groomed, free-flowing hair.

'Thank you.' Instinct warned the model had more on her mind than simple praise.

'No news on the wedding date?'

'We're working on it.'

'It must be heartening to know you meet Xandro's criteria for a wife,' Danika ventured silkily. 'I was seriously tempted. He's incredible in bed. My one objection was the breeding inclusion.' She ran a lacquered finger over her slender waist and hips. 'One's body never fully recovers.' Her eyes widened deliberately. 'Oh, dear, you didn't imagine *love* was part of the deal?'

Bitch didn't begin to cover it.

Ilana smiled, a gloriously stunning facsimile 'How sad,' she managed sweetly. 'There's nothing like a sore loser.'

Then she turned and made her way backstage where, to her relief, Micki and the girls had taken care of most everything.

'It was great, fantastic, incredible.' Micki threw her arms around Ilana's shoulders and led her in a short jig. '*You* are all of those, and more. We have appointments, promises of orders, and…ta-da,' she said with a flourish. 'Requests for further showings.' She drew back a little. 'Hey, why aren't you doing the happy dance?' Her eyes narrowed. '*Give.*'

'In a word…Danika.'

'Colour her green with jealousy?'

'You got it.'

Micki kissed a finger and held it in the air. 'Every time, babe.'

Ilana grinned. 'Precisely why you're in charge of business.'

'What say we transfer everything into the van, send it back to the workroom with the girls…and go reward ourselves with a latte or two?'

'Sounds good to me.'

Half an hour later Ben accompanied them a short distance to one of the many cafés lining the élite suburban street.

A recap of the afternoon resulted in Micki pulling the workroom diary from her bag and displaying the entries she'd noted therein.

'We may need to employ another seamstress part-time.'

'You think?'

'We'll see how it pans out over the next week or two.'

Ilana checked her watch and gasped at the time. 'I need to leave.'

'Big date, huh?'

She rose to her feet and collected her bag. 'Dinner.'

Micki retrieved her cellphone. 'I have a few calls to make.' She signalled the waitress and ordered another latte. 'Enjoy.'

It was a short distance to where Ben had parked the four-wheel-drive, and Ilana engaged in some idle window-shopping as they walked.

A passing reflection in a large glass panel caught her attention, and for a second she puzzled the shape, the angle… then everything happened in rapid motion.

She felt Ben push her vigorously to one side, followed simultaneously by the squeal of brakes, the thud as tyres jumped the kerb, and the explosive crash as the car hit the shop and sent plate glass shattering onto the pavement.

Ilana scrambled quickly to her feet and was shocked to see the car partially embedded in the shop window. Steam rose from a punctured radiator.

Ben caught hold of her shoulders. 'Are you OK?'

A little shaken, but otherwise fine, and she said so.

'What the hell happened?'

The sound of running footsteps became apparent, then Micki was there, her features pale and anxious. 'Perhaps you should sit down.' She eyed Ben. 'I'll stay with her, you go do whatever it is you need to do.'

He punched a code into his cellphone and spoke briefly, succinctly, then disconnected. 'Xandro is on his way.'

Ben took charge as people converged, and Micki assumed a protective role, requesting a chair, bottled water.

'I'm fine,' Ilana protested. 'I don't need a damn chair.' She waved it away as one was placed at her side.

'*Sit*.' Micki leaned in close. 'You need to know Grant is trapped in that car.'

The blood drained from her face. '*Grant?*'

'The one and only.'

The implications hit hard, and for a moment she couldn't speak.

Micki twisted the cap from bottled water and placed the bottle in Ilana's hand. 'Drink.'

The police arrived, closely followed by a fire squad and ambulance.

Then Xandro was there, and he hunkered down beside her. 'You're OK?'

She bore his scrutiny with a faint smile. 'OK.'

'Thank God.' The words were heartfelt as he cupped her face and captured her mouth with his own in a brief, evocative kiss.

His presence was reassuring as uniformed emergency crew took care of the situation with synchronised efficiency, using steel jaws to open a trapped car door, whereupon Grant was removed and transferred into the ambulance while two police officers began taking statements.

When they were done, Xandro led Ilana to the Bentley and saw her seated before crossing round to slide in behind the wheel.

Within minutes the powerful car was purring through the streets, and she sat in silence as she viewed the scene beyond the windscreen.

It was over.

Grant would be treated in hospital, then arrested and charged. She would return to her apartment and life could resume as normal.

So why wasn't she feeling relieved and happy?

Dusk began to descend, and soon it would be dark. 'We'll be late.'

Xandro sent her a quick glance. 'I've cancelled.'

'There was no need to do that.'

'We'll have a quiet evening at home.' He needed to hold her, keep her close, not share her in a restaurant filled with people.

She became aware they were taking a different route home. 'Where are we going?'

'A private medical centre.'

'Why? I'm perfectly fine.'

'Indulge me.'

'You're being ridiculous.'

'View it as a precautionary measure.'

Ilana threw him a dark look, silently damning him...which had no impact whatsoever.

'No.' Succinct, irrevocable, as if he read her thoughts.

'Telepathic communication, Xandro?'

'A calculated guess.'

Service at the medical centre was such she was sure he'd phoned in ahead of their arrival. The doctor was thorough, and, although there were a few tender areas, he assured they were merely contusions.

Ilana had the satisfaction of saying, 'Told you so,' as they left the medical centre.

'How do you feel about Chinese take-away?'

'Yum.'

'That's a *yes?*'

They ate out on the covered terrace while the food was hot, after which she retreated upstairs to shower and change.

There was a need to cleanse her skin, as if the action would somehow cleanse Grant from her mind.

Time, she rationalised, would gradually heal the mental wounds.

However, *nothing* would ease what she felt for Xandro.

Love could be a fickle emotion. For to love and not be loved in return...it wasn't enough.

So tonight she would stay...one last night to savour and remember. Surely she deserved that?

A faint movement momentarily startled her and she looked in silent askance as Xandro stepped into the shower.

'Communal bathing?'

He took the soaped sponge from her fingers. 'You object?'

Why should she deny herself the pleasurable experience? Heat coursed through her body as he shaped her breasts with the sponge, then he leaned in close and placed his lips to the sensitive hollow at the edge of her neck.

'Hmm, you do this so well.'

'I've just begun.'

It took a while…a long while, and became a celebration of all the senses. A gentle touching experience with lingering kisses in an exquisite foreplay that promised much, yet withheld sexual fulfilment until neither of them had the emotional strength to resist any longer.

In one co-ordinated movement Ilana wrapped her legs around his waist as he lifted her up against him and positioned her to accept his length.

He felt so good as she angled her mouth against his own in a deep, erotic kiss that mirrored the sexual act itself.

This was no hurried coupling, but slow and deep…so very deep it felt as if he invaded her womb.

She didn't want it to end…and felt like weeping when it did.

Together they towelled each other dry and donned towelling robes. A television screen lay concealed within a built-in wall cabinet, and Xandro channel-surfed cable until he found an interesting programme.

It felt so *right* to lie curled up in bed with her head pillowed against his shoulder, his arm curved across her back with his hand resting close to her breast.

The last thing she remembered was the light touch of his lips against her forehead.

In the early pre-dawn hours he reached for her, and she went willingly into his arms, loving the lingering foreplay before he moved over her with unbridled hunger, stroking deeply as she caught and matched his rhythm in a wildly inflamed coupling that knew no bounds.

Shameless, wanton, mesmeric. All of those emotions and

more, as raw desire assumed a treacherous primeval level…
and left them fighting for breath.

Afterwards they slept.

CHAPTER THIRTEEN

ILANA WOKE EARLY and lay quietly so as not to disturb Xandro.

So many weeks. So much anxiety…emotional, mental, physical.

But now it was over.

Ilana didn't know whether celebration or commiseration was the flavour of the day.

She was free to resume her life.

There was no need for her to remain beneath Xandro's protection.

She could return to her apartment.

So why did she hesitate?

Because she wanted to stay…for the right reasons.

Anything else was a compromise.

It was all or nothing.

Could she put it to the test?

Dared she?

Sadly there was no other way.

She'd wait until Xandro left for the city, then she'd go upstairs and pack.

Last night…she didn't want to think about the night and

their loving. Each time…was special, she allowed. But last night had been a feast of all the senses, evocative, primitive and impossibly erotic.

Breakfast was the last meal she'd share with him. Then she'd kiss him goodbye and pretend it was just another day.

She could do that, couldn't she?

How hard could it be?

The hardest thing she'd ever had to do, and her heart bled as she watched him walk out the door.

Don't think. Don't cry. Just go upstairs, collect your bags and pack. Make it quick.

How long would it take to bundle everything together? Ten, fifteen minutes?

Ilana completed one bag, and had just placed shoes into the other when a prickling sensation niggled between her shoulder-blades.

'What do you think you're doing?'

Xandro?

She spun round and saw his tall frame crowding the bedroom doorway. He had the soundless tread of a cat. 'I thought you'd left for the city.'

He'd driven a few kilometres before swinging the Bentley into a U-turn and heading back the way he'd come, caught by a deep instinctive premonition he couldn't ignore.

'That doesn't answer the question.'

He watched as she continued packing.

'I'm going back to my apartment.'

His voice was a dark growl. 'No, you're not.'

'The reason for me staying here no longer applies.'

'The hell it doesn't. What we share together…what's that?'

'Sex.' Very good sex.

'You think…just *sex?*' He sounded ominously quiet, like the calm before the storm.

'The ring is safely in the top drawer of the night-stand.'

'Stay with me.'

'I can't do that.'

'Can't…or won't?'

'It was great while it lasted,' she managed quietly.

'Dammit, I asked you to be my wife.'

'A convenient marriage.'

'I can offer you anything you want.'

Except the one thing I need. Your love.

Wrong answer, Xandro.

'I really appreciate everything you've done for me.' More than you'll ever know.

'You think I'll let you go?'

She looked at him steadily. 'You can't stop me.'

'What will it take, Ilana? Name your price.'

'There is no price.' Just three words…words from the heart. She collected the last item and closed the bag.

'Ilana.'

'I'm sure we'll see each other on the social circuit.'

For a long moment he stood looking at her, his gaze locking with her own, then he moved forward and collected a bag in each hand.

Together they descended the stairs and crossed to the garage in silence. She disarmed the alarm system on her BMW and opened the boot so he could stow her bags.

This was it. The moment she'd been dreading.

So do whatever it takes to say goodbye and drive away.

'This is what you want?' Xandro demanded, and she

inclined her head, not trusting herself to speak as she opened the door and slid in behind the wheel.

Go. Switch on the ignition, shift the transmission into *drive* and leave.

Afterwards, in solitude, she could cry.

The apartment seemed eerily quiet, and Ilana spent long hours in the workroom, refusing to take any personal calls except those from her mother.

She didn't accept any social invitations and confided only to Liliana the engagement had merely been a ruse to ensure Grant was caught.

Days became a week, and she told herself she was fine.

Except she ate little and slept less.

Each night she dreamt she was with Xandro, in his bed… and she'd wake bathed in sweat among tangled bedclothes only to find she was alone. And *wanting*.

Him, only him.

Work became a panacea, and all-consuming.

Liliana rang in the middle of a fraught day at week's end with an invitation.

'Darling. I have reservations for dinner tonight. A beautiful little restaurant where the food is divine. I'll pick you up at seven.'

'Maman—no. I—'

'Seven, sweetheart. I won't take no for an answer.'

She didn't want to go. Make that she *really* didn't want to go.

Twice she rang her mother to cancel, only to cut the call before it could connect.

So she'd leave the workroom on time, shower, dress, apply make-up, and go spend a pleasant hour or two and attempt to do justice to the meal.

At a few minutes to seven she took the lift down to the lobby, and found Liliana's Lexus waiting outside the entrance.

'Darling, you look lovely.'

Did she? It wasn't intentional. She'd merely selected an evening trouser suit in deep emerald, added stilettos and left her hair loose.

'Where are we going?'

'It's a surprise.'

OK, she could go with that, and Liliana enlightened anecdotes from a committee meeting held that morning, relayed a new boutique just opened in Double Bay which sold the most exclusive imported bags.

Fortuitous the restaurant happened to be in the same vicinity, her mother informed as she parked the car. They could examine the window display as they walked by.

It was almost seven-thirty when Liliana led her into a small, intimate restaurant where the *maître d'* provided an obsequious greeting, and offered a gracious invitation to be seated.

There were huge stands of flowers placed at regular intervals around the walls. Masses of them.

Ilana cast a puzzled frown around the room, for they were the only patrons present. It was most unusual, and she said so.

'Take a seat, darling. I need a moment to consult with the *maître d'*.'

Each of the tables bore a decorative lit candle, and she was led to a centre table by a hovering waiter.

'I will bring iced water, and the wine list.'

She had little appetite, but perhaps a glass of wine would provide the necessary impetus to do justice to an entrée.

A delicious aroma teased the air. Sautéed mushrooms? And was that herb bread?

Liliana was taking a while.

Where was the waiter?

She sensed movement, and glanced up…then she froze at the sight of Xandro walking towards her, tall and infinitely powerful.

The evening, the restaurant…suddenly it all fell into place. A planned conspiracy…but to what end?

For a moment she just looked at him, unable to tear her eyes away from his compelling features, and her stomach executed a slow roll in protest as all her nerve-ends tautened in pain.

'What are you doing here?' Stupid question. Why did she feel as if she stood at the edge of a precipice? It was crazy.

'Would you have agreed to dine with me?'

'Probably not.'

He pulled out a chair and sat down opposite her. 'Hence the subterfuge.'

'To what purpose?'

'To spend time together, drink a little wine, enjoy fine food…and talk.'

'We have nothing to discuss.'

'Yes, we do.'

'Xandro—'

'Bear with me.'

The waiter appeared and proffered the wine list, which Xandro handed to her.

'You choose.'

She shot him a quick questioning glance, which he met with a bland smile, and she deliberated a little before selecting a crisp medium white.

Background music lilted softly through hidden speakers, the instrumentals soothing and non-intrusive.

Xandro seemed in no hurry to order, and she searched for something to say.

'What was Liliana's part in this?'

'Merely to bring you here.' He indicated the room. 'The ambience is pleasant, don't you agree?'

She glanced around the empty room. 'You booked out the entire restaurant?'

'Yes.'

'Why?'

'Patience, Ilana.'

She shot him a suspicious look. 'What game are you playing?'

'No game.'

At that moment the waiter appeared with the wine, performing the opening and sample tasting with a practised flourish, then he retreated only to return and hand her a florist's box containing a single tightly budded red rose.

Ilana looked at him in silent query.

'For you, from the gentleman.'

There was a card tucked into an envelope, and Ilana extracted it with shaky fingers.

'With love. Xandro.'

For a moment her heart gave a crazy lurch, then settled back into a steady beat as she inclined her head. It could only be a thoughtful gift to set the tone for the evening, nothing more. 'Thank you.'

She'd take it home and keep it in a vase until every petal dropped.

The waiter returned with the menus, and Ilana made her selection, choosing an entrée instead of a main, while Xandro ordered both courses.

She spared him a surreptitious glance from beneath fringed

lashes, and wondered if the faint grooves slashing each cheek were a little deeper than she remembered.

His mouth…she skimmed it quickly, not wanting to linger on its sensual curve, for to do so brought too vividly to mind the pleasure it could bestow.

Worse, how much she hungered for his touch, the heat and the ecstasy. With him…only him.

Had he tossed and turned in his bed, craving her…as she craved him? Somehow it would be a divine justice if he did.

'You are well?'

How should she answer that? Admit she didn't eat or sleep much? 'Fine, thank you. And you?'

His shoulders lifted in a careless shrug. 'As you see.'

Ambiguity? He *looked* good. A little tired, perhaps, for there were lines fanning out from the corners of his eyes.

'Have you been away?' Such politeness was ridiculous, and she was tempted to say as much.

'New York.'

'On business?'

'Yes.'

The waiter appeared and presented their entrées, and Ilana viewed the artistically displayed food and wondered how she'd manage more than a mouthful or two.

It was obvious Xandro had an ulterior motive…but what? Meanwhile, her nerves were become more frayed with every passing minute.

She took a sip of wine in the hope it would help, then recalled she'd only had a small tub of yoghurt for lunch, and she reached for her water glass.

'You're busy organising another showing?'

'We work a season ahead.' She launched into an involved description that was definite overkill, although to give him credit he asked intelligent questions and accepted her explanations.

It took them through the entrée course and during the main.

How long before the meal was over and she could leave?

Ilana declined dessert and felt her nerves stretch to breaking point when he ordered a sorbet.

When it arrived he scooped a spoonful and offered it to her…only for her to shake her head in silent refusal.

'No?'

He was silent for several long seconds, then he replaced his spoon and pushed the sorbet dish to one side.

Ilana went suddenly still, her eyes held captive by his own.

'The woman I chose to be my wife flung my proposal back in my face and relayed…and I quote, it "sucked, big time".'

She wasn't capable of saying a word.

'Circumstances brought her into my home…my bed.' It was almost as if he reached into her heart. 'You changed my life,' he said gently. 'Loving you is more, so much more than I believed possible.'

It was almost too much to hope for, and she hardly dared breathe in case she had it wrong.

'Except nothing I said could convince you to stay.' A muscle bunched at the edge of his jaw. 'The most important moment in my life…and I failed.'

Ilana glimpsed emotion in the depths of his eyes…naked and rawly primitive. And she held back the shimmering tears threatening to well and spill.

'I love you. *You*. Everything you are. I want the privilege of sharing your life. By my side, with me for as long as I live.'

He slid down on one knee before her and took her hand in his. 'Will you marry me? Let me love you every day of my life?' He reached into his pocket and withdrew the diamond ring and slid it onto her left finger. His eyes met and held hers. 'It's back where it belongs.'

A single tear spilled and ran slowly down her cheek, and she couldn't have uttered a word if her life depended on it.

She watched in fascination as he rose to his feet in one fluid movement and reached for her, drawing her into his arms as he lowered his head down to hers.

His mouth was gentle, teasing a little, tasting the full lower curve, then he went in deep, and she clung to him as she became lost to everything except him.

How long did they stay like that? A few minutes? More? Ilana had no idea of the passage of time until he gradually eased his mouth from hers.

'I love you,' Ilana vowed simply. 'So much.'

He wanted to gather her up into his arms, take her home and into his bed where he would prove beyond doubt just how much she meant to him.

'There's just one more thing.'

'Yes.'

Xandro laughed softly. 'You don't know what I'm going to ask.'

'I don't need to know. The answer will be the same.'

He brushed his lips against her own, lingered a little, then reluctantly lifted his head a few inches from her own.

'When I take you home with me, I want it to be as my wife.'

She'd spent two lonely weeks without him, she didn't think she could bear being apart another night.

Ilana opened her mouth to protest, only to have him place a forefinger to her lips.

'I have the licence and a celebrant waiting with Liliana and Micki in the next room.'

Her eyes lit with a mischievous sparkle. 'You were that sure?'

He trailed a hand to cup her cheek, his expression intensely serious, almost vulnerable. 'No.' He'd spent sleepless nights gathering courage to plan this evening…and agonising almost every hour of every day how he'd manage to live without her if she refused.

'Just incredibly hopeful. And determined to do it right.'

Did hearts sing? She was willing to swear hers did.

'If you want the big deal, we'll do—'

Ilana placed fingers over his mouth. 'This is perfect.'

'You think?'

'Absolutely perfect,' she reassured gently as she reached up and brushed her lips to his cheek.

Xandro signalled the *maître d'*, and within minutes votive candles were placed on a nearby table, together with white orchids.

The celebrant was summoned, together with Liliana and Micki, who both held back tears as they shared hugs and kisses, then stood in position as the celebrant began intoning the words committing Ilana and Xandro together in holy matrimony.

It was touching and spiritual…and so very special.

Their vows were simple, yet profound…to love, honour and cherish for as long as they each should live. Liliana handed Xandro a wide diamond-studded ring, which the celebrant blessed before he slid it onto Ilana's finger. Then Micki handed Ilana a wide gold band so she could follow Xandro's lead.

When it came time for the groom to kiss his bride, Xandro bestowed a lingering, reverent salutation that almost brought Ilana to tears.

There was champagne, and laughter. A violinist appeared and began to play a medley of love songs, while the waiter presented more food.

Photographs were taken on Liliana's digital camera strictly for family use, and it was after eleven when they decided to wrap up the evening.

'I'm so happy for you.' Micki's words echoed those of Liliana as they bade each other good night. 'He's incredibly gorgeous.'

Ilana agreed, and cast Xandro a teasing look. 'But let's not tell him so too often.'

'My wife plans to keep me on my toes.'

Micki's laugh held light amusement. 'I doubt you'll mind too much.'

Xandro merely smiled, and caught Ilana's hand in his as they walked to where the Bentley was parked.

The vehicle whispered along the arterial road leading to Vaucluse, and she sat in reflective silence as rain sprinkled the windscreen.

'Nothing to say?'

She turned to look at him. 'I love you,' she said gently. 'So much.'

'It's reciprocal.'

The evening's events played over in her mind, and she savoured every detail, each nuance. And knew in her heart she wouldn't have wanted it any other way.

A soft laugh emerged from her throat, and he looked askance.

'Clothes,' she elaborated. 'I don't have any with me.'

'I don't plan on you needing them.'

'Promises, huh?'

'Believe it.'

Traffic was minimal at this hour, and it didn't take overlong to reach his Vaucluse mansion.

'Welcome home,' Xandro said gently as he switched off

the engine, and her bones melted at the passion evident in his dark eyes.

Ilana lifted a hand and cupped his cheek. 'Thank you. For everything. Being there, believing in me.'

He covered her hand with his own and turned his lips into her palm in an evocative caress.

They moved indoors and he paused at the foot of the stairs to pull her close, then his mouth captured hers in a kiss that reached right down to her soul.

She lost sight of where she was as he plundered at will in an erotic tactile exploration that had her clinging to him in mindless need.

He felt so good, and she exulted in his taste, his touch, and wanted more…so much more.

His hands slid to cup her shoulders, then slipped down to shape her breasts, easing each thumb back and forth over the tender peaks until they hardened beneath his touch.

It was easy to reach behind him and caress the tight muscles bunched beneath his trousers, to squeeze his butt and feel his penis engorge in reaction.

With one swift movement he swept an arm beneath her knees, lifted her high against his chest and began ascending the stairs, only to pause as she linked her hands at his nape and angled her mouth to his own in a kiss that shook them both.

'The bedroom,' Xandro announced huskily, 'will be infinitely more comfortable than the stairs.'

A soft laugh emerged from her throat as she reached up and caressed an earlobe, only to nip it gently and hear the breath hiss between his teeth.

They reached it and Xandro closed the door behind them before moving to the centre of the room, then he manoeuvred her body to slide against his own as he lowered her to stand on the floor.

Ilana reached for his jacket and slid it off his shoulders, then began unbuttoning his shirt and loosened his tie. Her hands went to his belt and he covered them with one of his own, then lifted her left hand to his lips.

His eyes were dark, so very dark with the promise of passion, and she swallowed compulsively as he cupped her face.

'My turn, I think.'

With leisurely movements they dispensed with each other's clothes, until the last silken shred fell to the carpeted floor.

He looked magnificent and incredibly male, his arousal a potent force, and she reached for him, lifting herself high to straddle him.

It was he who groaned as she settled her moist heat against his rigid penis, and the breath hissed from his throat as she rocked gently against him, causing a teasing friction that tested his control…as well as her own.

'Careful, *agape mou,*' he warned huskily. 'Even I have limitations.'

'Really?'

He adjusted her hips and held them as he positioned his length, then he entered her, paused at her faint gasp, and plunged deep inside.

Oh, my. She felt incredible. *He* felt incredible as she enclosed him completely, and sensation began to build, intensifying as her vaginal muscles began to contract and pulse around him.

When he began to move, she couldn't help the faint cry escaping from her lips, and she held on as he drove into her again and again, taking her high, so high she didn't think she'd survive the sensual ride.

Then his mouth covered hers, stifling her scream as she climaxed, and she shuddered in his arms, wholly captive to an emotion so intense she hadn't known its equal.

Xandro held her against him, and soothed her gently, passing a hand slowly up and down her spine, then he captured her head and brushed his lips against her own as her breathing settled back to normal.

It was more, so much more than she believed possible, and when he released her mouth she tucked her head into the curve of his neck.

For a while he just held her, then he shifted to the bed and carefully tossed back the covers and slid in between the sheets with her cradled in his arms.

Before her, there had been nothing…nothing to compare with the independent, sometimes gloriously stubborn young woman so beautiful in mind, body and spirit. So infinitely precious.

All of his future.

Everything.

His heart melted as a hand trailed around his neck and settled at his nape. Her lips parted against his skin and savoured a little, then stilled.

Xandro rested his cheek gently on her own, and slept as she did.

CHAPTER FOURTEEN

THEY ROSE LATE, showered together, dressed in casual clothes and ate a leisurely breakfast on the glassed terrace.

It was a beautiful early-summer's day, the sun shone in an azure sky and a slight breeze drifted in from the harbour, dappling the water's surface and teasing the tree-leaves.

Ilana's features softened as she reflected what a difference a day could make.

Yesterday she'd resigned herself to a life without Xandro. Only seeing him briefly at social functions, offering a polite greeting, a little perfunctory conversation before moving on. And burying the desolation she felt at having walked away from him.

To stay with him knowing she was a convenient wife and a suitable mother for his children wasn't enough.

Because she'd wanted it all…or nothing.

And consequently, she'd taken the biggest risk of her life.

What if she'd lost?

Xandro glanced up, caught her solemn expression and regarded her steadily for a few long seconds, then offered quietly, 'Not a chance in hell.'

'Mind-reading, huh?' she managed lightly, and caught his faint smile.

'I've become adept at discerning the way you think.'

'Am I that transparent?'

'Only to those who care about you.'

Ilana searched his features in an attempt to divine his thoughts, and failed to narrow them down to any *one*. 'You mask yours very well.'

'Plenty of practice from an early age.' His voice held an unexpected tinge of cynicism, and her eyes sharpened.

'My father succeeded beyond belief in the business world, yet failed several times at marriage.'

So few words that explained so much, Ilana perceived as she caught a glimpse of a young boy whose life had been torn apart by a clutch of stepmothers who had little genuine affection or time for him, and a father who was rarely there.

A childhood that had shaped him into the man he'd become.

She wanted to say she was sorry…but he wouldn't want her sympathy.

'Given his example, it seemed sensible to view marriage as a mutually convenient partnership based on trust and fidelity.'

'And deny yourself any deep emotional involvement.'

'I imagined it would work.'

'Except I didn't conform to your expectations.'

Humour gleamed in his eyes, softening his features. 'A slight understatement.'

'Yet you chose to protect me.'

'Yes.'

'For which I owe you my life.'

'Yet you left.' There was something in his voice that touched her heart and reached right down to her soul.

He'd suffered, just as she had.

'Is it so wrong to want to love and be loved for all the right reasons?' Her eyes darkened as she silently beseeched him to understand. 'It's the greatest gift. Beyond price.'

Xandro crossed to stand behind her, and Ilana leaned back against him as his hands slid down over her shoulders to intimately cup the soft fullness of her breasts.

He brushed his lips to her temple. 'You humble me.'

She covered his hands with her own and held them there. 'I love you.' So much. She wanted to give him the family he had never had. Children...dark-haired boys in their father's image, and little blonde girls he'd adore and protect.

'We need to go pack a bag.'

'We do?'

'I'm taking you to a small island off the coast of Greece.'

'Next you'll tell me you've consorted with Liliana and Micki on this.'

'Uh-huh.'

'OK.'

His husky laughter curled round her heartstrings. 'No questions asked?'

Ilana tilted her head to look at him. 'All I need to know is you'll be there with me.'

He covered her mouth with his own, lightly at first, then he lifted her to her feet and went in deep, taking his time in a sensuous exploration that had her clinging to him, wanting, needing more.

Xandro lifted his mouth from hers and she almost died at the passion evident in the depths of his eyes. 'Count on it.' His voice was gentle, inviolate. 'Always.'

With one agile movement he swept her into his arms and walked towards the stairs.

'Where are you taking me?'

'To bed.'

A bubble of laughter emerged from her throat as she linked her hands together behind his neck and held on. 'You said something about needing to pack a bag.'

He began ascending the stairs. 'Later.'

'The flight—'

'It'll keep.'

'Even you can't delay a commercial flight.'

He reached the gallery and covered the distance to their suite. 'It's a chartered jet.'

Of course it was. 'Oh.'

That was the last word she uttered for quite some time, and it was after lunch when they stopped off at her apartment to collect her clothes.

The sleek lines of a Gulf-Stream jet stood by as they cleared Customs and stepped out onto the tarmac.

Within minutes they boarded and sank into comfortable seats while a steward stowed their bags. The noise pitch intensified, then they were rolling out onto the runway prior to take-off.

'There.'

Ilana leaned forward as Xandro indicated a small island off the mainland. Too small for an aircraft to land.

'We'll need to take a boat from one of the larger islands.' That small?

'It's been in my father's family for a few centuries. Yannis loved to visit whenever he could. Two of his wives hated the isolation, and another demanded he build a modern edifice to make the sojourn bearable.'

Soon they boarded a small cruiser that carried them over an Aegean Sea which sparkled with jewel-like clarity. The air was fresh and clean and held the faint tang of sea spray, and

Ilana caught sight of a long jetty, crisp white sand and a stark white plastered home partially hidden by foliage.

'The original settlers' hut lies at the rear of the house. A middle-aged couple live there as caretakers. They'll take a break while we're here.'

It was breathtaking, a plantation-style home at variance with her expectation, yet in some strange way seemed to sit well in immaculate grounds.

The interior was cool with tiled marble flooring, spacious open rooms and elegant yet serviceable furniture and furnishings.

Xandro introduced her to the caretakers, then when the couple left he led her towards a staircase hugging an interior wall.

'Do you come here often?'

The main bedroom was enormous, with large expanses of floor-to-ceiling glass, tiled floors, a very large bed on a platform, two *en suites* and two walk-in wardrobes.

'It's an idyllic place to relax and unwind.'

Had he brought other women to this remote island?

'No.'

'You have no idea what I was thinking.'

He closed the space between them and pulled her close.

'Yes.' His lips brushed the sensitive cord at the side of her neck. 'I do.' His mouth shifted to cover hers in an evocative, slow-burning kiss, kindling a raw desire that made her want to pull him down with her onto that huge bed.

Reluctantly she eased back a little. 'Let's go explore.'

'The only exploration I want to do is of you.'

'Indulge me a while.' Her eyes gleamed with latent amusement as she pressed a finger to his mouth. 'I promise you won't regret it.'

'Minx.'

Ilana laughed, loving her ability to tease him as she pushed him to arm's length. 'No prevarications of a sexual nature permitted.'

Together they walked to the edge of the grounds and took a path leading down to a small sandy cove protected on each side by a rocky outcrop. Man-made, at a guess, given the neat assemblage of rocks.

The air was fresh and clean, and she slipped off her sandals, then rolled the length of her cotton trousers to mid-thigh.

Her eyes sparkled as she cast him a mischievous look. 'Where's your sense of adventure?'

Buried for too long beneath the constraints of business, and women companions who took pleasure in the sophisticated social life.

Something that was about to change beneath the hands of a delightful imp different from any female he'd ever known.

'Shoes. Socks. Trousers.'

Both eyebrows lifted in quizzical disbelief. 'Trousers?'

'Unless you want to damage Armani tailoring with salt water.'

It was a beautiful game, and one he entered into without reservation. 'And how do you propose I might do that?'

'Paddling in the Aegean.'

'*Sans* trousers doesn't come under the *no prevarication of a sexual nature* category?'

Ilana cast him a look of mock-severity. 'And risk shocking the natives?'

'I should remind you there are no natives.'

Xandro shucked off his socks and loafers, dispensed with his trousers…and hid a smile as he caught sight of the quick-ened pulse-beat at the base of her throat.

Ilana curved an arm around his waist as they traversed the water's edge from one rocky outcrop to the other, and she made no protest as he turned towards the path leading back to the house.

'Would you like a cool drink?'

She shook her head. 'The only thing I want is you.'

His slow smile held sensual warmth as she caught hold of his hand and began tugging him towards the stairs.

He laughed, a deep, throaty chuckle that reached her intimate heart. 'Pay-back time, hmm?'

They reached the bedroom and she melted into his arms. 'Count on it.'

It was she who took command, teasing shamelessly until he groaned beneath her touch and his heartbeat thudded against his chest as he sought control.

Liberties, she took them all, with a finger-light touch that drove him wild, only to increase the sensual torture with her lips, the edge of her tongue.

Just as he was in danger of exploding, she took him deep inside…and it was he who gained control, taking her high. So high she cried out as he held her there before tumbling them both over the edge in a mutual climax so intense it became more, so much more than they'd shared before.

Afterwards they lay limbs entwined in the aftermath, and Ilana sighed as Xandro drifted light fingers down her spine, shaped the firm globes at its base, then trailed high to cup her nape as he captured her mouth in an erotic tasting.

They shared wonderfully idyllic days, swimming a little, spending time on the small cruiser moored in the cove waters.

No social obligations, no need to dress up.

Together, they ate when they were hungry and made love when the sun went down.

Ilana lost count of the days, aware with increasing certainty she could be carrying Xandro's child.

There was the wisdom in waiting to have it medically confirmed, but she wanted Xandro to share with her the tentative excitement, the possible joy of their own personal miracle.

She left it until their last night on the island, and told him as they walked arm-in-arm in the moonlight along the cove's sandy foreshore.

His reaction was everything she could have hoped for, more than she believed possible as he caught her close.

'You're the sun and the moon,' he said gently. 'The very air I breathe. The love of my life. Never doubt it.'

'I'm yours,' she offered simply. 'Always. Forever.'

THE

Balfour

LEGACY

Eight Sisters, Eight Scandals

VOLUME 1 – JUNE 2010
Mia's Scandal
by Michelle Reid

VOLUME 2 – JULY 2010
Kat's Pride
by Sharon Kendrick

VOLUME 3 – AUGUST 2010
Emily's Innocence
by India Grey

VOLUME 4 – SEPTEMBER 2010
Sophie's Seduction
by Kim Lawrence

8 VOLUMES IN ALL TO COLLECT!

www.millsandboon.co.uk

M&B

A collection of three powerful,
intense romances featuring sexy,
wealthy Greek heroes

The Greek Millionaires' Seduction
Available 16th April 2010

The Greek Tycoons' Takeover
Available 21st May 2010

The Greeks' Bought Brides
Available 18th June 2010

Three volumes of gorgeous, hot-blooded Italian heroes

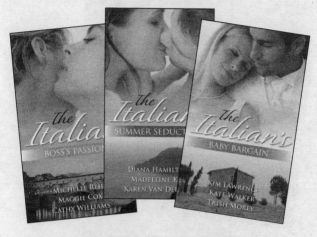

The Italian Boss's Passion
Available 16th July 2010

The Italian's Summer Seduction
Available 20th August 2010

The Italian's Baby Bargain
Available 17th September 2010

COLLECT ALL THREE!

www.millsandboon.co.uk

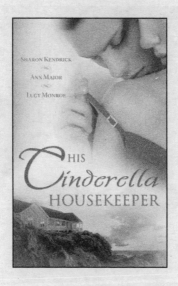

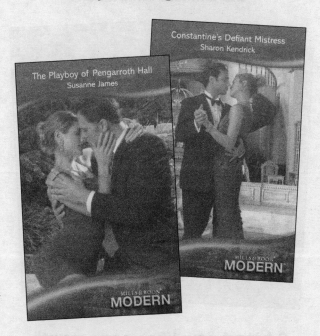

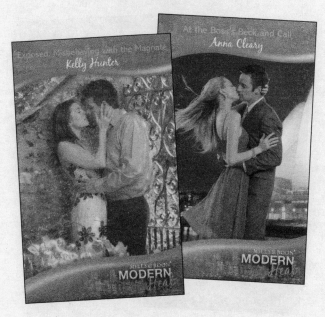

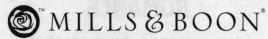